Vampire's Deception

IMMORTAL PROTECTOR

BOOK ONE

STEPHANIE FLYNN

Small Fish Publishing

USA

This is a work of fiction. Names, characters, places, and incidents either are the products of the author's imagination or are used fictitiously. Any resemblance to actual persons, living or dead, businesses, companies, events, or locales is entirely coincidental.

Copyright © 2022 Stephanie Flynn

All rights reserved. This book or parts thereof may not be reproduced in any form, stored in any retrieval system, or transmitted in any form by any means—electronic, mechanical, photocopy, recording, or otherwise—without prior written permission of the author, except as provided by United States of America copyright law. For permission requests, email a request to support@stephanieflynn.com.

First edition
Cover design by Stephanie Flynn
ISBN eBook: 9781952372575
ISBN Paperback: 9781952372568
ISBN Hardcover: 9781952372629
ISBN Large Print: 9781952372636
Library of Congress Control Number: 2022912350

Also By Stephanie Flynn

Find my catalog at StephanieFlynn.com

Immortal Protector series

0.5 Vampire's Distraction

1 Vampire's Deception

2 Vampire's Secret

3 Vampire's Promise

3.5 Elf Bound

4 Vampire's Demand

5 Vampire's Destruction

6 Vampire's Conquest

Immortal Protector Side Tales

Deer Holiday

Love Claws

Depths of the Heart

Matchmaker in Time series

0.5 Minutes to Live

1 Seconds to Act

2 Hours to Arrive

3 Days to Hide

4 Years to Savor

Pirates in Time series

1 Pirate's Prize

2 Pirate's Treasure

3 Pirate's Plunder

Time Travel Romance Shorts

Fateful Time

One Crazy Time

If you like your urban fantasy without the romance, too, check out Stephanie Flynn's other name, Marie Flynn!

I

The Rules

Oliver

I CONSIDERED MYSELF A simple guy. Throughout my hundred-and-eighty-some years on this earth, I had only two rules. The first was no harming my loved ones, which included torture and murder. The second most of us abided by most of the time: Keep the hidden world hidden at all costs.

Then, a body was left for humans to discover...with a pair of throat punctures. Now here I was, outside the city limits in northeast Wisconsin in my black wool suit, striped button-up, and patent leather shoes, zipping through the woods in the wee hours of the morning. This vampire needed a permanent lesson in self-preservation. Luckily for that fanged friend of mine, I was in a teaching mood. Although the more my suit sustained damage, the less patient I would be.

The canopy of trees overhead shrouded the ground in darkness, but my enhanced vision spotted all the nuances as if it were daylight. Unfortunately, I hadn't yet seen the perpetrator, but I could smell the murderous fiend—a mixture of moss and sweat, like a homeless man who'd slept in a cave. So unrefined.

Behind a broad maple trunk, I paused, listening, breathing in the air. A rustle, northeast about fifty yards, but I waited to pinpoint my prey's trajectory—oh, pardon me. I meant my student's trajectory. I was the monster other monsters feared, and my student was going to learn that as well.

Not much surrounded us but dense forest, a sprinkle of houses and cabins between towns, a few cornfields, and a major road system—Highway 41. The quiet land was prime pickings for vampire activity, but the Marinette area hadn't experienced a vampire as sloppy as the one I tracked. If I couldn't stop him, our hidden world was at risk of exposure, and the gruesome fiery hunt from over a century ago was doomed to repeat itself.

The rustle pricked my ears, and I mapped the change in my head. He'd veered toward the highway in view of the public. He must've been a new vampire in the thralls of bloodlust, incapable of thinking with anything but his fangs. Those were the worst.

I bolted off through the woods after him. Sunrise was not far off, so I had to finish this business and find shelter of my own before the fiery ball in the sky lit me up like a torch. Leaping over downed trunks, snapping twigs underfoot, and dodging branches before they marred my handsome face, my senses brought me to the clearing.

As a pickup truck disappeared around the bend, a family sedan approached. Quiet, as was common on a pre-dawn

Saturday morning. Still bathed in moonlight, I scanned the area to locate my student. He blew across the front end of the family sedan and disappeared into the woods on the opposite side. I headed after him, but while trying to avoid a collision, the small car lost traction and now fishtailed dangerously.

The driver attempted to regain control, but he was caught in the grassy median, heading straight for the overpass column. I could give chase to the reckless vampire I'd been hunting or grab a snack at the inevitable accident scene.

Typically, I abstained from drinking straight from the tap. In this modern world, I found it's an unnecessary risk, but it tasted oh so much sweeter than the bagged stuff, and the fresher it was, the greater our muscular endurance, capacity for rapid healing, and sharpness of our senses. I couldn't teach the vampire a proper lesson if I wasn't at my full strength.

Sod flew behind the tires as the driver tried to navigate toward the road without rolling the vehicle. At their speed, it was unlikely any would survive the inevitable impact. And if the humans died, there would be no heartbeat to pump my drink.

And that would be a waste of perfectly good nutrition.

Waste not, want not.

Daisy

THE LINE WENT SILENT, and I squeezed the cell phone against my ear as Dad's crushing words echoed in my head. Unlike him, I believed in second chances. We were all human. Even if every person on this planet thought they were perfect, everyone had a different definition of it, so by *that* definition, no one was perfect. See? Easy. So, if someone screwed up, they deserved the opportunity to make it right.

Well, I'd screwed up.

Medical school had been a bust, and my heavy student loans would be kicking in soon. Rather than wallow in pity with my useless bachelor's in biology and further disappoint Dr. Greg Barrett by remaining a bartender forever, I'd enrolled in an emergency medical technician program. It was a breeze after the unbearable strain of med school, and my fast success boosted my spirits. My new career might not be as prestigious as what my father envisioned for me, but I was proud, and I wanted my parents to be happy for my accomplishment.

The black sheep of the family didn't begin to describe where I stood with them.

Wheels hummed down Highway 41 on a far-too-early Saturday morning, and the headlights illuminated the long stretch to Green Bay. Darkened trees flew by the side window. The pre-dawn time and droning commute made me wish for coffee. Since my Aunt Lisa and Uncle Marc went far out of their way to pick me up and insisted bringing me along wasn't a burden, I wasn't going to ask for a detour.

Next to me in the backseat, my younger cousin texted her new husband on our way to our college graduation ceremony. She was all giggles and smiles. A stab of jealousy ran through me.

The call officially ended with a chirp.

"They aren't coming, are they?" Uncle Marc Barrett said from the driver's seat. He glanced at me in the rearview mirror with familiar pity.

Taking a moment to steady my voice, I said, "They don't believe there's any point."

"Well, we know they're both stuck-up snobs," Aunt Lisa said.

My cousin snorted with amusement next to me. I wasn't sure whether she reacted to her mom's statement or something her husband texted her. Either way, it was a reasonable response, and I smiled at her. She and Mike had been married for only a couple of weeks. It was a beautiful garden ceremony at night in her parents' backyard, where I was a bridesmaid. The youthful passion between them was sweet.

Despite having a boyfriend of my own, I had none of what Abby and Mike had.

"Lisa," Marc scolded and changed lanes to pass a slow vehicle.

"What? They are snobs. Daisy has two degrees now, but because she didn't earn the doctor title, she wasted her life.

They're unbelievable." Lisa looked over shoulder at me. "I'm sorry, honey. I don't know what got into your father."

"Stacey did," Marc said. "No offense, kiddo."

"None taken." My parents weren't the easiest growing up, and listening to my aunt and uncle chide them was validating.

"Greg and I had been competitive until it was obvious my older brother would surpass me in some ways. We were destined for two different lifestyles, but when he'd met Stacey, she'd insisted on a certain image for the Barrett household. I think it's unhealthy, which is why we only visit during the holidays."

My cousin snickered, this time clearly focusing on her phone. Abby had earned an engineering degree, and at twenty-one years old, she had her whole student-loan-free life before her with a husband who adored her. Mike worked in Green Bay, and he was meeting us there. He'd also said he had a surprise for Abby.

No one was waiting for me. My boyfriend, Pierce Evansson, was currently absent from the car, and he wasn't meeting us there either. Pierce had told me he couldn't switch shifts, but I didn't believe he'd tried all that hard.

I was a disappointment to my parents, the lowest priority to my boyfriend, and a pity case to my aunt and uncle. But I managed to find a career I liked, scraped together the funds to pay cash for the associate degree program, and I passed the licensing exam. Plus, I already had a job lined up in my hometown.

I supposed that was basic adulting—nothing to write home about.

"Marc, look out!" Aunt Lisa's shrill voice lifted my head.

Something rushed across the road, and my uncle swerved to avoid it. The tires caught on the gravel shoulder. With the differing heights of the ground, the rear of the vehicle fishtailed.

"What was that?" Marc white-knuckled the steering wheel, playing games with physics using a ton of steel. Stones pelted the wheel wells.

"I don't know. Something big. A deer maybe?" Aunt Lisa turned her head out the side window to check if they had hit whatever it was.

That was no deer. I'd seen a blur of clothing, which made no sense at all.

"It's too dark to tell. Get us back onto the road," Aunt Lisa added, worry in her voice.

"I'm trying." Arms rigid with the force, Marc yanked the wheel in a last-ditch effort to return to the pavement. Instead, the car skidded onto the grassy median of the divided highway. We careened straight toward the overpass column.

"Marc, do something!" Lisa shouted.

Abby furiously texted on her phone and dropped it on the floor. She cried out in pure terror. "Dad!"

Marc slammed on the brakes, sending the vehicle tilting sideways. I gasped. The column grew larger out of Abby's window, and my heart jumped into my throat. My eyes widened in disbelief. This couldn't be happening. This couldn't be how it all ended. I had a ceremony to get to and a fantastic job ahead of me. I had people to say goodbye to. No, no, this wasn't happening. My hands uselessly gripped Lisa's seat back in front of me.

The side of the car smashed up against the column, and darkness took over.

A searing pain throbbed in my head, and I opened my blurry eyes. I blinked and blinked again. It was dark. I should've been in bed. This was a twisted dream, and I needed to wake up. I heard a dinging sound, like a dashboard warning, but I couldn't see it. Where was I? Why was I stuck?

I found a seat belt. Car. I was in the car, but I had no strength to release it. Where were we going?

Aunt Lisa's blond hair draped over the seat back in front of me. Abby was buried under something. It looked like a blanket, and she was sleeping. Sleep sounded good. I was very tired.

Marc wasn't moving either. The car wasn't moving. His hands weren't on the wheel. He was sleeping too. Why was there concrete in front of Abby's window?

Accident. We hit something. At once, the tangy scent of blood hit my nose.

A cozy heat warmed my feet through the floorboards. Orange light licked up the side of the car.

Fire.

Gas tank.

I had to get out of here.

I was just so tired. My exhausted arm reached for the seat belt connector, and I tried to push the button again.

I couldn't.

My breathing quickened with my returning clarity. The car was on fire. I needed to get out. Smoke began curling in through Abby's broken glass. I coughed weakly.

A shadow approached my window. Pale gray eyes found me. A Good Samaritan had stopped for us.

"Help," I whispered, too weak to express urgency.

The man stared at me as if he'd seen a ghost. I was going to be one soon.

"Help me, please," I repeated my plea. I reached my heavy hand up and splayed my palm on the glass. Only friction held it in place.

I was a natural reactor in emergent situations, but the average person wasn't, and my rescuer struggled with what to do next. He looked down the highway as if hoping to flag down another passerby for assistance. *You're here now. Help me*, I silently pleaded.

I tapped the window weakly, and my arm fell to my side. That was all I could do.

The man brought his face close to the glass. "Turn your head away."

I did, and I received a fresh face full of smoke. I coughed.

The window shattered over my lap with a high-pitched bang and a pretty tinkling. He popped the lock on the door and ripped it off the hinges. The door flew off onto the grass. No, that couldn't be right. My brain misfired. I blinked, and the door still sat in the grass off a way. How?

"The car's on fire, but it's going to be okay," the man said, leaning over me.

For whom? My cousin, aunt, and uncle were sleeping.

"I'm going to get you out, Daisy." He ripped the belt right out of the connector and curled me into his strong but gentle arms.

He carried me from the wreckage as if I were lighter than a feather. If such an afterlife of eternal peace existed, I imagined it smelled like him. My face rested against his chest, covered in a soft fabric like a pillow, and I was tired again. "How do you know my name?" I murmured against his chest.

My rescuer lowered me to the grass, and he kneeled next to me. He wore a suit, as if he were on his way to the ceremony too. His eyes raked my body from toes to face, like a paramedic assessing my injuries. I was grateful for an experienced rescuer. But his demeanor was grim. I probably looked as bad as I felt. And that meant—bad news.

The sky paled with the coming dawn, lighting the man's features. He had dark shaggy hair falling over his forehead but trimmed neatly in the back. Thick dark brows complemented pale gray eyes. His prominent jaw was dusted with a five o'clock shadow. He was simply stunning.

Or I was delirious with shock.

A goofy grin of happiness lifted my lips. I reached out a tired arm and ran my fingers through his hair. Soft as satin sheets. "No need to sugarcoat it for me. How bad is it, Doc?"

Too far from the burning vehicle's heat, the chilly morning dew on the blades of grass gave me a shiver. I was cold and getting colder. Also a very bad sign.

My rescuer's graceful fingers slid along my face, brushing aside my sticky hair. White pain snaked down my body, and my head throbbed. I sucked in a breath.

"Daisy, you're dying—"

At the sound of that word, the rest of what he said blinked out of existence. The car accident. Remembering what had happened, I asked, "Where's my family? Where's Marc, Lisa, and Abby?"

"Marc Barrett is in there?" My rescuer looked at the burning car with sad resignation.

"You know my uncle, too?"

"We met at your cousin's wedding, but it's too late for him. For all of them. I'm so sorry, Daisy."

My family, whom I'd considered my real family, was taken from me. I'd never felt more alone in my life, but I couldn't process the gravity of the situation. I didn't want my rescuer to leave, so I desperately tried to make a connection. "How could I not remember you?" The idea was impossible. Anyone who laid eyes on this man could never forget him—sexy, refined, brave. He was the complete package.

So, probably not single, but I was in no condition to care. He'd decided by looking at me that I was dying.

A sad smile lifted my rescuer's lips. "I get that a lot." Shadows from the fire flickered across his handsome face, and he rolled his sleeve up to his elbow. Thick forearms were dusted with dark hair. My rescuer bit his inner wrist, and blood pooled on his skin. "Here we go. Drink up."

I stared. I must've been hit in the head really hard, because what he offered was disgusting. "Um, no, thank you?"

"I can hear your erratic heartbeat and your crashing pulse. You must drink, or you will die. Open up," he insisted.

I didn't understand how he could possibly hear my vitals, but I wasn't thinking or seeing clearly. I opened my mouth, awaiting a cup and assistance at the back of my head. Instead, my rescuer pressed his wet wrist directly against my mouth, and a warm metallic liquid squirted into the back of my throat. As I'd expected—not seeing clearly. I didn't like whatever this medicine was, but medicine generally didn't taste good, anyway. I tried not to gag.

In a gentle voice, he said, "Everything's going to be okay now."

With a single swallow, energy filled my muscles with a mega-jolt of caffeine. I had to force the second swallow, and my headache eased. That was enough. With a grimace, I pushed his arm away, confused and disgusted. I sat up straight, and his thumb rubbed my lip clean.

What the hell was that? How was I no longer in pain? I had my full strength back, and I felt mentally clear, but still, so much confusion persisted. "What was that?"

"Something to heal you, Daisy." My rescuer, nameless and so damn beautiful it should be a crime, smiled softly at me.

"What's your name?" I needed the name of my hero, who I shamefully couldn't remember from Abby's wedding.

"Oliver Rockwell, not that it matters."

"Of course it matters. How am I going to send you a gift basket if I don't know your name?"

Oliver laughed, lines wrinkling the corners of his eyes, and bright white teeth—a little on the sharp side—gleamed back at me. "That's not necessary."

"Oh, yes, it is. I have to get to my graduation." I climbed to my feet and checked my watch. "And I'm going to be late. You know, I'm going to rescue people for a living, just like you." I hoped to be half as effective. Whatever he gave me was some miracle juice. I felt pretty damn great, honestly.

Oliver glanced at the horizon, and worry knitted his brow. Purples and pinks filled the sky. The sun would be up soon. It was beautiful. "Daisy...I hope you never become like me."

With the ridiculousness of his statement, I scoffed, recapturing his attention. Pale gray eyes stole my breath. "Not that you need more compliments, because I'm sure you get them all the time, but you risked your life to save me from a burning car. For that, I thank you a million times." Oh, now they came, those damned tears. I blinked them away. "I couldn't even get my boyfriend to support me at my graduation ceremony. It's like he doesn't care at all, and yet you, a perfect stranger, cared entirely." Perfect, indeed.

Oliver Rockwell captured my hand in his, and a jolt of warmth threaded through me. "Daisy, you need to find yourself someone who lights a fire in your heart, who makes you sing when no one's looking, and who will always be there for you. That is someone you deserve, and it isn't him."

"Sounds like someone knows true love."

Oliver's eyes blazed an unnatural shade of bright red, and lucid hallucination or not, I gasped and backed up. "What's wrong with your eyes?"

The siren of an ambulance filled the air. Oliver gazed at the horizon for a moment and gripped my hands in his, eyes now a perfectly normal gray. I shook my head to knock free the last of the visual disturbances. He spoke urgently. "Daisy, listen to me. I must go now, but I want you to know you're going to be a fine EMT. Congratulations on your graduation, and I'm sorry you have to miss it."

A stranger had more heart than my own boyfriend, and no one else made it out of the car. A burst of loneliness surged through me. "Please don't go. Stay. Stay until the ambulance gets here. I don't want to be alone."

His hand brushed my face. "I need you to do something for me."

After all he'd done for me, I'd do anything. "Name it."

"Look at me." I happily gazed into his eyes, back to burning an unnatural but beautiful fiery red, as if the ambulance's lights reflected off them. "Forget I was here. You escaped that car yourself."

I stared blankly at the pretty sky, and only one thought filled my head—a very important thought. "I escaped that car myself."

The sun's rays projected across the sky, lighting the destruction. Flames fully engulfed Marc's car, and an ear-piercing squeal made me cover my ears a second before the explosion.

My family was dead, and I was alone. But at least I escaped that car myself.

2

The Mysterious Legacy

Three months later...

Daisy

HOLDING A FOOD STORAGE container of hamburger casserole, I stuck my head inside the front door of the home I grew up in. With stone and vinyl siding, a two-car attached garage, and a fancy front door surrounded by picture windows, it met the definition of cookie-cutter suburbanite. There was one important distinction. Mom and Dad's backyard was on the shore of the bay of Green Bay, and sunrises here were awe-inspiring. As a teen, I would dangle from a tire swing hanging from a thick tree branch with my cell phone. Placing the utmost importance on texts from friends, the enchanting view wasn't the only thing I'd taken for granted.

The house was also a stone's throw from the University of Wisconsin-Green Bay, Marinette campus, and my favorite jogging trail was down the block. Most of the time, it was peaceful here. From the outside, it was the enviable home of a successful family. The inside was something else entirely.

Even though I stopped by every day with a new meal prepared for Dad, it was weird to stroll in unannounced. "Dad?"

Dr. Greg Barrett didn't answer, but I wasn't surprised. I worked second shift, and Dad worked...all the time, including weekends. And even when he was home on Sundays, he still had paperwork to do.

I called to him as I stepped inside. "I brought dinner for later."

Still no response.

The house was kept orderly, almost like a sparse museum. Growing up, we never had pets, so everything in the house was exactly the same. Day in and day out, nothing changed, except everyone was gone now, and the house that was once so full of life was a husk, currently holding an open invitation for all the dust bunnies.

As I crossed to the kitchen, framed photographs of our happy family hung on the walls. On tables that served no other function than decoration, photos from charity benefits and weddings waited to be admired. After struggling to furnish my own house, I respected the extravagance my parents were able to provide, but I would've rather had more time with them. Maybe I could've explained my point of view better and earned their acceptance.

A photo from Abby's wedding a few months ago rested on an accent table, pausing my steps. My grinning cousin hugged her new husband, Mike, at their dreamy wedding. They were so happy, so young, with so much life ahead of them.

I couldn't blame Dad for wanting to be away as much as possible after his younger brother, sweet sister-in-law, and adorable niece died the same day Mom had died. Yep, I didn't want to think about Mom's accident being on the same day as mine. Maybe if she'd escaped her car by herself...

Dad must've been suffering her loss, but he never acknowledged what I'd gone through. I had no explanation for how I survived the crash without a scrape, but survivor's guilt was real, and I needed my dad and my sister. Instead, he spent even more time at work, and Lily had left. My sister never returned my calls or texts.

An emptiness I couldn't fill pervaded, like a gray cloud on my head and shoulders, an invisible weight. I still couldn't shake it months later. There were no photos of my graduation in the extensive collection on display because no one made it there. Not even me.

After I'd been carted off to the hospital and given a clean bill of health, my dad was less than sympathetic, as if their deaths were all because I wanted a pat on the head for my minor accomplishment. I'd said, "You were right, Dad. I should've skipped the useless graduation or gone alone. Then they'd still be alive. Maybe even Mom, too."

I was already thirty years old and just finding my footing in life. Then the rug was pulled straight out from under me. I'd landed flat on my face and taken everyone else with me.

Next to Abby and Mike's photo was one of me smiling with Pierce Evansson's arm around my shoulders. We had been in the wedding party. He was a fine-looking man, a fantastic medic—the best I'd ever seen, in fact—and friendly with Dad. I'd hoped having that sliver of approval was enough for me, but like many things in my life, it didn't work out. Despite an exterior package of bulky muscle and chiseled good looks, there was no fire between us.

I wanted Pierce to throw me onto the bed and ravish me like an animalistic teen pumping too many hormones. I wanted to pant and moan and embarrass my roommates. I'd begged for the little teases and flirty smiles my roommates got from their dates, and I'd explained my needs in explicit terms that would make any man lose control. But Pierce just couldn't do that for me, and after he made excuses for skipping my graduation, I swallowed back my loneliness, and I'd broken up with him. I deserved better.

Someday I'd find someone who lit a fire in my heart.

Unfortunately, I'd already accepted a position where Pierce worked, which sounded convenient and fun at the time, but now I actively avoided shift change pleasantries. With a sigh, I turned that photograph around. I wished Dad would get rid of it.

I opened the refrigerator. On the top shelf, I found yesterday's meal uneaten, and I sighed. "So stubborn and prideful, Dad. People have to eat."

Dad didn't accept handouts, even from me, but that wouldn't stop me from trying. I took the spaghetti to eat later and left him the hamburger casserole. On the lower shelf, he had one bottle of water left. I took it and drank it down, promising to buy a case later since I was the primary water connoisseur in the house. There was something unique about the kind Dad bought. The label looked ordinary, but it had herby notes in it—not too strong to detract from the otherwise neutral flavor, but subtle enough to be pleasant. It took me several weeks to even notice.

A door closed upstairs, and I smiled. "Dad? Are you here?"

Footsteps climbed down the stairwell, and I rushed around the corner to greet him.

"Hey, kitten. I have something for you." Dad, wearing his standard uniform of an off-the-rack suit, carried a medium-sized moving box.

"Where are you going?"

"This is yours, left to you in Lisa's will. It was tough to find in their cluttered house." He pushed the box into my arms, and my face twisted with confusion and a fresh wave of painful memories. "Doesn't mean anything to me, so if you don't want the stuff, toss it." Dad swept into the kitchen.

"Are you going into work today?" I followed him and set the box on the granite-top kitchen island, and I dropped onto a stool in front of it. Dad poured coffee into a travel mug from the Wi-Fi controlled pot. That answered that question.

Dad never sat still unless hunched over a microscope or focused on paperwork. His employer was Pharmaceutical Development Inc., where they discovered new ways to fight old diseases. I was to be his protégé, but when it was time to open my wings and fly, I'd landed face first on the ground.

I was beginning to notice a pattern here.

"We're on the verge of a big breakthrough," Dad said calmly. Breakthroughs were an expectation, not a celebration. "Oh, don't forget to take a bottle of water on your way out." Dad collected his briefcase, keys, and the mug.

"I just took the last one. Don't you get *any* time off?"

"Most people have no clue the threat is right in front of their faces. What I'm working on is going to save hundreds of thousands of human lives. It's revolutionary." *Bacteria, viruses, fungi, yeah, yeah. Heard the speech before.* "And you, my kitten, can finally be free to return to medical school."

My mouth dropped open. "I what?"

"You heard me."

"But Dad, I already have too many student loans, and they're not going to accept a dropout. I can't—"

"I don't want to hear excuses," he cut me off, and I shut down. There was no use in arguing with him.

Dad approached me, seriousness on his face. "I want you by my side when these big medical advancements are discovered. I want your name in the journals next to mine, and I want people talking about how you and I saved the world. So, think about that next time you drive around in your meat wagon and bring Aunt Ethel to the emergency room for low blood sugar. You're a Barrett. We're better than that."

Except I'm not. There were no extenuating circumstances in my academic disqualification. With a fake smile, I said, "I know. I'm working on it." Just not how he wanted.

"Good. I'm running late." Dad rushed out the front door.

Once again, I sat in the empty house. I wished I could be his priority. Aunt Lisa was so kind in comparison. My lower lip quivered. I missed her so much. I missed Mom too, but she was different. Like Dad, Mom worked all the time and cared about nothing but her image. At least Dad tried to make something of me. Mom just...appeared sometimes.

Exhaling a deep breath, I pushed the flaps of the box down and looked at what Aunt Lisa wanted me to have.

A couple of framed photographs of me with her, Abby, and my sister Lily smiling together on a girl's outing. I smiled. We'd rented a cabin, sparked a fire—with the touch of a button—and swapped man stories while sipping wine. Aunt Lisa had been vague in her details of my uncle, thankfully, but she did share stories of the previous men in her life. It was the best weekend I'd ever had.

I found a charcoal portrait, hand-drawn, of a trio of women from generations past. The artist's signature contained an O and an R, or maybe a K. The rest was wiggly lines, worn with age. But the year was unmistakable—1870. I shouldn't be touching this piece of real history without gloves. It was far too delicate. Whoever the artist was, the lifelike work was breathtaking in its detail. I gently set it aside, and when I got home, I'd hang both the photo and the drawing with my other art. A burst of excitement tore through me. These women were important to Aunt Lisa. I wanted to know who they were.

I was going to make a discovery. Wasn't that what Dad wanted? I smirked to myself.

Underneath the photos was a worn leather book with symbols on the cover. I lifted it out and paged through it, but I didn't understand anything in it. Like the portrait, the papers were delicate and old. Setting it off to the side, I found a smaller box, a little larger than the palm of my hand. It was wood with symbols similar to the book carved all around it, and the top had a metal latch, currently unlocked. I flipped open the lid, and inside rested a ring nestled between velvet inserts. It was an antique style that didn't fit my tastes, but I loved it anyway. A round ruby stone set in intricate swirls of silver, like curving vines. On each of the broadsides was a single daisy flower, like it was meant for me. I slipped the ring onto my middle finger and admired it.

I would rather have my aunt back, but at least I had something to remind me of her, something I could take with me everywhere as long as I wasn't worried about losing it. I picked up the carved box, and something poked out between the inserts. I slipped the paper free and unfolded it. "This is more valuable than it appears. Protect it. It's the last the Barrett family has. XOXO, Lisa Barrett. P.S. Be careful with the grimoire."

I didn't know what a grimoire was, but I assumed she meant the book. Tears rimmed my lower eyelids, and I brushed them away. "I promise I will."

I pulled out my phone and dialed Lily again. It rang and rang as usual, and her voicemail kicked in. My voice quivered with the pain of the accident being thrust back to the forefront of my mind. "Lily, please call me. I need you. I miss you. Just let me know you're okay."

I hung up and stared at the screen until it went black. Nothing was getting done sitting here. I rubbed my eyes clear and set all the precious valuables and Dad's uneaten leftovers into the box. I left the house, locking up behind me, and when I turned around, I knew the universe wanted to dump more pain onto my lap.

Pierce Evansson walked up the pathway, headed right for me with a friendly grin. I suppressed an audible groan. The frustrating man wore cargo shorts and a band T-shirt. Clearly, he was off-shift today. Deep brown eyes stared at me, but from my point of view, they were empty.

"Pierce, what are you doing here?"

"Looking for your dad. Is he at work?" Even after we'd broken up, Pierce and Dad remained buddies. I hadn't the foggiest idea why.

"He left." I hugged the moving box closer and squinted, waiting for him to get the hint.

Piece's gaze took me in from messy bun to sneakers and back. "You look good, Daisy."

I glanced away, not wanting any compliments from him. "Dad has a phone."

"He hasn't been answering."

At least I wasn't the only one getting the cold shoulder. "Big breakthrough at work again. You know Dad. His medical research is all-consuming."

"Yeah, I figured. I've been calling you, too."

And that was the prelude to the conversation I didn't want to have. "I know."

"I don't know what I did wrong, but I want to apologize either way." His words were calm, level, logical. He didn't appear stricken by being dumped months ago, only confused.

And that was the biggest problem. "We just don't...mesh well. It's not you. It's me, I swear, and that's not some silly line either. I mean it."

Pierce stared at me, processing what vague information I gave him. I couldn't stomach telling him the truth. It wasn't fair. Just because he wasn't the one for me didn't mean he wasn't for someone else. And she deserved a chance to meet him at his best.

"I wish I could fix it," he said softly.

"It's not something that can be fixed. I hope you find someone who makes you happy."

Pierce stepped closer, still unable to read between the lines. "You did."

He was a nice guy, really, but I couldn't deal anymore. He never gave up. For a moment, I almost considered taking him back, erasing the mistake. But that was loneliness talking. I knew that. I looked at the grass, avoiding his eye contact.

"Pierce..." I said dismissively, wishing he would leave.

"If you see your dad, let him know I need to talk to him. It's urgent."

Pierce touched my upper arm with the palm of his hand. It was gentle, but I flinched. He looked me in the eye, and his irises changed color to a pretty green. The lawn must've been reflecting off them. "I don't understand why we didn't work out. You need to change your mind about me. I miss you."

Longing spread through my bones. I missed him too; I really did. Pierce hadn't found a new girlfriend yet, and my childhood bedroom upstairs still had a spacious bed, just waiting to be disheveled. Neither of us had to be alone. We could make this work if I were willing to, and I thought I really did. I opened my mouth to tell him what I really felt, hope surging through me.

"Forget it. Forget what I said. Never mind." The green in his eyes faded back to brown.

Whoa, Pierce was too close. I backed up, pulling away from his awkward touch and uncomfortable with how close he stood. "I need to go, but I'll let Dad know you're looking for him."

"I still love you." Pierce turned away, dejected. I hugged my box.

3

The Snake in His Pants

Daisy

I swirled the breakroom's carafe of hot coffee in a tease for my closest friend and EMS partner.

"Do you want one?" I asked Megan. Since I'd started at Borealis Medical Center a few months ago, Megan had taken me under her wing. At first, she was intimidating—a licensed paramedic younger than me with years of experience, standing several inches shorter than my five foot five, with a blond bob straightened to perfection. Megan was self-assured, put-together, and on track for a great career.

I was none of those things.

"Kevin's in the emergency room tonight. I don't need an extra buzz." Megan bit her lower lip in anticipation.

That poor nurse was going to be flirted with until he combusted. If only Megan were a guy...

We had an hour left on our shift, and the moon was in full display, but the night was still young. I poured myself a cup from the coffeepot and mixed in generous sugar and creamer. It had been a quiet evening so far. Borealis Medical Center's emergency services department had only a pair of ambulances to serve a trio of small cities. There was a volunteer squad elsewhere in town, but I couldn't pay the mortgage with pats on the back. I couldn't pay the mortgage with just a paycheck either, so I had two roommates to help out.

Despite all my setbacks and less than generous paycheck, I loved my job. Accidents, injuries, and health complications brought all people to the same basic level: afraid. For their brief ride in my unit, we were equals, and we all wondered if this could be the end and what it all meant and what could we have done differently. I didn't have the answers they were seeking, but watching people expire on the regular—sometimes too frequently—kept those thoughts at the front of my mind too.

Especially after I'd lost most of my entire family in one day.

My job wasn't always doom and gloom, thankfully. Whenever a sick child slumped over with fever, and after a quick IV bag of fluids, they'd bounce back with sunny smiles. That helped me through the tougher days. Everyone in my unit was a warrior—fighting fear and uncertainty, and that kindness, innocence, and gratitude charged me through each and every shift—and coffee, too.

Naturally, there were bad apples in every city, and my home was no exception, but on the whole, people deserved second chances. They deserved help when they needed it...and sometimes when they didn't want it.

I gave Megan a sly smile, happy for her. "He's cute. Don't scare off the guy."

Kevin Fontaine was a young emergency room nurse, about twenty-five, with dark eyes, buzzed brown hair, and a smooth baby face. From the tales Megan had told me, he had a fabulous bedside manner and kept the flirty old ladies at bay politely and respectfully. I was happy for them, really.

"If he scares easily, then he's not my type." Megan headed for the door, on the prowl for younger meat.

A pang of jealousy tore through me, but I brushed it aside. I had my chance with Pierce, and since he didn't prowl after me—in more ways that one—I chose differently, and no matter how much I drowned my sorrows in drinks at Fully Loaded, I wouldn't succumb to the temptation of Pierce's empty bed.

The overhead announcement called for ambulance 9B to respond to an incident at one of our city parks. Megan froze in her tracks, face scrunching.

I laughed at her reaction as I rushed across the breakroom and tossed my disposable coffee cup in the trash. Megan shifted gears instantly, following on my heels as I pushed through the door and into the garage. I climbed into the driver's seat of our boxy unit.

"I guess Kevin has to wait," I said while my partner buckled in.

"The heart only grows fonder with time," Megan said wistfully.

"Yes, the heart is exactly what I was thinking of." I made a sarcastic snort and started the engine. I said into my radio, "This is unit 9B responding."

Dispatch relayed the vague information of the call, and I turned the wheel, steering us onto the county road, a short hop from a busy shopping center, which at this hour was mostly closed. The sirens and lights alerted the sleeping city of Marinette to the ambulance's race through town.

"Classes are starting soon for the paramedic diploma. Are you signing up this semester?" Megan asked.

My education was a sore spot for me, but Megan only meant well. "I can't swing the commute to Green Bay or the tuition right now. I could hardly cover the exam fees for my EMT license." Not long ago, I had to decide between making a mortgage payment on time or paying my exam fees. Debating between long-term and short-term goals, I swallowed the mortgage late fee. Things had been marginally better since then.

Until my student loan payments begin...

I focused on the road and yelled a few expletives at the distracted drivers ahead of me. The roads were thin this time of night, and eventually the cars moved aside.

"You won't be satisfied staying an EMT forever. Don't get mad at this suggestion, but it's an easy answer...why not ask your dad to help?"

On that heartbreaking call moments before my car accident, while trying to convince my parents to show up at my graduation ceremony, my dad had told me he refused to support me or help in any way unless I graduated from medical school. Apparently, any less was a pointless waste of my life. Even if I were capable of learning the material, that ship had long since sailed. "Negative."

"That's a shame. You'd make a great medic," Megan said with a sympathetic smile.

"I'm perfectly fine as long as I have you."

I turned onto a side street, and as we approached the park given by dispatch, I flipped off the siren. The sporadic streetlights made finding the victim difficult and assessing the safety of the scene even worse.

"Do you see anything?" Megan asked.

I parked the ambulance at the curb. "No."

"He's there." Megan pointed through the windshield and climbed out of the passenger-side door.

Spotting a shadow in the grass, I rushed around to the double doors of the boxy unit and dragged the stretcher out. Megan was already kneeling at our patient's side with the monitor by the time I rolled across the lumpy grass. The man, likely in his mid-twenties, wore athletic shorts and a tank top, like he'd just finished a pickup game of basketball on the other side of the park. Where were his friends? Who called this in and left him alone? *People suck.*

"He's not breathing, and the monitor's not picking up any activity." Megan swept his airway, but it was clear. "Bag him. I'm starting CPR."

"Hey, buddy. Can you hear us?" I asked, pulling on a pair of disposable gloves, but the patient didn't respond. "If you can hear me, I need you to squeeze my hand. Can you do that?" His hand was cold. I wrapped the mask over his face and connected a bag to it.

We counted compressions together.

"I wish the caller stayed to give us more information," Megan said, breathing heavily with the effort. A rib cracked, possibly more than one.

"Does he have a pulse?" I asked, squeezing oxygen into the man's lungs, hoping this guy could pull through. *Breathe, damn it. Just breathe.*

Megan paused and checked his carotid. "What the...?" She pulled back her fingers and gestured.

"What is it?" I shined a light at the man's throat. "This side of his neck looks punctured. I've seen plenty of dog bites in my day, but that doesn't look like Cujo."

Megan cleaned her gloved hand on a towel and mimicked the shape and distance of the puncture wounds with her fingers in the air. "More like a snake's fangs."

"Vipers don't exist in the wild up here. So unless the patient took a grumpy pet for a walk, someone wielded a snake as a weapon in a public park." Bizarre was an understatement.

"The world is becoming nastier by the day."

Good thing I was a night owl. "And weirder."

Megan resumed compressions, and I squeezed the radio button for the online physician. "Hey, control, it's Daisy with the bite victim. This guy is ten-seven, completely cold. Pallor resembling exsanguination, but no sign of blood in the grass. Unresponsive."

Control confirmed.

"Another one," Megan whispered with a tinge of fear in her voice.

There was no point in continuing life-saving measures. I pressed the button again. "We're on the scene, calling for cease orders from the physician."

The doctor on duty gave us the okay and said, "I'll contact the M.E. Standby unit 9B." The voice shut off.

"How many of these have there been now? Three? Four?" Megan asked.

"I think this guy is four." But I hadn't responded to the other dog bite victims. They'd always happened at night, but either off my shift, or the volunteer squad had responded to them. Now I knew what the wounds looked like.

While Megan adjusted the stretcher, I looked at his face, and sadness pulled me down. I wasn't a dog expert, but I really struggled to match a dog's bite to these wounds. Why wasn't the owner shouting for their dog? Why had the caller left him to die? Was the caller a victim too? I glanced around, looking for another shadowy figure lying in the grass, but I couldn't see much in the moonlight.

No one deserved this kind of cruel and pointless end. I wondered what my family thought right before they died. Had they been afraid, or had it happened so fast they didn't realize? This young man's family was going to be devastated, asking themselves endless questions and wondering what they could've done differently so he'd still be alive.

I had.

And here I had a chance to save this man, but I'd been too late. Crappy night all around.

While preparing him to be moved, the victim's eyelid twitched.

Great. Now I was seeing things, too. I needed a drink, and getting fully loaded sounded like a nice escape. "Are you heading to Fully Loaded after shift?"

"The minute that M.E. gets here, I'm going straight back to Kevin. Maybe another time." Megan paused. "Why don't you take Pierce?"

I raised my brows in surprise. I couldn't think of anything less appealing. "Would you take your ex out for drinks?"

"Wait, he didn't give you that ring?" Megan asked, puzzled.

I glanced at the ruby on my finger. "My Aunt Lisa."

"Oh, well, he's still hot. If you agree to a no-strings-attached *friendship*, what harm is there?"

I hadn't told Megan the primary reason we broke up, and this conversation was heading in the wrong direction. "The 'no strings' aspect is pointless."

"Is he gay?" she asked, confused.

I laughed, wishing it were that easy. "Let's just say he's not Mr. Energizer, okay?"

Megan cringed. "I never would've guessed he's a two-pump chump. All those fine looks going to waste."

For some reason, I felt the need to defend Pierce. He wasn't a chump. We just weren't compatible. "Put it this way, if you need a medic who can assess a patient, calmly talk down spinning anxiety, and start an IV without hands shaking, he's perfect. And his track record for saving lives is absolutely unmatched. But if you want to be kissed like there's no one else in the world or have your lights banged out, let's just say he likes to take things slow."

Megan scrunched up her nose. "Hmmm. Almost sounds like a challenge."

Perhaps Megan could teach the man some tricks, and that thought didn't bother me. "Be my guest. If you're lucky, Kevin will join you."

"That's...not a bad idea."

The patient's hand moved. "Did you see that?"

"What?"

"He's moving." I pointed and held my hand steady to make sure it wasn't me.

Megan checked the basketball player's pulse again. "I probably bumped him. He's gone, Daisy. I think you need that drink."

"You're right. Does Kevin have an older brother?"

Megan laughed. "We haven't got that far. I'll have to ask."

"Evening, ladies." A man approached out of the darkness of the park, startling me, and my breath caught in my lungs. "I see you found my friend here."

The basketball player's friend had dark hair gelled back, thick dark brows over pale gray eyes, and his strong jaw sported an enticingly handsome five o'clock shadow. Tearing my gaze from his, I noted the white dress shirt, partially buttoned, exposing the shadows of chest hair, and dark slacks. He wasn't dressed like the basketball player, but not every friend participated in the social event.

The man was simply stunning, unforgettably gorgeous—the kind of man no one forgot. There was something familiar about him, but I couldn't quite place him. I blinked and hid a shameful smile from the dopamine hit to the brain. How inappropriate! Stupid, stupid. I couldn't give him the bad news with a stupid smile on my face.

The stunning man tugged his pant legs up and began to squat beside our victim. With instincts back in full swing, I leaped up for the victim's protection, and I held out my hands. "Back up, please. We're taking care of him."

"I can help," he insisted, but he stepped back politely, and his eyes shifted to my splayed hands with amusement.

Yeah, I weirdly tried to push him back with my palms in the air like some crazed, unarmed bodyguard. "Unless you have a snake in your pants, please leave us room." And of course, I had to look...again. *Open mouth, insert foot.* Heat rushed up my neck and face.

The man chuckled, and he held out a hand to shake. "I like the way you think. I'm Oliver."

Out of politeness and some stupid need to know him better, I accepted his offer. Instead of a simple shake, he twisted my wrist and kissed my knuckles. Soft lips pressed against my skin. My heart sped up, and a shiver danced along my spine. I actively told myself to keep my eyes above his belt from now on, and I blew out a quick breath. He had no business being this hot in this small town.

Oliver's eyes lingered on Aunt Lisa's antique ring on my middle finger, and his demeanor shifted ever so slightly. "That's...a beautiful ring. Where did you get it?" He released my hand, but I didn't want him to.

I twisted the gem to recenter it. "Family heirloom."

Movement next to me stole my attention, and I sucked in a breath. Forgetting to be calm and compassionate in the face of fear, I stared. "Meg, how could the monitor *and* the BP gauge be wrong? Are your fingers numb too because he's moving? Tell me I'm not hallucinating."

"The odds are...astronomical." Megan stared at the stirring bite victim with wide eyes, too.

"If he's alive, we're in trouble for not following protocol," I said but still didn't move.

The victim's arm lifted and dropped over.

I should be jumping to assist a patient in dire need of emergency assistance, but for some reason, my feet were glued to the grass. Dead people didn't move that much, and my training had failed to mention zombies. "Did you see that?"

Oliver approached his friend, and this time I let him. Oliver cradled his friend's skull between his open palms and twisted it violently. The cracking sound was unmistakable.

Megan and I both gasped and took several steps back.

"No worries, ladies. He won't bother you anymore."

My brain misfired, disbelieving what my eyes were showing me. "I...I...I need to call this in. What the hell do I say to control? We need the police." This night was so damned confusing.

The body no longer moved, though.

Megan shook her head and backed toward the ambulance a few more steps. After a short pause, she dashed to the cab of the rig.

I reached for the radio at my shoulder to call for backup, but when I blinked, Oliver stood inches from me. My chest could almost graze his. That masculine scent—comforting and completely sexy—filled my nose, and my heart sped up faster. He was very close. Too close. This...completely mesmerizing *murderer* was too close. I needed to run, to call for help from the safety of the rig, but I couldn't move. His handsome guy was an ordinary human, not some dog with chase instincts. Why wasn't I running?

"Hi," I said awkwardly and finally managed a step back.

Oliver chuckled again. "Hi." His eyes reflected the brilliant flashing red from the ambulance's lights, and I was hypnotized by their beauty. "I didn't snap his neck. Don't be afraid."

Why would this sexy stranger say that? The only I was thinking was I needed a date tonight, and every inch of my body wanted him...all of him. My hand still hovered uselessly at my radio, and now I couldn't remember why I'd intended to call anyone. But I felt like I'd spent too much time not paying attention to my patient. My boss was going to have my head.

"Oliver, I need you to give us space to take care of your friend, but I'm afraid he isn't going to make it."

A sly smile reached his lips, but he still hadn't backed up. "Daisy, a dead body rests five feet from you, but the only thing on your mind is me."

I frowned. I didn't remember giving him my name. But my heart sped up with his words, and thinking of his hands on me, another flash of heat tore through my body. That ego was as massive as—my gaze snapped below his belt—damn it. How could he so easily distract me? "Have we met?"

The handsome stranger gave me a crooked smile, and I only wished to know what he was thinking.

"Abby's wedding."

That was it! Now I remembered the gorgeous guy in a fabulous suit...who hadn't seemed friendly with Pierce. That was about all I remembered...oddly. Now I understood why he was so strange—he knew me, but I didn't know him. "I thought you looked familiar. No one's a stranger in a small town. Look, Oliver, it's nice to talk to you, but I need to do my job."

"Then I'll leave you to it. But first, look at me." Oliver urged.

I met his gaze, and his eyes flashed red again.

"Daisy, he's been bitten by a dog. You did nothing wrong."

My patient was bitten by a dog. Honestly, Oliver didn't seem too distraught over the loss of his friend, but the two of them might not have been super close. People dealt with grief differently, and I had plenty of experience with that.

I scanned the area for a foaming Cujo, but with the moonlight and a few cones of light from streetlights, I couldn't make out much. If the dog carried a fatal bite, I didn't want Megan or myself or whoever Oliver was to be next. I turned back to warn him to seek safety, and to ask if he'd like to join me at Fully Loaded later. But Oliver was gone. How could he move so quickly and quietly? I spun around, looking for him, and exhaled a deep breath.

I glanced at the body, daring it to move again, but it didn't. The medical examiner's vehicle rolled to a stop nearby, and a police cruiser followed. Megan brought them over.

"The M.E.'s here, and I have a hot date tonight. Things are looking up," Megan said, unusually high-spirited considering a basketball player was attacked by a roaming dog and moved after dying. The human body was a science-defying marvel sometimes...or I just really needed that drink.

"I can take care of this," I told Megan.

"Awesome. Thanks!" My partner tapped away on her cell phone, likely texting Kevin, as she headed back for the cab.

The medical examiner squatted down and checked his vitals before filling out a report. The officer asked me questions, but I didn't have much to tell him.

"One's curious. Two's a coincidence, but four is a serial killer," the medical examiner said, tucking her pen behind her ear.

The end of this shift couldn't come fast enough. "We need to notify animal control," I offered.

"Until someone sees the animal in question, we can't go knocking on doors and swabbing jowls," the officer said.

I assisted the M.E. with shifting the body into the dreaded black bag, and she zipped it up over the patient's head. And on the count of three, we lifted him onto the stretcher.

This town just kept getting weirder and weirder, and despite that, I couldn't stop thinking about Oliver. I'd never met anyone who affected me like that. I never got a chance to ask him out or get his phone number, and I wanted to ask him about Abby's wedding. I remembered only a few flashes, which was so utterly...confusing.

Besides, I needed to inspect that snake in his pants, you know, for science.

4

It's Her

Oliver

A SINGLE CHOICE COULD change everything, and I laughed to myself at my good fortune. Rather than continue the exhilarating chase through the woods a few months ago, I'd chosen to feed on accident victims. And who should appear? Daisy Barrett. Now the rogue vampire—whose identity I had yet to verify—was leaving bodies in my town. So, I'd paused the chase once more to save another of his victims. And who should arrive?

Daisy Barrett, the lovely woman I'd been determined to find one day and sweep off her feet. But she still wasn't free for the wooing, and I had other problems. While lurking, my hypersensitive vampire hearing had picked up on where she was going tonight. And because Daisy Barrett wore something I'd been hunting for over a century, I would be there. Nothing—not even my mortal enemy—was going to stand between me and recovering the greatest weapon for vampires ever created.

First, I needed a place to crash during the daytime to avoid discovery or accidental death by sunlight, and I needed to change my suit and freshen up. My old house was just what I needed.

The stately three-story brick building commissioned in 1880 stood before me in all its grandeur, just how I had designed it. From the trio of rooftop dormers and the ground floor's oversized windows, glowing light sprayed across the darkened lawn like a cackling jack-o'-lantern. The imposing white columns of the front porch, with scroll flourishes at the tops and bases, were divided halfway with a balcony, the perfect scenic lookout over the river for entertaining or relaxing.

Bracing myself for the condition of my home, I climbed the concrete steps and opened the door. I reached out my palm at the threshold, and the mystic barrier refused me entrance...as intended. She was still here. She was still alive. I wasn't too late. Good news didn't come around that often.

I knocked on the doorjamb several times with no response. I'd forgotten how close to deaf humans were, but since I was in a fantastic mood tonight, I was surprisingly patient.

A salt-and-pepper-haired man in an off-the-rack business suit answered the door, puzzled. I wanted to rip his throat out for being on my property, but I couldn't reach him. Yet.

"It's a B&B, you don't have to knock," he said.

In my absence, I'd needed the property maintained and protected. A bed-and-breakfast wasn't my choice, but my niece claimed it would serve my purpose, make use of the excessive bedrooms, give her a purpose, and bring in an income. Despite not needing more income and rejecting the excess bedrooms descriptor, I really had no argument.

"Please send the hostess to me. I have something to discuss with her." Like needing to park my vintage car in the garage before some gawker or opportunistic squirrel scratched the paint.

The man shrugged and turned away. I waited outside on my own porch for embarrassingly too long. My exceptional hearing finally picked up her voice. She was annoyed by the interruption of *some door-to-door peddlers*.

The solid wood door opened the rest of the way with impatience, and when my niece spotted my handsome mug, her face blanked. Straightened gray hair hung below her shoulders, and the lines of time pulled at her skin. Like the businesswoman she'd been her entire life, she wore a floral blouse and dress pants. Her aged eyes still sparkled with the pizzazz of someone half her age. I shouldn't have stayed away for so long.

"It's me, Nicole."

Her head tilted to the side as she scrutinized me. Recognition and a wistful smile dawned on her features. "You haven't aged a day."

"I can't say the same about you." A painful reminder that in no time at all, another beloved family member would be gone forever.

She playfully swatted me on the shoulder.

"Please let me in and give your uncle a hug."

A warm smile touched her eyes. "Oliver Rockwell, please come inside."

"Oh, so formal." With the mystical boundary released, I crossed the threshold and held my arms out.

My niece limped closer, and I embraced her.

"How's the hip doing?"

"It doesn't get better with age, but never mind me. I haven't heard a word from you in decades. I was starting to wonder whether you were still alive."

"I'm not."

Nicole pulled away but kept a firm grip on my arms, as if she feared I would disappear for another four decades. "You know what I mean. How long are you planning on staying this time?"

"I don't know for sure, but I want you to stay with me." For as long as nature decided.

My niece's eyes sparkled with excitement. "I wish you would've relented years ago. I don't know if I want to be a limping vampire for all eternity."

Ever since Nicole was in her late teens, she'd begged for the change. She'd complain about all the human things plaguing her that I no longer faced, and she'd said keeping the gift to myself was unfair. She then begged me to promise that if she were ever gravely injured or mortally diagnosed, I would do it then.

Over the decades, I'd made two vampires, and both still haunted me. I'd never turn another human again, even the people I loved.

"That's not what I meant." I gave her a sad smile.

Disappointment had her turning away. "Come on. It's dark out there."

The Persian rugs on the floors and walls were clean. The cool-toned oak banisters were shiny with polish, and the matching wood beams running parallel along the ceilings were dust-free. Most importantly, the bar was stocked.

A pair of affectionate guests drank coffee by the crackling fireplace in my sitting room. The man who'd answered the door typed on a laptop on my chaise lounge. I glared at him. Now that I was inside, my anger toward him lessened. Lucky for him. But this invasion by humans wasn't going to do at all.

"I see you've kept the place going."

"It's going, but it's not as easy as it once was. Tastes are changing. Trends are on a constant roller coaster, and I'm afraid bed-and-breakfasts are out of style."

I glanced around my classically decorated home. "What do you mean, out of style?"

Nicole chuckled softly. "Only you, with endless time on your hands, can be so oblivious to the world around you."

I was aware. Technology changed faster than I could adapt. After the last thirty years, I wanted to throw my hands up in the air and turn my back on all of it. The struggle to keep up with change was one of the worst drawbacks. I tried not to dwell on it, since I never chose this life.

"So how bad is it?" I asked.

"Follow me into my office." Nicole led us upstairs, away from the prying ears of guests, where my bookshelves and statues were dust-free, and all my art remained on display. I appreciated Nicole's respect for my things. Some pieces were purchased from artists I admired and had to own. The rest were of my own hand. Drawing scratched a creative itch and allowed me a form of expression I couldn't speak out loud. I captured unwitting strangers together, smiling faces of children, and long-lost family. Always people.

Around the corner and down a corridor, she led me into my old bedroom. I'd left my furniture draped in sheets, but it didn't stay that way. "I hope you don't mind. No one was here to complain, so why not take the best? I had the bathroom updated to include a walk-in glass shower with four showerheads, and I replaced your threadbare bedding."

"Right this way," Nicole said, and sat behind my lacquered, hand-carved desk. She'd modernized my room and commandeered my desk.

I strolled over to the balcony. Outside the oversized windows and under the moon's glow, city lights dotted along the far bank of the silent and swift Menominee River. "Nice view for an office."

"I know." Nicole opened a laptop in front of multiple curved screens.

I ran my hand along the mahogany. "I bought this desk in 1882 at an auction. It was owned by the local trading baron before his doors shuttered, and he got it from France—"

"I know, dear," Nicole interrupted sweetly. She had heard the story behind every piece in this house. Sometimes I forgot, or perhaps I was just happy to talk to someone who understood me.

Nicole opened a file and pointed to lines on a spreadsheet. I sat on the edge of the desk and followed her finger so I didn't get lost in all the mayhem. "See this here? We're still in the black, but each year, the margins are getting narrower. It's a good thing you've invested well over the decades. With how little this place brings in, I'm surprised you want it to stay running."

"I appreciate your honesty, but that's why I'm here."

Nicole looked at me over her shoulder. She said, dejected, "I don't understand."

I stood up straight. "I'm moving back in, and I want the operations shut down at once. You know I don't like to share." With humans, anyway.

"Shut down?" Nicole rose in alarm. "If you're not staying, I could block out a vacation week so guests can't reserve that time. Then the place is all yours, but I still have a business after you leave."

"That's a great idea. Give me two weeks." That should be enough time to close off this rogue vampire issue and recapture my long-lost weapon from the beautiful Daisy Barrett.

"You've been gone forty years, and I'm thrilled you're back. Pardon my suspicion, but what's changed? Why return now?"

I rested a hand on her shoulder and leveled a gaze at her. "A vampire is in town."

My niece chuckled. "Yeah, I'm looking at him."

"Not me. This guy is sloppy, leaving bodies at random. I have to stop him before we have a repeat of Peshtigo, 1871."

Her hand covered her mouth, and she shook her head. Nicole hadn't been there, obviously, but she'd been told the truth of that devastating fire. "It's that serious? I can't believe it."

"If he makes his way here, don't let him inside. Nothing is worth your life, understood?" I couldn't live with myself if something happened to her—the only family I had left whom I loved.

Nicole nodded. "You seem certain it's a 'he', and you're warning me about him coming here. Do I even have to say his name?"

The rogue vampire carried the signature style of Soren Rockwell, my estranged younger brother. I never wanted to see him again, but if he were responsible for all those deaths, then I'd finally get my wish. He deserved much worse than a stake through the chest, though.

"Indeed, you don't. I have to get a few things before I settle in. By chance, is the refrigerator stocked for me?"

"My apologies, but I wasn't aware you were coming. I will have your favorite ready in the morning. A-positive, right?"

"I knew I liked you. If the staff at the blood bank gives you grief, let me know. I'll have your badge reinstated at once."

"Thank you." Nicole left.

I uncovered my bed. Nicole had updated the fluffy bedding, and that included a confusing number of throw pillows. Most importantly, my closet filled with custom-tailored suits was organized by color and dust-free. This was still home.

I slipped out of my clothing and inspected my white shirt for blood. Happily, it was clean. I went straight for the remodeled bathroom and fired up the four showerheads. This was one technological improvement I could agree with.

While I spent my free time hunting a rogue vampire, I was spending tonight on a date at Fully Loaded. I was getting my weapon back after all these decades, and I was going to enjoy Daisy Barrett in the process. I whistled while I lathered.

5

Flirty Tease

Daisy

BEFORE HEADING ALONE TO Fully Loaded, I'd showered and changed into jeans and a cute top. I left my heirloom ring tucked away in its antique box inside my dresser, since I didn't want it stolen at the bar. And I'd pulled my hair into a messy bun to pretend the nest on my head was on purpose. I wasn't here to attract attention.

I only wanted to forget and visit with a friendly smiling face. I pulled out a stool and dropped down at the bar. Fully Loaded was busy tonight. Sleek, modern gray and neon green accents filled the space with a masculine yet trendy feel, and it succeeded in attracting the twenties through forties crowd.

There was no live band on stage in the side room tonight, but people danced to the thumping sound system anywhere they had a place to stand. A pool cue cracked in the adjacent room, and people cheered. Others played darts nearby. Stupidly, one from their group sat under the dartboard, and they laughed at how close they were to hitting their friend with the metal tips. Idiots. I was finally off shift and not interested in assisting with foreign body removal.

A few people sat at the bar alongside me, but they kept their distance, which was fine. I wasn't in the mood to socialize, and others slid up to the bar for orders and left. I waited for my bartender to make her way over. Not only was this bar a convenient walking distance to my home, but I tried to be supportive of my roommate, too.

Allison Kincaid was a few years younger than me, and she too struggled to pay bills. Hence, roommates. Her light brown hair had sun-kissed highlights, and she wore thick-framed reading glasses when she felt saucy. Or she needed more tips. The librarian thing worked when slinging booze.

Allison smiled at me and set an empty glass on a cocktail napkin. "Rough night?"

"Another bite victim." I glanced over my shoulder at the idiots playing darts. "And that's looking like the next emergency call."

Allison followed my gaze and rolled her eyes. The dart thumped into the wall, entirely missing the dartboard and the drunk idiot standing in front of it. The group laughed.

"If you ever want to join me on this side of the wood again, the job offer is always on the table," Allison said. "Then you wouldn't have to do anything for those idiots but dial a phone number."

Tempting.

While working through undergrad, I had been a bartender alongside Allison, and because we got along well, she moved in with me. I liked the work, and to be honest, the tips were nice, but I felt a calling to do more with my life. Maybe it was Dad's influence, but I had no regrets. But after what I'd been seeing in the field lately, slinging booze and giving pep talks to brokenhearted men sounded like a vacation.

But vacations were temporary, and in no time, I'd be lost without my job. "I appreciate the offer, but I'm good. Thanks."

"Let's see, I'm prescribing you vodka with lemon." Allison poured the clear liquid into my glass and pressed a fresh slice onto the rim. I always let her pick. Eventually I'd choose a favorite to stick with, but until then, there were too many flavors to try before I knew which one fit me just right, the drink that announced this was me, fitting my personality to a T.

I downed the drink in two generous gulps. Warmth trailed down my throat and into my stomach. My roommate lifted a surprised eyebrow and refilled my glass.

Answering her unspoken question, I said, "Tonight's bite victim moved *after* he died, and I'm not talking about a postmortem muscle twitch. I think I'm losing my mind."

Allison frowned. "We all process breakups differently. Some people slide through the stages of grief right away; others experience a delay. Whatever is making you see unnatural things is likely as natural as they come. All that to say, you're not losing your mind. I tell you what, anytime I see that glass empty, I'll fill it. But you need to make sure you can get home in one piece, okay?"

"Deal," I said and made the second shot disappear with a pinch of my features. Alcohol burned my throat and zipped through my veins, calming the chilling scene in my head. I couldn't see anything natural about it, but Allison was rarely wrong. My bartender was too busy with other customers to notice my need for a third.

"Slow down there, Doc, or someone's going to have to carry you to the emergency room. I have a feeling you don't want to visit work tonight," a familiar masculine voice said.

My breath was swept away from me. I'd remember Oliver's smooth voice anywhere. I turned with butterflies warring in my stomach, and Oliver's presence stole my gaze. He'd changed into a fresh suit, minus a tie, and his striped button-down shirt was partially opened at the throat. I feasted on his exposed skin, drinking in the flecks of soft dark hair. Oliver rested his drink next to me and shrugged out of his suit jacket. Sitting on the stool to my right, he draped the jacket over his lap and rolled his shirtsleeves up, displaying his strong forearms dusted with more dark hair. Heat flushed my face.

I pictured Oliver carrying me to the emergency room, and after another thump of my heart, my inner spaz calmed. Pierce had volunteered to pick up a shift tonight. "You have no idea how right you are."

Oliver's eyes flashed with confidence, and his lips lifted in a self-satisfied tease. He took a sip of his drink, and as Allison moved near us, he glared at her for an instant. "Is it warm in here, or is it just me, Daisy?" Capturing my gaze, his fingers unbuttoned the next button of his shirt.

The roar of alcohol only made my hot flash worse. I turned away and fanned my face with my hand. I wanted to run my fingers all over his body. It should've been a crime to be so damned attractive. So flirtatious. With a face like that, he must've flirted with everyone. So either he was smashed himself, or he was looking for something.

The idea of an ulterior motive helped me focus. I gestured at Allison. "My roommate has her eye on me."

"Someone's awfully lucky," he said.

Agreed. Saucy librarian worked, capturing his attention. I sighed, resigned to my beautiful roommate stealing this guy's interest. I drummed my fingers on the bar, wishing she'd return with my refill.

"Can I buy you a drink?" Oliver asked.

Surprised, I turned to find him gazing at me, and only me. This was too good to be true. He was so far out of my league, there had to be a catch. I'd feel bad taking the guy's money and walking away. "Listen, I think you're great, but don't bother, okay?"

Oliver gestured for Allison's attention anyway. "Now why would I not bother?"

The liquor loosened my tongue, and I didn't care that I was being completely straight with him. "You're larger than life and absolutely hot. You can have any woman or man in this bar, so I don't know why you're bothering with me."

"Ouch," Oliver said, feigning insult. "What makes you think I want anyone but you?"

In a sea of sexy, gyrating bodies with lowered inhibitions, that didn't answer my question. Seeing right through his player personality, I snorted and changed the subject. "Someone's chipper for just losing a friend."

Oliver smiled, showing his bright whites, and he swayed on his stool. Okay, he was smashed, which was actually comforting, a normal reaction to loss.

"Your lovely roommate over there already introduced me to my newest friend. I'd like you to meet Jose Cuervo." He lifted the half-empty glass. "I think we should share him."

I smiled, no longer concerned about his mental health. He was grieving. "Oh, kinky."

Oliver laughed. "I like the way you think."

He'd said that before, and now I couldn't help but think he meant it. More heat flushed through me while Oliver gestured for Allison's attention again. She finally made her way to us. Round three and four became tequila, and the horrors of earlier now felt like a distant dream. A solid buzz energized my limbs. I had every intention of scratching an itch tonight, if I could hold Oliver's attention.

"I haven't seen you around town. Where are you from?" I asked, hoping he wasn't just passing through.

"Here and there, but I'm back for a little while." His eyes moved to my hands, and he watched me finish my next drink. More heat burned on its way into my bloodstream as if the fire in his eyes caressed my body with promises.

Oliver placed his elbow on the bar and faced me with his head resting on his fist, studying me, as if I were to only person in this bar. His eyes drank me in, and my heartbeat kicked into high gear. I didn't deserve this kind of attention from a man so far out of my league, but I wasn't going to push him away again.

I asked, "Are you here to thank me for trying to save your friend? Which I'm still sorry about, by the way."

Oliver leaned in close, his breath warm against my ear. I sucked in a breath. "A couple shots of my favorite drink is hardly thanks enough. What do you say we get out of here?"

With a growing throb between my legs, he didn't have to ask twice. I nodded and slipped cash out of my back pocket. Oliver stopped me. "I have it covered already. Let's go."

I wasn't in a position to argue with his generosity, and I certainly wasn't going to turn down a chance at those lips. When he offered his hand, I took it, but when I stood, I swayed. Perhaps I'd had a little too much too fast. But I was having fun for the first time in a long while, and both of us were on a mission tonight.

Oliver flung his jacket over a shoulder and wrapped my hand around his arm. Holding the front door for me, he led me outside. Streetlights dotted the thick air, instantly making my skin sticky. I pushed hair out of my face and stumbled on a crack in the sidewalk. Oliver caught me. Our eyes met, and his gaze was hungry, dark, and...sober?

Or I was just too drunk.

"Careful there. We wouldn't want to mar those tight jeans of yours," he said.

I sent him a dopey smile and hung onto his arm. We walked a slow, lumbering path toward the parking lot. It was almost bar close time, and Fully Loaded would be unloading soon. Privacy wouldn't last long. There weren't any alleys around, just individual brick buildings and the main thoroughfare through town. Not that I would do anything to this man in a dirty alley. He deserved better than that.

I deserved better than that.

Shouts of alarm came from the bar. Likely, the dart thrower's luck finally ran out.

"Did you drive?" he asked.

I pointed, unable to describe the direction to my house. "Walked, you?"

"I left my car at home, too."

We crossed the street with minimal traffic and lumbered down the quiet sidewalk. I tried hard not to think, why me? What did I do to get this lucky? But that was all that ran through my head.

A siren wailed in the distance, gaining on us quickly.

Oliver said, "It's headed this way."

"Idiots were playing darts. I'm off shift and not in any condition to help. Let's go." Besides, Pierce was on duty.

"What dragged you to the bar for a night of self-destruction?" he asked.

"Wasn't it for the same reason you were there?"

Oliver paused for a beat. "Oh, my friend's death? Yes, quite upsetting, but I don't see why he needs to affect you so."

I sighed heavily. "Sometimes a tough call gets under your skin, and it's hard to shake. I mean, the young guy was playing basketball with his friends—with you—and a dog came out of nowhere, chewed his throat out, and ran off. No one found the dog yet. That was upsetting enough, but the reason I needed the forgetty juice was—and don't take this the wrong way, I'm sure it's just me—I saw him move after he died."

I glanced at Oliver in alarm. I probably shouldn't have said that. Either I upset him or I sounded crazy. "I mean, you were there. Didn't you see it?"

Oliver leaned in close, and I breathed in his scent, helpless to resist anything about him.

"I'll let you in on a little secret. I don't know his name. I found him and called it in, and since he was in rough shape, I pretended to be his friend so he wouldn't be alone. So, I'm upset but not devastated."

He was only a Good Samaritan. What a rare breed. In surprise, my hand loosened from his arm, but Oliver quickly recaptured it as if I'd lost my balance. There had to be a catch. No one was this perfect. Since I only wanted one night to rival Megan's lust-filled evenings with Kevin, Oliver's skeletons would remain hanging in his closet.

The ambulance rolled by us, and I cringed, thinking Pierce could've seen me. We'd broken up—completely over—but still, I didn't want to rub a new guy in his face, even if Oliver was only for tonight.

When the sirens quieted enough to speak again, I said, "In that case, I'll let you in on a little secret, too. The basketball player wasn't the first victim."

"Oh? We have a murderous canine running the streets?" Oliver craned his neck around as if searching for the beast's approach.

Well, shit. I didn't think we'd be at risk ourselves. A trickle of fear sobered me quickly as we turned the corner to my block. "That one is me, the beige with...lovely...maroon shutters."

Picking up on my sarcastic description, Oliver smiled. "They are hideous, aren't they?"

I barked a laugh at his honesty. "Yeah."

"Truth be told, I have a soft spot for vintage styles. Someone once designed this place with their own eyes, using their heart and soul, hoping to make people feel like the world around them could still be beautiful, cozy, and warm."

His words were a melody to my ears, and I needed to confess. "I actually love my maroon shutters. Everyone I know thinks my house is ugly, but I secretly love it."

"You can be honest with me. I don't judge."

I smiled softly. He was just too perfect, and my soberness yanked away the beer goggles. Once again, I questioned his intentions. "What is it you're doing here with me? I don't want to be a buzzkill, but are you actually trying to get to know *me*?"

Oliver stopped us near my gate and turned to face me. With the nearby streetlights and soft glow from the moon, he was both menacing and handsome. His hands gripped mine. "Why wouldn't I? From the moment I met you, I knew you had a good heart. To put on your uniform every night, you'd have to. And our meeting again at the bar wasn't a coincidence."

I waited. His words were sweet, but I wanted to hear more.

"I can see when someone isn't happy. Like a sixth sense, it stands out to me in an obvious way. You weren't at that bar because of a disturbing bite victim. You lost someone recently, and a reminder tipped you over the edge."

I'd lost my whole family—Uncle Marc, Aunt Lisa, my cousin Abby, my mom, and effectively my sister Lily—all in one day. The bite victim had reminded me that loss could be unpredictable and wholly unfair. Oliver was perceptive, and a little unnerving in his accuracy, but still, I was glued to every word.

He continued, "You need someone who challenges you, who makes you proud but also angry with stubbornness. Someone who consumes your thoughts with their passion. Someone who makes you feel alive. You won't be satisfied settling for mediocrity." His eyes shifted to my lips.

"How do you know all this?" I asked breathlessly.

"Takes one to know one."

6

Catching the Snake

Daisy

I WAS SPEECHLESS. NEVER had anyone's words affected me so. Everything he said felt like he rummaged in my thoughts and put into words what I couldn't. Like he knew me, he saw through me. His stunning pale gray eyes held my gaze, and I was helpless to look away. "I don't know what to say."

Oliver's fingers lifted my chin, making our lips inches apart. "I mean it. You're beautiful."

My chest shuddered with shallow breaths as the throbbing down low continued to grow. Like a gentleman, he waited for me to close the distance between us. I moved closer. *Take me. Take me now,* I silently begged, but the words wouldn't pass my lips. He gazed at my mouth, and I trembled with need and flushed with desire. I leaned forward to bring us together, but I stumbled.

Oliver caught me, and his attention tracked to the edge of the darkness. He frowned.

"What's wrong?" I asked. Did I drool? Was I more drunk than I thought?

"Nothing. There's nothing wrong. Let's get you inside."

Great idea. He supported me as we passed through my gate and climbed the unusually difficult steps to my front door. I fumbled with the slick knob, and Oliver opened the door for me. Oh, yeah. Definitely too much to drink.

"You should keep this locked."

"Someone's always coming or going. Mostly, it's pointless."

Something in the darkness captured his attention again, and my stomach flipped with worry. Was the dog here? I didn't want to stick around to find out, and I didn't want to climb into bed alone tonight.

"Are you joining me?" I asked playfully. After all the teasing and sweet talk, I thought he was a sure thing.

Oliver stared off. I couldn't see anything, but I waited, listening. All I could hear was the pounding of my heart in anticipation, or was that fear?

He turned back to me, and the fire in his eyes returned. "Invite me inside, and I'll join you."

"You don't need to be invited," I said. I dragged a finger down his firm chest, and I walked backward into my living room with the sauciest lick of my lips I could pull off.

Oliver braced himself at the threshold, a half-smile tilting his lips. "You have to invite me first."

A tease indeed. I returned to him and unbuttoned his shirt, one little button at a time, while Oliver's eyes darkened.

"At this rate, the neighborhood is going to get the same great show as me, and that's not fair. Come in and save yourself an indecent exposure call."

Oliver's hands clamped over mine, and he stepped inside, walking me backward. He kicked the door shut and pushed me up against it. His nose touched mine, and my breath dragged in and out.

"Which room is yours? Unless you want your roommates to get a show instead."

"Upstairs to the left," I said breathlessly.

Oliver's lips touched the corner of my mouth. I turned my head to meet them, but he moved to the other side and touched again. Warm breath puffed against my face, and a warm throbbing built between my legs. Frustrated with the tease, I gripped his head between my hands and kissed him deeply.

A soft chuckle rumbled in his chest, and he pulled away for an instant. "That's how you want to play?"

"I like it hard, fast, and rough." And it had been way too long since I'd had anything remotely satisfying.

His eyes darkened with desire, and he gripped me by the hips and pressed me against him. A firm length pressed back. "Your wish is my command, Daisy."

His mouth recaptured mine, and I moaned as his tongue slipped into my mouth. Oliver lifted me up as if I weighed nothing. I wrapped my legs around his hips, and he brought us upstairs in a hurry.

At the foot of my bed, he stopped, and I climbed down. Oliver flung his suit jacket over a chair. My feverish hands finished unbuttoning his shirt, and I opened the fabric. The level of perfection in one man was simply unfair. To match his beautiful face and stunning eyes, his curves were in all the right places, from lean pecs to chiseled abs, and a prominent V. A happy trail of soft hair directed me from his belly button to what hid beneath low-hanging pants.

I totally didn't deserve a man like this, but since he was in my room, I wasn't going to let a defeatist attitude ruin this fantasy.

"Like what you see?" he asked.

I rested my palms on his pecs. "I want to see every last inch of you."

The corner of his lips lifted. "There's a lot of inches left to uncover."

I smiled deviously. "A full snake's worth."

Oliver kissed my lips again, and his nimble fingers worked at the button and zipper of my jeans. He pulled them down with practiced efficiency, and his fingertips caressed the skin beneath my underwear, my basic black underwear. I stifled a groan. I hadn't planned on hooking up tonight.

He didn't seem to care as his hands started on my shirt. I unfastened his pants quickly and tried pulling them down, but I had to stop. His rounded buttocks were a thing of glory. I gripped him tightly and squeezed. Oliver's lips pulled away for a moment to lift my shirt off, revealing my plain white bra. I hadn't bothered matching. Shame! Shame!

Oliver looked me over and pulled his own pants down, revealing his boxer briefs, and finally a satisfying, but not terrifying length, ready and primed for use. His arm wrapped around me, and with a twitch of his forearm, my straps came loose and my breasts fell free. His smooth hands slid the straps down my arms, palms caressing my skin, and he captured my breasts in his mouth. My head fell back in sweet ecstasy.

Oliver scooped me up and set me on the bed, never once breaking contact. Without a word, he gathered my wrists and pulled them above my head. With his free hand, he tugged the band of my underwear down, and my hips moved, begging to be filled with his length. I couldn't touch him—the biggest tease—and I ached to put my hands on him.

He admired my naked body, and heat rushed through me as if his own hands did the caressing. I panted in anticipation. "You're such a tease."

Oliver lifted his brows. "Oh? We have four hours until dawn, so there's no rush. Do you have any rubbers around here?"

I gritted my teeth. I hadn't thought of that. Hopefully they weren't extra crispy with age. I gestured my head toward the end table. "Top drawer."

Oliver released my wrists. "Don't move."

I chuckled. "I won't."

"Don't touch."

I grinned. Tease...

He slid open the drawer, read the label on the package, and tore it open. He rolled the protection over his length, moving nice and slow on purpose. I kept my wrists overlapped, waiting for him to resume taking me.

All wrapped up, he leaned over me and gripped my wrists, and I hooked my legs around his hips and pulled him closer. I wasn't skilled enough to aim him without my hand, but I rocked against him in silent pleading. Oliver leaned down and kissed my jaw. Light butterfly kisses trailed from my ear down my throat. He spent extra time at my neck, leaving me panting harder.

His thumb found my throbbing clit, and while he slowly built a steady stroke, his fingers penetrated. I tensed with a frenzied need to come all over his hand.

"That's right. Let it all out. I want to hear you scream."

His magic fingers ground against my sensitive skin, and short moans rumbled from deep in my throat.

Oliver's mouth trailed lower toward my breast, and the shot of hypersensitive nerves sent me crashing over the edge. I screamed out. His self-satisfied smile followed, and his fingers slowed to a stop. I wasn't done yet.

He repositioned himself over me, and this time, he released my wrists. My body trembled and pulsed, but still I needed more. When he lined himself up, I aimed him, and he slipped inside with a groan of pleasure. Giving himself a beat, I grabbed those round firm glutes and held him, relishing the fullness. He gently glided back and pushed in farther, and again and again until he filled me tight.

"You still want it fast?" he asked gruffly.

"Yes, please," I said, panting.

"Whatever the lady wants." Oliver thrust into me, no longer gentle. My body rocked on the bed frame, and for a flash of a second, I worried about my bed breaking. But if it did, it was worth it. A sheen of sweat covered his smooth skin. I gripped his glutes in my hands and helped him thrust. Not that he needed it. He kept going and going relentlessly, and his hand once again found my clit. His fingers stroked slowly at first and then built up a momentum matching his.

I pulled his face down to me and kissed his throat, nipping at the skin. He groaned and tensed, and his panting paused as a rippling orgasm pulsed inside me, but his fingers kept going until I too, froze with the explosion of heat.

His fingers slowed, and I panted and kissed the salty sweat off his throat.

Oliver's breathing slowed, and he relaxed, facing me with a lazy grin. "We still have three and a half hours left."

I laughed. "I don't know about you, but I'm a grouch without sleep."

Oliver pulled himself out and swiped his forehead. He unrolled the used condom. "Are you kicking me out? Because I make one hell of a naked breakfast."

Hell, no. "Not at all, but I need to use the bathroom. Be right back."

Oliver stretched out on my bed, hands behind his head, full glory on display, and I smiled in appreciation.

In the bathroom, I made sure to pee right away, and I brushed my hair and teeth. I gargled mouthwash to fight the stale liquor lingering on my breath. When I returned to my bedroom, he was sound asleep. I curled up next to him and threw a sheet over us. He was just perfection. Something had to be wrong with him, and I was determined to find out what it was. But that could wait until tomorrow. I fell asleep with my head on his chest.

7

Who is This Woman?

Oliver

Daisy—a beautiful, sexy, unexpected woman—was about to fall asleep next to me. She consumed my thoughts. As much as I wanted to give her the full 'hard, fast, and rough' experience, I could break her in half with my bare hands, so I had to keep myself in check at every moment. Hold back. Resist. Daisy was a fragile human, which, on the plus side, meant her furniture stayed intact. If she had been a vampire like me, we could've shifted up a few gears, reaching our potential with intimate blood sharing, a sacred bond between vampires. But those thoughts were far too premature, because after more than a century of searching for just the right vampire to bond with, it never happened.

As long as my younger brother was alive, it was pointless to try.

Soren Rockwell had teased me about the blood bond commitment, deciding long ago it was a waste of a vampire's heightened emotions. It drove a male vampire to recklessness and risked exposure of our entire hidden society. As if dropping bodies all over town wasn't a risk…

Once I thought I'd found a companion worthy of eternity, but Soren's teasing turned into vicious threats. Not believing him capable of such a heinous act, I ignored him to my own detriment. Now I couldn't bear to recall what had happened without wanting to break down, even a hundred-some years later. Having the woman I loved ripped away from me, I'd long since given up hope of finding a blood bond. I wasn't strong enough to survive falling in love and having it torn from me again.

It was easier to avoid it.

And so far, much more fun.

As her breaths softened into a rhythmic sleep, I faced Daisy. Definitely much more fun. So innocent. So naïve—or was she? What had Pierce told her, or had he compelled her to forget so much her brain was like Swiss cheese? My amusement at overhearing Daisy and the elf had broken up was enough for me to cheer her on, but what human could fight the allure of an elf? That spoke volumes about her. Add to that, Daisy wore my ring earlier this evening in the park, so she couldn't be blind to our world. Daisy Barrett had to know more than she let on.

Intrigued was an understatement.

Cautious was my new motto.

My body was spent and sated for now. Besides copious amounts of alcohol and coffee, which at my age metabolized far too quickly, sex was the easiest way to dull the hunger into manageable meals rather than an all-consuming driver. With any other human, I would've fed on her during sex, but I couldn't be certain what ran through Daisy's veins, and I took that caution seriously.

So I was hungry.

I slipped out from under Daisy's snuggled naked body, wishing to stay in her arms. Taking in her miles of smooth skin peeking behind mussed sheets, blood pumped hard through my veins. Just like that, I was ready for another round. The hunger gnawed harder. I'd been eager to find the out-of-control vampire and leave town, and Nicole hadn't stocked the refrigerator yet, so I hadn't fed in days. That was a mistake.

Her sleeping head tilted to the side, exposing her pulsing throat. I clenched my jaw as my fangs descended of their own accord. Control. I needed to regain control before this room became a crime scene. Focus.

Why was I here? I couldn't peel my eyes from her throat. My head pounded with the need to feed. Why did I risk myself and her tonight?

Daisy's hand shifted into her nest of hair, stealing my gaze from her intoxicating vein. The bare digits curled on the pillow. Daisy had something of mine—the one thing that would give me freedom from a life lived skulking in darkness like a loathsome creature of the night. My ring. I'd seen her with it. So where would she put it for safekeeping in the few hours between then and when I'd met her at the bar?

I'd rather cuddle with her naked and be offered a vein, but that was a road I wasn't willing to traverse right now. I had an opportunity I couldn't waste. The vampire meddling in my town was dangerously close by, and the sun was coming up.

I'd been very patient. Now I wanted what was rightfully mine. I scanned the room and picked the most obvious hiding place—her desk, but the top drawer was locked. In the lower drawer, she kept the keys.

Well, that didn't bode well for her ability to secure valuables.

I unlocked the drawer and shuffled through it, but it wasn't there. I checked the storage bins under her bed, but still nothing. On a bookshelf, I paused to admire the titles she owned. *Count of Monte Cristo. War and Peace. Moby Dick. Don Quixote.* Light reading. Either she enjoyed the heavy weight of these tomes, or she was trying to impress whoever she brought to her bedroom. The spines weren't bent. Taste in books aside, I was already impressed.

I touched behind the books, feeling for a hidden compartment or a latch or anything out of place. I lifted each book and checked for a cut out before replacing each one exactly where it was, leaving no trace of my search.

Still nothing.

Since her bedroom was on the second story and carpeted, I didn't believe she'd have a shifty floorboard underneath, and there was no way she'd leave a family heirloom in a shared space with her roommates lurking around...unless she didn't know what she had. Gritting my teeth, I returned to her bedside and reassured myself she'd remained fully asleep. I brushed a lock of hair out of her face, and her eyelids twitched.

I had time. I returned to my search. What was I missing? Frames on the wall caught my attention. As an appreciator of art, I approached the photographs of her family members holding each other and smiling. I recognized these faces from the fiery car accident a few months ago. I glanced back at Daisy, and for the first time, I wished I could've saved them too.

Brushing away that useless guilt, I looked further. Next to her collection of portraits was a drawing in charcoal on aged paper. I focused through the dim light, and I recognized the faces staring back at me. My mouth dropped open, and I touched the fragile paper. I thought it had been lost in the fire. How did Daisy get this? Intrigued was beyond an understatement.

With danger lurking near her home, I needed to keep her alive until I got answers, and that would become much more difficult if I didn't get what I came here for, and even more difficult if she turned out to be my enemy.

Was it possible? If Daisy knew about me, she wouldn't have invited me inside. Witches were no friends of vampires. I learned that lesson when I met a young Newton Reed who befriended me, and after earning my trust, he'd betrayed me by siding with the one person I couldn't trust—the one person I truly hated.

Brushing that awful thought aside, only the chest of drawers remained. I pulled open the top drawer, sifting through her lacy underthings with an amused lift of my lips. She owned these tantalizing pieces but wore practical underwear to the bar. So she didn't intend to bring someone home, and she brought me here all on her own. I didn't compel her.

But I had before. When I'd rescued her from the burning car, I compelled her to forget. If she were a witch, I wouldn't have been able to compel her. Did it work, or did she act like it did? Daisy might've been skeptical of me tonight, but now I was completely suspicious of her.

Drawer by drawer, I combed the contents. In the final drawer, under folded dress pants, a wooden box with ancient witch lettering engraved on its exterior sat in the corner. The latch had no lock. Bracing myself for the inevitable, I picked it up. My fingers sizzled like bacon on a griddle. Quickly, I fought to open the lid, but I couldn't budge it. This had to be where she kept the ring, a spell-protected box.

With a grunt of frustration, I returned the box to its resting place and shook my fingers as they healed. After all these decades, I was so close I could almost taste it.

Definitely smelled it.

The front door opened and closed downstairs.

Like Daisy, I didn't want to give someone else a show, but more importantly, I didn't want to be caught vulnerable. I picked up my clothes and got dressed.

I had patience.

Soon enough, I would have what was mine, even if I had to seduce it off her.

I leaped out the window, soundlessly.

8
Conflicted

Daisy

I'D DROPPED BY DAD'S house this morning before my shift, like always, but he hadn't eaten the food I'd brought him yesterday, like always. I'd left countless voicemails and texts. I couldn't remember the last time he'd been so excited about a medical breakthrough, so maybe his long absence was standard protocol. Hopefully, he was getting overtime pay. I'd also restocked his water myself and taken a bottle right away. Even though I bought the same brand, it didn't have the same notes in it, but I convinced myself I liked Dad's better simply because it was Dad's.

The last few days had been normal calls for me and Megan. No more animal attacks. Maybe Cujo had moved on to a different town, and just like Cujo's radio silence, I hadn't heard from Oliver either.

The best sex I'd had in so...many...years (ahem, ever!), and it vanished just like that. I didn't even know his last name, and I forgot to ask for his number, because he'd promised me a naked breakfast. After a quick search around my room, I realized he hadn't left it for me either. Maybe I wasn't good enough, or maybe he was just a master of seduction.

And no commitment.

I'd only wanted breakfast, not a ring. Sheesh. I'd have to say that while some regret had been stewing over the last few days, I couldn't wipe the grin off my face. Remembering all his slick curves and tight muscles and that devious snake in his pants set my body alight all over again. If nothing else, I had fantastic material for the rub club.

Going out for drinks tonight would only get me into more trouble, because no one would ever live up to that experience, and I couldn't handle the disappointment. Instead, I needed to go for a run to burn off these excess thoughts before I desperately dragged Megan into the broom closet. I didn't think she'd fight me on it, especially if I invited Kevin too.

Megan pushed into the breakroom, grinning with pink cheeks. *Speaking of broom closet...* I had only one guess. "Kevin?"

"Turns out he likes a woman on the prowl. Who knew?" Megan beelined to the coffeepot and poured herself a steamy cup.

"That's great. I'm happy for you." Our breaks were short, so I tried my best to take full advantage. I dropped onto the scratchy upholstered couch and lifted my feet to rest on the edge of the coffee table. The television droned on, but I couldn't bring myself to listen. I stared at my mug, trying to decide if I wanted to spill the beans, considering the unhappy ending.

"What's wrong with you?" Megan asked, sitting next to me with her cup. She sipped from it.

"You remember a few days ago, that guy who called in the basketball player?"

"That fine man wrapped in delicious layers of meat? The one you asked if he had a snake in his pants?" Megan bit her lip and smiled deviously. "No, I have no idea who you're talking about."

Heat flushed my cheeks, but her description of him was oddly Megan. "I don't know what to do now, I can't get him out of my head."

Megan beamed. "You need to spill now. Right now. That was one fine man, and I need details."

I glanced sideways at her and sipped my coffee.

"Relax, I dig Kevin. He has this way with his hands..." Megan trailed off and looked up at the ceiling. She sighed with contentment. "He doesn't tucker out, and he gets me, you know?"

And he came back for more, not that I was jealous or anything.

I set my coffee on the table and sat up straight. "Oliver was at the bar the same night as the call."

"Oh?" Megan leaned in with a mischievous grin. She whispered, "You found that snake, and you didn't tell me before now? I'm not sure whether to be proud or insulted."

I cocked a brow at her. "Let's just say he's sweet and *very* generous."

"Good for you." Megan patted my knee. "When are you going to see him next?"

I exhaled. "I'm not."

Megan set her coffee next to mine. "Why not? What's wrong with him? Don't tell me he has—" she trailed off and waved a hand near her crotch, insinuating STDs.

I shook my head and chuckled. "As far as I can tell, he's impossibly perfect, but he left that night and hasn't called."

"This is the twenty-first century. Call him, girl. Get what you want. Damn."

I snorted. "That requires having his digits, which I don't."

"Oh, that sucks. It's a small town. He can't hide forever. Maybe you'll run into him again."

I'd lived here my whole life and never run into him before. I had better odds of winning the lottery, but I gave Megan a blank smile of acknowledgment. She always tried to cheer me up.

"I'm glad you're over Pierce," she added. "Everyone deserves to be satisfied."

The mention of his name made me tense, and the last words he'd said to me ran through my head: *I still love you.* I didn't mind being friendly acquaintances, but his declaration after we'd broken up twisted me with discomfort. "Has he talked to you lately?"

"Not me personally, but he's never been chatty. Why?"

"He threw the 'L' word at me, and I don't know what to say to him, so I've been avoiding him since."

"You broke up, so you don't have to say anything."

If we didn't work for the same hospital system, perhaps that would be sound advice. But as it was, we had to coexist peacefully during shift changes and communicate about swapping shifts on the occasion it was needed. But we were both adults. "You're right, and I'm never dating a colleague again, if for no other reason than the discomfort afterward. They coined the phrase, 'Don't dip your pen in company ink', for a reason."

Megan frowned.

Open mouth, insert foot. "I didn't mean...Sorry. I'm sure you and Kevin will be great."

"With that defeatist attitude, no wonder you're struggling. Just walk straight up to Pierce and tell him how you feel. I'm sure the awkwardness is entirely in your head. And once that's settled, then you can go have more fun without the guilt."

"I don't feel guilt because of Oliver."

"But yet you kept that romp a secret for days." Megan glared at me knowingly. I didn't feel guilty, did I? "And don't worry about me and Kevin. If we don't work out, no problem. I can wave and smile with the best of them."

I wished I could shut people out so easily. For some selfish reason very likely attributed to the huge loss of Barretts lately, I didn't want anyone to leave me. But I didn't want Pierce to be in love with me anymore. Was there guilt because I had fun with a stranger while Pierce still pined over me?

"I need to solve the Pierce dilemma. Then I can enjoy my new freedom."

"And hunt down that sexy Oliver."

"I wish." I tried to keep the dryness out of my tone. Seeing that perfect man again was a pipe dream. He'd made it clear by disappearing before breakfast and not leaving his number. But Megan had helped me craft a plan to hurdle the roadblock of guilt. After work tonight, I'd go for a run and practice exactly what I wanted to say. Then tomorrow I'd drop by work a little early to catch Pierce...

The breakroom door opened. What were the odds Pierce also thought we needed an adult conversation to set some boundaries? Unprepared for the talk now, I swallowed thickly and turned my head. The man at the doorway was not Pierce.

My heart leaped into my throat, and I stared in disbelief.

Oliver swaggered into the breakroom wearing a sharp suit and clutching a bundle of flowers—ruby roses, golden sunflowers, and mauve blooms entwined with green leaves. They were whimsical, reminding me of an English cottage garden in full bloom. Not daisies, thankfully. Everyone always thought giving me flowers matching my name was clever. Okay, 'always' was a bit of a stretch. I'd received flowers twice, and they were daisies, but the anecdote still fit.

Oliver stopped in front of me, bringing a waft of sweetness with him. "You called?"

Megan winked at me and launched herself out the door to give us privacy.

I blinked and lifted my shocked ass off the couch. My palms sweated, and I rubbed them on my thighs. My mouth opened to say something, but only a ramble of incoherence flitted around in my brain like a drunk butterfly. I cleared my throat. "Hi." That was lame. Exhaling a quick short breath, I said, "I thought you forgot about me." That was better.

"How could I possibly forget about you?" His familiar fingers brushed aside stray hair from my face. I closed my eyes, streams of memories returning. Heat roared through me, kicking my heart rate into danger territory, and I rubbed my palms dry again. His hand slipped away, and he added with an amused chuckle, "These are for you."

"Thank you." I brought the flowers to my nose, and a grin pulled my lips wide. I couldn't relax the muscles in my face, but I noticed him checking out my hands, worried I'd drop the bundle. What could I put them in? I searched around the breakroom. A plastic cup wouldn't be strong enough to hold them upright.

"What's the matter?" he asked, watching me fluster.

"I don't have a vase, and I'm on shift for another hour." They were too beautiful to let them wilt.

"That sounds like the easiest problem I've had in a while. I'll be right back." Oliver dipped out the door remarkably fast, leaving my jaw hanging open. In the blink of an eye, he was simply gone. The only proof I didn't hallucinate him was the bouquet in my hands. Was this really happening?

9

Make it a Date

Oliver

With silent feet, I sped through the hospital corridor until I found the nurse's supply station. Using supernatural speed meant I wouldn't get caught, but if I did, then I'd compel the witness to leave me alone. But the more time that took, the less I had with the mysterious Daisy Barrett and my ruby ring on her finger.

Her reaction to my presence still amused me.

On a metal shelving unit, I found a suitable basin. Although beautiful flowers didn't belong in something built for containing human waste, I should've bought a vase to go with them. I lifted a new bedpan off the stack and rushed back to the breakroom.

Daisy bent over the coffee station cabinet, and I admired her curvaceous backside before interrupting. "This holds water, correct?"

She laughed, and I couldn't get enough of the sound of her happiness.

"It's designed to hold liquids. A little unorthodox, but it'll work just fine." Daisy took the bedpan from me and filled the basin with water and leaned the flowers inside. She carried them to the coffee table and took care to rearrange them in their new home. She stood back and admired them. "They're beautiful."

Despite my better judgment, allowing the praise of my enemy to affect me, pride filled my chest. A lightness lifted me, something I hadn't felt in decades, but I needed to check myself. I had a reason for being here, and the sooner I finished what I'd set out to do, the sooner I could leave.

But the way her eyes lit up when she saw me lifted me from the monster I was to a man she appreciated. I stifled the rising emotion in my throat. "A bedpan destined for disgust becomes a work of art, simply by being next to something extraordinary. Like you."

At my metaphor praising her, she frowned for an instant, and I was impressed she caught it. But her words were direct. "No one puts that much thought into a disposable shit bin."

That made me chuckle.

Daisy looked at me thoughtfully. "Is that why you ran out on me?"

Now I wasn't sure of her exact interpretation. I wasn't calling her the bedpan—I wasn't that pompous. The real reason I'd left? Sunlight almost trapped me in a home with only humans for food, leaving me vulnerable to a loss of control and discovery. Not knowing enough about her yet, I played it safe. "My sincerest apologies."

A blush bloomed on her cheeks. "Well, you owe me a naked breakfast. Truthfully, I'm wondering how you're not beating women off you with a stick wherever you go."

I chuckled again. Anytime I approached a woman who knew what I was, she'd wish for a stick, one whittled to a sharp point to get the job done. I was convinced Daisy was naïve, and that was the only reason she didn't wish for her own stick. Because if she were anything else, we wouldn't be having a flirty chat. I wasn't going to waste this opportunity. "You think I'm *generous*?" I lifted a suggestive brow.

Daisy smiled bashfully. "The confidence is back, I see."

I'd show her confidence. I closed the distance between us, placing my body inches from hers. Salty coffee and the unmistakable nitrile gloves filled my nose. And once again, her heart danced for me. "Are there cameras in here?"

Daisy glanced at the upper corners of the constricting, outdated room. "I don't see any obvious globes of glass spying on us, but I haven't had a good look at my boss's computer screen. I never did get your last name, Oliver."

I touched her jaw, drawing her face back to mine, wishing her memories could stay intact. "Rockwell. Oliver Rockwell. Don't forget me this time."

Daisy's arms wrapped around me, and she pulled me close. A deep stirring had my heart thumping in my dead chest.

Our lips grazed each other in the slightest tickle. She whispered, "You are unforgettable. I only wish we'd been properly introduced at Abby's wedding, because you are amazing, and very...distracting."

We had been. Twice.

"If I knew you weren't getting a call in the next ten minutes, I'd show you just how distracting I can be."

"Ten minutes?" she asked with a tease. "That's fast."

"When time is short, efficiency and speed are the name of the game."

"Kiss me," she demanded.

I brought my lips to hers, and for that amazing moment, none of the past haunted me, none of the mysterious events going on around us both interfered, and none of the worries for her future meant anything. There were only her and me. Our lips danced for what felt like far too little time before I pulled away slowly.

Turned out, the past couldn't be ignored. "Can I ask you something?" I whispered, intently focused on her flushed face.

"Anything, Mr. Rockwell."

I captured her hand and lifted it to my lips. The red ruby sparkled under the fluorescent lights. I was so close I could touch it. So close I could slip it from her finger and disappear. Unless she was my enemy. If Daisy were a witch, she would've felt the magic urging her to kill me. Either she was a powerful witch, capable of controlling her basic instincts, or she wasn't a witch at all. But she had my ring and my drawing, and most importantly, she was a Barrett. "Where did you get that ring?"

"I told you it was passed down to me."

"Can I ask who specifically gave it to you?"

"Well, the letter tucked inside the box said it was my great-great-great-grandma Henrietta Daisy Barrett's, who I'm named after, obviously. I don't know anything about her, but Aunt Lisa left it to me, and it was handed down to her, too. Like I said, family heirloom. Do you like history or something?"

"You could say that. You don't know anything else about this ring? Anything at all?"

Her face screwed up in confusion. "It's just a pretty rock. Why is this so important to you?"

Naïve, indeed. A witch would've given up the ruse and attacked me by now. And witches couldn't be compelled. I almost wanted her to attack. I wanted to know my suspicions were correct, and I wanted to shout *I know what you are!* Instead, I guided her back to the couch. "That's the thing, Daisy. It's not just any old ring. Sit down and let me explain."

"Okay, Indiana Jones, history buff with an affinity for old things." Daisy sat next to me on the couch, and amusement sparkled in her eyes.

This wasn't about ownership of an *old thing*, as she called it. This was about my quality of life for the next however many centuries I was destined to walk this planet. This ring was about my ability to feed myself without the risk of imprisonment or death. And yes, that meant I would become a bigger danger to humans.

I collected her hands in mine, and she gave me her full attention. This story had to break the ruse, bring out the witch ready to attack. Then, I would make my move. "A long time ago, three best friends secretly practiced something that would've gotten them killed had word got out. Neither their spouses nor their children knew the extent of their abilities. You see, the gene responsible for the skill resides in the mirrored replication of the X chromosome. Men, with their unfortunately uneven Y chromosome, are left out. They can, however, work hard to overcome that genetic fluke and enjoy the fruits of their gene pool too. I've known a few in my day."

Like Newton Reed, the bastard.

"I have no idea what any of that means."

I smiled gently and squeezed her hands. I couldn't feel any magic pouring into me. Either she was a master witch playing me or not a witch at all. Pierce played a jig in her head more than a few times. I gritted my teeth. Could an elf make a witch forget her abilities? Hide her natural instincts? I was fascinated by the premise.

Not that I needed yet another reason to despise the elf.

"Let me keep going and see if it clicks for you."

"Okay." She focused on my lips.

"Unfortunately for our three best friends, word reached the townspeople, who were irate at the heretic behavior. The townspeople hunted them down, and a great fire spread throughout the region, killing thousands of people. An unfortunate set of circumstances—drought, namely—led to more casualties than planned. And what was supposed to be a well-kept secret is now in the history books, with the truth twisted just enough."

Daisy flinched at my gruesome details, but those simple sentences hardly captured the reality of living it.

"What did these women do to deserve to be hunted and killed?"

"Witchcraft." I stared at Daisy, urging her to come clean.

Daisy looked at the ceiling and pinched her face in confusion. "The Salem witch trials were centuries ago, and this ring isn't that old, so what does that have to do with my ring?"

"Witch burning isn't ancient history. The three friends were Edith Johnson, Rose Watson, and..." I trailed off, watching her face. "Henrietta Barrett."

Daisy withdrew her hands from mine. "Are you saying my great-times-whatever grandmother was a witch who burned at the stake, and no one thought to tell me?"

Not wanting to break her trust and belief, I had to tread carefully here. "Henrietta Barrett might have survived. I don't personally know. However, when the fires receded, their sacred site had been lost, presumed by the blaze."

Footsteps approached the breakroom door, and I wished I could compel the interrupter to leave, but that would give me away to Daisy. She'd either expose herself as a witch and turn on me, or she'd be terrified of the monster I was. I needed more time. "I must go, but I have much more to tell you. Can we make it a date?"

Brow furrowing studiously, Daisy nodded. "Yes, absolutely. I need to know more, but I'm going for a jog tonight. Does Friday night work for you?"

"Sounds perfect. I'll come to your house. But Daisy, could you please skip the jog?"

"I could, but why?"

I leaned in close, and I caught Daisy breathing in my scent. "It's not safe, and I don't have time to explain."

"Is this about the serial killer dog?" Daisy swallowed thickly. "Okay, I won't go."

The breakroom door opened, and the one-and-only self-righteous elf walked in with a nurse at his side. As a vampire, I was immune to his glamour, so I could see the parts he concealed—pointy ear tips and feathered wings folded at his back, snow white with golden flecks.

Humans were none the wiser about the creatures prowling among them.

While wishing Pierce Evansson would smack his folded wings on the doorframe, I sensed something off about the elf's friend. He wasn't human at all. My lips curled into a smug smile. This just kept getting more and more interesting. So much had happened in this town while I was away.

I disappeared using hyperspeed, undetected.

Daisy

HAVING MY EX WALK into the breakroom as Oliver and I chatted was awkward, but when I turned back, Oliver was gone. Just like when he'd brought the bedpan. How did he move so fast? Pierce craned his head around as if he'd seen Oliver, too. That would be a relief, because sometimes I thought I was going crazy.

Kevin Fontaine dropped onto the couch and propped his feet on the coffee table, relaxing with the television. He completely ignored the flowers. Pierce gave me the side-eye as he strolled by me, headed for the coffee, and I stiffened. What I did with Oliver was none of his business. But, Pierce and I needed to have an awkward conversation.

Megan pushed through the door next as if she'd been following Kevin. She joined him on the couch, and she leaned into his ear and whispered.

I exhaled slowly and looked at my empty coffee cup by Kevin's shoe. I had an excuse to talk to Pierce, to clear the air. Steeling myself and channeling my inner Megan, I collected my cup and darted a look at the lovebirds. Megan nodded at me for encouragement, but Kevin didn't give me any indication he was aware of anything. It wasn't my place to kick my colleagues out of the breakroom for privacy. Steeling myself against a rain of embarrassment, I approached Pierce's shoulder. "We need to talk."

Pierce poured himself a cup and leaned against the small table. His eyes tracked over to Megan and Kevin. Was he envious of them? No! No guilty thoughts. His happiness wasn't my responsibility.

I glanced at my friend, and Megan grabbed Kevin and dragged him to his feet. She waved to me and winked as they walked out the door. At least my embarrassment would be a private downpour.

My ex sat on the vacated couch and hunched forward, leaning his forearms on his thighs, and nestling the steaming cup between his thick palms. I would've guessed he was bummed out, but since he always had this calm demeanor, it was hard to tell. He sipped while watching the television drone on, avoiding eye contact.

He said, "You're being weird. What's going on?"

I stood near the couch, mustering up the courage to do this, to crush a man's feelings again. "Mind if I sit?"

Pierce patted the empty cushion next to him.

I dropped down, holding my empty cup like an idiot.

My ex sipped from his cup and set it on the coffee table. His hand reached out for the beautiful bouquet Oliver had brought me, stopped mid-air, and retreated, as if its touch would show him Oliver's admiration, making my ex more miserable. Pierce spoke first. "I want to apologize for the other day. I was out of line."

My lips parted in complete and utter surprise. I didn't know what to say. "Thanks."

Pierce turned to face me, and he looked me in the eye. My stomach flipped with nerves. Something in his eyes sparkled, a green like no other, and a calming feeling washed over me. I held his gaze as if it were a relaxing drug, and I was helpless to fight. Pierce's fingers enveloped my hand.

"I shouldn't have pushed you, but I believe we're right for each other. You think so too, right?"

Not moments ago, my buzzing lips were only for Oliver, and breaking up with Pierce was absolutely the right thing, but now, his statement drove holes right through my certainty. Pierce said we were right for each other. *I think...I think he's right?*

My puzzled face met his, and he grinned with an excitement I'd never seen on him before, as if life itself pumped back into him. It was mesmerizing, contagious, and he *was* gorgeous. That had never been in question. Perhaps I never fully appreciated just how hot he was before. I thought...Yeah, I thought I was an idiot for dumping him, and I smiled at Pierce reassuringly. "Of course we are."

Pierce positively beamed. "I don't know how you got mixed up with that vampire again, Daisy, but forget you ever met anyone named Oliver. I'm taking you on a date." He paused. "Tonight."

I needed to burn off excess energy, but I couldn't remember why. "I'm going for a jog tonight. Does Friday night work for you?"

Pierce beamed. "Friday night. You and me. We'll grab dinner, and I know you'll love it."

"Okay," I said cheerily. "I know I'll love it."

"I'll pick you up. I love you." Pierce's glowing green eyes returned to normal, and he released my hand. Pierce patted my thigh and returned to the coffee station for a refill. He lifted the decanter and asked, "Refill?"

I smiled at him. "No, thanks. I'm good."

Pierce refilled his cup, winked at me, and left the breakroom. It took a lot of guts to ask an ex-lover on a date. Pierce was like a whole different man.

As if she were listening on the other side of the door, Megan rushed to my side. "What the hell was that?"

"We're going on a date," I said, a big smile plastered across my face. The man loved me, and he wanted to treat me to a fancy date. I couldn't be more excited about it. My bad luck had finally turned around.

Megan's face scrunched in disgust. "I heard, but why?"

"He says I'll love it." There was no other explanation. I thought that was obvious.

"After everything you told me, I don't think that's a great idea. What about Oliver?"

My head swam as if buzzing with alcohol. Attempting to retrieve the name left me dizzier. "Who?"

Megan rested a hand on my shoulder. "The sex god with the generous snake and magic fingers—and those gorgeous flowers." She pointed at the bouquet in a bedpan. "They're not even daisies! Are you okay?"

I remembered putting them in the bedpan, but that was it. My brow furrowed as I took a mental inventory of myself. No injuries, no soreness, no empathetic grief for patients—or my own family—lately. I couldn't feel anything off. And the buzz, as if I'd slammed a few shots down the gullet, was warm, comforting, but I was a little lightheaded from it. "I think I'm fine."

"Drink some coffee. It'll clear your head."

Megan's concern had me puzzled, but I couldn't figure out why she would be worried. Pierce and I had broken up, and we were both lonely, so that was clearly a mistake. There was no reason to deny the man who loved me a date. I couldn't draw up a single logical reason to turn him down, so I was going to make this the best date ever.

I know I'll love it.

IO

The Next Victim

Daisy

"Alli, want to join me?" I asked my roommate while bent over, tying my sneaker laces. I couldn't remember why I'd planned to go for a jog tonight, and even pushed back a date for it, but I remembered now. Nerves fluttered through me as if my date with Pierce was our first. What was I going to wear? Which way should I curl my unruly hair? How much makeup was enough to be tantalizing, but not overdone, like I was trying too hard? I couldn't sit still. I had a weird ball of energy that needed release.

Allison Kincaid beelined to the coat rack at the front door and lifted a cardigan. She had her hair teased into a thick ponytail, and the librarian glasses were perched on her nose. "I'm heading to work. I think Jamie's in class, and it's possible he has a gig tonight."

Jamie Harris, the blond, tattooed, bearded roommate, gigged as a dancer or stripper, depending on the private party's request. I remembered when I'd first met him at my cousin's bachelorette party. Allison had insisted he was excellent entertainment, although she'd averted her eyes when he took to the stage. Coincidentally, he'd answered my room for rent ad a few days later.

Whenever we'd cross paths in the house, I blocked the visual of him in uniform, dancing with so little fabric covering him. It was significantly harder when he casually walked from the bathroom to his bedroom with nothing but a towel around his waist. Allison and Jamie were my roommates, but also my good friends for the past couple of years.

Allison stuffed her bare arms into the sleeves and collected her keys.

"Happy tips." I waved and smiled.

"Have a good run." Allison rushed out the door.

I followed my roommate outside. While she climbed into her car—for safety, not necessity—I stopped on the front porch. Dealing with the bar crowd left Allison paranoid, while the people I dealt with on a daily basis left me more compassionate.

From what I've seen, people on the whole were good, and the ones frequenting the bar, myself included, were typically hurting for one reason or another. Sure, bad things happened sometimes, but Allison felt the need to always carry good luck charms. My paranoia extended to leaving my aunt's ring at home in its box. If I lost it on a grassy trail or down a city sewer, I couldn't forgive myself.

I tucked earbuds into my ears and slipped my phone into my armband. Pulse-pumping music filled my head as I stretched my hamstrings. Putting one foot in front of the other, I set off, pushing through my front gate and keeping an even pace down the cracked sidewalk. At this hour, people nestled in their homes watching television or gathered around fire pits in their backyards, drinking alcohol, and telling quiet stories. Something about the dim blanket of soft city light and a sprinkling of lazy cars rolling down the street relaxed me.

And since the serial killer dog seemed to have moved on or met its match, I was even more confident in my town's inherent safety.

Shutting out the world and focusing on the task at hand, I pumped my legs around the corner and veered onto a paved walking trail through a wooded park. My footsteps matched the quick rhythm of the music as the trail swallowed me in the darkness. Moss and decaying plant matter filled my nose with peace. Even though I was in the center of the city, it felt like being one with nature. Just me and the sleepy world filled with innocent nocturnal creatures rustling in the underbrush.

When the song pounding in my head peaked at the chorus, a surge of energy hit me. I punched the air and mumbled the words to the song. With only sporadic streetlights penetrating the trees and no other joggers, I was free to be weird.

And completely off-key.

The trail ended at a street intersection, and I emerged into the orange light of the city once again. My feet carried me around the block, and I looped back toward home. My legs burned from the exertion, and my chest pumped air in time with my steps. Closing in on my front yard, a dark figure leaned against my front gate. The height and build suggested a man resting on his forearms. He wore a hoodie pulled low over his face and dark jeans. Running shoes.

He was too tall and lean to be Pierce.

I slowed to a walk and pulled out my earbuds, trying to calm my breathing to hear better.

"Can I help you?" I asked with a friendly note in my voice.

The shadowy stranger stood upright and faced me, but I still couldn't make out his features. His head turned from side to side as if looking for witnesses. A creepy-crawly sensation skittered along my limbs. The gate I loved for the false sense of security was now a hindrance to me getting inside faster.

"Daisy Barrett?" the unfamiliar voice asked evenly.

I could only guess he was a recent patient working through an existential crisis. I said warily, "I am. Can this wait until tomorrow?"

"Excellent." He approached me slowly. "No one will mind a taste first."

"Huh?" I asked, backing up a step.

Instinct told me to run, that I had finally encountered one of those bad apples. My body tensed to flee when a searing pain stung my throat as if I'd been lashed with a leather belt. After a single blink, the creepy visitor was at my throat, and I couldn't lift a finger.

From the neck down, I was completely immobile. Paralyzed. The wound was hot and wet, and my face crumpled in pain, but I couldn't scream. My mouth hung open in silent agony. Blood pumped hard through my veins, swished in my ears.

From a bite on the throat.

I was the next victim. The perpetrator had never been Cujo. What kind of *man* bit a person on the throat? Why me? I helped people. I loved helping people. This wasn't happening.

I panted, willing my body to run away, to push him off me, but it didn't happen. I willed my voice to scream. Not a squeak came out. *Someone, anyone, please find me. Help. Help me, please!* I screamed in my head, but only the void inside me echoed the words. My heart pounded harder as panic lifted all the hairs on my body.

Just as fast as he attacked, the man released me, and, helpless to catch myself, I fell to the sidewalk. My phone tumbled out of my armband and clattered to the ground, and I scraped my skin and leggings on the concrete. My brand-new leggings. What kind of sick asshole—?

The man standing over me chuckled, smearing the back of his hand across his mouth. He bent down and fisted my ponytail and dragged me through my gate like a rag doll, farther from my phone. The pain on my scalp distracted me from my surging adrenaline fighting the paralytic.

In full tachycardia now, I was in grave danger from blood loss. No matter how much I fought to calm my breathing, I couldn't. My body was desperate to move oxygen-rich blood to my limbs and brain. The distant sound of my music faded to nothing. Second by second, I was dragged farther from my phone with no hope of getting it back when I needed it most.

The attacker dragged my limp body up the porch stairs, and the edges scraped my spine. In front of my door, he dropped me and leaned over my face, but I still couldn't see his features. Not enough to pick him out of a lineup. He could be wearing full clown makeup for all I could tell. I wanted to gouge his face with my fingernails for a DNA sample, but I still couldn't move.

What had I done to deserve this?

My breathing continued to increase, and my attacker pushed his sleeves up his arm, exposing his bare skin. No tattoos or other identifiable marks. My limbs tingled as feeling began to return, and I scooted hard to get away, but I only managed a few inches. What I wouldn't give for a few of Allison's good luck charms now.

I blinked, and my attacker was gone.

I craned my neck to find him and held my breath, hoping to become invisible.

A bang against my house turned my head the opposite way. It was so hard to move, exhausting to try. Out of nowhere, another man shoved my attacker against the exterior wall, smacking his head against the vinyl siding. For an instant, I wished my house was brick.

Oliver

I RIPPED THE VAMPIRE away from Daisy and slammed him against the siding, rage pulsing through me. As much as I wanted to tend to her first, I had to neutralize the threat, and with my predatory speed, I could get the job done without a significant risk to her life.

Pressing my forearm against his throat, I pinned the feral vampire. Standing only a couple of inches taller than me, he snarled in my face. Time to unmask the reckless vampire who'd been putting my home at risk, our kind at risk. I pulled back the hood obscuring his face, prepared to meet, taunt, and kill the threat.

See? I could be a good teacher.

Mossy green eyes stared back at me with familiar hatred. I'd had him pegged by the field of dead and his feral stench in the woods, but I should've guessed by his usual jeans and hoodie. The man never changed his preferences. Self-satisfied at my correct identification, I still hated to be right.

"Little brother, long time no see. I thought you were smarter than this."

Soren leaned forward, and I used my free hand to reintroduce his skull to the siding. Soren flinched. His upper lip curled back into a sneer. "What are you doing here?"

"I've been following your trail of bodies. You know the rules, brother, or should I remind you?"

"If you had any sense at all, you'd let me go. You have no idea what's going on, and interfering is a bad idea."

As I held him pinned, my jaw clenched. Vampires were faster than elves, but they could fly and hit like their fists were made of steel. Vampires were faster and stronger than witches, but those bitches had spells, if they were quick enough to deploy them or experienced enough to have them on hand.

Despite all that, Soren had always acted like vampires were the superior species, careless in his feeds, drawing unwanted attention. The one rule we all agreed on was that the hidden world needed to remain hidden, and after discovering firsthand what happened when that rule was broken, I was a full supporter.

Soren had disregarded that rule once again, and since he was my brother, I'd punish him with a stern tongue-lashing, but attacking Daisy, who I had a special interest in, was where I drew a new line.

I humored his threat while deciding on my next move. "Or else what?"

"You don't want to find out." His face curled into a feral snarl I hadn't seen in years, as if the man I once knew had been lost.

"Soren, I don't want a repeat of your escapades from forty years ago. I thought I'd made myself clear. If you returned and started killing again, I would stop you."

"My escapades?" Soren chuckled. "Always rewriting history to suit you. As usual, you have no idea what you're talking about."

"Wrong answer." I gripped Soren by the arm. Flipping him over my shoulder, I slammed his body onto the concrete porch with a bone-splitting crunch. It wouldn't kill him, but he'd have a walloping headache for a while, and he'd need a few hours to heal. By then, sunlight would've returned, buying me another day.

It was the least punishment he deserved.

Soren climbed to his feet with a hand pressed against the back of his head. He brought his bloody fingers forward to inspect the damage, and a sneer twisted his lips. "Can't kill me, brother? Nothing stopped you last time."

I intended to kill whoever was dropping bodies carelessly around town, but confirming my own brother was responsible had stopped me. I couldn't truthfully do it.

While distracted by his words, Soren shoved me back with a bloody hand onto my white pressed shirt. I lost balance for a split second, and Soren sped away into the night.

At least he left Daisy alone. For now.

I'd honestly thought the drifter had gotten bored with the selection and left. But tonight, he targeted Daisy specifically. Soren had been right. I had no idea what was going on.

But interfering was the only way to find out.

II
A Handsome Rescuer

Daisy

WITHIN SECONDS OF MY attacker getting slammed against the concrete, he vanished, but I didn't relax. I lost too much blood, and I needed an ambulance. At this early hour, the day shift team would respond. Pierce would come. I didn't want him to see me like this, regardless of our date this upcoming Friday. Not much happened in this small town, although that seemed to be changing rapidly, so I'd be breakroom gossip for at least a week, probably two. Swallowing my pride, I'd rather be gossip than an obituary header.

"Hello?" I weakly called out, unable to see anyone around me. My rescuer wouldn't leave me after saving me, would he? Concerned that was the case, my pulse kicked up higher, and my breathing quickened further. My phone was too far away. I was helpless. Mustering up the strength, I cried out, "None of my roommates are home, and I need an ambulance."

I stared up at the ceiling of my covered porch and noted the peeling paint, adding a paint job to my mental to-do list and wishing I'd left the light on. A light I could stare at while my vision narrowed into a tiny point, just before blacking out from blood loss. No, I wasn't willing to give up yet. I called out again, "Anyone? Please call EMS. Hello?"

I glared at the dark bulb above me. I wanted the light on. I wanted to gaze upon its beautiful light, like a bug drawn to the comforting warmth of the light. I wanted it to take the pain away from my aching body and drain away the paralysis holding me hostage in my own body.

"Help," I said to no one and everyone at once. *Help me see the light.*

My rescuer leaned over me, popping into my view, but the moonlight shrouded his face in darkness. I could make out a bloody handprint on his dress shirt, but that wasn't enough to identify him. He tilted my head to the side, and his fingers brushed against the stinging wounds on my throat. He leaned closer.

Who was he? Why wasn't he saying anything?

His hand enveloped mine, and at once, compassion poured from a simple press of his hands. A dazzling comfort rushed through me, and I knew I'd be okay. The only person I knew who had the ability to fight off an attacker so effortlessly came to mind. This amazing man had to be... "Pierce?"

My rescuer stilled, hovering over me. His tone was clipped. "You need help, but we don't have time."

Not Pierce. Of course not. Pierce was at work. This man had to be a neighborly Good Samaritan. Giving the proper thanks to my rescuer was useless if I didn't survive. "Hurry, please."

With a soft growl, my rescuer squeezed my hand and said, "You lost too much blood. I'm sorry, but I don't have a choice."

The things he said made no sense. What choice? Why was he sorry?

My heart pounded hard, fighting against the insufficient volume. My blood pressure was dropping, and I was so tired. Soon I'd pass out and die of cardiac arrest. I was thirty years old. This wasn't how my life was supposed to end. I had too many things I hadn't done yet and too many people to make amends with.

Like my sister, Lily.

My rescuer lifted me off the porch as if I were a feather, and he gently settled me on my couch. He stood over me, and with my living room light on, I could see his face. His beautiful, stunning face. Like seeing a celebrity crush, my lips curled into a goofy grin. This man was too perfect to be real, and I couldn't properly thank my rescuer if I didn't know who he was. "What's your name?"

He closed his eyes slowly and pressed his soft lips thin. "I need you to drink. It's the only way."

"Drink what?" I asked, confused. He wasn't holding a glass.

Delirium was setting in. I was cold. Too much blood loss. It was just too much.

He rolled up his sleeve and pressed his wrist against his lips before bringing it down to my mouth, and the unmistakable taste of warm, bitter copper splashed into my mouth. My face pinched in disgust, and I refused. Bloodborne pathogens and diseases crossed my mind. How many tests would I need tomorrow from exposure?

"Drink," he ordered.

I refused and fought a gag. I glared at him wide-eyed in horror. I'd been bitten by one man only to be fed blood by another. What was this world coming to?

"If you don't, you will die. Look at me, Daisy."

Fighting my disgust, I looked, and all I saw was gifted bone structure, a strong clean-shaven jaw, and a pile of dark shaggy hair. My rescuer's pale gray eyes met my gaze, and I couldn't look away. He was an angel with impossibly gorgeous eyes, the last sight I was going to see.

But clearly, he had a serious kink I wasn't on board with.

"Drink this, Daisy, and I promise you'll be okay." A worried smile lifted his lips. He knew me, but I didn't know him. With no other option than to trust him, I swallowed the liquid in my mouth, and I cringed at the awful taste.

Delirium was the only explanation.

Oliver

SATISFIED I HADN'T BEEN too late, I sat next to Daisy on the couch. I brushed aside frazzled hair clinging to her face, freed from her ponytail during her valiant attempt to fight back. I held her ring-free hands. No human ever bested a vampire; it wasn't the nature of the species. I held her hand for comfort as my blood worked its way through her system. My brother couldn't enter her house, so for now, she was safe.

"I won't let Soren get away with this." I promised as Daisy drifted to sleep.

She didn't acknowledge my words. I'd given her enough blood to heal her wounds on the inside and replenish what her body needed to survive. Vampire blood only accelerated human healing, like a fast-forward button. There were no tricks up my sleeve to erase the impending scars on the outside. In a few short hours, she'd be like new. Better than new, except for the marks left behind, reminding her forever of what my brother did to her, and that was my fault.

Daisy didn't remember me yet again, and when she'd called me the elf's name, it was like a stake to the chest. With Pierce showing up at her workplace, I had a feeling he was up to something. He'd messed with her head at least twice before. Sneaky, head-violating bastard. Yes, vampires compelled humans too, but we did it for the human's own good. Elves did it for their own personal gain. The selfishness of the winged bastards made me sick.

It was clear the elf was keeping Daisy close under his wing, as if she knew something he couldn't allow her to remember, and my intrigue with Daisy just grew exponentially. Hunted by a feral vampire, controlled by an elf, possessor of my drawing, keeper of a spelled ring.

My spelled ring.

All the mystery around her suggested she had to be a witch, and then I owed it to vampirekind to kill her instead of heal her, but I couldn't. If she were a witch, her mind wouldn't be susceptible to compulsion, so the question remained: Who was Daisy Barrett?

Innocent human trapped in a supernatural world she didn't understand or my enemy with her powers hidden from her? Either way, I had to do right by Daisy. She deserved to be the real Daisy Barrett, not some shell of herself. Besides, I preferred fights against formidable opponents, not unconscious, helpless women. And if that meant Daisy would be forced to kill me, then I'd just walk away, sparing her the guilt.

Standing up, I removed her shoes and tossed a blanket over her. My predatory eye caught the smeared blood at her throat. Peppered with the fresh, salty sweat of her jog, her blood had been seasoned to perfection, an intoxicating, delicious scent.

At her accident, an easy meal—even risking the dietary side effects—had brought me to her car door, but her bloodied face, familiar and terrified, had me helping rather than feeding. Just as then, I looked upon her familiar face once more, and I was lost. Knowing what I know now, with all the risk on the table, I'd still save her all over again.

The surging of her new blood while it healed her possessed me. I wanted to take her and ravage her in the blood bond ritual, but her vampire blood was temporary, and I would never lay a hand on her without her consent. I didn't survive in the human world by being impulsive.

Patience was my best virtue, and right now, I was fighting an invisible war against an elf.

Fuck that guy.

I wet a washcloth and cleaned up her throat, so when she woke, she wouldn't see anything terrifying. There wasn't much to do about her shirt, though. I tossed the rag into the bathroom to allow a roommate to take the blame for the remaining mess.

The sun would be up in a few hours, but I didn't know how much longer until Daisy woke. I couldn't stay. "You'll be safe in here. Just don't invite any strangers inside," I said to her sleeping face. I touched her jaw.

The front door creaked as it was opened.

Damn it.

I needed to find a way into her spell-protected ring box, and I needed to remove the elf's control over her. But tonight, I was out of time. I disappeared in a flash out the back door.

I didn't get to erase her memory of the attack or my feeding her blood.

Damn it.

12

Losing My Mind

Daisy

I EXPECTED A HOSPITAL bed, IV fluids, Allison with sympathetic flowers, and a droning television. But I woke up on my couch with a blanket instead. Was that unbelievable attack a dream? I reached for my throat wound and felt nothing at all. With a groan, I dragged myself up, and a white fluffy feather tickled my ankle. I picked it up and twirled it between my fingers. I swore it had gold flecks in it—a fancy feather for a leaky down pillow.

I stood up, surprised to still be in my jogging clothes, and grumbled at the scrapes on my knees. I'd worn these leggings only once.

I dropped the feather into the trash and approached the mirror in the hallway. My hair was a mess, of course. I tilted my head to see my wounded throat, but I found nothing. No marks, no blood, nothing. But how?

Some psycho bit me...

And my gorgeous, mysterious rescuer fed me his blood, which arguably was psychotic all by itself.

I went to the medicine cabinet in the kitchen and downed some painkillers with water. It had to be a very lucid dream because people didn't drink or feed on other people's blood. That wasn't a thing. Nowhere in any medical textbooks was it mentioned.

Yep, a dream. I had no idea what that meant about the current state of my psyche, but I didn't want to analyze it. The psycho who'd bitten me had issues. I didn't.

I swore.

I cleaned up in the shower and braided my hair away from my face. I slipped into my work uniform for my shift today. Needing a little aunty comfort, I kneeled in front of my bottom dresser drawer and opened the antique box containing my heirloom ring. The inscription on the box was old, and that was all I knew about it. But since it was hers and she wanted me to keep it, I'd take great care of it. Wearing it made me feel like I had a piece of Aunt Lisa with me. I slipped it on my finger and smiled at it.

My roommate Jamie shuffled out of his bedroom, looking far worse than I did. Cotton pajama pants hung low on his carved hips. He didn't wear a shirt, but in this summer heat, I didn't blame him. Besides, he was nice to look at, but too young for my taste. He kept his vanilla hair trimmed short, and he grew a thick blond beard. Tattoos covered one arm and shoulder.

"Rough night?" I asked him, leaving my room.

Jamie perked up when he saw me. "Hey, Daisy. Why did you sleep on the couch?"

Considering I'd never, it was a good question. "I don't know. Maybe I dozed off while watching something on TV." Because getting bitten by a grown man did not happen.

"In your jogging clothes?" He arched a brow.

I shrugged, unable to conjure a believable story. "Who knows? I'm making breakfast. Do you want any?"

"It's noon."

I smiled and asked, "Does the package say you can only eat waffles at certain times of the day?"

Jamie laughed. "I can't say I read the directions."

"I'm not surprised," I teased.

"Let me get dressed. I'll join you downstairs."

I slipped past him on my way to the staircase. Jamie slapped the frame of his bedroom door as if a thought had come to him. I turned back expectantly. "Oh, Daisy, you had a visitor last night. I wasn't sure if you were awake."

I froze, and my heart stopped for a moment. In my head, I pictured Pierce, but something pulse-pounding wanted it to be someone else, someone that confirmed what I'd dreamed had been real. "Who was it?"

"Pierce. Sat with you on the couch for a short while, and I don't want to alarm you or anything, because I don't know the current state of your relationship, but he had his hands on you, hands splayed over your..." he trailed off and cleared his throat. "Chest and neck. I'm no doctor, but nothing he did looked...textbook, and the part that weirded me out was you looked asleep. Pierce sounded worried, and I offered to call an ambulance, but you know Pierce."

My hands curled into fists, and my lips pressed tightly together. My ex-boyfriend was an exceptional paramedic, but I was fuming. I'd agreed to a date I just knew I was going to love; I didn't agree to whatever the hell he did while I was unconscious and unable to consent. "He did what?"

As I was about to explode with an outburst, Jamie held his hands in the air in surrender. "Not that I was eavesdropping on you two or anything. I'd just got home from work, and I was passing through. It looked weird to me, so I hung out for a little to make sure you were okay, and that he didn't try anything, but like I said, it was weird. You know, it's not any of my business, but I get why you two broke up. Something about him is just...off-putting."

I wasn't going to explain my complicated relationship to my young roommate. In a quick tone, I said, "I'll start the waffles."

Taking the hint, Jamie slipped into his bedroom to dress, and I went downstairs. The audacity of Pierce coming in here uninvited and putting his meaty hands on me. The violation angered me, but a jarring thought about our date tonight kept flicking a switch in my head. Too many things lately made no sense. Nothing fit together in a way I could process logically.

A date I would love, but I didn't know why. Confusing.

Abhorring the touch of my ex-boyfriend. Normal.

A blood-drinking attacker who wanted me dead. Confusing. And possibly imaginary.

A handsome rescuer who fed me his blood, but I couldn't remember his name. Doubly confusing, and also possibly imaginary.

Megan had asked me about a man...Oliver?...who I couldn't remember. If I'd told her about him, he must've made an impression, but I couldn't remember him. Part of me felt like I wore a bedsheet over my head, unaware of my own life, and the frustration bubbled just under the surface. I ruffled through the freezer and grabbed the waffle box. I loaded the toaster and shoved the lever down harder than necessary.

I knew where Pierce was today, and I would be there to confront him and demand answers.

Daisy

I'D SHOWN UP FOR work early to catch Pierce at the end of his shift, but of course, my ex had taken the day off. I didn't have enough time to hunt him down before clocking in, which left me on edge all evening.

I scrubbed the exterior of the ambulance with a soapy push broom, working out my frustrations. The street grime didn't deserve to have its clingy paws all over the shiny paint. Every patch of splatter was scrubbed, hosed clear, and scrubbed again if there was any residue left, and sometimes even if there wasn't.

"Slow down there, Cinderella. The rig doesn't hate you. Go easy on her." Megan approached, holding out a cup of coffee. Night had fallen outside the garage, but I would never turn down coffee.

I leaned the broom against the other team's ambulance and captured the coffee between sore hands. I sipped, enjoying the jolt.

"What's got you so worked up?"

"I fell asleep on the couch last night, and Pierce dropped by. He had his hands all over me while I was unconscious. I wouldn't have found out except Jamie caught him."

"Pierce did what?" Megan leaned forward with disgust on her face.

"I don't feel different, and I woke with all my clothes on, but still. I trust Jamie, and since Pierce wasn't answering his phone, that tends to scream guilt. And I couldn't unleash my anger on him."

"What a scumbag. And here the whole department loves him."

And now I can't figure out why.

"Just because someone is good at their job, doesn't mean they aren't a sleaze in sheep's clothing," I said, and that was truthfully how I felt about him.

"Don't get angry with me, but I don't understand why you agreed to go out with him." Megan sipped her coffee, confusion twisting her features.

That was a puzzle. "Honestly, I have no idea. He just looked at me, and...I don't know. Was it pity or a thread of hope that he could be what I've been wishing for?"

"Sounds like you have some deep introspective issues to work through. Let me help. Which one makes your heart flutter when you see him?" Megan asked with a spark of fun in her eye.

"Which what?" Seriously, I was already lost.

Megan shook her head in disbelief. "Okay, your choices are sex god Oliver and sleazy Pierce. And...I think I answered for you. Ignore my bias and choose of your own volition, please."

As enticing as it sounded, sex god Oliver rang no bells in the tower. "The only thing I remember about an Oliver is that you mentioned him before."

"You're kidding, right?"

I sipped my coffee. "Not at all. Someone must've drugged me or something. I've been struggling with areas of memory loss since I woke up."

"Oh, girl, we need to get you a urine test. If Pierce roofied you..." Megan trailed off and grabbed my arm as if she meant to bring me directly to the lab.

"That was last night. I'm fine now." And I didn't want to have upper management in a tizzy since the perpetrator was possibly another employee. Somehow I had a feeling *I'd* be the one in trouble.

"Come on, you can't ignore something that serious. Come with me." Megan pulled again, but as an older, taller, and stronger woman, I resisted.

"Seriously, it's speculation right now, and I don't want to involve our employer in my personal business, but I will have a talk with Pierce after my shift." Besides, shoving test results in his face wouldn't change anything, only risk my job. He couldn't avoid me forever.

"Waiting that long to take the test means that your results will be less likely to detect anything. You're missing your chance to protect yourself."

"The lab is open twenty-four seven. I have to hear an explanation from him, but if he lies, then I'll do the test, okay?" I looked at my watch. "Three hours, tops."

Megan frowned. "I hate to picture him capable of something like that, but I'm seriously concerned for you."

"I'll make him fess up in a safe public place."

Despite Megan's warnings, and the wise whispers in my ears, something told me that regardless of what I wanted, I had to go on this date with him Friday night. It sounded completely nuts in my head, and since I couldn't explain it or convince Megan that Pierce wasn't the danger she made him out to be, I smiled and kept my mouth shut about it.

Megan pulled me into a hug. "Just know I'll always have your back. If he bothers you, tell me."

"Thanks, Meg." My best friend's earlier description of the two men had me curious. "Sex god, huh?"

Megan released her embrace and quirked a smile. "You didn't give me the details, but from the lovely description you offered, yes. Don't let that one go."

I didn't know I had him, but rooting around in my head and heart, I felt a shadow, a hollowness where a memory should've been, like the drugging had blocked a slice of happiness from me. I couldn't wait for it to wear off.

"Now," Megan said with a friendly smile. "How about we—"

The overhead alarm went off, calling our unit and interrupting Megan.

"Get going?" I finished for her with amusement. "Always great timing."

Taking my coffee with me, I rushed into the driver's seat, and Megan jumped in next to me. Dispatch relayed another dog bite attack at the intersection of two streets.

We both exchanged a look.

I flipped on the siren and lights, and recognizing the location, I said with dread, "That's by my house."

"We have to catch this thing. How can a dog get away with this kind of damage and no witnesses?" Megan said, exasperated.

Because it's a deranged man. I answered silently, refusing to utter the words out loud. I shivered at the ludicrous thought while rolling the behemoth out of the garage and down the darkened county road.

We cruised by the shopping center and through several red lights, and as I swung into my own neighborhood, I shut off the siren. Red lights flashed across sleeping houses.

"I think the neighborhood watch is dead at this point," Megan said as we turned a corner.

"Not many people are on the lookout for a rabid dog. They're more concerned with teenagers slinging toilet paper or grown-ass adults stealing porch packages."

"True."

"The patient is somewhere around here." I searched the shadowed area, wishing someone would stand near the road and flag us down.

"There." Megan pointed through the windshield.

A woman had collapsed on the sidewalk in front of my gate. I pulled over, and we rushed to assess and assist.

"She's alive!" I yelled.

While Megan started on her vitals, I brought over the stretcher.

"Confirmed bite victim. Check this out." Megan pointed to the woman's throat.

The woman wasn't moving, but her eyes shifted with panicked fear. Almost as if she were paralyzed.

"Get the c-collar on her. Looks like spinal cord damage. This has to be one massive dog." I wanted to believe my own words, but they rang hollow in my ears.

"But it leaves such dainty bite marks." Megan countered. "I think you were right the first time—it's a snake. Just like the basketball player, remember? At this point, a man wielding a snake as a weapon sounds more realistic than an invisible dog."

I didn't want to think of a human walking around with fangs in his mouth, sucking blood like a horrifying man-mosquito.

My partner strapped the collar around the patient's neck, and we secured her to the immobilization board. "Ready to lift?"

On the count of three, we shifted the patient onto the stretcher and rolled her into the ambulance, where I had good lighting. I started an IV in the crook of her elbow, but my hands trembled.

"Can you tell me your name?" I asked the patient, distracting myself with the task at hand, while Megan watched the EKG tape and charted in the mobile computer system. "Do you know what day it is?"

Her panicked eyes shifted around, unable to speak.

"It's okay," I reassured her, taping the tubing to her arm. "We'll get you all patched up. You're going to be fine."

"No, she's not." A familiar deep voice lifted my head, and I froze in complete terror.

A man wearing jeans and a hoodie pulled low, obscuring his face, stood at the rig's bumper. He was the same man who'd bitten me like an animal. I hadn't been dreaming at all. My worst nightmare was about to be repeated, and I was helpless to stop it.

The deranged man snarled like a feral animal.

13
Devastated

Daisy

THE CLOSE QUARTERS OF the ambulance were stifling. I wanted to dash out the side door, but to what purpose? Megan and our patient would be left to face two-legged Cujo by themselves. While Megan lifted her palms forward in defense of herself and our gravely injured patient, I reached for the radio at my shoulder.

"Touch that thing and die," the hoodie attacker said, standing in the darkness at the rig's bumper.

My hand froze. I didn't have to have almost died from his last attack to believe him. Mirroring my partner, I raised my hands in the air as if we were under the threat of gunfire.

"We don't want any trouble. Let us help our patient," I said slowly, calmly.

"We only want to treat her," Megan added. "We don't want to interfere with your business."

"Too late." The hoodie attacker grabbed Megan in a flash and pulled her out of the ambulance. I couldn't track his movements. He was impossibly fast. I blinked, and the attacker held Megan in front of him. He opened his mouth wide and bit Megan's throat.

I screamed.

Megan stiffened under his control, and like watching my nightmare repeat before my eyes, her mouth gaped open in fear and blood trickled down her throat.

I was no match for this monster. I couldn't fight him off—I'd already tried once and failed. And waiting around for the mysterious rescuer to reappear took time Megan didn't have. I might not be able to fight him, but there was something I could do.

I slipped my cell phone free from my pocket and snapped a picture of the monster, but without the flash to illuminate his darkened features, I feared my attempt was useless.

The monster pulled his head away and sighed contentedly. Blood stained his lips, and he licked them clean. "Much better."

Megan stood eerily still, as if paralyzed. She didn't try to run. She didn't cry out. Megan was helpless. I knew that feeling.

The monster smirked at her terrified face, and his hands gripped the sides of her head, almost as if he intended to plant a kiss on her lips, but I doubted that.

He twisted violently, and a crack rang out. He didn't just...?

"Megan?" I whispered.

The monster released her like discarded waste, and Megan crumpled to the sidewalk. She didn't move. She wasn't simply paralyzed. I knew what that crack meant.

While I stared at my best friend in shocked disbelief, the monster climbed into the back of the rig slowly, like a predator. I scooted back farther into the ambulance, but the space was small. Tears flooded my eyes. "Why? How could you? She was only trying to help. We never did anything to you!"

"Thank her for sating my hunger. Now I don't have to bite you again." The monster paused in his tracks. "Unless...you want me to. I wouldn't turn down a free meal."

"What? Never! Let me go," I said, gaze bouncing between the monster and Megan. I hoped to see movement, any movement. I begged and pleaded that what I'd just seen was only a figment of my overactive imagination—a projection of my own fear.

"Daisy Barrett. We have some things to discuss." He reached out to me.

I cowered back. The minuscule curiosity of how he knew my name and what he wanted to talk about was nothing compared to the terrifying speed and destruction this man was capable of. I wanted only to run away, but I knew I didn't stand a chance if I tried.

"If you play games with me, you won't like it, but I will. Choice is yours." The monster pulled back his hoodie, and there was something familiar about him. I didn't know the guy, but his pale green eyes, his bloodstained lips, that prominent jaw. It tugged at me.

I wasn't quick enough to use the radio at my shoulder, and if I tried, he'd kill me. Besides, whatever help might've been on the other side of the line would be too late to do any good. My sense of self-preservation wanted me to put distance between us. I shifted to the side door. A niggling thought with no clear origin had me wanting to run into my house, and if I could get inside, I would be safe.

"Daisy, look at me. Look me in the eye, and I'll tell you what you want to know," he said.

Needing answers, I gazed into the monster's glowing red eyes, and at once I calmed down, waiting to hear what I was missing.

"You're in the wrong place for sucky-sucky." A familiar voice called nearby, instantly stealing the attention of the monster. His neck craned toward the back of the ambulance.

I blinked, suddenly aware of the window of opportunity. I checked my patient's pulse, and it was fading fast. Too much blood loss, and I realized none of it was on the sidewalk. She had been drained. Exsanguinated. Like Megan. I couldn't take my paralyzed patient with me.

I jumped out of the ambulance's side door. Instinct told me to run, but I couldn't leave Megan. I had to check on her. With distance between me and the monster, my fingers itched to call for help. I needed a second ambulance and a police unit too. Or six.

The attacker snarled at the man interrupting him. "Get out of here or I'll kill you both."

He meant me. A lump caught in my throat, and I tried to swallow, but my mouth felt like cotton. My heart pounded in my ears, and I crouched next to Megan. I felt for a pulse at her throat—the clean side—and I found nothing. I couldn't carry her, and both the monster and his distracter stood between us and my gate.

"I always knew you had a thick skull, but even I expected more from you," the distracter said.

It was too dark to see his features, but he was dressed almost formally in a button-up and dress pants, maybe. He didn't look like he was a tough-as-nails fighter. No, a Good Samaritan about to get his neck snapped like Megan. Damn it, I needed help.

He kept talking, continuing his distraction. "Are you just passing through town? Because if you planned to kill her, you would've already done it, so I'm guessing she's more important than dessert."

I was *dessert*? They were...the main course? I'd always thought nothing was more confusing than my calculus final exam after a week of partying instead of studying. I'd already been accepted into medical school at that point, so I'd wanted one last hurrah before cracking down on the books again. But unlike that damned final, I knew why I was lost and confused. Right now, I couldn't make heads or tails of anything these two were saying.

I wanted to find out who this Good Samaritan was, so I could get him to report the monster's crimes to the police, but I couldn't fight off the cotton gumming up my tongue. And even if I could, returning the attention back onto me wasn't a wise choice. Frankly, I didn't think this Samaritan was going to live another five minutes, and all he wanted to do was help.

"This is none of your business," the monster said and gritted his jaw. He stood an inch or two taller than the Good

Samaritan, and pure hatred rolled off his menacing posture. I had no intention of unleashing it on me and Megan, so I kept quiet, absorbing what I could. Trying to be a good witness, for whatever that was worth.

"You showed up in my town, and you made it my business. I'm giving you one chance, Soren. Get out now and never come back." The Good Samaritan sidestepped the monster and approached me and Megan. These two knew each other personally, and now I had a name for the monster.

Soren chuckled with amusement, but the sinister tone gave me the chills. "You can't stop me. Get out of my way, and I'll be gone by morning."

"You have my terms." The Good Samaritan had balls of steel, truthfully, but he was stupid to instigate this psychopath. He stood like a shield in front of me and Megan.

"So that's it then? We're at an impasse." Soren stepped closer.

Two unstable men hovered next to us. One of which smelled great, and the other, not so much. I just wanted to collect my two patients and rush back to the emergency department, hand them off to qualified physicians, and go home. I tried to relax the trembling in my hands.

The Good Samaritan gripped Soren's shoulder. The monster reacted, and I took that second to lean out of the way while protecting Megan's head. Grunts, thumps, and various fighting noises came from behind me, but I only focused on my best friend. I checked for a pulse again, but I still didn't find one. *No, Megan, no. You can't leave me. You can't.* I didn't have time to sob. I lifted her eyelids, seeking any sign of life, but there was nothing. She felt cold to the touch. Also drained of blood. This couldn't be happening.

Huddled over Megan, keeping my movements out of sight, I reached for my radio and pressed the call button.

A painful squeeze crushed my hand against the radio, and I cried out. The ironclad fist released my hand, and I cradled it to my chest, swallowing back sobs of desperation.

"I warned you," Soren said with a snarl.

If he were paying me any attention, I hated to think what had happened to the Good Samaritan. Not even five minutes had passed. I found him in the middle of the street, knees in the air, the kind soul pitched with pain.

No, damn it!

A meaty hand fisted my polo and lifted me to my feet with no effort at all. "This is going to be much more fun for me now. So thank you for that."

Soren's mouth opened wide, and two sharp teeth elongated, like a snake's fangs. What the hell? I couldn't make sense of what I saw. "Please don't. Don't hurt me. Please, please, stop." Air pumped in and out of my lungs in short, quick breaths. The trembling of my hands spread through the rest of my body.

Soren wrenched my head to the side, exposing my throat, and I yelped, heart pounding in my ears. All I could do was wait for the inevitable piercing pain I'd already experienced. Then the rapid heart rate from blood loss. Followed by the impending coma and cardiac arrest. All while paralyzed. My entire nightmare replayed in my mind because it was about to happen again.

This wasn't a nightmare. This was real.

A force twisted us both, and my head hit my gate, but Soren released me. Woozy, I pressed a hand against my spinning head.

The Good Samaritan slugged the monster with blurry, impossible speed. Soren's head rang against my gate, and a crack followed. No human could take that kind of skeletal damage and remain functional. He should've been knocked out. He should've been lightheaded and confused, on the ground bleeding and moaning. Instead, he returned to his feet, posture ready to fight.

How?

I crawled back to Megan and checked her throat again. Her eyes were lifeless. Her pulse non-existent. That monster had killed Megan. With a spinning head, I crawled into the back of the rig and checked our patient, but she, too, was dead.

Our serial killer Cujo turned out to be a man with fangs who drank human blood. Such a thing didn't exist. Was this a new viral disease? A human version of mad cow? Whatever possible explanation I conjured only made me more fearful.

With Soren still occupied, amazingly, I pressed the button on my radio. Despite the crunching damage, it still worked. "Dispatch, send all available units. We have victims down. One is our own. The perpetrator is on site." I gave her my address, and she confirmed the units were en route. I leaned back against the interior of the ambulance and closed my eyes. The police station was only six blocks away, but the cracks and thumps of the continuing fight were too surreal.

Monsters existed.

One of them killed several innocent people, including Megan. For what? To drink their blood. *Dessert...*

I folded my elbows on my lifted knees and rested my spinning head back against my gate. Sirens wailed within moments, and relief washed through me. I looked up to see how the men reacted to the approaching authorities, hoping the murderer would sit and turn himself in. Fat chance.

"I'm warning you for the last time. Stay way," the Good Samaritan said, panting. He deserved a better title than that. He was my rescuer and the only reason I was still alive. Blood smeared his face, and his shirt was torn and stained.

Soren chuckled and swiped his bloody lip with the back of his hand. In the blink of an eye, he disappeared.

My rescuer turned in place, looking for him. He paused, tilting his head as if trying to listen for Soren's retreat. No one was that fast, but I couldn't see him anywhere.

The monster got away.

My rescuer sat next to me on the sidewalk, and he leaned against the gate, pale eyes capturing my breath. His dark shaggy hair was matted with blood, and a five o'clock shadow covered an otherwise beautiful face. My rescuer was an angel, minus the wings...

Although I'd meant that metaphorically, with the strength and speed he displayed... If he had wings, I needed a drink. I looked behind him and squinted to focus. I didn't see any, but I had taken a good knock to the skull.

"Are you okay?" he asked.

My gaze flashed to Megan, crumpled in my lap, and a fresh wave of tears washed down my cheeks. I wasn't okay in the slightest. "I don't understand any of this. Why did Soren kill Megan and our patient? Why did he *drink* her? What was he?"

"Daisy, look at me."

I captured my rescuer's gaze, and pale gray eyes caught my breath. My last name was embroidered on my polo. Not my first. "How do you know me?"

My rescuer sighed heavily with frustration. "Did Soren make you gaze into his eyes?"

I shook my head and immediately regretted it. I placed a palm against my aching, floaty skull. "He said he was going to tell me what I needed to know, but you showed up before he told me anything."

My rescuer grumbled under his breath, but I couldn't make out the words.

"Who are you?" I asked.

He turned to face me and collected my hands in his. "We met the other night in the park and again at the bar."

I'd gone to Fully Loaded, and Allison relieved me of my mood, festering over a basketball player's dog attack, which now wasn't a dog at all. I remembered some idiots throwing darts at the person standing in front of the dartboard, and I remembered going for a walk...but someone was with me, wasn't there? I'd gone inside my house, up to my bedroom, and I woke up alone with messy sheets. That was it.

"I brought you flowers at Borealis."

I remember pretty flowers in the breakroom, but not who brought them.

"I don't remember any of that, but I do know there are pretty flowers in the breakroom. I'm sorry." And I really meant that. He was gorgeous.

Then I remembered Megan had been pushing me to choose...my ex or Oliver, the sex god with the snake in his pants...that I'd told her about. No wonder I'd gushed about this guy. I wished I knew how far things went between us, and now awkwardness settled in my gut.

"Are you Oliver?"

He nodded and pressed his lips thin, clearly disappointed. "Someone got inside your head again."

I frowned. "Again? What are you talking about? No one screwed with my head." Just bashed it against my gate, but that wasn't the right kind of damage to mess with memory, especially selective pieces of memory.

Sirens closed the distance, and Oliver looked over his shoulder. "Listen, I can't stay for the police. Just know I'm looking forward to our talk." Oliver climbed to his feet. "And I'm relieved you're okay."

"Wait—" I started, but he vanished as fast as Soren had. I finished weakly to myself, "I don't have your phone number."

My rescuer was gone, and I was alone with two bodies, one of which was my best friend. The two-legged Cujo was now identified, and he wouldn't get away with this.

14

The Unbelievable Forever

Daisy

After everyone alive had vanished but me, I'd given the police my statement, but when I explained the attacker's descending fangs, they hid their chuckles. I'd begged them to check Megan's wound to corroborate my story, but they'd refused. One of them mumbled something about drugs. I bet anything they tore up my report.

I'm not sure I believed my own report.

It was date night with Pierce, but I wasn't in the mood. Something told me I was going to love it. To delay, I begged to pick up a shift, but my boss had told me I needed the time off to process Megan's death, and he wouldn't take 'no' for an answer. I'd countered that without me and Megan, he'd be short-staffed. The boss had brought in temps from another station. He had it all covered, apparently.

As the hours ticked by before my date with Pierce, I needed a distraction. I called my sister Lily, hoping to hear her voice and not expecting any answer. As usual, I got her voicemail.

She didn't even record her own voice for the greeting, leaving the default robotic instructions.

I exhaled and left another message. "It's me again. I don't know how to tell you this other than spitting it out, so here it goes: Megan passed away. She was attacked on duty, and I can't explain it. I'm not sure I believe what I saw. Anyway, her funeral's coming up, and I'd like you to be there. For me."

I pulled the phone from my ear and ended the call. I inhaled a deep, shaky breath. Now was not the time for tears—I'd just finished swiping the final layer of mascara on my eyelashes. I checked the time on my phone. In three agonizingly short minutes, my punctual ex would be here.

I tucked my phone inside a black clutch, and the doorbell rang. A flurry of nerves shot through me. I trudged down the stairs, shouting to either of my roommates, if they were home, "I got it."

I opened the door and Pierce stood before me, holding a bunch of daisies, wearing cargo shorts and a polo. So a casual place then? I'd overdressed. I wore a little black dress that reached halfway from my hips to my knees. Red high heels lifted me up a few inches, and my brown hair curled around my shoulders. I even put on fake eyelashes and topped off my look with Aunt Lisa's ruby ring.

"You look good, Daisy," Pierce said and pushed the flowers at me.

"Thanks," I said quietly. I took the flowers and brought them to the kitchen. I didn't have a vase, so I found a tall glass, filled it with water, and dropped the stems inside. At the door, Pierce looked around like he'd never been here before.

"Did you or your roommates have new friends over lately?"

Could he smell a new perfume or something? Weird. "Maybe Jamie had a date over. I don't know."

Pierce grunted and held out his arm, inviting me to join him. "Let's go."

I wrapped my arm around his and fought a creepy-crawly sensation. Pierce led me down my pathway and held open his SUV's door. Happy to release him, I struggled to climb up while trying not to flash anyone. Thankfully, it was dark out. While I buckled in, Pierce dropped into the driver's seat and steered the vehicle into light traffic. After a few blocks of silence, Pierce pulled over at the curb randomly.

This couldn't be right. There was nothing around but the empty city park. "Why are we here?"

"Picnic in the park." With a small lift of his lips, he climbed out and popped the hatchback. I stumbled my way out of the SUV and followed him to the back end. Pierce picked up a basket and tucked a blanket under his arm before shutting the hatchback again. He captured my hand and led me down the sidewalk and into the grass, right through the spot where the basketball player had died. I pulled his hand to avoid walking there, and my heel caught on the grass. I almost lost my balance, but Pierce's firm grip held me upright.

"What are you doing?" he asked.

I didn't want to explain why I avoided that spot. Paramedic or not, he'd either not believe my story of the dead-but-moving basketball player or he wouldn't care anyway. But his question pissed me off. Who asked someone out for a date and didn't warn them it was in the park? I was a drunken monkey in heels on grass and one step from a sprained ankle. "My ankles are unhappy with these shoes."

"You should've worn sneakers."

Pierce's practical but short-sighted answer angered me further. "If you would've told me, I could've worn appropriate clothing."

"You always wear comfortable clothes, and the park is your favorite place. Where else would I take you?"

The park was my jogging sanctuary, not my favorite place, date or not. But if that was his logic, then he didn't know me all that well. "How is it a special date if you take me where I always go?"

"I thought you'd feel more comfortable here." He turned to face me directly, and at once his eyes lit up green in the darkness. Impossibly green. I couldn't explain how or why. "Have patience. You'll love this."

The words felt true, but they didn't ring true. I didn't know if that made sense. Frankly, my mind felt like it was dragged through sand. One minute my thoughts were soft, natural, comfortable and the next they were rough and abrasive. Grief was messy, and I didn't think I was handling Megan's unusual death well. The words popped out of my mouth before I could filter them. "You're right. I know I'll love it."

Pierce dragged me along the uneven grass, and I had to focus on preserving my ankles. But that wasn't distraction enough. All the silence was deafening. "Did you have any dog bite victims on your shift lately?"

"No, but I heard about it," Pierce said absently. He scanned the park while we headed toward a grassy area not far from a streetlight. "There's trouble in every town."

I agreed with that. "Don't you think we should go somewhere else, then? I don't know. A poorly lit park alone at night doesn't seem...wise. I mean, the dog could come barreling out from those bushes at any moment." I didn't mean to psych myself out, but now I glared at the bushes, hoping I hadn't jinxed us.

No one had caught Soren yet, but since my report was laughed at...I didn't think he would be.

"We're fine. Trust me."

My ankles wobbled painfully on the uneven grass, and just when I was about to put a stop to this ridiculousness, Pierce released my hand and bent over, setting the basket on the ground.

Sweet relief, this was the spot.

Pierce shook open the blanket, set the basket on one corner, and sat down near the middle. With shadowed features, he gestured for me to join him. Until a couple of weeks ago, I would've appreciated this.

But now, it was terrifying. A chill seeped into my bones, and I wrapped my bare arms around my body. "I don't know if I can do this."

"Nonsense. You're right here. Sit down." Pierce gestured again.

I hesitated, scanning the area for dangers, like Soren lurking in the dark.

"If you insist on going back to the truck, you'll have to go alone in those heels. You're already here. Just sit."

I rolled my eyes at his lack of chivalry. Trying to sit on a lumpy blanket with high heels catching the fabric and a short and tight skirt was beyond frustrating. Adding a dash of ex-boyfriend in a darkened city park where not-exactly-animal attacks had occurred, and I would've rather been anywhere but here. *Seriously, sign me up for a root canal.*

When was the 'I love it' part supposed to begin?

Pierce opened the lid of the basket. "While you gaze at the stars, I'm going to feed you grapes. Lay back."

I wasn't hungry now, and I had no intention of making myself deliberately more vulnerable. "Oh, no thanks, really."

"Are you sure?"

"Yeah. I had a late snack." It was a lie, but I didn't care. I filed that in the harmless white-lie category.

"Okay." Pierce popped grape after grape into his mouth, and the popping sounds made me clench my teeth. "Hey, if you want your paramedic license, classes are starting soon."

Seriously? Not him, too. I couldn't be upset with Megan for harping on me about it since she only encouraged me, but why couldn't everyone else leave me alone about my career? Wasn't I good enough just the way I was?

There was no use arguing with Pierce. He'd logic his way through it, leaving me angrier. "I can't."

"Why not?"

"I just can't, okay?"

"Is it your dad? Because I can talk to him if you need me to," Pierce said calmly.

Always calmly, and that irritated me more. I shifted my aching hips, patience running thin. "I can handle my own dad."

Pierce brushed his hands clean and rummaged in the picnic basket again. This time, he pulled out a little velvet box. "Daisy, I have something I need to ask you. Something I should've asked you a long time ago."

That better not be what I thought it was, because with the way I felt right now, I'd shove it down his throat until…

"I know we've had our ups and downs, but that's what every relationship has. It's normal. And that's what a commitment is: surviving the ups and downs. In good times and bad. Daisy…" Pierce faced me and paused. "Will you marry me?"

Before I could string together an appropriate response, he pushed the box at me, and in the yellowish light of the streetlights, a small reflection resembling vomit flickered in front of me. Not that his gem of choice had any impact on my decision.

If I'd had a grape in my mouth, I would've choked. Instead, I wanted to swallow my tongue and faint from asphyxiation. "I don't know what to say, Pierce. We broke up because things weren't working. They still aren't. I don't know how else to clarify that for you."

"You agreed to date me tonight."

He was right, but I didn't think I wanted to. The patience I'd held onto slipped from my fingers.

"Marry me, Daisy."

I tried to conjure images of a domestic life living with Pierce. Sharing the kitchen, preparing meals. I was messy. The kitchen needed a cleanup crew to make it presentable when I was done, but the food always tasted great, so no one, not even Dad, complained. Pierce was neat, clean, a perfectionist to a fault. In a word: bland. Same with the living room. Movies on shelves and plants in a row. No throw pillows haphazardly lounging on their own accord.

We'd slept together numerous times during our relationship, but I'd always left shortly after the deed was done. His things were always orderly. The sex perfunctory. I pictured his logical arguments to every quip I made, every point of view I had. While dating, it was something easy to make an excuse for, but Pierce being my last relationship forever and ever? If I weren't wearing heels, I'd literally run away. "I don't know how else to say this, but I can't. I'm sorry, Pierce."

Pierce's eyes glowed impossibly green in this lighting. Mesmerizing. His tone was firmer than he'd ever used before. "You will marry—" his statement cut off, and he fell over, not clutching his chest with a heart attack, not pinched-face with blunt-force trauma. He just fell over, like he'd fainted mid-sentence.

For one second, I allowed myself to bask in the relief that this was over.

Now I was terrified. Since Pierce was about a jug of protein powder away from a bodybuilder, my heart raced with fear, not for his health, but as bad as it sounded, I was afraid for mine. Chest pumping air, scolding myself for wearing these stupid shoes, I frantically looked around for Soren. I took one heel off and gripped it as a weapon, while I scrambled to my knees and fought my tight dress to stand. My hip sparked with pain from my uneven stance.

And just like that, Pierce was completely gone.

Terror officially taking over, I gasped, scanning again for Soren. Who else could lift Pierce and vanish into the darkness with him? In front of me stood a shadowed figure. Not Soren. Not Pierce.

Oliver Rockwell, my rescuer, was wearing a striped button-up shirt and a pair of dark slacks. On his feet were a pair of flat leather shoes, and envy tore through me. He'd kicked Soren's inhuman ass and now somehow disabled Pierce and disappeared him.

My instincts said to run, but these shoes would make a dreadfully embarrassing and ineffective attempt. I stepped back and looked over my shoulder for either Soren or Pierce. Neither was in sight. "Oliver, you..." I couldn't figure out what to say.

Pierce had the keys to his SUV. Since I didn't want my cell phone destroyed like my shoulder radio, I kept that in my clutch. So, a full sprint down the sidewalk was my only escape.

"We have much to discuss. Starting with why you're here with him," Oliver said, nodding where Pierce sat last on the blanket. His tone was clipped, not nearly as gentle as when he'd fought Soren off, a monster Oliver knew.

I stiffened, but I lifted my chin in a display of mock courage. "We're on a date. Why? Is Soren back? Did you follow him here?" I glanced over my shoulder again. A tingle of nerves skittered along my exposed skin.

"I'm here for you."

I frowned. A good way to lose my trust was to kidnap my date. "Where's Pierce?"

"He's fine. Daisy, I don't know how much you understand or what you remember, but I don't want to scare you," Oliver said carefully.

"Well, start by telling me where Pierce is."

"He's safe," Oliver said and gestured behind me. "He's in the bushes."

"Why did you kidnap him?" I took a step away from Oliver and toward the street...a long distance away.

"He's not hurt, I promise you. He's out of the way, so we can talk."

Pierce was a bulky dude, and from the looks of it, Oliver wasn't big enough to take him on so easily, so silently. But remembering him fighting Soren made me wary. "About what?"

Oliver sighed. "It was cute the first few times, but this is getting tiring. Daisy, we had a date planned for tonight. I was going to finish telling you the story behind your ruby ring. Do you remember anything about it?"

"You interrupted my date to ask about my ring?" Everything he said puzzled me further, and the ludicrous direction this conversation headed only angered me.

"Do you trust me to help you?" Oliver held out his palms in a surrender gesture.

The last thing Pierce had said was worrying, and there was still that unknown incident with his hands on my body while I'd been unconscious. Oliver had saved me from Soren. Weighing who to trust more, I asked, "What does your help entail?"

"I want to look into your eyes, that's all. May I?" Oliver took a step closer.

"Sure, but don't try any funny business." Such a strange and innocent request to ask permission for. Since I'd described him as a sex god to Megan, my guess was we'd already been that close. I just wish I could remember what happened between us...and the main event itself. He was unbelievably handsome.

Oliver approached cautiously and collected my hands in his. They were strong and warm, and a sizzle of energy heated me, as if my body remembered something my head didn't.

Oliver stared into my eyes, and I gazed right back, waiting for him to give me logical answers. After locking eyes for several seconds, he pulled back. "Someone tampered with your free will."

With a frown, I pulled my hands free of Oliver's, and the instant cold gave me a shiver. "You can determine that with a look into my eyes, and you expect me to believe that? I don't know what I'm doing here, and at this point, I don't care anymore. If your word is good, and Pierce is fine, then I'm out of here."

I managed two uneven steps before something unexplainable pulled at me, urging me to stay by Oliver's side.

That wasn't my instinct. But being vulnerable in the dark with Soren still roaming free wasn't wise either.

"In exchange for a favor, I can help you remove the influence, and everything you forgot will come back. Everything will make sense," Oliver said.

Humoring him, because deep down, if he was honest, I was tempted. I was missing too much. "What kind of favor?"

"Giving me that ring." He pointed at my hand.

I protectively cradled it. "This is my family heirloom. It's my job to protect it, and it's mine. I'm not giving it to you. What a weird thing to ask for."

"I know what it really is, and where it belongs."

After seeing what Oliver was capable of, I wouldn't be able to stop him from taking it, anyway. The more he talked, the more I hoped the missing pieces of my memory might fill in. "I'm listening."

"Many years ago, a trio of witches placed a spell on that ring for good fortune, but they didn't know the spell's side effect."

That explained everything. He was nuts. "You expect me to believe in magic?"

"There's magic all around you. Choosing to believe or not doesn't change whether it exists. That ring's side effect helps people like me. It was made for me."

"People like you? What does that even mean?" I was semi-curious about this confused rambling, but I took another step toward the street.

"I am different from you, but you won't see it unless I want you to."

I had no response to that.

He added, "That ring was in my family, and I've been searching for it for a very long time. I need it back, please." Oliver held out his hand expectantly.

I scoffed. "You just show up in the dark, kidnap my date, and expect me to hand over something precious to me? How dare you? Stay away from me." I'd had enough. I spun and marched through the grass, intending to look tough and dignified, but my wobbly ankle and bare foot had me stumbling all over the grass. I paused and took my other shoe off, cursing Pierce under my breath.

Pierce. I hoped he was fine, but I was in no mood to nurse him. And I better not encounter Soren, or he'd be running from me.

15

The Deception

Daisy

A SMALL PART OF me wanted to find out why Oliver thought my ring, handed down for generations, was owed to him. I wasn't related to any Rockwells. The Barrett family kept detailed records of the family tree going back to the early eighteen hundreds.

Instead, I put one bare foot in front of the other, staring at the ground immediately before each step. Cool grass chilled my feet. The farther I got, the clearer my intentions were. I wanted to go home, get a drink, and sleep. So much sleep.

I bumped into Oliver's chest, and with the unexpected impact, I almost fell over. Oliver caught me by my elbows, and my hands pressed against his firm pecs. A tingle of pleasure danced along my nerves, like a blocked memory fighting to surface. I made a fist, so he couldn't slip my ring free, not without a fight at least, and I was in the mood to fight. I ripped my arms free of his body. How did he get ahead of me so fast? He didn't make a sound.

"Why isn't Pierce over here?" I demanded and scanned the dark area for my date again…that I was about to abandon.

"I gave him a piece of his own medicine. He'll be fine in a few minutes." Oliver held out his palm, still expecting me to turn over my ring.

"You're not getting it," I said.

"Not so fast, vamp," Pierce said behind me. I wanted to be relieved. I think I was—of the obligation to be sure he was okay.

Oliver glared at my date.

For just one instant, I was sympathetic to Pierce's ordeal, but then I remembered him basically telling me I needed to do better in my career, because I wasn't good enough the way I was, and then the whole embarrassing proposal.

The anger returned. I faced Pierce and replayed what he'd just said. What the hell was a *vamp*?

"You know the rules, *Pierce,*" Oliver enunciated the name with disdain.

These two knew each other.

"Screw the rules," Pierce said, uncharacteristically angry. "You can erase her memory, and I'm sure you've done it. Just so we're clear, she's mine. I claimed her. Back off before this gets ugly."

What the hell did I just hear? This wasn't the usual mellow Pierce I'd always known. The way he talked about me as if I were some prize he owned pissed me off. My anger rose to flood levels.

"What did you just say about me?" I snarled at Pierce.

"Hold on, Daisy, let us figure this out," Pierce said in a condescending tone. He stared down Oliver, refusing to acknowledge me as an adult.

That was the straw that snapped my poor camel in half. The anger burned so hot that perspiration coated my chest and back, and a headache throbbed through my skull on a ripple, souring my mood further. Suddenly, whatever warm-and-fuzzies I felt for Pierce were gone. I was certainly *not* loving this date.

I marched up to his chest and pointed a very annoyed finger at his face. "You don't get to figure out anything. I'm not yours. I never wanted this date, and I have no idea why we're here, because I can't stand you. And that's a 'no' on the proposal if that wasn't already crystal clear."

A flash of pain enveloped my head, and I folded in agony. I dropped my shoes, and my knees crashed onto the cold grass, adding even more agony. My face pinched, and I pressed my hands to my temples, trying to stymie the explosion of C4 in my skull. Every inch, every corner, lit up, but just like that, the pain stopped.

"No, Daisy!" Pierce yelled, frightened.

Selfish jerk, mad at my pain instead of helping me. The smoke in my skull cleared, and I understood why. Images assaulted my brain as if an explosion blew the lock off a chest full of memories. Things familiar but forgotten.

Oliver.

In my bedroom.

The sex god with the snake in his pants.

Kneeling in the cold grass, my eyes widened, and I panted. Heat bloomed through my body. How could I forget? How could Pierce make me forget? How did Pierce force me to agree to this date? None of this was possible.

Arms reached under me and lifted me easily to my feet. I turned, and my heart swelled. Oliver had helped me up. I gazed upon his beautiful pale gray eyes. Oliver had fought off Soren for me, saving my life twice. Oliver, the man who brought me gorgeous flowers. Oliver, who was a complete gentleman, walked me home when I'd had enough to drink. Oliver, the Good Samaritan, helping with the basketball player. *Oliver*, whose stories I'd told made Megan blush. Burning heat tore through me at the memories of my rumpled sheets. The fear evaporated like the smoke had. I whispered, "I remember."

The corner of his lips lifted. Not with amusement. Gratitude, and I wanted nothing more than to kiss him until dawn, but I turned on Pierce, feeling pretty damned feral myself. "What the hell drug did you use?" I snarled at Pierce. I figured roofies, but I didn't want to help his answer, and since he was a paramedic, he knew all the same useful drugs I did.

Pierce stepped forward. His assertive demeanor was suddenly apologetic. "I tried to make you happy. We are right for each other, but we had an obstacle." His eyes darted to Oliver. "So I did what I naturally had to do."

I panted with uncontrollable anger and a sense of violation. "None of that makes sense. Tell me what the hell you were doing in my house the night I was attacked."

Pierce held out his hands in surrender. "I only helped you."

"All I see is manipulation. I didn't want this date. How did you make me do it?" It was frightening knowing someone I disliked could make me agree to whatever he wanted, not to mention the missing memories. The most terrifying thought was how far he would have taken the drugging. Until after we were married? After we had kids?

Pierce shared a glance with Oliver. "It's not me you need to worry about."

I looked to Oliver for help. "What does he mean?"

"Nothing. It's nothing. Let's get out of here," Oliver said, seeking my hand.

I pulled free and glared at Pierce. "You're a paramedic. You know the dangers of drug interactions and allergies. You could've hurt me or killed me, and I can never forgive you for that. What did you use?"

Pierce shifted forward again. With his softened features, he intended to make amends. I wasn't interested. "I didn't give you any drugs."

The pile of lies kept growing, along with my frustration. "I'm tired of waiting for someone to tell me the truth. You want trust? Stop lying to me."

Pierce glanced at Oliver again.

Oliver shook his head.

"What? What is it?" I demanded, losing all patience for both of them. "What are you keeping from me?"

"He's a vampire," Pierce said.

With pounding anger, hurt, and violation stirring in my head like a smoothie, surely, I misheard. "I think I hallucinated. What did you say?"

"Daisy," Oliver said gently. "He's right. I am what he says."

I pinched the bridge of my nose, and a chuckle-snort, like someone whose head just split in two, popped from my delirious lips. To clarify just how far my head had split, I asked, "A blood-drinking, sunlight-avoiding vampire?"

Oliver nodded solemnly. He focused on my face gravely, as if worried about my reaction.

Did he think I was stupid? "Vampires don't exist. I can't believe I'm entertaining this bullshit. You're wasting my time. Tell me the truth. This is your last chance, I swear."

Oliver paused, reflecting. He darted an angry glance at Pierce and returned his focus to me. "He forced my hand. I wasn't going to do this until I knew how you'd handle it, but I can see I'm out of time. I'm going to show you now, and I understand if you can't accept it. Please don't be afraid. You are not in danger."

Standing at my side, as if he wanted to see too, Pierce laughed. I ignored him.

Humoring Oliver, I waited for the magical proof fictional creatures existed here in Marinette, Wisconsin.

Oliver's eyes glowed red as rubies glinting in the sun, and his jaw opened wide. I blinked. Morbid curiosity rooted me to the grass, and I was unable to peel my eyes away. Unusually sharp canines descended as if on command. Two narrow points...

Like the fangs of a snake...

A monster. A vampire.

I shook my head, unable to tear my eyes away. This wasn't reality. Vampires didn't exist. I had to be dreaming. A series of terrible dreams caused by a recent traumatic event. I needed to make an appointment to talk to someone. Better yet, I needed to visit Allison at the bar.

I needed a drink.

I had no words to express the jumbled mess in my head. I swatted the air as if sweeping away everything I'd just heard and seen, and I stumbled away, barefoot through the grass.

"Daisy?" Oliver called after me, worry in his voice.

I stopped and turned around. Pierce had a self-satisfied smirk on his face. Oliver once again looked like the normal handsome guy I remembered. The pale gray eyes were back, and flashes of our incredible night together ravished my brain, spinning my head with a confusion cocktail that had no sign of clearing up.

I wanted nothing to do with this.

"I've heard enough. Pierce, stay the hell away from me. I never want to see you again. Oliver? I..." I trailed off as the heartbreak was clear on his handsome features. "Stay away from me." I walked down the sidewalk in the dark, carrying high heels in the crook of my pinky finger all alone.

I never hated my shoes, but I did tonight.

16

Finding Answers

Daisy

I'D TOSSED AND TURNED all night. Unable to process what I'd seen, trying to piece together something that resembled sanity. Wearing comfortable jeans, a T-shirt, and smart shoes, I dropped heavily onto a stool inside Fully Loaded, the television in the background droning on. The bar crowd was thin during the day. Only a pair of men in need of showers played a game of billiards in a side room. A lone pinball machine flashed lights, and the line of gambling machines enticed users to drop in coins with mesmerizing automations.

Allison placed a drink in front of me. I wasn't allowed to return to work yet, but even if my boss approved it, who was going to be my partner?

"Day drinking, huh? You look like you have something on your mind. Care to share with the class?" Allison asked, leaning on the bar and bringing her face close to mine. She had an ease about her, a gentle smile and kind eyes. I needed to say something before I exploded.

"I haven't slept." I swallowed down the whiskey sour and didn't taste a drop of it.

"Clearly. The answer I hoped for included why. Is Pierce being a dick again?"

That was news to me. "What do you mean?"

Allison propped her face on her fists, resting her elbows on the bar's surface. "Come on, like you haven't noticed. He's always trying to make you do what he wants, when he wants. He doesn't listen to you. And I heard from Jamie that he was at our house the other night. That guy is the textbook definition of red flags."

After what I'd seen last night, his hands-on escapades while I had been asleep were the lowest priority to unpack. He'd helped me, was all he'd admitted. I think I hated Pierce, so it was surprising Allison picked up issues, too. It wasn't just me, and I truthfully never wanted to see Pierce again, but I wanted answers. He'd used something to block my memories and agree to his date, but he never said what. I couldn't help but feel like I was missing something right in front of me.

"Pierce and I are over. If you see him lurking around and I'm not aware *again*, kick him out." Especially after his insulting rant at Oliver and treating me like a child who had to be controlled.

Allison stood up with a frown. "Are you saying what I think you're saying?"

I didn't want to rehash the entire evening or even begin on the shitty proposal. "I honestly don't know what he did—he wouldn't say. All I know is it wasn't consensual." I should've taken that test, like Megan said, and now it was too late.

"Asshole!" Allison worked furiously at the well, mixing me a drink like it was a sword for battling my personal demons. "You know, I never liked him." My roommate slid a shot of something across the wood to me, and I didn't even care what it was. "This one's on the house."

I tipped it back happily and relished the burn on the way down.

"And I promise he won't get back in the house again," Allison said.

I raised my empty glass and said, "Cheers to that." I slammed back the remaining drops at the bottom. It still counted.

My head swam with the alcohol, and all I could think of was going home and destroying all evidence of Pierce, but I wasn't in any condition to drive, and I wasn't sure how straight I could walk at this point. And I wasn't walking alone.

I slipped out my phone. I considered momentarily, for just a flash of an instant, one tiny lapse in judgment, drunk texting Pierce and demanding answers.

Still considering.

It was a bad idea.

I scrolled on my phone, finger hovering over his name.

Still a bad idea.

I stared at the glowing screen. His name disgusted me, but with a momentary surge of resolve, I swiped the app away, stopping myself from making a mistake. Instead, I could delete all the photographic evidence of Pierce on my phone, and I opened the file library.

What I found stilled my finger. The last photo I took was from the night of Megan's attack. I drew a long, slow breath and stared at the image. Using a pair of fingers, I zoomed in, unable to comprehend what I was seeing. What my eyes couldn't capture, my lens did. Ruby red glowing eyes on Soren as his mouth fastened to Megan's throat. I covered my gaping mouth with my hand.

Soren had bitten me, and Megan, and our female patient outside my house. Oliver had fought—and matched—his impossible strength. My nightmares of Oliver's feral glowing eyes and elongated fangs weren't nightmares at all. It was real. Vampires were real. We lived among monsters, and Pierce was totally okay with it. Knew about it, even.

"You okay? You look like you've seen a ghost." Allison cleaned the spots off a glass, eyeing me suspiciously.

Allison wouldn't believe me if I told her. The police didn't. Hell, *I* didn't believe myself. "I...I'm fine." By fine, I meant not bleeding or dying. Otherwise, my existential crisis would like a word with my fibbing tongue.

"Let me know if you need anything—another drink or a ride."

I nodded and thanked her absently.

Screw my judgment. I texted Pierce. *'How did you know vampires exist?'*

I waited for a response. When Allison returned to offer me a refill, I shifted my phone away so she wouldn't bust me. She gave me a whiskey sour, and I nursed it, focusing on the tiny keyboard of my smartphone, because as smart as it was, my phone's auto-correction really flubbed some of my words on the regular, and I wanted Pierce to think I was clearheaded and angry.

Instead of drunk and scared.

'Meet me at your house,' he texted back.

I glanced at Allison, guilt filling me as quickly as the whiskey she poured into a glass. She'd promised to ban Pierce from our house, so I couldn't cave so soon. *'Meet me outside Fully Loaded.'*

'K.'

I paid for the non-gifted drinks and nodded to Allison that I was heading out. She waved and silently mouthed 'Good luck' to me.

I was going to need it.

Daisy

PIERCE'S SHINY SUV ROLLED into the parking lot at the bar, and I rose from the outside bench. My stomach sloshed, and my head floated. I stuffed my fingers into my tight jeans pockets and slowly walked over to him, so I wouldn't appear quite as drunk. He climbed out of his vehicle, wearing the usual cargo shorts and polo. He smiled the usual cool Pierce smile. I was so over it.

"You look good, Daisy."

I pressed my lips thin, suddenly hating that phrase. "Just answer the question."

"Walk with me. There're too many ears."

Errr, okay. I had on sneakers, so I could mostly follow a straight line. Maintaining a comfortable distance between our shoulders, I kept pace.

"I was hoping for a chance to talk to you," he said, looking straight ahead down the sidewalk of the residential neighborhood. Nobody was outside that I could see, but someone nearby was starting a lawnmower in their garage.

I didn't humor his lead into an apology. I wanted the truth, and nothing more. "You're not like Oliver, are you?"

Pierce chuckled. "Clearly not. It's daytime."

I didn't know why, but that was a relief. "Vampires can't be out in daylight?"

"Direct sunlight burns them like a match tossed on a gasoline fire. A nasty way to go, but convenient, because they only leave behind ash."

Picturing it, I darted him a look of disgust.

Pierce backpedaled. At least he could read that on my face. "That's what I heard, you know. Not that I personally burned any vampires."

I shook my head, refusing to picture Pierce—the perfect healer—being a murderer. "And Soren and Oliver are both vampires?"

"Yeah."

"How many more are there?"

Pierce shot me a look, but I stared back in challenge. "Far more than you care to know."

"I can't believe any of this. How could I not know what's lurking all around us? Tell me how you knew he's a vampire."

Pierce blew out a long breath. "The animal attacks. The bites are clearly not canine, and there's always a pattern. Once they start, many of them can't stop, and some don't care to."

Unsatisfied, my face pinched in frustration. "I responded to one of those animal attacks, but my first thought wasn't, 'Oh, those darn vampires again', so I'm going to ask you again: How did you know Oliver was a vampire?"

Pierce held up his hands in surrender. "Alright, alright. My family and his are sort of...enemies."

"What? Why?" I didn't think getting answers would only create more questions.

"Let's just say our family rivalry started with a deadly fire and an inexcusable betrayal. When we spot one of the family, we are expected to destroy them, in keeping with the secrecy laws of our culture."

"One that you broke by telling me Oliver was a vampire."

"I made an exception for you, Daisy." His face softened, as if trying to win me over again. I wasn't having any of it.

Curious about my new world, I tried to extrapolate. "Your family holds a grudge against his for something both your ancestors did centuries ago, and that justifies killing each other to this day. Am I understanding this correctly?"

Pierce shut down. His walk became stiff, and he looked straight ahead like a soldier walking into an unwanted fate. "Yes."

I shook my head in complete disbelief. "Grow up."

Pierce stared at me, brows knitting.

"You heard me. Something vague happened centuries ago, and you think that justifies killing each other now? Do you know how ridiculous that sounds? You can both hate each other, if you could even call it hate, but stop this nonsense before one of you ends up in prison."

"I can't."

I stopped, and my head swam. "Why not?"

"The Rockwells are the ones killing people here, and I'm required to stop them." Pierce unfastened a pouch in his baggy shorts and revealed a sharp stick.

I was mildly unimpressed. "What are you going to do with that?"

He slipped it free and showed it to me. "This is the only thing that kills a vampire. Wood stake to the heart. Decapitation works too, but it's extremely difficult to do even on a willing participant."

My stomach rolled at the visual. "You're serious?"

Pierce slipped the stake back into his pocket. "You witnessed Soren in action."

I suddenly felt sober, and I swallowed a lump in my throat. "Then what does that make you?"

That question startled him. His words were punctuated with uncertainty. "Uh, I'm a...hunter. You know, a vampire hunter like on TV, except for the dusting thing. That's not real. Dead vampires leave dead bodies. Younger ones stay fresh, humanlike, for a while. Older ones desiccate pretty quickly. As I said, sunlight does the job and cleans up the mess. No one bats an eye at a pile of ash."

"Enough," I said, holding my hand out. I had a strong stomach as an EMT, but I didn't need a play-by-play of gruesome deaths. The glowing red eyes at the park picnic—because I refused to call it a proposal—returned to the forefront of my memory. "If this whole rivalry is required, why didn't you stake Oliver?"

Pierce continued walking, and I kept pace. "We both suffered losses at each other's hands. To keep the peace in our town, he and I forged a truce, if you will."

"So there is a possibility of burying the hatchet?" If a few conversations were all that stood between me and more bodies with puncture wounds, I was interested.

"Not exactly. And don't tell anyone because I could get in trouble for it."

"Who am I going to tell?" I just fell into this secret world, and I didn't know anyone else in it, but my roommate was my closest remaining friend. "Allison would only think I'm crazy anyway."

"Leave your roommates out of this, okay? Especially her. Working at the bar gives her eyes and ears that most people shouldn't have access to."

After everything I'd learned in the last couple of days, I needed an outlet to unload, so sharing with Allison wasn't going to stop now, even if I had to cherry-pick the details. To get it straight in my head, I summarized, "Fine. So you're a hunter, along with your family. Oliver and Soren are vampires, two of many around. You're supposed to kill each other over a long-standing rivalry going back to some big fire, and you aren't allowed to stop, but you have a secret truce anyway."

"Look, the less you know, the safer you are. And no matter what he does, don't give Oliver your ring."

I glanced at the ruby stone on my finger and turned it, reassuring myself it was in place. I had no intention of giving anyone my aunt's ring, but his firm tone piqued my curiosity. "Why?"

Pierce stopped. "We should head back." He turned around, back toward the bar's parking lot, and the neighbor with the lawnmower began the droning process of trimming the grass.

"You didn't answer me." I turned too fast and swayed. Too much movement. I pressed a hand against my forehead, wishing to sleep off this whole crazy ordeal. I caught up with him and kept pace.

"That ring allows him to become much more dangerous than he already is. Don't give it to him, no matter what he says." Pierce stopped again and held out his palm expectantly. "You know what? You should give it to me. He's going to compel it from you anyway."

I felt like I stood on the edge of this sheer cliff. The safe side was my life as I'd always known it—fighting to make my dad proud, fighting to earn my family's respect and my sister's love. And trying to find a man who gave me all three. On the other side was an abyss, a dark tumble into a world unknown, and each tidbit of information Pierce and Oliver told me pushed me closer and closer to that edge.

A world I may regret ever seeing.

A world I may not survive.

But I knew too much now. I could never walk away and forget what I'd seen. I had to know, regardless of the consequences. "Compel? What's compel?"

Pierce dropped his hand and hooked his thumbs through his belt loops. "It's a skill all vampires have to make hunting their prey easy."

"That sounds...awful, but it doesn't tell me what it is."

Pierce sighed. "They can change people's behavior and alter their memories, giving the vampires the ability to feed on humans and leave their victims alive without any witnesses. It makes them ghosts, very dangerous ghosts."

Oliver had said someone messed with my head. He wouldn't have told me if he had been responsible for it. I ticked off all the things that had been locked away and suddenly released: the forgotten date with Oliver, Oliver's bedpan flowers, the forgotten romp in my sheets, and the drunken walk home from the bar with Oliver.

I frowned, and for the first time, I was heavily suspicious of Pierce. I squinted at him. "Change behavior and alter memories? Like how you *forced* me to go to that picnic?"

His hands went up in defense. "I'm not a vampire, I told you. If I were, I'd be dead." He pointed upward. "Sunlight, remember?"

I wasn't satisfied. He'd compelled me to go on a picnic with him. It was the only explanation of why I'd agreed. I touched the wound-free side of my throat. I'd been attacked, but there were no wounds. "You were in my house the night Soren bit me. My roommate caught you with your hands on me. What did you do and what are you?" It didn't occur to me until now that accusing my ex-boyfriend of being inhuman could cause me trouble.

Pierce sighed and tipped his head back. "I didn't want to do this, but you're forcing my hand here. Daisy, look at me."

I already was looking at him—glaring and frowning in frustration, disappointment, and suspicion, to be exact.

His eyes glowed a brilliant green. They were like green fires flickering, mesmerizing, beautiful. "You will forget this entire conversation."

A vibration in my head, quite like another drunk, dizzy spell, had me swaying. I blinked, and next thing I knew, Pierce briskly walked toward the parking lot, and I didn't know why I stood there. A man cutting the grass waved at me, so I waved back. I jogged up to Pierce and nearly tripped over my own feet in the process. "You didn't tell me how you knew vampires are real."

Pierce said, while still moving and not meeting my eyes, "My friend was killed by one once. They're dangerous."

That wasn't as useful as I'd hoped, but I tried to sympathize. "What happened?"

"I don't want to talk about it."

We reached the parking lot, and Pierce climbed into his SUV without looking back. He rudely drove away, leaving me pining for answers. He'd driven a long way just to tell me he'd also lost a friend to a vampire.

Something didn't make sense.

I wished I had Oliver's phone number, because calling someone allowed me to get what I wanted at a safe distance. Marinette was a small town—not so small everyone knew everything, but not so big you couldn't play six degrees of whoever-you're-looking-for and get an angry ex-girlfriend or a parent's address.

I returned to the bench in front of Fully Loaded, waiting to sober up enough to walk home, while half-heartedly wondering if I could just ask everyone coming and going if they knew Oliver Rockwell.

That would make me crazy.

17

Prepare for Battle

Oliver

During childhood, when a developing vocabulary failed to properly express one's disgruntlement, squabbles were inevitable. And regardless of the child's changing ability to communicate, as children grew in size, so did their squabbles. War was inevitable, permeating history books with its regularity, but many battles were invisible, hidden, lost to time. Unlike humans, I lived long enough to understand war was pointless and to choose a different path.

Until today.

I had nothing good to say about Pierce Evansson. The despicable elf was selfish and vile, manipulating women's free will for his own personal use. He and I never saw eye-to-eye, but we coexisted peacefully, mostly while I was away.

My brother was much worse, having betrayed me by deliberately breaking my number two rule. From vast, unwanted experience, reasoning with Soren was useless. He was a child, forever using squabbles to settle differences, only his led to spilled blood. Soren had been given enough warnings and enough chances to make amends, but my patience over the decades had waned. If I knew Nicole Rockwell would be safe until the end of her natural days, I would simply leave now. I'd turn my back on the endless, pointless fighting.

Except I met Daisy, who made me wild with desire, and she was trapped in the middle of this three-way squabble: my brother attacking her, Pierce manipulating her, and me... Well, I wasn't sure where I stood anymore, but one thing was clear: she wasn't a witch...at the present time. If she were, that whole episode at the park would've ended differently.

Daisy might not want a vampire in her life, but I would fight for her in secret, in the shadows, invisible. No one would lay a finger on her without her permission. She'd always have me, her immortal guardian.

I declared war.

Every good soldier went into battle prepared with full strength, proper weapons, and a plan. Next stop: across the river to the Menominee Blood Donation Center.

Everyone had a favorite time of the day. For many, it was happy hour when drinks were discounted. For others, it was clock-punching time at the end of a grueling shift. Then there were those people who lived for dawn and an early morning jog. I didn't understand them at all. For me, the best time was after the sun had set but before business close, although happy hour came in a close second. Dusk was the only time I could get errands done, and since the window of opportunity was slim, I had to be quick. Thankfully, vampire speed allowed efficient checklist completion, and tonight was no exception as I pushed through the glass doors of the blood bank.

I headed straight for the only person in view, a woman in scrubs behind a tall desk. Her blond hair was pulled back into a ponytail that many hours ago was likely smooth, but now a halo of frizz ringed her head. Lines shadowed her tired face, and an empty coffee mug sat by her keyboard. I didn't know her, which meant I was far overdue for a visit.

The badge clipped to her breast gave me easy access to her eyes. "Evening, Lola," I said with a friendly smile.

The charge nurse sized me up and down from the false security behind the desk, and her eyes sparkled with flirtation. It wasn't my veins she ogled, although hers weren't so bad. After a hundred and eighty-odd years, I was used to the attention. Frankly, it annoyed me much of the time when I tried to stay hidden. But in times like these, I found the easy attraction a handy trait.

"It's too late for a donation tonight. We're closing soon, but I can schedule an appointment for you," she said, leaning forward and staring into my eyes.

"I'm not here to donate. Is Nicole Rockwell an active employee of this facility?" I rested my arms on the raised desk between us and charmed her with a smile.

I'd granted my niece an employee badge and compelled the workers to think she was out on sabbatical, allowing Nicole full access to the blood bank's fresh donations to replenish my private stash. Keeping a fridge full of juice bags and a bar full of booze kept the cravings at bay and reduced the likelihood I'd go off the rails and leave bodies around like Soren.

No small town needed *two* out-of-control vampires.

But every so often, new management cycled through and tried to verify Nicole's credentials. Figuring her name was a 'test' account or the IT department had lapsed on its routine check, management booted her from the system. When I needed Nicole's services, I returned to correct the misunderstanding, because telling management outright to allow my niece unrestricted, unquestioned access to the donation refrigerators brought more questions than I wanted to answer and too many people to compel into compliance.

"Let me see." Lola focused her attention on the computer before her, eyes shifting as she searched the information. "Yeah, I see her here. She's still active."

"Perfect." I leaned forward to recapture her attention.

"But I've worked here for several months, and none of us have met her."

"Lola, can you let me inside?"

The charge nurse looked up at me suspiciously. Now was my chance. I hyper-focused on her eyes, rewiring the fragment of her mind making her own decisions. "Lola, let me inside and forget I was here."

She stared at me, confusion knitting her brow.

Was I too weak for a simple compulsion? I thought back to when I'd last fed on the fresh stuff, and...no one since I'd returned to town. Before I lost her gaze, I repeated, firmer, "Let me inside and forget I was here."

Blankly, she got up and opened the door for me with her ID card. I strolled right by her and down the hall. Since the blood bank was closing, only a fraction of the lights were on.

A door on the left of the hallway led to a bank of commercial refrigerators, and today's haul from willing donors.

With a greedy smile, I found a transport bag and filled it to the brim, choosing all the A-positives I could find, and topping off with less preferable flavors. I zipped the bag shut and flung the strap over my shoulder. As I passed by Lola, I gave her a polite nod. She watched me go with that same blank look on her face.

Vampires had enough difficulty surviving in a human world. Having compulsion at the ready was one small mercy, and when it didn't harm people, I had no issues taking advantage of it.

I opened the trunk of my beloved car, a candy apple 1967 Shelby with white racing stripes from bumper to bumper, and I dropped in my haul next to a case of Jose Cuervo before closing the lid. I slipped into the driver's seat, and the V8 purred as I cleared the parking lot and headed home.

Most miserable and angry men drowned their troubles at the bottom of a liquor bottle. I wasn't most men. After parking in my B&B's garage, I shouldered the donation bag and hefted the case of tequila and carried them inside to my private bar. I restocked my shelves with booze and filled my fridge with blood bags. Since the public got the boot, I didn't have to hide my stash.

I immediately cracked a bottle and tore off a collection bag's port. Since my own fang was too short to reach, I used a custom keychain to puncture the seal. If I were a wild animal, I could've mowed the bag straight, but I wasn't, so I didn't. I licked the spike clean and mixed my drink hard. Since I was in a hurry, I drank it fast. Warmth permeated my cool tissues as energy awakened the muscle fibers that I'd allowed to atrophy. Big mistake. I almost couldn't do a compulsion tonight. I needed to keep my strength up, especially now. With a satisfied sigh, I slammed the empty rocks glass on the wood. Refill time.

"Bad night?" Nicole asked, sliding her arms to rest on the bar.

"You have no idea."

"Pour me one of those." She sat on the stool with a grunt of pain relief and added, "Without the human body parts."

I sent her a crooked smile while pouring her an ounce. I handed her the glass and placed a coaster in front of her.

She sipped with her eyes closed and held the glass between both palms. "Marathon runners carb load before a race. You've got something big going on. Talk to me."

I always enjoyed chats with my niece, especially now that she'd aged. Wisdom and maturity came from her years of life, and although we were as dissimilar as two family members could be, I appreciated her advice and our differing world views. Thanksgiving was always a treat with her around. I needed to be here more often. We didn't have much time left. "I found my ring."

Nicole coughed, held a fist to her chest, and coughed again. "You what?"

I mixed another potent vampire cocktail. "Daisy Barrett has my sun ring."

"Oh, you actually found it. Is that why Soren's lurking around?"

I swallowed down half the glass, and Nicole glanced aside. She accepted me for who I was, but she usually avoided watching me drink human blood. Out of respect, I'd be more tactful about it, but I was on a time limit.

"If Soren knew she had the ring, he would've taken it or at least mentioned it. Daisy says she inherited the ring, making her a witch. I mean, she's a Barrett, but her instincts didn't kick in when she learned what I was. She apparently has no knowledge of the paranormal world at all."

"So she's a pre-witch," Nicole said. "And her family has kept her in the dark about it."

"I think so. Now she's caught in the middle of something pretty big between Soren and the elf, but the two of them having any interest in her puzzles me completely."

"Elves don't go for witches."

"Right. So either he shouldn't want her in the first place, or he expects to prevent her witch side from activating." The idea made my stomach curdle. He really wanted her to be an empty-headed...ugh. "And as for Soren? I don't know the game on the board, but I'm going to be the game champion."

Nicole chuckled. "But like the two of them, she's also *your* enemy. You must really like this woman to go through all this trouble."

My mouth dropped open. Closed. Opened again. Word vomit spilled from my tongue. "I guess, yeah, I do. But really, Soren attacked her, and I'm just keeping her safe, and I want to do everything I can to spite the elf."

Nicole sent me a knowing smile.

I added, "Because I need my ring."

"Oh, dear." Nicole swallowed down the rest of her drink, and I refilled it without her needing to ask. "One of the benefits of your long life is you get to experience history in the making."

My chest inflated with the incoming compliment. Hell yeah, I made history.

"So when you see it repeating, you don't screw up the second time," she finished flatly.

Pop went the bubble. "What do you mean?"

Nicole leveled her gaze at me. "Don't let Daisy become Evangeline."

My heart skipped a beat as her name floated through the air. I hadn't heard those syllables in what—forty years? "You don't have to worry. Daisy knows what I am and wants nothing to do with me." The words were bitter on my tongue, and I wanted to change the subject. "On the plus side, she seems to hate Pierce."

Nicole's smile fell. "The elf is Pierce Evansson?"

"The one and only." And on that note, I filled another stiff drink.

My niece's nose wrinkled. "That's bad luck."

"Tell me about it." I slammed down another drink and started to mix a third.

"Let me," Nicole said, taking the bottle of tequila from me. "I'll mix it stronger for you. You're going to need it."

"Thanks."

Nicole squeezed a portion of blood into my glass and topped it off with the clear liquid. My drink looked like a pink, fruity tropical number. I wished I had those tiny umbrellas.

"So what are you going to do about it? Compel her to hand the ring over?" Nicole drank from her glass, watching me intently.

I'd thought about it since the moment I laid eyes on the ring. It would've been so easy. *Give me the ring. Forget you ever had it.* I couldn't do it. "Remember that accident on the highway a few months ago where the car exploded?"

"The one where you gushed over this pretty little thing and wanted to stay after sunrise—"

"Yeah, that one," I interrupted, regretting having to stop by for a change of clothes, but not regretting seeing my niece again. "That was Daisy."

"Oh, dear," Nicole repeated and tossed back her drink. Her hand rested on my shoulder. "If she wants nothing to do with you, coming clean will help. If someone else tells her first, you'll lose her forever."

"Trying to make myself look better by throwing others under the bus only looks worse on me."

"But it's the truth."

"Doesn't matter. Only the perception does."

Nicole smiled and pushed her glass away. "Then you've got it all figured out. Sweep the girl off her feet the old-fashioned way and try not to get her killed in the process..."

I'd tried that several times only to be deleted by the elf.

"Or...compel your ring off her before Soren does and deal with him. Then, for Daisy's sake, stay the hell out of her life. Poor Evangeline." Nicole stood up and strolled away. She called over her shoulder, "The tequila always loosens up the joints. Good luck."

Evangeline. My Evangeline. I'd loved her, but like all things, vampires and humans couldn't be together. Soren had taught me that lesson clearly, and since her, I'd sworn off human women entirely. But there was something about Daisy Barrett I couldn't push from my mind. I'd already vowed to protect her, and the best way to keep Daisy safe was to get my ring back and deal with Soren's blood-fueled rampage.

When I'd become the game champion, I had to let Daisy Barrett go, witch or not, because I was what she feared—a monster.

18

Hidden in Plain Sight

Daisy

IN MY DARK BEDROOM, candlelight flickered against the peaks and valleys of a naked Oliver straddling me on my bed. Keeping my hands firmly on his round ass, my heart pounded in my chest. Tangy lime from the slice between my teeth dripped into my mouth.

Oliver's soft lips licked a swatch of salt off my throat, and I moaned at his feathery touch. His hands glided down my bare breasts and cupped them while his mouth moved from my sensitive throat down between my breasts to my exposed belly button, and he sucked up the tequila floating in my navel. Oliver shifted up to my face and kissed the lime slice from my lips. Juice dripped down his chin and landed on my chest.

With a grin, Oliver swallowed a squeeze of juice and set the slice aside. Leaning over my naked body, he picked up a canister of whipped cream and a truffle. "Are you hungry, or do you want another body shot?"

Both were equally tempting. "Body shot. Tell me something sexy while you pour."

Oliver leaned back and poured chilled tequila into my navel. "Something sexy...? Let's see." Oliver smiled while he considered. "I made dinner. It's hot and ready whenever you want it, and the kitchen is clean—from the dishes all the way down to the floor."

Oh, yeah, baby.

"So clean you can eat off it," he added.

"There are other things you can eat off," I said suggestively.

Oliver's lips flashed a hungry grin.

Sex, body shots, and a man who could cook and clean up afterward. I had to be dreaming. "You know the right thing to say, as always."

"Here's the lime. Give it a bite." He brought a fresh slice to my lips.

"If I'm biting, then you're next," I teased and gripped the tangy slice between my lips once more.

"Where do you want it?" His fangs descended in anticipation.

I tipped my face away and touched my throat, begging for that rush of wet warmth and jolt of rushing endorphins.

Oliver's mouth spread into a grin, showing his fangs.

Yes, yes, do it!

A knock on my bedroom door had me drowsily lifting my head and squinting at the daylight spilling in through the windows. Ugh, it was a dream. Oliver Rockwell's chiseled abs, tireless fingers, and his generous desire to push all my pleasure buttons left me quaking with heat. Generous, indeed. He put my battery-operated-boyfriend to shame. So much shame.

I needed that man in my life.

Correction—I needed that *vampire* in my bed.

Even thinking the sentence sounded so...unreal. If I didn't have a raging headache, I would've slapped my forehead to knock some sense into me. Oliver drank human blood to survive, which alone was repulsive. But the inhuman strength, and that his brother was a literal monster, only made the dream worse. The only difference between Soren and Oliver was in who had better self-control.

I blinked, trying to drag myself from the twisted depths of my dream. Did I ask Oliver to bite me? Why would I ever want a monster to bite me on purpose? Remembering the terrifying paralysis alone was enough to cause a panic attack, but the searing pain and easy death by exsanguination made me nuts for dreaming about him in a positive light.

I needed to back off the booze because too much confusion swirled in my brain on a good day. Annoyed at being woken up early, but thankful for ending that twisted dream, I plastered a loopy smile on face. A bearded, bright-eyed Jamie leaned into my room, knuckles still in the air, prepared for the next knock. Morning people were annoying some days. Like today.

"Good afternoon, Daisy. How're you doing?"

Afternoon? I twisted my neck and grabbed my phone off the end table. I lit up the screen and checked the time. Huh. Mid-afternoon it was.

Jamie didn't normally pop in unannounced, especially when my door was closed. Whatever he needed had to be important. I pulled my sheet up to my chest and sat up. My pajamas—T-shirt and underwear—weren't exactly roommate friendly, even though Jamie had seen absolutely everything possible on a woman's body in his line of work.

"What's going on?" I asked and rubbed an eye.

Jamie strutted into my room and sat on the corner of my bed. I scooted my legs up. "What's up?"

"You want some waffles?"

"It's kind of late for that, no?"

"Does the package say you can only eat waffles at certain times of the day?" Jamie said, copying my line.

"Waffles sound great." I smiled and shifted to get out of bed, but Jamie didn't move out of the way.

"Actually, I came up here to find out how you were handling things, you know, with Pierce and Megan."

It was comforting to know Jamie cared enough to ask. "Handling? I'm taking Megan's loss one day at a time. Whenever I think of her, there's a crushing pain in my chest." And talking about it made it worse. I swallowed back the waves threatening to pull me under. Instead, I focused on something easier to process. Anger. "What about Pierce?"

"The other night, he had his hands on you. I just wanted to make sure you got that sorted."

Our conversation yesterday had been cut short, strangely short, so I didn't get to ask. "It doesn't matter. I don't want to see him again, and Alli promised he won't be allowed in the house anymore, especially if I'm not awake."

"Perfect. Come downstairs and get some grub. Oh, and Alli needs you." Jamie rose and closed the door behind him.

Need was a strong word. What would've sounded innocent to me weeks ago now left me uneasy, which was silly. I'd known Allison longer than Megan. My roommate didn't keep any secrets to justify the swirling in my guts.

I dressed quickly in clean jeans and a T-shirt, but not the same ones. I did have several of each type of clothing. I brushed my hair and checked on my aunt's ruby ring. Still in place on my finger.

I bounded down the wooden staircase and found Allison sitting on the carpet in the living room with various objects laid out before her. Jamie was in the kitchen, and the toaster popped. He caught hot waffles and set them on plates he'd laid out. He shook his fingers from the burn and stuck them in his mouth. I cringed. Hopefully, he didn't do that after every batch.

"Over here, Daisy." Allison waved at me to join her. "Sit down across from me."

I lowered myself cross-legged where she'd instructed. "What is all this?"

A fancy silver goblet rested between us, and white candles circled it. She tore up what looked like fresh herbs and sprinkled them into the goblet. In her lap rested an open book similar to the one Aunt Lisa left for me—tanned pages with faded lettering and symbols I didn't recognize.

"You want Pierce to stay out, so I'm doing just that." Allison flicked on a flame at the end of a long-handled lighter, and one by one, she lit candles in a circle.

Despite years of college and medical school requiring my nose to be glued to textbooks, I'd still carved out time for movies, television, and yes, binging a couple of urban fantasy books. I also wasn't oblivious to the different belief systems around the world, so I had an inkling of what I was seeing, but as a woman who'd dedicated her life to science, my skepticism raised its hand to argue. "And this is going to keep him out?"

"Yep."

Allison had never mentioned this practice of hers, nor had I seen her do it. "What exactly is this?"

My roommate glanced over her shoulder at Jamie, and she called over to him, "What do you think?"

Jamie opened the fridge and quickly shut the door. He popped open the bottle of maple syrup. "She survived dating Pierce for months. She deserves to know."

I knew something fishy was going on around here. "Know what? What are you hiding from me?"

Allison turned back to me. "This is witchcraft."

Vampires, then witches. I wasn't sure if I should be relieved or even more afraid. And that thought epitomized how messed up my life had become. When Megan and I had found the basketball player victim in the park, who *moved after dying*, I'd fallen into an alternate universe. I no longer knew anyone I thought I knew, and so far, I wasn't liking it. But to believe literal witchcraft could manifest physical change was a massive pill for me to swallow.

Oliver was a vampire, which, based on the little I knew, was merely an extreme version of xeroderma pigmentosum, a hypersensitivity to sunlight, in combination with an unknown viral infection, causing the brain to incorrectly seek alternative food sources. Both were treatable with medical intervention. So, although Soren had made some poor choices, he and Oliver were treatable. And afterward they could return to normal lives, and I could...perhaps...invite that *man* into my bed.

I smiled. I knew I could figure out what was bothering me so much. Their claimed vampirism was simply a medically complex disease that no one had treated yet. I'm sure Dad could figure something out with his medical breakthroughs at the lab.

I paused my logic train. But what about the descending fangs or the glowing red irises? Those topics weren't covered in the hematology class I'd taken. Then again, I was a med school dropout. If I'd completed my courses, extreme cases like Oliver and Soren's might've been addressed. Loosely based on medical science, their condition was explainable and believable.

But witchcraft was so speculative that I had to remind myself to keep an open mind, and the only way for me to learn was to ask. "I don't mean to be crude, but are you serious?"

Allison laughed. "I've known you long enough to know what you're thinking. I assure you I take no offense. Over the years, I've heard some nasty things come from people's mouths. At least you're calm about it."

I was so far. "How long have you been practicing?"

Allison shifted the lighter to the last candle, holding the flame in place until the wick caught. "Since I was a girl. It's not something we announce publicly. Ever since Salem, real witches have kept things on the down low."

"The witch trials?" I asked, remembering women accused of witchcraft were burned or drowned.

"One of many throughout time." Allison set the lighter aside.

"Why are you showing me this now?"

My roommate tore a different herb and sprinkled it into the goblet, a seriousness passing on her face that I'd never before seen. "You've somehow found your way into our world. So rather than leave you blind and unprotected, I—"

Jamie cleared his throat, interrupting her. He held the empty waffle bag in his hand.

"*We* decided to bring you into the loop," Allison corrected. "This spell will keep all supernatural creatures out of your house, witches being exempt naturally."

Jamie nodded, satisfied, and tossed the bag into the trash. "Breakfast is ready."

"This won't take long. Give us a minute," Allison said.

"Wait," I said, trying to process quickly enough. "Exempt because witches aren't supernatural, or exempt because they are?" I didn't like details dangling.

"Witches are natural. We can find and use the magic within, and when we deplete ourselves, communing with nature replenishes it. Knowing our limit is critical, because if a witch uses too much, it can kill her, so we always have to be careful."

I had no evidence to refute that, so I filed it away somewhere in my disbelief center, one notch closer to understanding and several away from acceptance. Jamie knew about Allison's witchcraft before I did, and they decided together to rope me into it. But why Jamie—a college student and part-time stripper?

"When the food's cold, I call first dibs on the microwave." Jamie wiped his hands clean on a kitchen towel and sat next to me on the carpet, legs crossed, and the three of us formed a triangle around the goblet.

Allison glared at his intrusion.

"What? Two is stronger and faster than one," Jamie said with a shrug.

"Two what?" I asked.

"We're both witches," Jamie said. "It doesn't come easy, trust me."

Allison turned to me. "For women, magic activates after a stressful moment in our lives, like a trigger, which, if you remember high school, is a common occurrence pretty young. The gene is dormant in men, so Jamie's been working on finding his power most of his life. It's a steep learning curve once you've been exposed to our world, but don't worry, we'll watch out for you, starting with this."

My head swam with information. My own friends—roommates living under my roof—were complete strangers. Witches and genes. Magic and science. My head exploded. "Magic is genetic?"

"Yep," Allison said proudly. "And Jamie and I are stronger together than apart, because we're related."

My gaze flicked back and forth between the two. She had light hair, and his beard and brows were blond. They were both attractive, objectively speaking, and they shared the same brown eyes. Why didn't I see it before? "You're siblings?"

"Half-siblings. Raised by a witch mom. We carry on her legacy." Allison slipped on protective cloth gloves and turned pages in her book as if it were ancient and delicate. She pushed her glasses up her nose. Today's choice was thin wire frames, nearly unnoticeable.

"Don't worry," Jamie said, collecting my hand in his. "We know what we're doing."

"Does it work?" Not that wielding magic wasn't the coolest idea, but my skepticism had me wishing I were elsewhere right now, doing something that could make a difference, like seeing a lawyer to send a warning letter to Pierce to stay away. Concrete problems had concrete solutions.

"Witches come from a bloodline of people destined to protect humans against supernatural forces, things humans can't fight fairly. We are soldiers without guns or knives. We are shields, keeping our world a secret. And yes, it does work. You'll see," Allison said, eyes on the book.

"But why the secrecy? If we knew what's out there, we could protect ourselves better." And not get mixed up with vampires in the first place.

Allison stopped turning the pages, and she took my hand and Jamie's. "People panic when the world they know is turned upside down, so while we protect them from the supernatural, we also protect them from themselves. Hundreds of years ago, when ignorance and fear ruled, witches were burned at the stake. But a couple of decades ago, during a time of advanced technology, and easy access to the internet, and endless information, people still panicked over

Y2K, thinking their computers were melting down. How do think people would react to vampires and elves?"

I pulled my hands free. "Hold up. Did you say *elves*? Santa's little toy makers?"

Jamie chuckled. "Every culture has a caricature rendition of the truth, but I can tell you real elves are not merry, not small, and most suck at making toys. The important thing is you don't want to get tangled up with one. They only lead to heartbreak."

I drew a blank trying to picture what an elf looked like. "You're painting all of them with wide strokes. They can't all be like that, right?"

"We consider them enemies of mankind, but their intentions aren't as extreme as it sounds," Allison said. "They only want what everyone else does. To survive."

My head swam with the new information. Evil elves, murderous vampires, and in my own living room, witch soldiers. After the last few nights I'd had, I was willing to be extra open-minded, hoping for logical explanations to what I'd witnessed. But *elves*?

How was I going to reconcile all these pieces, which didn't fit into the world I knew?

Allison turned a page. We were performing some sort of witch ritual...to keep *Pierce* out of our house. I squinted. "Are you telling me my ex-boyfriend is one of those things?"

Allison nodded. "For your own good, I'm glad you figured it out and allowed us to do this."

"What is he?" I'd seen Pierce in daylight, so I had a feeling I already knew, but I wanted her to say it.

"He's an elf," Jamie said.

I'd never seen fangs on Pierce. "He doesn't bite?"

Allison laughed. "No, but to make the differences between elves and vampires easier to understand, consider elves like foxes with wings—pretty, stealthy, but dangerous. Compare them to vampires, who are more like wolves—rough around the edges, terrifying, and something you want to stay far from."

Suddenly feeling hoarse, I cleared by throat. "Did you say 'wings'?"

"Big white wings like goddamn angels," Jamie said. "Where do you think the stories came from? They use a glamour to hide their wings and pointy ears, and when they fly, their entire bodies become invisible to humans."

I pressed a hand against my forehead, trying to stop my brain from doing laps. When I'd woken up after Soren attacked me, my wounds were gone, but there was something else... "A white feather."

"They shed worse than cats," Jamie said.

Well, if I couldn't figure out anything, I knew I didn't want to be bitten in my sleep, and I didn't want feathers shed all over my house. And I was grateful to have someone to talk to about it all, who understood, who respected me enough to explain what the hell was going on and wanted to help me. I really, really appreciated my roommates right now. I recollected their hands for their ritual. "What do I need to do?"

Allison glanced at the picture window in the living room. Daylight faded quickly. "Just focus. Listen to my words. We need to get this done before nightfall."

"Why?"

She shushed me and began chanting. Jamie closed his eyes. So I copied him and listened to her words. The flames made an explosive noise, and extra heat licked my face. I kept my eyes shut, focusing on the sounds, and trusting my roommates. But it was tough not to freak out about my living room being on fire. I had no idea if my homeowner's insurance covered spells gone wrong.

Jamie joined the chanting. It was awkward not knowing the words, but I sat there listening, pretending to know what the hell was going on. At once, the flames went out, and both my roommates turned silent. I opened my eyes. "Did it work?"

"I'm sure we'll find out soon enough," Allison said dryly.

Jamie stood up and headed to the kitchen. "Microwave's mine."

"You're not going to help clean up?" Allison said, gesturing at the melted candles, sprinkles of herbs all over, and other supplies she'd dragged from storage.

"Nah," Jamie said, holding his plate and opening the microwave door.

I snorted. Yep, a man who helped clean up could only be a dream.

19

Unexpected Surprise

Daisy

Disappointed, I slipped my phone back into my pocket. No response. Lily had never read my texts pleading for her to be here today. I shouldn't have been disappointed, but I was. Lily had claimed I looked too much like our mom, and that was why she had to leave. That didn't make sense, but everyone grieved differently. I hadn't heard a word from her since, but Dad kept reassuring me she was fine.

Well, *I* wasn't fine. I wanted my sister back.

A stately Victorian house had been converted into a funeral home and re-carpeted wall to wall with blood red crushed velvet flooring. A little tongue-in-cheek and excessively dreary. The sterile carpet wash scent didn't help any. Megan's mom picked out a pair of matching floral arrangements, but it would take so much more to cheer up the space. But the flowers worked hard to overcome the heavyhearted atmosphere of silence punctuated by sniffles and sobs. I inhaled a deep, shaky breath and exhaled slowly as I approached the cold, shiny casket.

Forty hours a week, plus weekends, overtime, and occasional bar closes, sharing laughter, tears, and life plans. Megan had been crushing on the emergency room nurse Kevin Fontaine for weeks, and she'd just started dating him. I'd never seen her happier, and she gushed about him at every chance. Megan's parents planned to move here to be closer to her, and Megan's older brother had a baby on the way.

One gruesome attack and the earth tilted on its axis. Families torn apart, memories tainted, hopes and dreams dashed, pain...so much unbearable anguish. Megan was gone forever. All her hopes and dreams vanished, just like that. Snuffed like a candle. No more life plans. I hoped she was somewhere looking down on us, laughing at the useless grief rolling through this macabre building, trying to tell us life was short, too short. Enjoy each day to its fullest, and when it was over, it was over. Make sure there were no regrets.

I already had regrets.

Like letting Megan exit the rig first for our patient. If I'd been first, Soren would've gotten me and whisked me away to whatever he had in mind, leaving Megan and our patient alone. But no, Soren had done her dirty, snuffing out her vibrant life before she'd hit her stride. I swiped tears pooling on my lower lids—tears of sorrow, tears of anger.

Exhaling a steadying breath, I looked into the open casket of my best friend and fondest colleague. I traced the curve of her smooth face, her closed eyelids, her stoic lips. The makeup was a little heavy-handed, making her appear so full of life, ready for a party. I watched her eyelashes, waiting for the tiniest hint of movement, hoping for the gag where she'd fold upright and laugh.

I kept waiting, wishing.

Jamie approached and squeezed my hand. Red rimmed his eyes from hidden tears. He'd agreed to be my emotional support human if I agreed to watch the Indy 500 race this weekend. The deal seemed so tactless at the time, but I was desperate for a hand to hold, since Lily was missing in action. Seeing how Megan's death affected him so, I think he wanted to come along. He just didn't know how to be upfront about it.

The cosmetologist did a fantastic job patching up the gory wound in Megan's throat. No one out of the loop would suspect a thing.

"How could a dog be so vicious and not get caught?" Megan's mother asked, holding a handkerchief to her nose and mouth. "A senseless murder. If a person did this, he'd be in prison, and I'd be rooting for the death penalty. But because it was a dog, it runs free until the next attack, and there's nothing I can do about it." She sniffled, and her husband rubbed her shoulders from behind.

Even if Megan's mother knew the truth, she still couldn't do anything about it. "It's a small town. Eventually it'll get caught."

Or run out of town.

With stakes.

A flicker of movement caught my eye. I released Jamie's hand, and to both him and Megan's parents, I said, "Excuse me a minute."

Her mother ignored me, her father nodded in acknowledgment, and Jamie watched me move through the crowd, most of whom I'd never met. A sea of strangers who loved Megan. When I'd die someday, would this many people show up for me? Would my dad? Would my sister finally come back to town to pay her respects? Because as of right now, I was honestly concerned at the quantity of people willing to appear at my funeral.

And that was the most depressing thought I'd had in…fifteen solid minutes.

I followed the movement out of the stifling velvet room, around a corner with fake plants, and down a hall. There in a nook out of direct sunlight, I caught him standing in front of an upholstered bench. Oliver Rockwell's bright pale eyes caused my heart to flutter, and with dark hair gelled back, and wearing a fine suit, he was stunning and respectable. Breathtaking.

The last time I'd seen him, he'd shown me his true face, the predator face, and I'd abandoned him and Pierce at the park, unable to accept what I'd learned. What I'd believed to be the only difference between him and Soren was Oliver's level of control. But that wasn't true. He'd rocked my bed and saved my life.

Much had changed since that horrifyingly confusing night. "You're the last person I thought I'd see here."

"If you want me to leave, I understand."

I'd only just dipped my toes into his scary world, and my witch roommates didn't think highly of vampires or elves, describing them as stealthy, dangerous, and terrifying.

I should've told Oliver to leave, but I had questions and no vampire phone number. "Please sit."

Oliver folded onto the upholstered bench nestled in the nook. He gestured for me to join him, and I sat down. His body was inches from mine, and my skin hummed in his presence, like I finally felt...safe. And that made no sense at all from what Jamie and Allison had told me.

"I wanted to see if you needed a shoulder to lean on," Oliver said. "How are you doing?"

Someone nearby broke into sobs, and sadness clogged my throat. My fingers wrestled with each other as I fought the anxiety trying to burst free. I choked out, "Not good."

Oliver rested his palm over my restless fingers. "It shouldn't have happened. I'm so sorry. If I could've done anything..."

Tears welled in my eyelids, and I blinked them back. "But you did." I sniffled through a sad smile. "You saved me."

Oliver squeezed my hands reassuringly. "I've lost many people over the years. It never gets easier. If you want to talk about it when it's not so raw, I'll be here."

A sob broke free, and I fell against his chest. Oliver embraced me, and I cried while his hand made soothing circular motions on my back. His thoughtfulness didn't align with being a monster. "Can I ask you something?"

"Anything."

I lifted myself off his firm chest, wondering if that was a mistake. "My roommates said Pierce is an elf. Is that true?"

Oliver rubbed the back of his neck. "Yeah, it is."

"They also said elves were worse than vampires. I saw Soren in action. I can't reconcile that with Pierce. What do they mean?"

The glass doors opened at the end of the hall, with late mourners arriving to pay their respects. Oliver exhaled. "That's a conversation for a place with fewer ears. And right now, we have incoming."

"Huh?" I wiped my face clear and followed Oliver's gaze. My heart stopped. For a solid, no-questions-asked, ten seconds, I had no pulse. Oliver squeezed my hand like he'd sensed it.

"My sister," I breathlessly muttered to myself in disbelief. I stood up on shaky knees. "Lily?"

My younger sister, with her shiny brown curls and dark blue eyes, stood before me in a navy pencil skirt suit. She was so beautiful. My face twisted with another sob, and I collapsed against her. Lily bent down and hugged me back. I missed her so much. "Where've you been all these months?"

"I had to leave," Lily said, pulling away too soon. "But I got your messages. How are you doing?"

I shook my head. The pain she'd inflicted by abandoning me stung, and with Megan's death, I was raw to the core. "Dad's never good at emotional stuff, you know that, and when I needed you most, you left. I had to process Mom's death alone. The day I lost her, I lost you, too. At least you could've called me and told me you were okay."

"You wouldn't understand." Her cold condescension tore through me. Lily glanced at Oliver behind me, who patiently waited with a sad smile. At least he stayed through our awkward fight.

"I wouldn't understand? Are you kidding me? You wouldn't believe the things I've—" I cut myself off and glanced at Oliver. His face was closed off, not happy with what I'd almost blurted. My newfound open-mindedness wasn't mine to share or to boast, and those who knew about it were at risk. Picking a fight at a funeral was hardly appropriate.

By Lily not giving a shit about me, she'd driven a knife through my chest. I wouldn't repay her with the same disregard, but I could prove she couldn't hurt me anymore, because I didn't need her. I plastered a smile on my face to show I'd moved on, started a new life, and accepted my sister wouldn't be in it anymore. Her choice, not mine.

"Lily, I want you to meet Oliver, my—" I fumbled for the word to describe whatever was going on between us, because we hadn't had that talk yet.

Oliver stood and held out his hand. "Friend," he finished for me. As happy as I was to have a reliable friend by my side, I didn't like that title for him. It felt understated and insufficient, but 'monster I slept with' didn't quite ring true. "Nice to meet you, Lily."

"Likewise." My sister shook and glanced over her shoulder at the funeral crowd with an uncharacteristic nervousness about her, like she didn't want to be here. I couldn't fault her. She didn't know Megan, and Oliver was intimidating. Besides, funerals weren't exactly rainbows and unicorns, and our first five minutes together almost caused a fight. Like usual.

Their hands released, and Lily turned to me. "What happened to Pierce?" She glanced at Oliver apologetically. "No offense."

Oliver dipped his head in acknowledgement. Always the gentleman, if the word could be defined loosely.

"We broke up," I said and glanced at Oliver, sending him a silent message that we needed to talk. He held my eye contact as long as I offered it. I think he got the message.

"Good," Lily said. "That's great news. He wasn't right for you."

I pressed my lips thin at everyone having an opinion. My turn to be short with her. "So I hear."

"My ears are ringing." Pierce approached, and ignoring Oliver, he brightened with a smile. "You look good, Daisy. Hi, Lily."

That damned phrase again. Oliver straightened his spine next to me, and Lily stiffened, eyes widening. Pierce wasn't the hugging type, but I had the feeling if he went for it, Lily wouldn't appreciate it. The tension between the three of them was thick enough to cut. What was going on around here?

Lily turned away, pale as a sheet. "I have to go."

"Wait, what?" I asked my sister. "I haven't seen you in months. Can we get dinner later?"

"I can't stay." She almost looked afraid. "It's good to see you. Say 'hi' to Jamie for me and be safe."

"Lily, wait!"

My sister rushed right out the door. I wanted to chase after her, but I'd done that before. She would vanish without listening to me. I would be standing alone, rejected, in a funeral home parking lot. It was a useless urge, and I had more dignity than that. Instead, I needed to referee Oliver and Pierce. Since Megan was his colleague too, I tempered my desire to throw the elf out. Maybe Pierce knew why Lily acted the way she did. "What was that about?"

Pierce shrugged. "I don't know, but I'm sorry about Megan."

"Thank you," I said honestly, but I itched to get away from him. Since Pierce had known Megan longer than I had, I could shoo him away for a while. "Go pay your respects. She's in there."

"Where all the people are?" Pierce cocked his head in the direction of the gentle murmurs.

"It's good your powers of observation are intact." I didn't mean to be snarky, but the guy deliberately ignored my hint to leave.

"In that case, my powers of observation say you look miserable." Pierce stepped closer to me, arm reaching out to touch me. He finally acknowledged Oliver with a warning glare.

I stepped back just as Oliver positioned himself between us, shielding me. "No need to touch her. You heard the lady."

I definitely didn't want Pierce's hands on me again, awake or not, and like with my sister, fighting was highly inappropriate at a funeral. I asked Oliver, "Do you want to get out of here?"

Oliver smiled gently. "You go ahead. I'll make sure you're not followed." He glared at my ex.

"What are you going to do about it, vamp?" Pierce hissed, keeping his voice low.

"Stop it. Enough," I said, repositioning myself in front of Oliver. "Pierce, go see Megan. She would want that."

Pierce gazed at me, and I watched his eyes for signs of green, like he was attempting to manipulate me again. But his baby browns stayed dark. Pierce turned on his heels and slipped into the crowd.

I sighed with relief and looked through the glass doors. Daylight. "You can't go now, can you?"

"Not yet." Oliver gave me a small smile.

"Can we talk?" I asked.

Oliver glanced down the corridor. "If you want privacy, we won't get it here."

I could be quiet, and, feeling emboldened in a public place, I whispered, "What does it mean to be a vampire?"

Oliver backed up, as if afraid of where his conversation headed. "You want to know?"

I stepped closer, unafraid. "Tell me. Are you like wolves—rough around the edges, terrifying, and something I need to stay far away from?" I used my roommate's definition as a starting point.

"That's fair."

I waited for more, but he didn't continue. "And?"

"We are what you think—blood-drinking creatures of the night who kill to survive, and you are my prey. You should stay away from me." He was confident and cocky, and by the definition of his food source, he could be called a predator, a monster.

I took in Oliver's expensive suit, his gelled hair, and glinting eyes. He'd shaved his handsome face today. He looked like the kind of man who was a CEO with a private jet. I supposed that still fit the image of a monster in many circles. If he spent his nights hunting people for food, then yeah, he was someone to stay away from. Oliver was exactly what he'd said. He was what my roommates warned against.

Now that I'd slept and was clear-headed and fully sober, I wasn't afraid of him. Oliver wasn't a savage beast prowling in the night. He'd saved me, and now, daylight trapped Oliver in a funeral home because he was amazingly thoughtful and supportive. Would I call him a creature? No, only a victim of a rare disease, xeroderma pigmentosum. "You're nothing like Soren. You've been in town how long, yet none of the victims were yours, right?"

Oliver shook his head. "Technically, no."

"I haven't forgotten all you've done for me, and it means a lot that you came here today. Refereed too."

Oliver stepped closer and lifted his lips briefly. "I'll always stand between you and him. Anytime you ask or anytime you're afraid, I'll be there."

My own personal bodyguard. I smiled in appreciation. Oliver was so damned hot right now. "And that's why you're not a monster."

Oliver exhaled deeply, as if he didn't believe me. He cupped my throat with his palms, holding me gently, and I fully trusted him not to hurt me. His forehead touched mine. "You don't know me well enough to make that determination."

"I'd like to make up my own mind on the matter."

"You deserve that much."

His lips pressed against my forehead, and images of his mouth all over my body assaulted my brain, sending sparks of fire flashing through me. While we worked on whatever this was between us, I wouldn't mind another go-around in the sheets. That dream with the body shots and lime wedges kept me roaring ever since, and I knew only one person who could satisfy me. "Then what do I need to do to get you close?"

"You don't know what you're asking for, but I'll play along. How close?" Oliver returned the tease, bringing his face closer to mine.

"Very," I whispered. Heat pooled low, and my heart rate increased.

Oliver grinned.

I asked, "You can hear that, can't you?"

"It's like 306 horsepower went from idle to pedal-punched-to-the-floorboard."

And I was suddenly thankful humans couldn't hear heartbeats. "Right now my horses are lifting the front chassis and leaving burned rubber down the asphalt."

Oliver closed his eyes and groaned. "Car metaphors are my nitrous oxide, damn sexy. Kiss me."

I wanted to so badly. I leaned in close, but a tap on my shoulder made me gasp and back up. Pierce returned. Just great.

"It's a funeral. Seriously?" With a look of scorn on his face, he walked around me but shoved Oliver's shoulder immaturely as he passed by.

Oliver straightened. "There's more ceremony for you to attend at the cemetery, and I can't be there, but I'll see you soon."

I had one question before forcing myself to walk away from his fine mouth. "What kind of car has 306 horsepower?"

Oliver's sexy grin had me regretting where we stood. "Mine."

"You'll have to show me sometime." I walked away, but looked over my shoulder at Oliver, whose fiery eyes had me flustered. He was the perfect distraction to get me through the day. And I didn't know how to properly thank him for being so damned perfect. Besides the bloodsucking vampire disease and a million questions to go along with it.

I detoured into the visitation room and collected Jamie. He was uncomfortably sweaty in his suit, but it was chilly in the room. "Are you okay?"

"Just keeping the peace." He adjusted the tie at his throat and gathered my hand. "Let's get out of here."

After we pushed through the glass doors, I asked, "Were you doing a spell?"

"A vampire, an elf, and a witch walk into a funeral home. It's the start of a very bad joke."

I cringed. "Do I want to know the punchline?"

"We avoided it," Jamie said and opened his car door for me.

Now I knew why he wanted to go. Did it still count as a favor? Because I wasn't in the mood to hold up my end of the bargain.

20

The Replacement

Daisy

I THOUGHT I WAS going to be excited to return to work and dive into the distractions of my normal routine, but I was glad my boss had made me take a few days off. Walking through these halls, I kept looking over my shoulders, irrationally hoping to see Megan and Kevin sneaking around. But that would never happen again. Despite the stabs of sadness every few minutes, I had to get back in the saddle and get that rig moving.

I had others to think about.

And that included meeting and training my new partner. Not being super experienced myself, I was nervous about meeting her. I went into my boss's office and closed the door behind me. My boss smiled at me from behind his basic desk, stacked high with knickknacks, photos, and files. His comb-over needed brushing as it stuck up and flopped over. Sitting across from him in a plain upholstered chair was who I presumed to be Megan's replacement.

"Daisy, this is your new partner, Kayla," my boss said and gestured to the woman.

As I approached, Kayla stood up and offered her hand to shake. The leggy brunette smiled politely, but she seemed as nervous as I. A partner was serious business. We had to get along because mistakes were made when partners miscommunicated.

She said politely, "Nice to meet you."

With a friendly smile, I accepted her hand. "Likewise."

"Kayla joins us from Antigo, another small town an hour and a half west of here. I think the two of you will be a great team. Daisy, show your partner around our highly important department." He gestured for us to leave.

"Come with me," I said, all cheerful. Antigo was a similar-sized town, so I was curious to know the call volume and types of cases she'd responded to. Plus, she wasn't Pierce, so we were already off to a good start. I led Kayla back down the corridor. "So tell me, what was your weirdest call?"

"Weirdest?" Kayla's eyes scanned everything as we passed through the emergency department, taking in all the sights like a new person would. "I responded to a vicious animal attack at a school."

"Oh?" Perfectly relevant and I tried not to grin.

I was glued to her every word, bubbling with excitement at the possibility of having someone else to discuss the weird world I'd just learned about. I scrutinized her as we turned a corner, and I realized I had no way to tell if someone was a vampire, elf, or a witch. But Oliver had made it clear their world was not to be discussed, so I'd have to be absolutely certain she knew something before I tipped her off.

"It was quite harrowing." *I bet*, I thought, eating it up. "The poor kid was traumatized."

Okay, excitement over.

"An elementary school student smuggled her pet cat in her backpack for show and tell. As you can imagine, the cat wasn't thrilled, and when the teacher fought to shove the cat into a box, it scratched her good. She hollered about rabies, and demanded all sorts of things from the administration, and she threatened the poor kid with a lawsuit."

Disappointed, I said, "That is weird."

"I know, right? All cats like boxes."

Maybe, just maybe, I wasn't the last person on earth to learn about the hidden world around us. That was a small consolation. "And through here, as the boss requested, is the most critical place you need to know." I pushed through the final set of doors.

Kayla looked around at the couch, television, and coffee station. "I don't get it."

"The breakroom." I headed straight for the coffeepot and poured myself a cup.

My new partner frowned, and her lip curled in disgust. Okay, the budget for the breakroom left everyone wanting, but since the coffee was free—so far—I wasn't complaining. She asked, "The breakroom?"

And I got myself an overachiever, likely with a serious case of naivety. I so missed Megan. I lifted a clean cup for Kayla. "Want some coffee?"

"No, thanks." Kayla wandered the breakroom, pausing at the bulletin board to read the ads.

I glanced at the door leading to the emergency department, wishing Megan would push through and regale me with steamy tales of her and Kevin in the closet. I never wanted to forget Megan, but when would the aching hollowness go away?

"Everything okay?" Kayla asked, approaching me.

Tight-lipped, I smiled. "Yeah, why?"

"You didn't answer me." Bright green eyes stared at me with concern.

"Oh, sorry. I was distracted. What did you say?"

"I was invited to a party, and since I'm new here, I don't know anyone. I was hoping you'd come with me. Introduce me to some hot guys, you know, have some fun?" She bit her lower lip suggestively. "You are single, right?"

I didn't personally know anyone I could introduce her to, but if someone else was buying drinks, why not? "Sounds fun. Where and when?"

"Tomorrow night. Give me your phone." Kayla held out her palm expectantly.

I placed my phone in her hand, and she tapped away before handing it back. "You've got the address. I'll meet you there."

I looked at the address and smiled. Close to my house and on the river. I could have all the fun and not worry about driving home. "Sounds great."

The overhead announcement alerted us to a call. We listened and took off running.

"The good news is," I said to her as she kept pace, "I showed you the most important area in this place before the first call, just like the boss requested."

Kayla laughed.

Daisy

THUMPING BASS PUMPED DOWN the neighborhood, so I was getting close. I checked the time on my phone while keeping an eye on the uneven sidewalk in the dark. Yeah, I walked. *I know, I know.* Soren had disappeared, and there were a lot of people out tonight, so I wasn't worried.

I'd worn cute but comfortable wedges, capris, and a cute top. Since I was older than the typical party crowd, I wasn't sure what to expect, and butterflies danced in my stomach. I didn't want to disappoint the new woman in town, with whom I had to spend forty hours every week.

When Kayla had given me the address, I'd recognized the street as being near my house and on the river, but I didn't realize it was the bed-and-breakfast—a fancy, old-world styled building with imposing columns and light beaming from massive windows. With paying guests inside, why would the owners allow such an event?

Man, if I were on vacation, hoping for some rest and relaxation, and someone threw a party like this? Call me miserly, but I'd be shaking my cane at those hooligans. Since

I wasn't and I'm not, I walked past the tipsy people in the grass carrying red party cups and kept an eye out for my new partner.

A clearly intoxicated guy turned, and I stopped before he splashed me. I shifted a step, and he guzzled down the drink in his hand, dribbling over his chin and down his shirt. He belched and strutted away with arms flailing for balance.

So this was *that* kind of party. I was a little overdressed.

Steeling myself for whatever awaited me inside the stately mansion, I marched up the concrete porch and stepped through the wide-open door. The interior of this place was stunning. The old wood accents, including the parallel beams overhead, were so uncommon these days. Laser lights shifting around sprayed the room with bright colors, altering the natural hue, and a smoke machine obscured the floor. It was a dizzy but fun atmosphere.

People socialized in small groups, shouting into each other's ears over the din, holding more red plastic cups. I searched the faces for Kayla, but so far, no luck. Our colleges in town didn't have on-campus housing, and fraternities weren't a thing here—too small of a city. And since this was clearly not a business event, I had no idea who hosted this random party filled with people in their twenties and thirties. Other than being sober, I fit in just fine.

I weaved my way through the crowd, trying to focus on faces, not gorgeous architecture. I was damn near a regular at Fully Loaded, so I had to see someone I recognized. In the large dining hall, I admired a sparkling chandelier overhead. I wanted to explore every room of this gorgeous house, and it was a shame the antique woodwork was getting sloshed with beer. While checking out the crown molding running along the ceiling, my eye caught on the leggy Kayla sandwiched in the corner.

I flagged her down, and she broke off from a guy to approach me. Kayla was all broad smiles and shiny jewelry, skinny jeans, and a frilly top. She was stunning. Why did she want me to help introduce her to people? She didn't need it.

"I'm glad you're here. Come, I want you to meet someone." Kayla pulled me by the wrist, and I went with her, absorbing her high energy and excitement.

In the corner where Kayla had been, she stopped me in front of a tall man, a little over six feet in height, sipping from a glass—a real one, not a red party cup. He wore a white button-up rolled to his elbows, slacks just a little too short, and black shoes with grass stains. He definitely didn't dress like most of the partiers, and he made me feel underdressed. Something about his short, trimmed hair and pale green eyes was familiar, but I couldn't place him. His dazzling smile relaxed me, and he held out a hand, which I politely shook. "You must be Daisy Barrett. I've heard so much about you."

I exchanged a glance with my new partner. She winked suggestively and strolled away. For not knowing the woman, she sure took strides to hook me up already. The man had authority and confidence oozing off him, and he wasn't hard on the eyes. I noticed he still held my hand, so I asked, "And you are?"

"The host of all your fun tonight. Dance with me." He gently tugged me away from the corner. We stopped underneath the chandelier I'd been admiring, and the music switched to a slow song as if waiting for his lead. His arm wrapped around my waist, and his hand held mine up in a frame. Older music...a classical waltz—filled the air.

Oliver's sweet face filled my mind, and I wished he was here so I could be in his arms. Since we weren't anything official, I could dance with this guy, and I wasn't doing anything wrong. So why did it feel wrong?

"I don't know this dance," I said. "In fact, I'm terrible at this." At least with anything requiring steps.

"You're doing just fine. Follow my lead."

Those butterflies were back. This fancy house and classical music were like walking into a storybook.

"Relax. You're stiffening up." His hand pressed me closer to him, and we circled the room. I concentrated on not stepping on his shoes because with these wedges, one wrong move would mean a sprained ankle, and I had to walk home. Why couldn't sneakers be socially appropriate all the time?

A few others joined us, but most were talking and drinking. Some were confused by the choice of tunes, as was I, and I wished I had a drink. I searched the room for Kayla, but I couldn't find her, and I didn't know anyone else here.

"How do you know Kayla?" The party host's mouth was right by my ear and, rather than a tingle of sensitive nerves at his breath, a shiver ran through me. I chalked it up to the waltz, forcing me completely out of my comfort zone, but talking helped distract me.

"I just met her. She's my new EMS partner. How do you know her?" Wheels turned in my head. He was staying at a bed-and-breakfast for travelers, and she was brand new in town. Were they a couple looking to socialize with their new community? Trying to decide if they should stay here? Now dancing with the guy was even more uncomfortable. My foot landed wrong, and my shoe tilted a little too far sideways.

My dancing partner laughed and held me straight. My ankle didn't hurt, but it was too soon to tell if I was going to have trouble with it later, so I ignored it.

"She's a friend," he said.

I wouldn't have guessed that. So what was this party for then?

"Enough about me," he added. "I hear you're a paramedic."

I pressed my lips thin. Every time someone assumed I had a higher skill level than I did, it stung. Maybe they thought I was capable of more and didn't want to insult me by assuming less. I didn't know. *Thanks, Dad, for making me feel so damn inadequate, and Pierce for reminding me, and Megan for bringing it up.* "EMT."

"Well, I'm sure your father is very proud." The host grinned at me like he'd dug deep for that compliment. Instead, it was a slap in the face.

I kept my tone even and light, wishing I'd found a drink before finding Kayla. "Not exactly. He expected me to become a doctor like him."

"What's his specialty?"

I smiled, thrilled someone normal in the real world cared enough to ask about something so mundane. No chatter about witches hunting vampires or evil elves. No drama. Just real life. This time Jamie would give me a thumbs-up for having safe, non-vampire, non-elf fun.

"He's a medical researcher in a lab in Green Bay, trying to discover new medicines in the war against disease. Dr. Greg Barrett wanted me working by his side, but I wasn't smart enough to hack it, so an EMT I am." I tipped my chin up, proud of myself for what I had accomplished, even if no one else was.

The party host grinned. I was fairly certain he was trying to flirt at this point. "Oh, I don't believe that. You were smart enough to come here. I bet if you tried again, you'd discover you can do it."

What did attending a party have to do with my ability to earn a Doctor of Medicine degree? I furrowed my brow at the illogical leap. The host poked a sore spot, and I couldn't hide my snippiness. "No, I can't."

"I can prove you wrong. What if someone accidentally sliced themselves open right here? Could you save their life?"

Strange turn of questions, but the conversation worked to distract me from my two left feet. "It depends on the patient's condition—are they calm or panicking? That's a major factor. It also depends on how quickly the paramedics arrived, of course. But I would staunch the blood flow the best the patient would allow, and if there was glass or anything caught in the wound, I'd leave it be to prevent excessive loss and minimize the chance of infection. This feels like a quiz."

My dance partner nodded, completely entertained, and gestured with his head at a guy wearing jeans and a Packer's jersey, holding a drink. "If that man over there tripped and ripped his throat open, you'd call for an ambulance and apply pressure. While waiting, you'd give him pointless platitudes to help calm him down, but by the time medics arrived, he would die no matter your feeble attempts at a rescue."

The morbidity brought the chill back, and I didn't appreciate being insulted once again. I tried to pull out of the man's arms, but he resisted, his grip like steel.

"What did you say your name was?" I asked, snippiness firmly in position.

"Soren," another voice said from behind me.

21

The Party Cut Short

Daisy

MY BREATH CAUGHT IN my throat. *Soren*? The vampire who'd bitten me and dragged me by the hair? The vampire who'd ripped out Megan's throat? *That* Soren held me locked in his embrace in an elegant dance in a beautiful house by the rolling river. *No, no, no.* There was no way *that* monster was the same as this semi-creepy Mr. Fancypants. I wanted to get away from him without drawing too much attention. I pulled, but I couldn't free myself from Soren's brutal arms. His grip was literally like steel—cold, hard, inescapable.

But just as I wished it, Soren was torn from my frame, and I stumbled a few steps. I turned to find Oliver with a nasty scowl on his face, nose to nose with Soren. Relief flooded through me for an instant until fear washed it away. They were going to fight. Last time Oliver tussled with him, Oliver ended up in the street, on his back, knees swinging in the air in agony.

Oliver snarled. "Stay away from her."

"Just because you're older doesn't mean you get to boss me around," Soren said with calm menace.

"Yes, I do. Who are all these people? What are you up to?"

While waiting for his reply, Oliver glanced at me with an apologetic look. I didn't know whether to flee or call for help. I looked around to see if any other muscle would be willing to intervene before things got messy. But the others around ignored the increasing tension.

Where was Kayla? More importantly, how did she know *Soren*? Pierce had said there were more vampires than I realized around. Was Kayla one?

The monster said, "I wanted to learn more about Daisy here. She's quite humble and shy. Not what I expected, considering—"

"That's enough," Oliver said, interrupting him. "Daisy, come with me."

He didn't have to ask twice. With a challenging glare at Soren, Oliver brought me to a side room, while the partygoers continued their murmurs and drinking. Soren didn't follow.

Oliver asked, "What are you doing here?"

I frowned. Like I wasn't *cool* enough to be invited to this party? For that matter, if Oliver was invited, why didn't *he* invite me? For an instant, I wondered who in this crowd was his date, and anger flashed through my body. I folded my arms across my chest. "I should ask you the same."

Oliver smiled. "We need to talk, and since it's unbecoming to stand in the middle of a party, dance with me." Oliver held up his arms in a frame, inviting me.

My heart fluttered, but we did need to talk, and dancing brought us closer, making it easier to hear each other over the loud music. I stepped into his frame. I fit into his arms so perfectly, and despite not knowing the steps, I felt safe in his arms and tried to remember the pointers Soren had given me.

"I hope your date won't mind," I asked, fishing for information.

"I suppose she doesn't."

"What does that mean?" I glanced around for any death glares, but no one paid us attention.

"You are my date."

I couldn't help but smile. "Cute. Why would you come to that monster's party?"

Oliver leaned in. "This is my house."

Admiration flooded through me. This place was gorgeous. "I thought it's a bed-and-breakfast."

"It was. I converted it back to a private residence recently."

Oliver looked to be about my age, thirty-ish. To obtain and control an asset like this at our age, long enough ago to *convert* it, either he had an amazing business mind, or he came from old money. Based on some of the artwork on the walls and the dangling chandeliers, my guess was on the money.

I fished for more answers, curiosity getting the better of me. "You mean your parents converted it?"

Oliver's hand at the small of my back pressed me closer to his chest. "They died a long time ago."

Inheritance. At least he was smart about it. "I'm sorry. I know what that's like. My mom died a few months ago. It's hard, and I miss her so much. Every time my phone rings, I still hope to see her name on the screen, even though I know better. And when I walk into my parents' house, I search for her in the kitchen, making cinnamon rolls and getting icing on her work documents. I really needed her after the car accident where I lost my cousin, aunt, and uncle. I was the only survivor, and I'm always asking myself how I managed it and why me. I'm sorry, I didn't mean to ramble about my losses. I just meant...I get it."

Oliver squeezed me tighter, and a flutter of warmth filled my chest. "Our house burned down a while ago, so I don't have that reminder."

My heart broke for him. "Do you have any siblings to rely on?"

Oliver snorted. "I have a brother, but he's a piece of work. I can't trust him at all. In fact, I hate him."

I didn't believe that. "You can't hate your family. Despise what they do, sure, but you can't hate the person. Case in point. After Mom died, my sister disappeared. You met her at Megan's funeral. That was the first time I'd seen Lily in months. But she just vanished again. I hate that she abandoned me. I hate that she won't grieve with me, but I don't actually hate *her*. If she walked through that door, I'd give her the biggest bear hug, shed several tears, and then yell at her until I was hoarse."

Oliver chuckled. "Well, my brother is a special breed. I don't agree with anything he does. He's selfish, reckless, and he tends to hurt people in ways that aren't forgivable."

I believed everyone deserved a second chance, that everyone was redeemable and worth saving, so for Oliver to completely turn his back on his brother was so foreign to me. How could he justify it? "What did he do?"

"I had a girlfriend a long time ago. He found out that I cared about her, and he hurt her, just to hurt me."

I frowned. "That sounds worse than the typical sibling rivalry."

Oliver shook his head in memory. "It was. He's...unstable, more so lately. I don't know where it comes from, but I've tried helping him over the years, but nothing stuck. So now I do my best to avoid him, but sometimes he just pops up when I least expect, and then I'm left cleaning up his mess."

"That sounds awful."

"It's his cycle. I've learned to adapt and avoid."

A scream cut through the party, and the music stopped with a screech. Did Soren return and bite someone else? Oliver gripped me tight, serious eyes seeking the source of the woman's panicked cry.

"What was that?" I asked, pressing against Oliver like he was my personal shield.

"Stay here." Releasing me, he rushed across the room, and the cold air chilled me. I looked around at the gawking bystanders, hoping to see Soren, innocently away from the commotion, because if it wasn't him, there was another vampire attacking people. Or...maybe it was a spilled drink, or a cheating significant other, or anything but what I feared.

A man's voice yelled for emergency services.

Instincts kicked in, and I pushed through the people leaning in tight. I found Oliver kneeling at the partygoer. I joined him.

Kayla.

She held her hand to her throat. Blood seeped between her fingers. Kayla's panicked eyes crushed me. "Kayla, can you tell me what happened?"

Her lips moved to speak, but no words came out. Her eyes were wide with terror.

"Kayla, you're going to be okay. Don't move. Just relax, okay? An ambulance is on the way." To lighten the mood, I smiled. "You know the routine, right?"

She didn't acknowledge my words. I searched for something nearby to press against the wound, but only expensive vases, hand-woven rugs, and red plastic cups rested within range.

Oliver tore a piece off his shirt with surprisingly little effort, and I took it, bunched it up, and pressed it against her throat. "Hang in there. Help is almost here."

Kayla's blood soaked the fabric. For her comfort, I gripped Kayla's hand in my own. This was grim and getting worse by the second.

Partiers gathered closely around us, whispering.

"Back up. Give us air, please. We need space," I said.

They didn't.

Kayla's wild eyes shifted to the faces all around her. Lips moved, but no words came out. I leaned down to her mouth with my ear. 'S' sounds were all I could make out.

"I'll give you two guesses, but you're only going to need one," Oliver whispered.

Soren? It had to be Soren.

"Daisy, I need you to trust me. Can you do that?"

I had a small trust circle, and Oliver had proven to me he belonged in it. "Yeah, why?"

"Distract everyone. I need them to be looking elsewhere."

I hesitated. "My hand is slowing her bleeding. I can't let go."

"I'll take over." Oliver positioned his hand next to mine, and on the count of three, we switched.

I stood and opened my arms wide. "Show's over. Everyone, get out of here. The paramedics need space. Move back and move out, please." Some people left, while others continued to stare. I got in their faces. "Go to the other room or refill your drinks. Just go now!"

After a few ugly glances my way and some mumbled snark, the rest left.

I rushed back to Oliver's side and found his wrist pressed against Kayla's mouth. Her eyes relaxed, less panicked. What was he doing? I collected Kayla's hand in mine again and waited. There was nothing more I could do.

A siren approached the front lawn, and Oliver moved his wrist away from her mouth as footsteps rushed up the porch. There was blood everywhere.

Pierce and his partner stood over us. I stiffened. I should've realized who would respond at this early hour.

"Step aside. Let us take over," Pierce said, setting down the yellow backboard and kneeling by Kayla. My ex-boyfriend shot a nasty look at Oliver, who was coated with blood. It somehow got on my clothes, too.

Pierce whispered to me, "What the hell are you doing here?"

Ignoring his invasion of my privacy and the useless question, I said to Kayla, "The paramedics are here. You're going to be okay."

"I warned you to stay away from vampires," he whispered. Pierce's partner spoke over the radio, not hearing the sensitive conversation.

"The only person I'm avoiding is you, but apparently I haven't done that well either," I whispered back.

"You don't know everything about him," Pierce said, indicating Oliver with his grim features.

Oliver said with a bored tone, "I can hear you."

"And I don't care, vamp." Pierce hissed the word like it stung in his mouth. He stabilized Kayla and secured her to the backboard.

"We had a truce," Oliver said.

"That only entails not killing you. I don't have to play tea party with you, and I don't want you anywhere near Daisy. She's better than that, better than you. Stay away before you get her killed."

Disgust tore through me. The only person who acted out of line around me was Pierce. The assumption dripping from his words was obvious and insulting. "Oliver didn't do this, and you don't get to tell me what to do. Stay out of my life and out of my business."

Pierce glanced at me as if my words were empty. He and his partner collected and loaded Kayla into the back of the ambulance in record time. He shot me one last warning look before climbing into the back of the rig, and the ambo lumbered away.

Oliver and I stood together at the doorway, bloody and sticky.

"She's not going to make it, is she?" I asked him, remembering Soren's twisted prediction.

"She'll be fine."

I turned to him with a raised brow. "You don't need to sugarcoat it for me. This is what I do for a living." It wasn't like I'd never buried a partner before.

"I know, and she'll be fine." Oliver sent me a reassuring smile.

But how could he be so sure?

The partiers poked their heads around the corner from the other rooms.

"What happened to her?" one asked.

"Cut herself on something?" another answered with a lilt of uncertainty.

"Let's wash up and get out of here," Oliver whispered into my ear.

I nodded and followed him into a guest bathroom on the first floor. I washed my hands, and then Oliver scrubbed his. The white porcelain sink turned pink with Kayla's blood.

Looking at him in the mirror, I said, "Your shirt is ruined." Torn and bloody.

Oliver glanced down at himself. "Don't worry about it. There's plenty where that came from." Oliver plucked a fresh, fluffy white towel from the towel bar and wiped the sink and surrounding area spotless, now ruining the towel too. He turned to assess me. "You're a mess too. Let me drive you home."

"I walked here. How about you walk me home?" I wanted more time with him, to get to know Oliver better, to understand his affliction, and to see if I could help. I stretched my ankle from side to side, and it felt fine.

"What about my 306 horsepower?" Oliver lifted his brows, teasing.

The drive home was too short. "Rain check."

Oliver slipped his hand over mine and led me back through the house to the front door. The music quieted down as the party dwindled. People were leaving, but a few beelined for refills. What a strange night.

"Are you sure you want to leave? These people probably need supervision, or they'll break your stuff or steal," I said as we climbed down the front steps.

"Things are replaceable." Oliver brought me to the sidewalk, and we stepped into the darkness.

"Soren, the party host, was the same guy attacking people all over town, right? The vampire ripping out people's throats. The one you fought with."

"The one and only...I hope," Oliver mumbled.

"I didn't even recognize him," I said to myself, surprised at my naivety. "I danced with a murderer, and I had no idea, and it wasn't until he'd told me his name I realized."

"He can make people do what he wants regardless, so don't be hard on yourself. He probably compelled Kayla to stay quiet until he was done feeding."

My face twisted with disgust, and I made sense of all the unusual events. "Kayla, my brand-new partner, introduced me to Soren, and he insisted on dancing with me, which, fine. I can see how a guy would want time with me."

Oliver shot me a look of jealousy, and I had to admit, I liked it.

I added, "But Soren asked me personal questions about my dad and his research, which was weird enough, but he also asked me what I would do if someone hurt themselves. I think he planned to kill her the whole time."

"The question puzzling me is, why risk it in public?" Oliver said. "I mean, he's impulsive, but that's high-risk even for him."

"The whole thing is weird."

Oliver held my hand, and we strolled down the darkened sidewalk extra slowly, as if neither of us wanted the night to end. "Daisy, I don't know why Soren was interested in you tonight. I mean, besides the fact that you're beautiful."

I smiled at him, heat rushing up my cheeks.

"But since he attacked you before, can you do me a favor and stay away from him?"

"Gladly."

"And can you avoid being alone at night?"

"That's two favors," I said with a chuckle.

Oliver darted me a look.

"I'm kidding. Of course, I'll be careful."

"Soren can't be reasoned with. Please take this seriously," Oliver said ominously.

"It sounds like you have a lot of experience dealing with him."

"Unfortunately, I do."

We reached my house, and he walked me all the way to my front door. On my darkened porch, his fingers brushed the hair back from my face. A gentle smile lifted his lips. "I'm sorry you had to see that, and I'm sorry Soren got that close to you. I promise I won't let him hurt you."

"He didn't."

Oliver's eyes met mine, and he stared at my lips. My breathing picked up with anticipation.

"I want to kiss you," he said.

Electricity crackled around us. Memories of his hands on my body sent shivers along my spine. I wanted him. I want to touch and taste every inch of him. I wanted that morning dream to be real. "Then do it."

Oliver waited, watching me closely. Expectation pounded in my chest. I needed to feel his arms holding me close. I needed his hands on me right now. My breath hitched in my chest, the wait driving me wild. *Please*, I begged silently. *Please put your hands on me now.*

22

Pieces of the Puzzle

Oliver

I STARED INTO THE depths of her gorgeous eyes. Our lips were so close. She trembled with need, and my body hummed to be inside her. The A-positive pumping through her veins had me salivating to taste her. My fangs tingled to be satisfied, and they descended without my permission. Just one tiny tilt of my body and we would be together again. I would make her come all over my hands and face until she screamed with hypersensitivity, and I wouldn't leave until just before daybreak. Blood surged through my body, demanding I take her inside, demanding I take *her*. Those dark brown eyes begged me, and I could hear every breath in and out of her lungs.

Off in the darkness, a suspicious noise turned my head. We'd left the party on foot, and I'd expected some patrons would walk home too, but those noises weren't drunk humans. They were the careful predatory footsteps of a vampire on the hunt.

Soren fed exclusively on live humans, and I...avoided it, for dietary reasons. But I'd been heavily feeding from bags to increase my strength to fight off Soren, should the occasion arise. If he attacked me or Daisy now, I wouldn't be able to stop him. I almost didn't stop him last time. She was too important to jeopardize unnecessarily, and until I could best Soren, I needed the element of surprise to protect her.

Which I didn't have now.

"It's not safe," I told her, wishing that wasn't the case. "Go inside and don't invite anyone in."

Before I could change my mind or she could protest, I used my superhuman vampire speed to tear off into the darkness. Following the carefully placed steps and the rapid changes in the position of my prey, I shifted from tree trunk to tree trunk, hunting the threat at Daisy's doorstep. There, behind a tall bush hanging over the alley, I tracked the blur of a vampire's head. I gave chase, and when I reached the perpetrator, I gripped his shoulder and spun him to face me.

"What are you doing out here?" I snarled at Soren's casual face, holding him in place with a fistful of his shirt—my shirt. He'd gone shopping in my closet for the party.

His lips curled into a smug smile. "Just keeping an eye on sweet Daisy Barrett. Someone dangerous might come knocking. Humans aren't a good look on you. Don't you remember?"

I remembered all right. Every day in my dreams, I vividly recalled what this monster had done to Evangeline. If Soren thought he could use Daisy to control me, he was so very wrong. "Are you threatening me?"

Soren chuckled and pointedly glared at my fist, balling up his shirt. "I'm not here to fight."

I released his shirt and smoothed it for him. I didn't want to ruin my own threads.

"That's better."

"Then what do you want?" I asked.

He shrugged. "This or that."

He could be so damned aggravating sometimes. "Enough games, Soren. Your fun caused enough damage. This is my town, and I want you gone."

"You're demanding I leave?" Soren laughed. "Oh, you have no idea what's going on. Here's a tip fresh from the live feed: Stay out of my way. When my business is complete, you won't see me again."

"Is that a promise?"

Soren's face curled into a sinister snarl, one I'd seen dozens of times before, and it never ended well for me or those around me. "That's the best promise you'll get."

With his track record, something was going to happen, and it wasn't going to be good. Soren vanished into the night. I'd declared this town to be my territory, and I was going to stay until this was settled.

Daisy

My body thrummed with need the next morning. I didn't get any satisfaction after the party. Oliver had vanished so quickly I wasn't sure if I had hallucinated him on my porch, and I was left a twisted mess of frustration.

I cozied up on the couch with Jamie, popcorn, and a case of beer. As far as owed favors went, this wasn't so bad. I swigged from my can of hops, watching cars drive in circles on the television while crowds cheered and an excited man shouted stats and speed. My mind was with Oliver on my porch, inches from kissing him and dragging him to my bed. But Oliver had said kissing me wasn't safe, so I stood, gaping mouth, in his wake. He'd disappeared into the darkness. Something had him spooked, and I woke up flustered over my lack of release.

Every encounter I'd had with Oliver filled my thoughts throughout the day, making my promise to Jamie easier to bear, which led me back to Megan's funeral. If Oliver couldn't be out in daylight, how did he get there for the service? He had to have spent the whole day there—from before dawn to after dusk—surrounded by grieving, sobbing people at the worst time of their lives. The thoughtfulness and kindness didn't fit with what everyone else kept telling me about him. Sure, Soren was a murderous monster, but Oliver wasn't by any stretch of the definition.

A shelving unit surrounded the television, and I gazed at a framed photograph of me and Pierce. That photo needed to go.

"You're going to miss the best parts," Jamie said, noticing my disconnect.

I glanced at the screen. "Where the white car passes the green car on the curve?"

With a big bowl of popcorn resting in his lap and a can of beer in his hand, Jamie nudged me with his elbow. "Very funny. We had a deal. I stopped a bloodbath at a funeral in exchange for an Indy 500 buddy. I think I got the short end of the stick on that one."

Pierce's empty smile caught my eye again. I couldn't believe I'd dated an *elf* for several months, and I never knew what he was. My witch roommates had told me elves were worse than vampires, but I couldn't reconcile how Pierce could be worse than Soren. "Tell me more about elves."

Jamie emptied his can and crushed it in his fist. "I don't think you want to know."

"I'm asking. Can they erase memories?" I had a few I'd be willing to part with, like Megan's brutal murder, and Mom's car accident, and my crash, taking Marc, Lisa, and Abby from me.

Jamie cracked a fresh can with a hiss. "Alli and I can sense elves and vampires. All witches can, so the supernatural can't hide from us, but until you knew what was going on, we couldn't ban them from your house. That would only raise questions on your end that you weren't ready for. But I'm glad we're past that now, so I can properly warn you that vampires and elves both can interfere with your free will and eliminate memories. The reasons they do it are very different. Vampires erase your fear so they can feed without a struggle, while elves compel you to make you like them. After what you've gone through lately, I know what you're thinking. You can't trust either of them to take away your pain. Don't even consider it for another second, Daisy. They're both so damn dangerous that witches have to exist in the first place. Trust me when I say stay the hell away from them both."

Did Jamie know about Oliver? I didn't recall introducing them, and I didn't think they were ever in the same room together for Jamie to 'sense' him. Was there another vampire he referenced? "What do you mean by *both*?"

Jamie slurped from his beer can. "You're not convinced yet. Use your imagination and picture the worst things a person could do with no remorse. That's a vampire's lethal combination."

My curiosity wouldn't let me drop the elf thing, and since Jamie kept focusing on vampires, my fascination only grew. "And an elf's?"

"They don't focus on killing, if that's what you mean." Jamie tossed back another bite of popcorn, training his eyes on the race.

"Then how are elves worse?"

"You don't want to know. Trust me."

Jamie's vagueness was frustrating, but the more he resisted, the more I needed to know. If I pushed too hard, he'd shut down entirely, so I needed to let him take the lead. "Is there anything else I should know?"

Jamie nodded and swallowed. "You should know how to kill one. No offense, but if I haven't made it clear enough by now that they can and will do whatever they want with you, I need you to protect yourself. First, vampires are allergic to the sun, obviously, and vervain, a purple flowering plant. Small doses can knock them on their asses, but a strong enough dose can cause a coma for a short while. From that point, decapitation or a wooden stake to the heart will kill it. Walking around with a sharpened stick tends to raise brows, though."

"They really are strong." Inhumanly strong.

"Then wait until you hear about elves." Jamie swigged more beer. "Wood and vervain don't bother them anymore than they bother us, but elves have weaknesses too. It's all about balance. They have an allergy to black nightshade and iron. Iron alloys like stainless steel are still effective. A knife to the heart drops them dead, which is convenient because a long folding knife can do the job, easy to conceal and carry. But if they sense you're going to attack, they can fly away, and when they take flight, their whole bodies are cloaked from human sight. They might not move as fast as vampires, but elves are still hard to kill."

"Nothing else kills them but a stab to the heart or decapitation?" Impossibly, inhumanly strong and formidable.

"Nothing in the known world can kill a vampire besides a stake. Well, you could always pick one up and throw it into the sun, if that's an option; it works." Jamie chuckled. "Seriously though, fair warning—don't even attempt a decapitation. It's far more difficult to pull off than you'd think, and they are inhumanly fast and quick to anger. So, find yourself a suitable stake and knife that fit in your purse. Use as you see fit, but remember the element of surprise." Jamie winked.

I had no intention of attempting to kill a vampire or an elf, not even Soren if given the chance. I wasn't a murderer. How would that make me any different from them? A small part of me envied their invincibility and flight. "Not even a car accident that severs an artery?"

Jamie chuckled. "Don't get all medical on me, but no. Vampires are susceptible to injury, but they heal impossibly fast."

Oliver had fought Soren outside of my home, leaving Oliver in a daze on the street in clear pain, but he'd sprung back within moments and chased Soren off. He'd healed his injuries that fast—within seconds.

"And that's why you need the element of surprise and a direct hit. Otherwise they'll heal, and they'll be pissed."

I couldn't help but wonder what their blood could do for human healing. Perhaps Dad needed a new subject matter, like supernatural blood, to create a vaccine, boosting human's healing and preventing accidental deaths—like car accidents. Could their blood heal disease? Cancer? Arthritis? Alzheimer's? I pictured vampires voluntarily going to blood banks and donating pints for medical research. This information could change the world. Dozens and dozens of car laps continued while I restlessly pondered the possibilities.

But all Jamie seemed to want me to know was how to kill. With this world-changing information, what was I supposed to do now? Why hadn't Jamie done anything with it? Anger burned in my veins. "That's it?"

"What's it?" Jamie tossed a pinch of popcorn into his mouth.

My life was flipped ass-over-teakettle, but Jamie was so nonchalant about it. Like I was expected to absorb and catalogue all this for a *Jeopardy!* episode, but otherwise accept it as fact and continue on as if everything was normal. "All you and Alli have done was place a spell on my house, blocking Oliver and Pierce from coming inside, and that's it?"

Jamie frowned. "Where are you going with this?"

"The extraordinary healing power of vampire blood could heal people. Medical research on their abilities could've prevented so much human illness or accidental deaths, but yet, you want me to kill one if they give me trouble or pretend they don't exist. Why haven't you don't anything in all these years?"

"Daisy—" Jamie started.

"Don't *Daisy* me. Answer me."

"Witches, elves, and vampires maintain a truce. No one does anything in view of the public precisely to prevent things like the Salem witch trials from reoccurring. But, from time to time, someone breaks the rules, which is why, with tensions so high between you and the vamp and the elf, I went to the funeral. We have to keep our hidden world hidden."

This was unbelievable. "Because you, the vampires, and elves decided humans didn't have the right to know about you, we have to suffer and die from preventable and treatable afflictions?"

"You're making humans the victims here."

"You're the one telling me to kill supernatural beings to protect humans."

Jamie set aside his popcorn and shifted to face me. "A human needs protection, yes. They're inherently as formidable as Jell-O. But you've heard of the Peshtigo fire of 1871?"

A great blaze had eliminated the entire town of Sugar Bush and destroyed Peshtigo, killing twelve hundred or more innocent souls. "Who hasn't?"

"That was one of many such events where people discovered the supernatural."

Aware of Peshtigo's annual historical festival to commemorate the event, I distinctly remembered no one mentioning elves or vampires. I asked, "Then what really happened?"

Jamie watched the cars go around and sipped again, taking this entire conversation as casually as a chat about changes to garbage day. "Not that I'm advocating you do this, but if you want a firsthand account, Oliver would be the one to ask. He was there."

The words pinballed in my head as I struggled to comprehend. I pinched the bridge of my nose. "Wait. Stop right there." Did he just say...? I exhaled a deep breath. How was any of this possible? "Oliver Rockwell *himself* was at the fire in 1871? How is that possible?"

"Weren't you listening? Nothing kills vampires and elves but a stake to the heart or decapitation," Jamie said, eyes meeting mine.

I blinked. Yes, I remembered those words.

Sensing the disconnect, Jamie added with a frustrated sigh, "They're immortal. Not even old age kills them. The story passed down goes: using vervain, our witch ancestors rounded up some vampires who'd been snacking in the area and burned them. Unfortunately, some escaped, and three witches were caught in the crossfire. In the history books, the entirety of the story revolved around a drought, bad burning practices, and a bunch of innocent humans, but I suspect there was some truth in there."

I'd pictured witches as sweet little old ladies cooking dinner for their hungry families and playing with herbs and candles like Allison had, not running around with stakes and snarls. That was horrible. "Your witch ancestors *hunted* vampires?"

Jamie snorted. "Vampires feed on people. Witches protect people, remember? The fire wasn't supposed to get out of hand and kill so many innocent people, though. It's a blemish on our history."

The more he told me, the more I didn't understand who was essentially good or bad. "Doesn't the irony bother you?"

"I'm sorry?" Jamie asked, swallowing half the next beer.

"Your kind survived persecution in the sixteen hundreds, but you perpetrated it yourselves in the eighteen hundreds. Didn't you have any empathy? And by you, I mean them...unless witches are immortal too." I side-eyed Jamie hard.

Jamie's friendliness shut down, and his tone was curt. "For the record, since this is starting to feel like an interrogation, I'm twenty-four years old. I'm one of you, born like all humans. On the other hand, vampires on a whim force their victims to turn into abominations like them, and in the process, kill their victims violently. Now you see why my sister and I, and other witches, accept our jobs without complaint. Due to the unpredictable nature of the work, sometimes there's collateral damage."

Twelve hundred innocent lives lost in a great blaze, all in the name of hunting and murdering vampires. So much for protecting humans. "Collateral damage? But that's the opposite of what you stand for."

Jamie squished the next empty beer can with extra force than necessary. "Everything has a cost. Sometimes winning a battle is more important than focusing on the war, which is why we placed a spell on your house to keep you, your friends and family, and all of us safe. The humans in your life are worth saving, and they deserve to be protected, but the effort is a waste if you choose to associate with vampires and elves from this point forward. Don't be stupid."

I turned away from Jamie. Once I'd learned witches existed and they wanted to help me, I trusted Allison and Jamie, but now, I wasn't sure. My roommates apparently hated Oliver and Pierce, but neither did anything to me to warrant being *murdered*. Sure, Pierce was a jerk, and he threw Oliver under the bus to win favor with me—but it didn't work. Pierce also messed with my memories, forcing me to forget Oliver, which I could dismiss as supernatural-style jealousy. Jamie had outright said Pierce and Oliver were evil and not to be trusted, but of all the confusing pieces of the puzzle, only Oliver never said a nasty word about anyone. And having never messed with my memories or free will, he treated me with kindness and respect, which I couldn't say for the others. What did that mean?

Did Oliver manipulate my mind to accept him as he was? Did he erase the memories in my head that would make me cower in fear of him? Did he make me believe he hadn't?

I needed a drink. Oh, there was a warm beer in my hand. Good enough. I swallowed down the rest of the yeasty hops and got up as the race ended.

Jamie wasn't excited about the race results, and I couldn't care less if I spoiled his fun. He spoiled mine. I tossed the empty into the recycle bin and collected my purse.

Unable to sit still, I needed answers to the growing list of questions now.

23

The Deepest Gift

Daisy

After Jamie's pile of information, I was determined to find out the truth from the source. It was daylight, so Oliver had to be home. I headed out my front door, but this time, I took my car to make the trip quicker. Since Oliver's massive house was only a few blocks away, I arrived in minutes and pulled into the driveway. Cautiously, I steered along the narrow asphalt path, passed under the porte-cochere, and parked just into the grass. A three-car garage was attached to the back of the bed-and-breakfast, and I parked out of the way, curious about Oliver's 306 horsepower. Was he literal or figurative?

That was one mystery I intended to solve.

I climbed the steps to the front door, admiring the antique columns with their detailed scrollwork in the daytime, and knocked. There was no sign that a party had ever happened here. Oliver had said the bed-and-breakfast was his private home now, but no one answered. I continued to knock, not knowing what else to do, and in a flash of desperation, I tried to open the door, but it was locked. I turned to leave, completely disappointed and wound so tight I was going to snap.

I trudged down the expansive stairs and sighed. The rumble of the river caught my attention—a broad and deadly flow with a dam upstream, and countless islands dotting along the river. Commercial shipping was farther downstream. Beautiful, deep, dark, and deadly. I shivered.

A rattle behind me made me turn. The front door opened, and an older woman in her sixties popped her head out. For a second, I thought I had the wrong place. Sunlight glinted on her fashionable, sleek silver strands. "Can I help you?"

If Oliver owned the place and his parents were dead, who was this woman? Had I hallucinated the whole night? Vampires and elves could erase memories. Could they invent them too? I approached and said, "I'm sorry to bother you. I know this is a long shot, but I'm looking for Oliver Rockwell. Is he here?"

"May I ask who is calling upon him?"

I think that meant yes. "Daisy Barrett."

"Wait one moment." The door closed, and excitement gripped me. I was so close to getting answers.

The door swung wide again, and this time the woman said, "Oliver is waiting."

She backed up, giving me a wide entrance, and watched me as I stepped inside. The beauty of the place was as I remembered it from the other night. Certainly, I couldn't have imagined these details. Carved wood, antique brass fixtures, and shiny hardwood floors. Since I didn't know who this woman was, I played dumb, so Oliver wouldn't get in trouble. "It's beautiful, like stepping into a different century."

"I'm Nicole Rockwell, owner of this fine establishment. Since we are no longer a bed-and-breakfast open to the public, I've been missing those compliments. So, thank you for brightening my day. Right this way."

But if she was the owner, had Oliver lied? I asked, "Are you his mother?"

Ms. Rockwell chuckled. "You'll have to ask him."

I took that as a no, but still, her reaction had me curious. She led me up a curved staircase with hand-carved finials, and I slid my fingers along them. At the top of the stairs, the hallways in both directions were filled with art. Paintings, drawings, sculptures, busts of historical figures that I couldn't name off the top of my head. My eyes widened. Even if Dad would've allowed me to spend allowance or time on artistic endeavors, I never had the skill for it, but I sure did appreciate it.

I recognized a few famous pieces, and my knee-jerk reaction was that they had to be reproductions. But deep down, I had an inkling they were originals. And Oliver walked me home, risking a house full of partygoers having sticky fingers with this value hanging in clear view. Okay, reproductions they were.

I paused at each piece, and Ms. Rockwell was patient with me, waiting with a gentle smile on her lined face.

Piece after piece was stunning, and it took me no time at all to recognize the theme. Each one featured smiling people in various locations, like city parks or parking lots, all drawn with a soft hand in charcoal. They reminded me of the one I inherited in Aunt Lisa's box of belongings, the one I hung up right away.

"Take your time, dear. I'm sure he won't mind."

Oliver was waiting. It was rude to stare at all his things while he waited. Why didn't he meet me at the door? "Sorry. I just couldn't help myself."

"Right this way." Her words were soft, almost a whisper, and Ms. Rockwell gestured at the correct door. It was cracked open, and I looked at her for permission.

She nodded encouragement, and I gently pushed the door, nerves suddenly getting the best of me.

I froze in the doorway while Ms. Rockwell's uneven footsteps gradually faded. Art filled this room too, some framed, some newly completed and lying around—the same charcoal and soft hand. A wall-length bookcase filled the far end of the room, stacked floor to ceiling with books. A fluffy rug anchored a huge bed piled high with pillows. Across from the bed was a set of patio doors opening onto a balcony. A cozy fireplace with upholstered chairs and carved wood was centered on the other end of the room. Classy, antique, jaw-droppingly beautiful.

Just like the man busy in the middle of the room.

Oliver hunched over an easel, forearms shifting with careful strokes.

"Is it bad luck to interrupt an artist at work?" I asked playfully.

The pencil clattered, and Oliver spun on his stool. He stared. This was the first time I had seen him wearing a T-shirt and sweatpants. So unlike him. Confusion tilted his head. "Daisy?"

That wasn't the reaction I'd been expecting. "I'm sorry, I shouldn't have..." I turned away, face hot with embarrassment.

Oliver met me at the doorway so inhumanly fast, eyes glittering with a look I couldn't quite place.

"I told you it was dangerous," he said, reaching a hand toward my face. I waited for his contact, but his hand stopped just short of my cheek.

"I've never been one to listen."

Oliver ushered me inside and closed the door behind us for privacy, but Ms. Rockwell had already left.

I glanced at the piece he'd been working on, and my breath caught as realization dawned on me. The artist of all these charcoal drawings was Oliver himself. "This is your work?" I turned in place, admiring the portraits around the room. There was a clear feature in all of them: cheerful people. His massive house was almost entirely empty. Was this his way of filling it with happiness?

"I have excess time on my hands."

Immortal, Jamie had said. So many questions warred in my head, but I didn't want to scare him off. I wandered through the patio doors to admire the view of the river, and Oliver followed me. I'd decided on a simple question that wouldn't make him shut me out. At the party, he'd told me his parents had long since passed away. "Your mom's house is stunning, like a museum."

Oliver didn't respond, so I turned around. He stood behind the sharp line of shadow cast by the enormous columns.

"She's not my mom." Sadness returned to his features.

"You also said this was your house, but Ms. Rockwell said otherwise."

Oliver raked a hand through his disheveled hair. "Daisy, what are you really doing here?"

"Isn't it obvious?"

Oliver sighed. His tone was of clear defeat. "Soren murdered Megan. He attacked you. He also tore out Kayla's throat. So I escorted you home from Soren's party for your own stubborn safety. After all that and Pierce assassinating my character, I thought you'd never want to see me again. Yet here you are."

His disheveled vulnerability, so opposed to his usual well-groomed, confident swagger, was so sexy. Those loose sweatpants hung very low, and his T-shirt showed off arms that I wanted around me. I stumbled over my words. "I want...uh, I want..."

In a blur, Oliver closed the distance between us, his chest nearly touching mine. I could feel the heat radiating from him. "You were saying?"

My train of thought completely derailed with him looking like that while this close. Memories of that dream with lime wedges in my bed returned, flustering me further. Oliver's intense gaze made my heart thunder in my ears.

He could hear that. Just as I could hear an odd sizzle, like bacon on a hot frying pan. He'd crossed out of the shadow.

Vampire. I cleared my throat and reminded myself of why I was really here. "Uh, answers."

The sizzle made me uneasy. I returned to his bedroom, expecting he'd follow me back to safety, and while calming myself, I had a choice of a king-size bed or upholstered armchair for seating. The bed was closer, and that was the only reason I chose this spot to get comfortable. I expected disheveled, mismatched sheets to go with his look, but a modern geometric quilt with layers of coordinating pillows led me to believe he hadn't used it.

Oliver sat next to me and followed my gaze.

"That's a lot of pillows," I said.

"Nicole always had a flair for style. She claimed the guests wanted a modern feel in an antique atmosphere, but I didn't see how that mattered in here. But she said she wanted my bedroom to be cheery for when I returned someday. I envy her optimism."

My skin hummed with him so close. I didn't want to talk about interior design. "You were right, you know, about all the dangers you listed. Everyone around me warned me to stay away from you—"

"And you didn't listen," Oliver said lightly.

I had the urge to defend him. "But Pierce took away my free will and erased you from my memory. My roommates are witches who are perfectly fine with human lives lost in the name of hunting vampires. Soren *is* a monster—no one's debating that. But of all these people, you're the only one who never got into my head, who never badmouthed anyone else, who never attacked anyone or killed for fun. I trust *you*."

Oliver glanced at the floor.

A sinking feeling curled in my stomach. "What is it? What are you keeping from me?"

"You believe I'm not a danger, and you're absolutely right. I would never hurt you, Daisy. I promise."

I believed him. "Then why does everyone else warn me away from you?"

"As Pierce said, I'm a vampire, a natural enemy of witches and elves. It's their duty to protect humans from us. I can't blame them for their shortsightedness. They were raised with the beliefs they have, and I can't change them, so they aren't worth the effort to try. There's only one opinion I care about, and that's yours."

My heart skipped a few too many beats while I met Oliver's bright, pale eyes. Sunlight beaming through the windows reflected in the dark strands of his shiny hair. It was beautiful. His five o'clock shadow on a strong jaw made him irresistible, but it was his heart that captured mine. Monster or not, he was the kindest soul I'd ever met.

Wait. I touched a strand. "The sunlight burns your skin but not your hair?"

"Special glass coating." He positioned his hands into the sunlight. "The only time I can feel the warmth of the sun."

That sounded miserable—living in the darkness or being trapped indoors forever. "There's no other way for you to be outside during the day?"

Oliver steadied his gaze on me. "There is."

"What is it?"

He pointed at my hand. "My ring."

I cradled my hand to my chest. "Why do you keep calling it yours?"

"My mother and her friends were witches. They'd create spells for fair weather, bountiful crops, and healthy families. To channel the magic, they placed it inside rings. One for each family member. Since witchcraft was forbidden, they performed their rituals in the woods and hid their supplies and materials before returning home. One October night, unusual winds kicked up during a drought, and a devastating fire wiped out a full town and barreled down on Peshtigo like an angry hurricane sent to punish us for our heathen ways. My mother collected my siblings and me from the fields, and we rushed into the woods to escape the wall of flame. Father stayed behind. He tilled the earth around our cabin to destroy its fuel and tossed wet blankets onto the exterior walls."

I recognized some details. "The Peshtigo fire of 1871."

"That's the one."

Now I could reconcile Jamie's story with Oliver's. "You really are that old," I said in total awe. "I didn't truly believe him. Wow..." The possibilities were breathtaking, and I found my excitement returning. "You're older than my great-grandparents. The things you must've seen over the years—wars, famine, financial crashes, prosperity, changing technology. I want to hear all your stories."

Oliver smiled at my amusement. "Well, I was born in 1841, if we're being exact, and I hate technology, if I'm being honest."

I chuckled. A walking, talking museum of firsthand accounts in history. I marveled at him. "You look damn fine for your age. Don't let anyone tell you differently."

Oliver laughed and looked at the floor. "You're beautiful yourself, Daisy."

His pale eyes met mine, and I wanted to kiss him, but I also wanted the rest of the story. "Did it work?"

"Did what work?" He continued staring.

I was lost in his eyes. "The wet blankets."

Oliver broke contact and sighed as the memory returned to him. "Sheets of fire hundreds of feet high hurtled at us. Smoke quickly overwhelmed the escaping townsfolk. Friends and neighbors were coughing and dropping all around us, lungs burning with the heat. Babies cried in the night. Trees exploded. While running away, our skin bubbled with blisters. Flames chased us, hopping from treetop to treetop, carried swiftly by the winds like a fire demon. My family and I managed to find a cave in the woods, but in the darkness, we discovered a young man was already inside. My mother pleaded with him to allow us to share, and he agreed, saying he was delighted to find other survivors. But that's when things went sideways."

I hung on every word, enthralled by the tale.

"The young man bit my throat. I later figured he saw me, the eldest, as the biggest threat in our family, and that's why he chose me first. As you know, I couldn't fight him or shout, and in the darkness, my family had no idea. They were also distracted by the blaze. Then I'd heard the cracking of a neck, and that meant lights out for me. The whole thing was a short blur I couldn't process at the time."

Hearing about Oliver's murder was surreal. He really was dead. My mouth dropped open, dumbstruck. "How could someone be so cruel?"

"He was a vampire, and he was hungry," Oliver said simply. "However, he turned me rather than leave me to perish. As I stirred, my family worried about my sudden change in health, and they wouldn't leave my side. If there hadn't been a raging inferno, I could've left instead."

I read between the lines. "You turned your own family?"

Pain radiated from behind those beautiful eyes. "Now you know my greatest shame. I wish I would've gotten a look at that young man's face. If there was any vampire I could stake, it would be him, without hesitation."

"I'm so sorry he did that to you."

"No need to apologize on his behalf, Daisy. Once I learned baby vampires couldn't control the bloodlust, I only hated that vampire even more for his recklessness. The fire raged until dawn, keeping us prisoners of the cave, our skin now incapable of feeling the sun. Thankfully, in no time at all, my mother recalled her last spell. She'd infused the magic of good fortune for the coming winter's darkness into a set of rings. She didn't understand the warnings at the time, but after discovering what we'd changed into, it made sense to her. She'd said the ruby rings offer protection from the sun for those who walk in the dark."

I looked at my hand. "My ring allows vampires to be in daylight."

"Upon nightfall," he continued, "my mother ran for her sacred space, needing those rings for us, but she never returned."

"Oliver, I'm so sorry." I touched his shoulder.

"Just when we'd given up waiting, a woman appeared looking for missing loved ones, and my siblings and I shared her. I don't regret what we had to do, but I wish we weren't so hungry when she happened upon us."

My face twisted, picturing several starving vampires attacking a helpless woman, just as Soren had.

"After I was sated, I set off to find our mother and the hidden cache of sun rings. When I found the correct area deep in the woods, the rings were gone. I've searched all this time, and until I found you in the park with that ruby on your finger, I thought all hope was lost."

"Why not ask a witch to make you a new one?" Not that I believed he hadn't exhausted all possibilities.

"I later learned once I turned my mother, she'd lost her power and her allies. Witches never consent to helping their enemies, and vampire compulsion doesn't work on them."

I gazed in awe at the treasure trove of history on my finger. How had Aunt Lisa come into possession of such a valuable piece? I pulled the gem off my finger and held it out to Oliver. "Here. It's yours."

"I can't take that from you," Oliver said, pushing it away and shaking his head. "You don't know if I manipulated you. I could be a total monster, ready to destroy every human in my path, and you just offered me the perfect weapon—my freedom."

I frowned. This vampire, by definition or not, was no monster. "If you wanted to take it, you had plenty of opportunity to compel it off me and make me forget it. I do love the ring, but it's yours. For all I know, my ancestors raided your mother's sacred space and stole it. It doesn't belong to me." I held it out to him, the stone glinting in the sunlight through the protected window.

Tears glistened on Oliver's eyelids. He closed his eyes, and his body sagged with relief. "You have no idea how much this means to me."

"I think I do," I said with a gentle smile. I took his hand and pushed the ring onto his right ring finger. "And it fits you perfectly."

Oliver's hands found my neck, and he pulled me in close. He studied my lips, and his breathing hitched with emotion. "Thank you so much."

I closed the narrow distance between us and pressed my lips against his. Salty tears slipped onto my tongue. All the warmth and memories of the time we shared my bed rushed through me in an instant surge of need. Keeping my lips moving, I straddled his hips, and a growing tingle pulsed along my body.

Oliver groaned, his kisses deepening. A pressure grew beneath me as his desire surged. Dark hair fell over his forehead, and I brushed it back, raking my fingers along the dark silky strands. I lifted onto my knees and pushed him back onto the bouncy mattress. Pillows tumbled all around us, swallowing us whole. I swatted one aside and then another.

Oliver chuckled under my lips.

I broke contact. "Why are there so many?"

Oliver swatted a few aside and laughed. "You'll have to ask my niece."

"Oh!" I said excitedly, sitting up. I pictured Oliver painting a young girl's nails, braiding her hair, and playing football with her, and my heart melted. "Is she around? I'd like to meet her."

"You already did." His lips pressed against my throat, immune to the distraction, and I moaned.

Regaining my senses, I asked, "Who was she?"

Oliver released my throat. "Nicole. My great-great-great-grandniece, technically. I think that was the right number of greats. On paper, she owns the building to keep unwanted vampires out, but it's mine."

I froze. The dignified gray-haired businesswoman limping through the halls with kindness wrinkling her eyes. It was so jarring to think this handsome young man was so much older than her, older than me.

"I hope you don't have a problem with mature men," Oliver said with a quirk of his lips, as if he'd read my thoughts.

"Not right now, I don't." An idea struck me. "Come with me." I climbed out of the pillow quicksand and stood up.

"Where are we going?" Oliver sat up but otherwise didn't leave the bed.

"It's a surprise. Let's go."

"Not all of us can shift gears in an instant," Oliver protested. "I need a minute to drop the stack." The visual of him comparing the engorged swell in his pants to a convertible car's raised top made me chuckle.

I strolled over to the patio doors. Warm arms wrapped around me, hugging me from behind. "What is it you wanted to show me?"

Something firm pressed against my backside. "I think the stack's still lifted."

"If we aren't leaving the room, it's not a problem."

"You don't want your niece to see that."

Oliver released me and scratched his head. "That's a quick way to fix it."

I laughed and gripped his hand. I led him down the hall and stopped at the front door. "What happens if it doesn't work?"

"Like an electrical burn from the outside in, I catch on fire. The time to reduce a vampire from a steaming corpse to ash depends on the intensity of the sun. Dawn versus noon versus dusk all matter."

"Like how the moon is just reflected sunlight, but yet the moon doesn't bother you?"

"Correct. The smell isn't great either. Hard to wash out of your hair."

My face fell in horror at how flippantly he'd described that detail. "That's awful."

"It's an unfortunate way to go."

I pointed to the ring. "How much do you trust it?"

"Enough to allow you to take me outside."

I opened the door and walked onto the porch. Oliver's hand slipped free of mine. He hesitated before reaching his fingers into the sunlight slowly, as if testing the ring's power first. A smart move.

There was no sizzle. "It's working?"

He flipped his hand over and back. "Yeah," he said breathlessly.

I offered my hand to him, and he took it. I pulled him outside. While deep, strained breaths clogged his throat, the sunlight lit his beautiful face. He squinted and shielded his eyes. "I don't remember it being this bright."

"Don't look directly at the sun. That hasn't changed."

"Duly noted." With his eyes closed, he tipped his face up to the sky. "For the first time in over a hundred and fifty years, I can feel the sun directly on my skin. I forgot how warm and comforting it is." His face tilted back to me. "I will *never* be able to thank you enough. The gift you've given me pales compared to sunshine itself."

My chest bloomed with his affectionate compliment, and I laced my fingers through his. A smile lifted my lips. "Just don't lose it, okay?"

"Never."

His lips recaptured mine, but I pulled away. "Take me to your bed."

Oliver groaned in anticipation. "Your wish is my command."

24

A Devastating Truth

Daisy

STANDING AT THE FOOT of the heavily decorated bed, I palmed his abdomen and slid the cotton T-shirt up over his firm chest. Oliver lifted his arms, but I couldn't reach to pull it clear of his head. After I exposed his mouth, I left the remaining fabric to block his view. Oliver tried to tug it off, but I stopped him. "I saw this in a movie once, and I always wanted to try it. Granted, it's not raining, and you're not upside down."

Oliver smiled, a willing participant.

I kissed his lower lip and then the corners, his short beard prickling my skin. I moved to the softer skin of his throat.

He groaned and gruffly said, "I like this game."

I grinned. Blindfolded with his own shirt, his nipples hardened while I teased him, enjoying the control but wanting to switch sides. I wanted the vampire to dominate me with his endless strength...and stamina. I said playfully to the blinded vampire, "You like 'pin the tail on the donkey'?"

"I can pin anything while blindfolded," he said, but tore his shirt free anyway. Oliver smiled hungrily. "But I want to see you."

"Is that so?" I said in my best teasing voice, taking in the soft dark hair dusting his smooth skin and trailing below the waistband like a roadmap.

Thick muscles in his sexy arms flickered as he placed his hands on my hips. With quick vampire speed, he slipped my shirt free and unfastened my bra. It dangled loosely on my shoulders. In the blink of an eye, I was half-naked. "That's cheating."

"It's not cheating if it's all natural."

I dropped my bra on the floor, and Oliver gazed at my exposed breasts. I wasn't shy, and he'd seen them before, but that time had been dark. "Now that's a beautiful sight worth spending hours staring at, and yet kids these days can be entertained by television. I don't understand it."

"No kidding. Jamie watches cars drive in circles for hours. I'd rather look at boobs myself."

Oliver pinched the bridge of his nose, as if I'd said the wrong thing. "We need to set some rules right now. First, no talking about other men while I'm getting you naked."

"Okay, check." I swallowed a laugh.

"Two, save all boob talk until the main event."

"What, you don't want to discuss the uneven sway when I move? It's like they have their own personalities. This one prefers to move first, while this one jigg—" An index finger pressed against my lips.

"You are incredible. Kiss me."

"I can't," I said through the pressure of his finger.

Holding back a laugh, Oliver released me and took my lips with his. Using slow human speed, he unbuttoned my jeans and tugged them down. I easily gripped the stretchy band of his sweatpants and slid them down, careful not to snag his jutting length.

His kisses trailed down my neck and to my collarbone, while his hard penis pressed against my hip. I panted, needing more and needing it now. I positioned us at the edge of his bed, and I pulled him down on top of me.

Oliver straddled my hips, holding himself above me on his elbows. His fingers brushed a lock of hair out of my face several times while fighting the quicksand of home décor. His pale eyes searched my face, inspecting me as if I were the only thing in the world that mattered. "Careful, Nicole means to drown us in pillows. I may not come up for a while, so yank my hair if you can't breathe."

"What if I want to yank it anyway?" My fingertips raked through the floppy locks.

"I expect you will." He winked and resumed kissing my body.

"No shortage of confidence in your skills, huh?" His lips found a nipple, and I sucked in air before groaning.

"I've had centuries of practice," he said between kisses, "to learn that every woman...has her own...pleasure buttons. If I press too hard, feel free to scream."

A throaty laugh came from my chest, hiding a flash of insecurity. I was not nearly as experienced. How could I compete with a vampire alive in the nineteenth century? "You are just too much."

Pausing from his kisses, he said on a serious note, "Vampires are much stronger than humans. If I do *anything* that makes you uncomfortable or hurts you in any way, let me know immediately. I never want to hurt you."

I grasped his beautiful face between my palms and said, "That's the sexiest thing anyone's ever said to me."

Oliver turned his face and kissed my palms. "And that's a shame that speaks for men everywhere...unless...you said you like boobs. Are we lumping other women into that pool?"

"I prefer to drive a stick."

Oliver grinned. "I happened to have a manual transmission all fired up and roaring to go for a drive."

"Let's not keep the engine idling."

Oliver winked and trailed kisses down to the cleft between my legs. He had been right. I wanted to grip his hair and grind against him, but I resisted. As his tongue lapped at my swollen, sensitive clit, I found myself holding his head and carefully rocking against him with restraint but an urging to keep going. Pooling heat flooded my body, and right at the edge, at that cliff, my muscles tightened. I gripped his hair and held my breath. So close. Just moments more and I wouldn't be able to stop myself from losing control.

"Come for me," Oliver said.

I wanted to. More than anything. I wanted to tip over the cliff for him. To him. Oliver's tongue moved faster, ordering me to let go. To give in to him.

I did.

My body locked up, and my breath hitched as the waves of pleasure crashed into me. Oliver slowed to a stop, carefully avoiding the hypersensitive spot. And as the waves eased, Oliver popped his head up from between my legs. "How many do you want? Two? Three?"

"Two is fine with me." I crooked my finger at him to urge him closer so I could kiss him. He wiped his mouth on my inner thigh and climbed over me with a hungry grin. I fastened my legs over his hips and pushed him over, rolling us both together. I straddled him and trailed kisses from his ears down his throat.

"Neat trick," Oliver said.

"Does anyone ever say you talk too much?" I asked playfully, pausing at his collarbone.

"My brother does."

Curious once more about the tragedy that befell his family, I sat upright. "At the party, you'd said you have a reckless brother you don't like. I think you even said hate. Tell me about him."

Oliver's eyes cast aside. "I try to avoid mentioning him."

"Yet he keeps coming up."

Still avoiding my gaze, he said, "I just didn't want to see that look on your face when you found out and assumed he and I were peas from the same pod."

I had a feeling I already knew him. "Who is he?"

"Soren is my brother." After a long beat, Oliver met my eyes.

I couldn't believe what I'd just heard. I climbed off him. "That *monster* is your brother? The vampire who killed my best friend, attacked my partner, and slaughtered innocent people all over town? He attacked me!"

Mood ruined, Oliver rolled out of bed and gathered his pants. I crawled off the fluffy bed—not without effort. I took to cue to dress. Fun time was over.

"What's wrong?" I asked, confused about why the truth made him clam up.

Oliver pulled his shirt over his head and paused, back facing me. "He *is* a monster. A selfish, reckless, untrustworthy monster. And I hate him."

I no longer overestimated his animosity. "I understand, but I don't see what the problem is."

Oliver turned to face me. Sadness drew his features. There had to be more. Being related to a monster wasn't enough to explain his sudden withdrawal. "What are you not telling me?"

"He and I are the same, Daisy."

I had a feeling he meant more than vampires. I stepped back and frowned. His words felt like a warning, a punch to the gut, a stab to the heart. Why did Oliver think so little of himself? "What do you mean?"

"Daisy," he said with a breathless sigh. "What we have is great, but it's never going to work."

That was not what I wanted to hear. Did I say something wrong? I needed to fix this. "You haven't hurt me or those I care about. That was him, not you. I saw the real you. Ten minutes ago, that was the real you—generous and sweet. But if something in the past is standing between you and me discovering what this could be between us, then I want you to know I believe in second chances."

"I turned my brother into the monster he is. Everything he's done is, by extension, my fault."

"You didn't have a choice," I interrupted. "That wasn't the real you."

"Your judgment is clouded. You want to know the difference between me and Soren? The Soren whose actions you describe with such eloquent gruesomeness?" Oliver asked with a hardened look in his eye. "I don't leave bodies lying around. That's it."

Trying to reconcile Oliver's actions with Soren's only caused me more confusion. Did Oliver torture, harass, and murder, too? Did he care enough about being caught to hide the bodies of his victims? If Soren had been responsible for all the animal attacks, I couldn't think of any evidence that Oliver was just like him. "Are you saying you kill people?"

"Not lately," he said, arms crossing over his chest.

I was losing him, but I still didn't know why. "Like days? Months? Can you give me a ballpark?"

Sharpness filled his voice. "Would it make a difference?"

"Yeah, actually it does. I mean, if your last victim wore huge puffy sleeves and bloomers under long skirts, that's one thing, but if you killed my basketball player patient, that's something else entirely."

Oliver didn't react.

"Explain to me why you suddenly feel that this—whatever this is between us—needs to end before it begins. I don't understand."

"You haven't seen everything I've done." Oliver approached. His posture was...defeat? He was somber, perhaps ashamed. I couldn't figure out what the big deal was. He rested his hands on my upper arms. Leaning down slightly, his eyes captured my gaze, and Oliver's irises glowed as red as ambulance lights flickering across the darkness. He said evenly, "Remember the basketball player."

Images assaulted my brain like a barrage of lightning bolts. I gasped and backed away, covering my gaping mouth with my hand. The memory I didn't know had been missing returned in a head-splitting onslaught of rapid-fire images. Megan and I had responded to the basketball player in the park, down with an animal bite. He was dead, but he *moved*.

Now I remembered. My face twisted with disgust at the deception. How could he do that to me? I'd trusted him. "You killed my patient. Right in front of me, you casually walked over to him and you...you snapped his neck." I glared at Oliver. Learning he'd murdered a man and made me forget was a punch to the gut and a violation I couldn't forgive. How many other murders had he covered?

Oliver had been right about himself. He *was* Soren, but cleaner, craftier...but more dangerous because he'd covered his tracks with compulsion. And there was the missing link to the truth. The witches had warned me. The naïve bubble I'd lived in popped, showing me a reality more frightening and dangerous than I'd realized. How could Oliver switch from sweet and generous to cold and callous right before my eyes? I could take a neon-sign-flashing hint it was time for me to leave.

Oliver stared at me without an ounce of emotion on his face, but he didn't defend himself. He didn't say anything at all.

There was no excuse for what he'd done.

I gathered my keys. "You know what? Here's what I learned: vampires kill the innocent. Witches purposely set a fire that killed *thousands* of innocents. You're both equally bad, and it was karma that you turned into your own enemy."

Oliver's face fell, but I ran, heart breaking piece by piece with each step I took. I wasn't sure I wanted to know how elves could possibly be worse.

25
Unwanted Visitor

Oliver

AFTER A CENTURY PLUS of searching, I finally possessed my sun ring once again. The feeling of the rays on my face, of Daisy in my arms, of Daisy on my face—I had everything to be happy for, but that was just the rub, wasn't it? Nothing was ever going to get better than at that moment. I peaked in life, so the only way to go from there was down, and I'd just slalomed uncontrollably into a tree. Daisy and I had always been doomed. I'd known that. So when I trudged out of my shower, why did my feet feel like concrete blocks?

A vampire and a human...it never worked. My brother was everything she feared, and if Soren discovered my feelings for Daisy, then I might as well have placed the target on her head myself. To keep her safe meant I had to let her go, and showing her the truth of what I'd done pushed her to make the decision. I'd rather she hated me than cried over me, and now Soren wouldn't hurt her just to torture me.

Again.

Even if I could stop him once and for all and win Daisy back with years of dedicated groveling, we were still doomed. Unlike me, Daisy wouldn't live forever. Watching the people I cared about die was a given, and living with the pain—an expectation. I sighed. Everything was better this way. I didn't trust Soren regardless, so I'd watch over Daisy from the shadows, a silent and formidable private protector until the end of her natural days—or Soren's unnatural ones.

I wrapped a towel around my waist. I appreciated Nicole's having remodeled my bathroom. Who knew four heads were so much better than one? I didn't deserve such luxury. In my walk-in closet, stacked floor to ceiling with pressed shirts, suit jackets, and slacks in a variety of dark and powerful colors, I picked out black slacks and a white-collared dress shirt. I brought them to my adjacent bedroom.

I swiped my feet on the fluffy rug centering the room and set my clothing on the bed. Movement in the corner of my eye stilled my hands. I didn't have a stake at the ready, but I shouldn't have needed one in my own protected home. I made sure vampires couldn't get in here. So, the one sitting at my crackling fireplace on my favorite lounge chair, sipping my favorite drink, had me both impressed and curious. And silently fuming because when he'd thrown a party here, I'd forgotten to discover and close the loophole.

Vulnerable while naked, I casually said, "Soren, pleasure to see you here. To what do I owe your gracing me with your presence?" I stuffed my legs into boxer briefs and the slacks, hoping he wouldn't notice my ring. It was too late to take it off or hide it.

Soren laughed. "I'm not here for you. I'm just enjoying a break from my exhausting work." He gazed at me, observing my clothing, and lifted a brow. "After all these decades, you wouldn't remember what a hard day's work consisted of, would you? Unless lifting a drink to your lips, scribbling with a pencil, and reading a book counted for something."

That loophole was now critical. I'd given Nicole a vervain bracelet. Vervain was a native perennial flowering plant with purple petals, the only known toxic plant to vampires. Ingesting it was poisonous, debilitating even at low doses, and touching it burned like fire. Since it grew prolifically in our area, we had to keep it and ourselves a secret for obvious reasons. But if a human, as in the case with my niece, wore the flower, the plant's effects prevented a vampire's compulsion, and if a human drank it, well, the hungry vampire was going to have a no-good, very bad day.

So how Soren skirted around Nicole's defenses was intriguing, and something that needed rectifying immediately. "How did you Trojan-horse your way inside?"

Soren sipped from his drink, knees crossed, foot bouncing in the air. The amusement at besting me radiated from him. "You see, our little Nicole is not as witty as you thought. One simple 'accident' sent her hobbling outside like her insurance depended on it. Humans and their insufferable liabilities. Ripping off the bracelet was child's play, and then I only had to ask to get inside. Seriously, brother, you underestimate me, and after all these years, you still haven't learned."

Knowing Soren, his story gave me cause for concern. "What did you do to her?"

"Me? Nothing. She's useful after all. You know, to keep out the riffraff." Soren smirked.

My brother no longer looked like his usual filthy creature prowling the streets, someone easily recognized as a danger. He'd styled his hair, and his clothes were pressed. *My* clothes and *my* shoes to be precise. In broad daylight, he looked clean, refined, a silent predator to unsuspecting victims, just like me. "You took my clothes again. Why not compel someone to give you a five-finger discount and a free hotel room?"

Soren shrugged. "Do you know how difficult it is to find lodging without intrusive sunlight? Humans just love that view. Don't flatter yourself, brother. Necessity brought me here, and opportunity sent me to your closet. Although both impositions were equally repulsive to me, I find it's better to look and smell like you than the alternative. But dear God, Oli, can't you own a single leather jacket or pair of riding boots? You always dress like you're going to kiss ass at a board meeting. Gag me, please."

With pleasure.

I slipped into the white button-up shirt and fastened it closed. "Congratulations. Today was the first day you found my life to be less vile than living like a sewer rat. And now that you've had your makeover from steerage to first class, Jack, what is it you want from me?"

Soren laughed. "This place, such a disgusting display of wealth. You remember our real home? The one we helped Father build? The cabin that burned to the ground, displacing and destroying our family? Oh wait. Was the loss of our home the reason or what it...I don't know...you?"

Vengeance. Got it. I filled my pockets with my wallet and keys. "I'm glad my four showerheads offer restitution."

Soren shook his head. "I like the way you think. But don't worry, once the sun sets momentarily, I'll be on my way. My chicken is ready to be plucked, and her master is hungry."

Soren had a plan, and that meant he wasn't murdering sporadically on a whim. A glimmer of hope sparked for my despised brother. Rather than toss him aside, I needed to know what he was up to. "And who is the lucky main course?"

"Daisy Barrett." Soren swigged and swallowed with a satisfied sigh.

As I'd feared, the target had been placed. I'd gotten too close. I'd waited too long to sever our electrifying connection. This was my fault. Since I'd promised I'd never hurt her, and I'd always keep her safe, I had to fix this thing, regardless of what she thought of me now. I settled my shoes by the closest chair and stuffed my feet into them.

"Why do you want her?" I asked casually.

Soren finished his glass. He set it on my lacquered end table without a coaster. Unrefined animal. "Wouldn't you like to know?"

"What's that supposed to mean?"

My brother strolled over to me. I tied my shoes and met him face to face, not wanting to be left in a vulnerable position.

His sinister green eyes met mine in warning. "Know this," he said, tone dripping with menace. "I have a job to do. Anyone who stands in my way will be put down. I won't be lenient with you again, Brother. You can't save everyone." After a pause, his smirk returned. "Or *anyone*. Poor Evangeline."

Evangeline's name pierced my chest. She had been my last and only attempt at finding love, and the reason why I had to stay away from humans...from Daisy. There was nothing I could do to save Evangeline's life—as a human or vampire. The insult and surging pain reeled my fist into a right hook, and I clocked my brother in the eye.

Soren's head snapped back. He collected himself with the smirk still in place, touching the wounded flesh.

Jaw clenched, I said, "You forced me to kill her."

"Suppose I deserved that."

"Leave the past in the past," I warned him.

"Perhaps one should take one's own advice. Two minutes ago would've been ideal." He rubbed his sore eye, and it healed in seconds.

Something about this conversation was off. Soren had mentioned a master, which I'd brushed off as an improvement in his personality, but now he had a job to do. This long game of planning and stalking was the opposite of his style. And Soren didn't take orders without a good reason.

Somehow, someone pinged Daisy on their supernatural radar. Since witches couldn't be compelled by vampires or elves, Daisy wasn't a witch. But clearly, I wasn't the only one interested in who she really was.

I hadn't placed that target on her head, so I no longer needed to stay away from her. Just the opposite: I couldn't let her out of my sight.

"This isn't you, Soren. Who put you up to this? Who's the 'master' you referred to?"

Soren's smarmy grin twisted his features. "Oh, brother, someday you'll learn."

"Speak plainly." I insisted.

I was too late. I'd always underestimated him. In a flash of vampire speed, he seized my hand, and his eyes brightened at the ruby bauble on my finger. "Look what you've got here."

"No!" I shouted, squeezing my fist tight and wrenching away, but his grip was too strong. Soren drank directly from the live tap, which gave him far more strength than me and my blood bags.

His right hook slammed into my jaw, and instinct had me moving back and covering the injury. With more vampire speed, Soren slipped my sun ring free of my finger and vanished down the hallway.

I glanced out the window. Daytime. I couldn't give chase without igniting like a pile of paper doused in gasoline, so I did the only thing I could. I paced, footsteps clattering on the hardwood. Somehow, I had to get to Daisy before my brother did, but he had a severe advantage.

Sometimes the only way to protect the ones I cared about was to become what they feared, what I was at my core. I marched through the house on my way to the basement, calling to my niece. I opened the door to my commercial-sized refrigerator. Rows of blood bags filled the unit, recently restocked by Nicole.

"What's the matter, Oliver?" Nicole asked, concern in her tone.

"I need more time here. Clear the guest calendar for another two weeks." I slammed down a bag with more lined up, so my compulsion would reach its highest strength.

Nicole watched me with a critical eye and a pinch of disgust as I engorged on bags as if I'd been starving for years. "Sure thing."

"Oh, and Nicole?"

She turned but kept her eyes away from my dinner.

"Replace your vervain bracelet. We'll figure out something more Soren-proof when I get back."

Nicole checked her wrist. "Soren! He got inside? I'm so sorry. I'll take care of the calendar."

I engorged bag after bag greedily, taking solace in knowing these were filled by volunteers. After all these years of abstaining from the live tap, I needed full strength tonight, and I didn't want them to remember they hadn't volunteered. Hopefully, Nicole wouldn't need vervain at all when I returned, but I knew Soren's strength. My efforts had to be enough. I needed enough.

26

Ambushed

Daisy

Before heading out for a jog, I stopped by Dad's house. He hadn't returned my calls or texts for a while. I wanted to know if he'd heard from Lily since she'd run away from Megan's funeral. There were no cars on the driveway. Either Dad's commuter car was still parked in the garage, or he wasn't home. Holding a food storage container, I stuck my head through the front door. "Dad?" It was sunny outside, so I couldn't tell if any lights were on. "Dinner's here."

As usual, no answer. I walked inside, listening for sounds of him getting ready for work upstairs, but all I heard was the humming refrigerator. I opened the fridge and found my less-tasty water bottles and the food I'd brought yesterday. Strange. This time, I checked the date on the milk carton. It was expired. He hadn't been home for a week or more. What kind of medical research breakthrough required him to sleep at the lab for a stretch at a time?

I left the new food next to the old food, planning on grabbing it after my run. Dad's house was in a sweet area on West Bay Shore Street, near a University of Wisconsin campus. His backyard overlooked the bay, and the Wildlife Nature Walk was nearby—a secluded public jogging path. Today I was clearing my head there for a change.

After Jamie's warnings turned out to be correct, I took extra precautions. First, enjoying the fresh air while it was daylight. Second, Jamie had happily given me a vervain bracelet. And just in case of something four-legged, I had pepper spray in my armband.

I was safe to be a normal, boring human again.

I took a water bottle and chugged half of it, making a face at the bland flavor, and left it on the counter to pick up on my way back through. The trail wasn't long enough to need refreshment along the way.

I stretched my hamstrings and quads and closed the front door behind me. I set off, pausing only for traffic as I crossed the street. My feet ate up the short distance to the trail, and I swerved onto the path, keeping an even pace. I focused on my footsteps and listened to my breathing, trying to avoid my head returning to Oliver's bed.

But my body was still singing from his touch, his lips, and his *tongue*. I didn't judge him for what he was—a vampire, perhaps a colloquial term for whatever unusual disease he had—but he killed my patient and violated my head to hide it. That was unforgivable.

Aunt Lisa would be so disappointed I'd given away her ring, but no one more so than me. In fact, I was pissed I gave it to a monster. I was stupid for falling for Oliver's touch, his smile, his warmth. He'd convinced me the story about the fire and the cave was the truth—that the ring had always been his. I frowned. Supposedly left in a witch's sacred space? Gullible. That was the word I'd been looking for. So, did he compel me to give it to him?

I just couldn't deal with the violation. The lies, the deceit. How could a person trust someone after that? The answer was: you didn't. Oliver wasn't alone in his transgression. Pierce had his feathery hands on me while I'd been unconscious. He, too, had meddled in my head.

Jamie and Allison had warned me, but I didn't listen. For that, I'd lost some dignity...and a family heirloom. *I'm sorry, Aunt Lisa.*

My dad wanted me to be someone I wasn't—a fancy-titled, well-respected, famous medical researcher like him—well, famous was subjective. Throughout my teen years, I'd thrived to become like him, but that build-up only crushed me harder when I failed. These days, Dad might as well not exist.

Mom had always been out of the house—worried about her next real estate sale. She wasn't great at being supportive or available. And my mom died on my graduation day, which was still a fresh stab to the chest every time I thought of it. My sister disappeared after Mom's death. I couldn't blame her for needing to get away, but someone had to make sure Dad was okay. So I stayed. I fought to keep Dad in my life, but his job was clearly more important. Always was.

But Aunt Lisa and Uncle Marc were so kind. They loved me for who I was, which made the loss of her ring even more painful. Although there was tension between their daughter Abby and me, a healthy competition where she clearly won, they felt like my real family. Now they were all gone. My best friend Megan, too. For a brief moment, I thought I could have Lily back, but she vanished at Megan's funeral without another word.

I couldn't trust my roommates, who completely accepted the loss of human lives in the name of the greater good. That was something I didn't think I could ever wrap my brain around.

I couldn't trust Pierce. I still didn't know exactly what he did to me the night I was attacked.

And I couldn't trust Oliver, who blocked my memories of him murdering my basketball player patient, even though he warned me away by himself.

Then there was Soren. On top of all the brutal things he'd done, when he'd attacked Kayla, she'd quit. I'd brought her flowers at the hospital, but oddly enough, I couldn't see any wound on her throat at all, and she didn't seem to remember much of the incident. The whole interaction was...cold, and I could take a hint.

I had no one—not a single soul I trusted—to give me a hug and tell me everything was going to be okay. An ache carved a hole in my heart. Tears pressed against my eyelids, but a moderate breeze dried them while my legs pumped down the trail. Clearing my head wasn't supposed to make me feel worse.

I turned a corner on the homestretch back to the sidewalk, and a man stood at the trailhead. I slowed to a walk, panting with the exertion. Other people used this trail on the regular, and under normal circumstances I'd pay no attention, but something about him tingled in my gut. For instance, he just stood there, wearing a button-up shirt and pants. He wasn't dressed for a run, and he didn't have a dog with him.

I slyly removed the pepper spray from my armband, keeping it securely in my palm, and approached with caution. As I closed the distance, I got a better view. His slightly too-small dress clothes were strange, but maybe he'd had a bad day at the office and needed to walk off his thoughts. Completely normal. Not everyone in public was a danger.

The man started toward me, face tipped down and hands in his pockets, like he was working through something. See? Normal. The thick trees in the immediate vicinity wouldn't allow me to run off the trail, though. So, I strode with a purpose and a sweaty-palmed grip.

Something about him was familiar, but I brushed it off. I probably met him at a party or at Fully Loaded and completely forgot his name. His ignoring me was a favor, so I wouldn't embarrass myself, and that was that. I strolled right on by him with my chin up.

Until arms clamped onto me from behind. In surprise, I gasped and struggled to free myself, but I couldn't. A pull and a snap at my wrist had me exclaim in pain. Then I heard the sizzle.

Like bacon on a frying pan.

Iron-like fingers pried my hand open and gingerly took the canister. That was when I saw it. My ring. Aunt Lisa's ring. But this wasn't Oliver. And just like that, I'd been de-armed in broad daylight. Before I could attempt any kind of escape, a searing pain stung my throat. I opened my mouth to scream, but the familiar paralysis took over.

Soren.

I was helpless to fight him and helpless to cry for help. At that moment, my phone was taken from my armband and tossed off the trail.

What did he do to Oliver?

Daisy

THE FEAR OF A paralytic shutting down my body, forcing me to watch helplessly as a monster dragged me by the hair, was hands-down the worst. Adrenaline uselessly pumped through me as Soren tossed me into the back of a commercial van—the plain white kind with the windows blocked out, the kind that if it had a sign advertising free candy, to run away. That kind.

My arms and legs weren't tied, and I wasn't gagged, but I was still as useful as a rag doll. Soren didn't know the first thing about kidnapping someone during the day with a suspicious vehicle, but with his toxic fangs, he didn't need to be clever about it. Under my terror, embarrassment at how effortlessly he'd taken me stung.

The doors slammed shut, swallowing me in temporary darkness. The back end of the van was empty except for me, splayed out. Between me and the vampire were two rows of seats and nothing else.

Soren started the van and maneuvered us down the city streets. He drove like an ordinary grandmother—slow and cautious, so he didn't turn heads. But when the engine roared to get up to highway speeds, my heart sank while my breathing pumped in and out of my panicked lungs.

Southbound on Highway 41, the location of my accident with Uncle Marc, Aunt Lisa, and Abby. Images of the crash flashed across my mind, further eroding my ability to think straight. After what felt like ages bumping against the hard floor in a vehicle in desperate need of new shocks, I flinched.

I...*flinched*.

I could finally move. Straining against the effects of his venom, I painfully shifted onto my knees and looked out the front window. Yep, we were headed toward Green Bay. At this speed, I couldn't just jump out.

"You're awake," Soren said, glancing in the rearview mirror. "Might I remind you not to do anything stupid?" His eyes flashed bright red, warning me of his intent to compel me to behave. "I never had the chance to thank you for such a lovely dance, Daisy. Too bad it was cut too short."

I pulled my cottony tongue free. "What are you doing with me? Where are we going?" My throat clenched as we approached the location of the fiery crash. I hadn't been down this way since then. All I could think about was getting a seat belt. My pulse kicked up again.

"Relax back there or I'll make you calm down," Soren said in a bored tone.

After what Pierce and Oliver had done to my head, I believed he could, but calming down on command was impossible. "I am relaxed," I lied.

"I can hear your heartbeat."

I shivered. Still creepy. "Talking helps me calm down."

"Really?" Soren grinned. "Well, did you know I have some history here? Dates are a little wishy washy for me. After so many decades, it all runs together, but this particular morning I remember clearly."

I held my breath, fearing what he was about to tell me.

"Not too far from this exact location, a car came out of nowhere and nearly hit me. It was, frankly, a miracle I survived."

I knew it wasn't a deer that early morning on the drive to my and Abby's graduation, but a man didn't make sense. Vampire hadn't been in my vocabulary yet. That morning, I'd pulled myself from the wreckage, but I was too weak to save my family. And because I'd been too weak, they died.

Because Soren had been in the road, they died.

My throat squeezed, but I needed to know why. "What were you doing on the highway?" I asked curtly. It wasn't every day that I could get answers to such haunting events.

He said lightly, "Following orders."

My lips twisted. That wasn't the answer I expected. "You don't seem like the type to take orders."

Soren's eyes wrinkled with a hidden smile. "I'm not."

"So what are we doing on the highway now?"

Soren frowned. "Following orders."

Whatever those orders entailed likely wasn't to my benefit. "For whom?"

"You have witchy friends. You should've been asking them questions while you had the chance. It's too late now, of course, and hindsight always offers that frustrating clarity. But here's a tip, from one puppet to another..."

Puppet. I hung on to that word tightly.

"Witches can spell vampires and elves, like compulsion on overdrive. They—your friends—are the most dangerous beings on this planet. Too much power, too easily blended in."

What did Allison and Jamie have to do with my being kidnapped by a vampire and brought to Green Bay? Now I just had more questions than anything. "What do you want with me?"

The corners of his eyes wrinkled again. "What I want doesn't matter."

Weird deflection. "Then let me go."

Soren chuckled. "We'll be there in half an hour. Be quiet, or I'll make you."

He kept threatening me with compulsion, but he couldn't do it while driving, and I had more questions. "I saw you kill Megan, and I know you attacked me. I assume you attacked Kayla too, but it was hard to tell in the crowd. But it was you and only you who killed those other people in town—the animal attacks, if you watched the news. Why? Why did you do it? Why not take what you need and erase their memories, leaving them alive? That's less suspicious than leaving bodies."

"I thought your innocence was a clever cover, but now I'm starting to think you really are that stupid."

I cast my gaze down. After I failed out of med school, Dad reminded me almost daily in many creative ways how stupid I was for not hacking it. But in his way of apology, he'd tell me to try again, since I had all the material and answers in advance. *Sure, Dad. I'll just apply, and they'll welcome me with open arms.* Way to kick someone while they were down. Then my favorite, he'd tell me he'd keep this little blemish a secret. The image he maintained for his colleagues was more important to him than my happiness.

Soren chuckled. "I hit a sore spot, didn't I? To answer your question, yes, I could take a sip and erase it." His eyes glinted at me in the rearview mirror.

For some crazy reason, I wanted desperately to change the subject. I'd just accused Soren of many terrible things, but he didn't deny any of them. "Do you remember the basketball player? He was a vampire victim not long ago. I assume one of yours?"

"Doesn't sound familiar. Who was he to you?"

"I responded to the scene. The man had been attacked, and Oliver snapped his neck in front of me."

Soren laughed. "What a shame. We could always use more vampires."

That sounded like Soren knew nothing of it. So, Oliver had admitted the truth. He killed the man. I couldn't figure out whether that was good news or not. I swallowed a lump.

"Are you staying the neck snap prevented him from turning into a vampire?"

"Humans in transition keep all the same human weaknesses, like the density of their bones, so a neck snap would mean lights out for good. But without feeding on a fellow human, he was going to die anyway. Oliver made the choice for him."

When I'd seen it, I jumped to murderer, but if he was preventing the creation of another monster, I couldn't fault him for that. "If he didn't want another vampire running around killing people, when why did he drink so much from the basketball player that he'd died in the first place?"

Soren laughed. "Oliver drink from a human? Hot and fresh? Now you're funny."

Soren...always capable of disgusting me. "How can you justify being so flippant about this? People are dying because of your kind."

"Vampires are a predatory elite race, sweetheart. We let you live and procreate. *Usually*. We gotta eat, too."

Throughout the drive, Soren didn't once speak ill of his brother, but the deathmatch in front of my house wasn't a friendly, brotherly brawl either. Besides, Oliver had point-blank stated he hated Soren. I'd assumed the feeling was mutual. "Then why do you and your brother hate each other?"

Soren exhaled slowly. "Look, I'm a vampire, and I fully embrace it. When the urge strikes me, I eat whomever, wherever I want. I'll kill if I want to or when I have to. It makes no difference to me. Oliver... Well, he tries to pretend he's human, which is a disgrace. Forty years ago, I tried to teach him otherwise, but he's a stubborn ass. A family trait, really."

"And what lesson was that?" I was afraid to ask, but curiosity got the better of me.

"My human-pretending brother tried to have a relationship with a human woman. I showed him that wasn't possible and saved him a lot of pain. Possibly even saved his life, but he doesn't see it that way. But I don't know. Maybe he finally realizes I've been right all along." Soren gave me that smirk that said he knew more than I did.

If he was referring to my breakup with Oliver... A—how did he know? And two—I walked out on Oliver. Soren hadn't been a factor, so he didn't get to take credit. The more we talked, the clearer my head became, and I realized with a sinking feeling, the farther he took me from home, the lower my chances of survival. I had to do something.

"Whatever happened between Oliver and me had absolutely nothing to do with you. That bloated ego of yours must leak from your bodily orifices, which would explain the smell. And here you'd called *me* stupid?"

Soren slammed on the brakes, skidding the tires. My body flew forward against the seat back. He swerved the van over the rumble strip and into the gravel, and I tumbled against the side wall, like I was a high-scoring pinball. I cursed the lack of seat belts.

The van stopped on the shoulder, thrusting me forward again. I was going to feel that in the morning. Soren shifted into park and got out of the driver's seat. Now, my heart leaped into my throat. What was I going to do? The monster circling around to the back was faster than any known animal. At this hour, traffic was too thin to wait for help against a superhuman being. Woods were all around us, but I had no chance on foot.

However, he left the keys in the ignition.

I scrambled over the seat backs just as the back doors swung wide behind me.

Soren said, "You have no idea who you're messing—" The vampire cut off when he noticed me moving.

I dropped into the driver's seat, and before I situated myself, I slammed on the gas pedal and yanked the steering wheel, trying to control the vehicle's movement from the gravel shoulder onto the paved highway without Soren being able to climb inside.

Getting the wheels to catch on the blacktop, I glanced in the rearview mirror, and no one was there. With a smile, I scooted myself into the proper driving position. The back doors swung free, and I checked the road behind me to make sure nothing fell or was being dragged, endangering other drivers.

Soren was not back there—in the cab or dragging on the pavement.

I thrummed with energy at my success. I did it. I escaped. My lips pulled into a broad grin, and I pushed the gas harder. I couldn't have been prouder of myself than at this moment. I might not be med school material, but underestimating me was a mistake, one Soren was likely kicking himself for on the shoulder of Highway 41 all by his lonesome. Up ahead in Oconto was an emergency vehicle crossover, and normally I'd never consider it, but this was an emergency, and I was willing to risk the fine to save my life.

I drummed the steering wheel with impatience, heart thundering in my chest, and a grin aching across my face. Keeping my eyes peeled for the crossover, I fought the urge to pump the air with my fists. I saved myself, and I wasn't going to let others control me anymore. I was going to do what I wanted and when I wanted it. Humans weren't useless against monsters, after all. I wasn't useless, and I definitely wasn't stupid.

27

Bite Plans

Oliver

As dusk pulled the sun below the horizon, I had one final task to complete. On the top shelf of my walk-in closet, I lifted a small shoebox. I hadn't opened it in decades, and I never intended to again, but I needed protection for Daisy. Pulling back the lid, I dragged in a breath. A black and white, torn and aged photo of a smiling Evangeline Brant. A shaky sigh passed my lips, and I closed my eyes in painful memory. Screams and gurgles of death made me cringe. That night, I'd promised her I'd never turn another person again. I'd never broken that promise, and I never would, either. Pushing aside the awful image, I freed a lead-lined jewelry box and lifted out the locket.

The locket contained a pinch of both vervain and black nightshade, and the silver chain burned my flesh like a live flame. The silver itself was inert to my kind, but the vervain imbued the whole necklace with a layer of protection. One herb against vampires, and the other against elves. I had been too late in giving it to Evangeline, but I wouldn't make that mistake again.

I gritted my teeth against the singeing burn, while I dropped it back into the lead-lined box and slipped it into my pocket. My stinging hand healed within seconds. I returned the shoebox to its safe place and glanced out the window.

Night had fallen.

No longer would I pace this house like a caged animal. Plans and preparations were almost finished for me to take on the most gruesome vampire I'd ever met. My own brother, Soren Rockwell. Now I would finish this once and for all.

The bags of blood I'd engorged myself on lifted my superhuman abilities to the artificial limit. Now I could hunt properly and fill myself with the highest quality blood—fresh from the tap. Only then did I stand a chance against Soren. I dashed out my front door and took a detour through the city park. Daisy wasn't the only jogger who liked to clear her head in the darkness. I approached a man who jogged so slowly I kept pace by walking behind him.

I tapped him on the shoulder, and he turned with a start and tugged his earbuds out.

I gave him a friendly smile. "Didn't mean to scare you, but I need to ask you something."

The jogger panted, eyeing me warily. "Like what?"

He was far too trusting when faced with the ultimate predator. His arteries sloshed the delicious nectar of nature in a symphony, calling me to satiate my baser needs. I'd lived on juice bags for decades. They'd kept me alive, but didn't quell the urge to feed. Hard liquor suppressed that, my preference being tequila. I hadn't fed from a live person in so long, I only hoped I could stop myself before killing him. "Have you had any dairy lately?"

The jogger frowned. "What kind of question is that? Leave me alone." He reached for his earbuds.

"Look at me." I activated my compulsion, connecting me to the neural pathways delivering messages in his tiny brain. I sent him an order. "No screaming. Stand still. Answer me honestly."

The jogger nodded.

"Dairy?"

The jogger twisted his features but stood still. "I...I don't know?"

I sighed. "Ice cream, milk, cheese, butter. Any of that ringing a bell?"

"I had cauliflower tacos for dinner."

I perked up. "You're vegan?"

"Yeah, and I only sprinkled a little Edam on top. Gave it a nice nutty flavor."

I grumbled. Damn it. I turned on my power of persuasion again. "Stand still. This won't hurt, and you won't remember it."

I tilted his head to the side, exposing the addictive channel. The straw for my meal only needed a pair of punctures. Then, the gracious heart delivered the nectar to my mouth, as if obeying me. Nature was willing to give me the ultimate strength—with a mild case of indigestion.

If I took too much, his heart would panic, pumping harder to deliver oxygen around the body, but the pressure would drop. Instinct caused a new vampire to draw harder, pulling as much as possible from the victim, but that pressure would only cause the artery to collapse, shutting off the supply entirely. And the human would die. I had to get what I needed without allowing myself to take the victim that far, but I was out of practice.

I opened my mouth, and the fangs descended in anticipation. My irises glowed, reflecting off his clothing, and like a snake, I bit down. At once, two channels of blood leaked from around my fangs. I retracted them, and the spurts from his heart fed me. I swallowed mouthful after mouthful, but the more I took, the more I wanted. The more I needed.

When a food became an addiction, the best course of action was to avoid it. When that addiction also killed the food, the best plan was to stay the hell away from it. As a vampire, I had to have it. The craving—the addiction, the urge to survive—never went away.

I drank and drank, the need driving me to take more. My sensitive hearing tracked his heart rate. It kicked up in panic. I had only a few more seconds left before this man's life on was the line.

But I wanted more.

If I took more, I would be no better than Soren. A murderer. A killer for a drink that wasn't necessary for survival, not since bagged blood. Daisy's smiling face came into my view. Her voice... What would she say if she saw me right now? Her complete horror and disgust tore me from the jogger's throat.

His hand clamped onto the wound and drew back blood. "What... What just happened?"

"Nothing. You're fine."

He stumbled away, my paralytic having been at the weakest dosage. The jogger pulled back more blood on his hand. Complete and total confusion kept him from facing me.

I didn't spill any blood on me; I wasn't an out-of-control sloppy fiend like my brother. I licked my lips clean, and the level of energy surging through me had me grinning. For too many years I lived with mediocrity, brooding over the constant dilemma of wanting the best food source but avoiding exposure and murder—and indigestion. In the case of Daisy's car accident, I'd merely intended to take advantage of a situation not of my making, but even then, I hadn't partaken.

The fresh tap made me feel alive, but I was terrified. Wielding this kind of power was a challenge with practice. I had to be careful not to get drunk on it, not to get lost to the cravings. Because drunk meant sloppy, and I had to find Daisy.

With lightning speed, I rushed up her porch and pushed open the unlocked front door, only to be blocked against an invisible shield. The witches had blocked my entrance. The timing couldn't have been worse.

"Hello?" I called into the dark house. "Anyone home? I need to see Daisy."

No response.

I slapped the invisible shield in frustration. "It's urgent. I need Daisy now." Before Soren got to her. Knowing my brother, and he was quick, the dark house gave me the impression I was already too late. How had my brother crossed this threshold? "Someone? Anyone? She's in danger."

A light flicked on, and a woman appeared in a navel-grazing T-shirt and baggy cotton pants. Her long, wavy hair was tangled from sleep. Allison the witch bartender from Fully Loaded. "Get out of here, vampire. Can't you catch the hint?" She folded her arms across her chest and stood just out of reach.

"Is Daisy here? She's in danger."

"No shit, and I'm looking at it." Her eyes sized me up with a frown. "Daisy already made her choice, and it was to stay far from you."

"Allison, it's not me she has to worry about. Soren's in town, and he's after her."

"Why?"

Exasperated, I said, "I don't know. Is she here?"

Allison blew out a breath and gazed over my shoulder as if expecting her return. "She went to her dad's house as usual and then went for a jog. At this hour, she'd be at work."

That wasn't good enough. Something wasn't right. I could feel it in my old bones. "Call her work phone. Just tell me she's there."

Allison folded her arms across her chest in defiance. I couldn't compel her even if I wanted to. Damn witches. "If you're so concerned, you call her."

"I don't have a phone."

Allison rolled her eyes and leaned to the side, collecting a cell phone off the table by the door. She dialed, and I heard every word of the short conversation. Daisy wasn't on shift tonight.

Daisy was missing. My heart thundered in my chest, and I itched to kill something, someone. *Think, think, think.* She'd told me Soren had asked about her dad's work at the party. It was a long shot, but I had nothing else to go on. "I need to know the location of her father's lab."

Worry knitted her brow. "You think she went there?"

"No, Soren has her. He must. It's all connected somehow. It has to be."

Still skeptical, Allison said, "Her dad works in Green Bay, but they aren't open right now."

That didn't matter one bit. "Dr. Greg Barrett hasn't been home in days. He's either at work or he's dead. Please, Allison. It's the only lead I have, and the only lead that makes sense."

Allison started, anger twisting her features. She lifted her palms skyward, as if preparing to cast a spell. "And this is why Jamie and I protect humans from your kind. You are all despicable creatures who bring nothing but death and destruction wherever you go."

She wasn't wrong.

"And this is all your fault, vamp. If Daisy gets hurt..." Allison trailed off, steaming pissed at me.

I didn't blame her. Regardless of whoever had given orders to Soren, if I'd never met Daisy, she wouldn't be in Soren's mitts. I hadn't been careful enough, and I should've given her this vervain locket a while ago.

Her upper lip curled in anger. "Get her home alive, or I will kill you."

"If I can't get her home safely, I'll come looking for you to kill me." It was a statement I hadn't expected to say, but I felt it was true. Daisy hated me right now, but I had endless time to grovel. Picturing a future without her, even with her hating me at arm's length, crushed my chest like a ton of bricks poured from a dump truck. I just needed to get to her in time.

Allison eyed me with suspicion. "Deal." She told me the address of Pharmaceutical Development, Inc.

I couldn't go barreling into the secured building alone. If Greg Barrett had been colluding with Soren, then who knew how many of what I'd be walking into. I had to be careful, and I needed backup. "Can I borrow your phone?"

Allison dropped it into my hand. "Break it, and you buy it. And stay out of my banking apps."

I dialed a number I despised, but my issues with him had to be set aside to keep Daisy alive.

"Hello?"

"Listen here, elf. You want to kill a vampire? Get your stake. I'm coming to pick you up." I ended the call, dropped it back into her surprised hand, and vanished into the darkness to get my car. My darkness dragged Daisy into this mess, and I was getting her out of it. Even if I had to stoop to low places for help.

Daisy

HANDS GRIPPING THE WHEEL, stomach fluttering with butterflies, I anxiously awaited the emergency crossover. Until then, I had nothing to entertain myself with—to distract myself with. So my thoughts ripped through my whole kidnapping conversation, over and over. I felt like I was missing something. What had Soren meant when he'd called us both puppets? I truly hadn't the foggiest, but I was curious.

And it turned out Oliver was an innocent vampire, if those words could make logical sense together. He didn't feed on humans. Was that a consolation or a confirmation of what I'd already known? I wished I had my phone to tell people I was okay, but all things considered, it could've been worse. The sign warning people that the crossover was for emergency use only appeared up the hill. I was safe and headed home.

Keeping the van steady down the highway, the back doors lazily clattered. I needed to pull over and close them before the police flagged me, but if I jammed on the brakes hard enough, they might close themselves. I signaled to change lanes to the left, ready to slow for the median, and I checked the rearview mirror to make sure I wouldn't brake-check anyone.

A shadowed figure rested his folded arms on the backrest next to me. I yelped in panicked surprise, and my hands jerked the wheel. The van swerved, and half the tires rumbled on the gravel shoulder. No, no, no, this was not going to happen. I was not going to relive the crash that had stolen my family from me. Trees flew by as I focused on fixing the van's traction. On a deep exhale, I steadied the lumbering vehicle and with a final jerk, I shifted it back onto the pavement.

"Not a bad attempt, Daisy. Props, seriously." Soren laughed. "But hey, I got some peace and quiet for a good chunk of the ride. Now pull over."

My blood ran cold, and I whispered, "No."

Soren sighed impatiently. "If I pull that wheel sideways, the van will flip, turning into a log as it spins down the highway, flattening everything in its path. Only one of us would walk away. Hint, it's not you."

Hands shaking, I changed lanes back to the right and slowed the vehicle to a stop on the shoulder. The crossover was within arm's reach, but with the dangerous cargo I couldn't shake, it didn't matter. I glanced in the rearview mirror again. But Soren was gone, and the back doors were properly closed. Before I could consider a repeat, he'd opened the driver's side door.

In a flash, Soren gripped my chin and pulled my face to meet his bright red glowing irises. "You won't try to escape again. Get in the passenger seat."

He released me, and I climbed over and buckled in. My stomach swirled with nerves.

Soren lowered himself into the driver's seat. With a glance at me, he said, "Now let's get this over with." He shifted into drive and moved us back onto the highway, quickly gaining speed. I watched the vehicle fly past the crossover with painful sorrow. My eyes fell to my fingers in my lap. A human couldn't outsmart or outrun a vampire. We were their food, prey, and no match against them. Their strength and abilities were unparalleled. Vampires were a superior species. It just sucked to admit.

I glanced at my captor, hate pulsing through my veins. On the steering wheel, the ruby gem sparkled on his finger. Oliver wouldn't have given up the ring voluntarily. Although we had issues to discuss, I didn't want to see him dead. "What did you do to Oliver?"

Soren glanced at me. "You believe I'm a cold-blooded killer, so you tell me."

His own brother wasn't as forgettable as the people he'd attacked around town. I was certain he would've bragged if he'd killed Oliver, which meant the better of the two brothers was still breathing. And so was I. Soren had also mentioned the puppet thing. I didn't believe he'd give me a straight answer about that, as usual. Perhaps he meant he wasn't in control. I certainly didn't feel in control. With all of that, I had to believe Soren wasn't pure evil. "He's alive. The two of you are at odds with one another, but you can't hate your family. Despise what they do, sure, but you can't hate the person."

Soren's hands tightened on the steering wheel. "A simple human with a short life, who can't begin to scratch the surface of what it means to be alive without purpose, to lose everyone you've ever met and cared about. What could you possibly understand about hate? But yes, my brother's alive and mighty pissed off. Now you, on the other hand, are interesting to me. After spending so much time with him, he should've given you vervain, but my brother never learns."

"You've said that before. What do you mean?"

Soren smirked and asked with unusual excitement, "He never told you the story?"

"No, but I think you're going to."

Soren laughed and cleared his throat as if honored. "The year was 1880, I think. Don't quote me on that. Oliver is better with the years than I am. Anyway, we'd had a few years to learn about our new lives and how to adapt when one day he met this pretty little lady, Evangeline Brant. If the situation had been different, you know, humans, I would've liked Evangeline as a sister-in-law. She was strong, capable, independent, but completely oblivious to my and Oliver's true nature. How he managed to have a relationship while only seeing the poor thing at night still baffles me, but somehow, he pulled it off. The woman was simply smitten with him. Now can you imagine how well a Puritan girl's parents would accept a demonic abomination like my brother as a husband? He couldn't give her children!"

I didn't know why that obvious piece of information made me so sad. Vampires were dead. Of course, they couldn't have families of their own. Vampires had to be made, which was what Soren had meant by my basketball player victim being a vampire in transition. I rubbed my bare arms with my hands.

"Oh, I know what you're thinking. Yes, Oliver is a sap. Always was and clearly still is." Soren eyed me as if he knew something I didn't.

"Anyway, she and my brother loved each other, blah, blah, blah. But there was no way it would work." That also sounded familiar. "Either she found out his secret and ratted us out to the pitchfork brigade, or he admitted it to her. The secret couldn't remain a secret. Obviously, Evangeline had to die either by his fangs so they could stay together, or by mine, so we wouldn't be hunted by the aforementioned brigade."

I couldn't help but realize Soren's clear warning message: Vampires and humans didn't mix and couldn't find a happily ever after, no matter what. That was why Oliver pushed me away. He'd told me he'd killed my patient, so I would hate him. In this story, I was Evangeline. I didn't choose Oliver's fangs, but I didn't choose Soren's either. I had a feeling I was going to be treated as the pitchfork brigade, regardless.

"I gave my brother the choice—he turned her, or I killed her. Like an idiot, Oliver refused to turn Evangeline without her permission, and that wasn't a risk we could take. So when I was hungry, I grabbed the first convenient throat. It happened to be hers, and even after my warnings, my big brother never bothered to protect her with vervain. Serendipity, I suppose, or was it fate? I try not to overanalyze my choices."

I wondered why and avoided rolling my eyes.

"Wearing vervain prevents the effects of compulsion," he added, apparently having a blast explaining this all to me. "But it's easy to remove, as you know."

I rubbed my wrist where he tore my bracelet off. Jamie's concoction was no match for Soren's strength.

"And drinking it leaves a human inedible. Not that I usually volunteer that information, but I'm not worried about you."

Gee, thanks.

"It burns like fire through your insides, the worst pain imaginable, but no worries, we heal." Soren sent me a friendly smile, and his nonchalance grossed me out.

"Why are you telling me all this?" Divulging vampire secrets seemed...careless? Sloppy? I didn't know, but it was weird.

"You aren't getting away from me, if that's what you hoped for."

"I think we're past that."

Soren smiled. "Now, how are you supposed to understand the impact of Oliver's mistake if I don't tell you just how stupid he was? Since Evangeline was unprotected—a colossal mistake—and my brother didn't heed the consequences I warned him about, I took matters into my own hands. I personally saved them both the pain of waiting for that inevitable day of another large-scale hunt."

I recalled Jamie's creepy story while we watched the car race. "You're talking about the witches hunting vampires?"

Soren brightened. "Precisely. You do know your history. Well, I had myself a lovely meal and left her to die. It would've been a mercy had she, but no. Evangeline was terrified, and with the blood loss, incoherent. Oliver refused to live without her, so in desperation, he fed her his blood and snapped her neck."

I gasped. "Why not just heal her and leave her be human?"

"Pitchfork brigade. Aren't you following? Must I speak slower?"

I frowned at his insult, but Soren was happy to continue. "You should've seen the tears when he killed the woman he loved. Oliver wanted Evangeline for the rest of his life, but he'd never told her what he was. Following his own selfish desires, he made the call. Spoiler alert: It was the wrong one, and there has never been another woman like Evangeline scorned."

I could imagine Oliver's desperation, and my heart broke for him. He only wanted his love to last. "I couldn't help but notice your use of the present tense."

Soren sighed. "Let's just say if you think I'm a cold, murderous monster, I have nothing on Evangeline Brant."

I swallowed a lump in my throat. I hoped I would never encounter her. "Where are we going?"

"Turns out dear old daddy needs motivation, and you're a bargaining chip."

I frowned. "What does my dad have to do with anything, and a bargaining chip for what?"

"If your father wants to see you alive, he will obey."

Dad had been gone for too long. I knew something either very right or very wrong had happened. "Obey what?"

Soren shrugged. "Enough talk. I want to listen to music. Less grating on the ears."

The vampire turned the knobs and found a radio station. I didn't figure him to be a hip-hop fan, but I didn't know Soren at all. I sat still with my hands in my lap, watching trees and exits roll by. They chose me as a bargaining chip, but I wasn't sure if using me to motivate Dad would work.

And then what would they do?

28

Truce with the Enemy

Oliver

I ROLLED MY CANDY-APPLE red 1967 Shelby to a stop in front of my enemy's house, wishing to partner with anyone capable but him, but beggars and choosers and all that. I wasn't an elf fan by any stretch of the imagination, but I couldn't deny their inherent strength—and supreme healing ability, which might come in handy tonight.

The passenger-side door opened, and Pierce Evansson dropped into the black leather seat, crushing my cushions with his heft. That actually gave me pause. I should've taken the Mercedes.

We had too-little time to change plans. "Are you ready?"

Pierce patted the side pocket of his cargo shorts and buckled in. "When you called me from Allison's phone, I didn't know what to think. But then I remembered you're caught in the sixties, so you had to borrow her phone like a damn Luddite."

"Not all of us see a need for such trackable devices." Especially when one could move unnaturally fast and draw unwanted attention.

Pierce rolled his eyes. "But then, you didn't clarify which vampire needed staking—of course, they all do. And for a brief moment, I thought I knew what you wanted from me. The immense guilt for destroying my proposal to Daisy had you needing me to relieve you of your endless misery."

He'd have to take a number if things didn't go well. "Look, you know my stance on what elves do, and I don't apologize for interfering with your compulsion. I never will."

"Pot, meet kettle."

At least we agreed on one thing. Satisfied he'd cooperate, I released the clutch and motored my 306 away from the curb and through town, wishing to fly wide open. I didn't want to deal with the authorities slowing me down, so I gritted my teeth and tried to focus on anything else but what might be happening to Daisy right now.

Like defending myself to my enemy. "Feeding to survive and erasing the horrific memory of the experience is a mercy, and not remotely comparable to what you do."

"Sure, whatever, vamp. Anytime you feel like stepping into the sun, just think of me first," Pierce added dismissively.

"I need you to take this seriously."

Pierce folded his thick arms across his massive chest. "When staking is involved, I don't need details to volunteer, but you never told me what we're doing."

"Soren kidnapped Daisy."

Pierce visibly stiffened, and his fists clenched.

"I called you because I believe you care enough for Daisy to help me, and that our decades-old truce will supersede whatever we're walking into. Am I right, or do I need to turn around?"

The last thing I needed was for the elf to stab me in the back and run off with Daisy under mind control. I slyly touched the lead-lined box containing the black nightshade and vervain locket in my pocket.

Pierce darted me a look of indignation. "Well, I need your word that if I kill your brother, you won't turn on me."

I would do anything to stop Soren *and* save his life, but if I could only choose one, my mind had already been made up. "My brother crossed a line for the last time."

"And I need your word that if Daisy gets hurt, you won't attempt a repeat of Evangeline Brant," Pierce said.

We stopped at a light on Marinette Avenue, and the highway stretched into darkness before us. I squeezed the grip on the wheel. Evangeline's name still haunted me from the grave, but that was one mistake I'd never repeated. "That won't be necessary."

"Are you sure about that? We can't have another bloodlusting murderer running free. This isn't 1880."

"You should have more faith in Daisy than that."

"When people turn, they change," Pierce countered and rested his palms on his knees, looking straight ahead as we barreled down a tunnel of darkness. "I get you two had a thing. I was with her first, but she always felt so far away."

The elf had compelled her to forget me. I didn't know how many times. "Not that I agree with it, but why didn't you compel her to stay with you?"

Pierce lifted his lips in amusement. "I tried all the time, but something was blocking me. Only in the last couple of weeks did my compulsion finally work, but I was too late." He glared at me accusingly.

"What are you going to do now?" I asked, trying to decide where the two of us really stood.

"There's someone out there willing to give me what I want," Pierce said. "I just have to find her."

I relaxed my grip. "In that case, I promise I won't stake you after we're done tonight."

Pierce acted surprised. "You planned to break our truce?"

"It's not a truce if you're dead." Technically, true.

Pierce shot me a dark look. "You're asking me to hunt your vampire brother, who, by the way, is a soulless murderer, and rescue the woman who rejected my proposal—a woman you want—and you're joking about killing me after I help you?"

"Your panties are bunching." I hadn't made a plan, but I wouldn't turn down an opportunity.

"You couldn't take me anyway, vamp." Pierce grumbled. "But you're tempting me. Watch it."

I'd be lying if a fair fight hadn't crossed my mind. A few days ago, Pierce could've seriously injured me, but now? I was older and therefore inherently stronger. "And that's why I picked you."

Pieced eyed me suspiciously.

"I need someone almost as strong as me to get Daisy out of this."

Pierce scoffed. "You wish. You know it's your fault she's caught in the middle of this, right?"

I was well aware. My body tensed, and I shifted gears, roaring my 306 horsepower. "And I'm going to get her out of it."

Even if I had to rip the throats out of everyone in the building.

Daisy

MY EYELIDS FLUTTERED OPEN and closed as I fought groggy unconsciousness from dragging me back down into nothingness. When I finally found clarity, there was still nothingness. Not a wink of light penetrated wherever I was. The floor underneath me didn't move, and there were no engine sounds. I was no longer in the van. But cleaning supplies stung my nose. Bleach, definitely bleach nearby. I tried to sit up, but my hands were tied behind my back and a ring of plastic dug into my wrists. I twisted and pulled, trying to free myself, and I knocked over something. A wood clatter of a broom handle, maybe?

I was in a janitor's closet.

In the dark.

Tied and alone.

The last thing I remembered was Soren asking about my dad's work, and he'd said I was a bargaining chip. I gasped. The Pharmaceutical Development lab. "Dad? Hello? Anyone there? Dad?"

I struggled in my binds.

I'd already dealt with an elf and a vampire mucking about with my free will, and then Soren had forced me to be obedient in my own kidnapping. When I escaped, I was done with vampires and elves for good. But I couldn't fight him. And he'd been around for over a hundred years, so he must've picked up a trick or two in human behavior. How was I going to outsmart a supernatural creature—a superior species—with amazing abilities and no human conscience?

The closet door opened, flinging bright fluorescent light into my eyes. I squinted.

"Oh, looky here. She's awake. Come with me," Soren said and grabbed me by the hair to stand me on my feet.

I thrashed, protesting the needless pain. "Seriously with the hair pulling! Stop!"

Soren gripped my arm and effortlessly pulled me into the lab and shoved me down onto a stool. I grimaced at him as he walked over to the corner, and he watched me like a twisted gargoyle. My scalp ached, my wrists hurt, and my knee was sore. But for now, he appeared to leave me alone, so I took in my new surroundings, already planning my escape. Rows of cabinetry with sinks, Bunsen burners, microscopes, stacks of petri dishes, and other lab supplies and equipment filled the vast space. Glass-front refrigerators with blinking lights, monitoring conditions, lined one wall. To my right, rows of plain white doors filled another, and what looked like offices took up the rest. That was a whole lot of doors to check for an exit.

From one refrigerator, Dad carried a tray of test tubes to a countertop near me.

"Dad!" I squeaked. My voice was hoarse. Had I been yelling?

Dr. Greg Barrett ignored my plea. He pushed his wire-framed glasses further up his nose and slipped one vial free in the series. He held it up to the light like a jeweler searching for impurities.

"Dad, help me. What's going on?"

Soren didn't make a move, thankfully. But neither did my dad, as if both of them couldn't see or hear me. "Let me go. These hurt!"

Dad cleared his throat and said, "That's not necessary. I have the product here. Let her go."

Bargaining chip. I glowered at Soren while speaking to my dad. "What's going on? What did he make you do?"

Dad didn't answer. He must've been compelled. Soren—a more vile creature couldn't possibly have existed. He attacked, murdered, maimed, played with, and manipulated at will. The world was his personal twisted playground. The least of his offenses was theft. He wore my ring, but since Soren had claimed Oliver was fine, then he'd been complicit. Was all of this to con me out of my ring, sleuth out my routine, and kidnap me for whatever the hell this was? Seemed like an awful lot of effort when a compulsion did the trick.

And if Oliver had been complicit, where the hell was he?

I felt like an idiot for worrying about him. Everything I'd shared with him—my bed, the swoon-worthy dance, the sweet walks at night, the silly banter. It was all a lie to weasel my ring from me. He'd taken advantage of me; he'd toyed with my head, and least of all, he'd torn out my heart.

I wished I didn't care.

And now Dad was in trouble too, because I got mixed up with selfish, heartless vampires.

Dad swirled the red liquid in the test tube, staring at it with his analytical eye. That was blood.

"Are you certain this version works?" A strange voice came from a strange man, who appeared out of nowhere. He was tall and lean with a mop of gray hair and a fan of wrinkles at the corners of his eyes. The way he moved with authority, accepted the vial with expectations, and inspected it against the light made me believe this dude was Dad's boss.

The man in charge.

My dad pushed his glasses back up his nose. "It's been tested thoroughly, Mr. Reed, and I think you'll find the results satisfying."

"Let us see for sure, shall we?" This Mr. Reed—why not *doctor*?—turned to Soren. "Be a pet and come over here."

Soren obeyed without complaint, but his usual animated chatterbox was gone. He just...obeyed, like a puppet.

Mr. Reed offered the vial to the weirdly complacent vampire. "Drink this."

Soren slammed it down in one gulp, no questions asked. He handed back the glass and stood waiting, as if expecting his next order. What kind of man could wield that much power over a vampire?

A witch? But according to Allison and Jamie, they usually weren't men.

Mr. Reed frowned and turned to Dad. "I'm not satisfied so far."

Dad glanced at Soren's unchanging stance. "Mr. Newton Reed, I'd explained that some specimens take longer. There are variables in age and diet that affect the process, but I promise you'll be satisfied."

A banging turned all our heads toward one of the plain white doors. It sounded almost like metal thudding rhythmically against concrete.

"And that one is one of the longer specimens," Dad said, answering everyone's unspoken question. "She's had the serum in her system for a few days now. She's declining, but it's taking longer than the others."

"What are the effects?" Mr. Newton Reed asked.

Dad cleared his throat. "In the event of a fired projectile, the tissue surrounding the wound darkens, then the veins blacken from the wound outward. If a subject drinks the serum, like our pet here, there is no wound. The fatal serum appears as a darkening of the veins, beginning with the extremities and working its way to the chest and head. Fever, confusion, fatigue set in as the circulatory system fails. Lastly, the capillaries go, turning the specimen dark like a burned husk."

I gaped, horrified for Soren. Despite the grim news, the vampire continued to stand still like a zombie, hearing but not listening to the torture that would come.

"Sounds painful," Mr. Newton Reed said with a lilt of satisfaction in his tone.

"I assure you it is," Dad said without concern either.

And I thought I'd already heard the worst a human could do to another.

Mr. Newton Reed checked his watch and gestured for Soren to raise his shirt. "Let's see the progress."

Soren lifted his T-shirt without hesitation and continued to look straight ahead for the next order. He really was a puppet. None of his actions were his own. And the darkened veins slowly coated his skin like a spider wrapping its meal with inky webs. Soren didn't have much time.

Mr. Newton Reed smirked and gestured for Soren to lower his shirt, which he did as expected. "I see we have success. Dr. Barrett, go ahead."

Dad rushed over to me and reached for my wrists.

Mr. Newton Reed shouted over, "Not so fast. You can chat, but she's not free. One successful demonstration doesn't mean the work's complete."

Dad's forehead broke out in a sweat as he leaned close. Pain, regret, worry—all crossed his features. He whispered, "I'm sorry about all this. You weren't supposed to be involved."

"What is all this?" I whispered back.

"There's so much you don't know, and I don't have time to explain."

I couldn't believe my own ears. "According to that guy, I'm not going anywhere, so throw me a bone."

"The serum is a chemical weapon against vampires. Awfully uncomfortable if touched, but fatal if ingested."

Soren was going to die. In a flash of sympathy, I glanced at the doomed vampire. He remained standing, but now he squirmed in pain with the serum working its way through his system. Creating a bioweapon was against everything my father stood for in the name of medicine. I hissed at my dad, "How could you?"

"That's enough," Mr. Newton said. "Back to work. I need more doses."

As if obeying his master, Dad returned to his station at the microscope, shattering my image of the highly reputed medical researcher who did nothing but push me to be my best—*his* best. No wonder we'd always butted heads. I was nothing like him, and I never would be.

And I was no longer ashamed.

29
Betrayal

Daisy

When responding to an emergency services call, the first rule of thumb was to assess the safety of the scene. Fire safety codes demanded two exits out of every room. This lab didn't have an emergency exit sign, but it did have a whole lot of unremarkable doors. The janitor's closet was a dead end. The door with the metal thumping noises I wouldn't touch with a ten-foot pole, so that left...a series of identical others. But which one was the right one?

The situation was bleak. Soren was dying, and I was tied up on a stool. Every time I attempted to twist free, it felt like the plastic bit deeper. My wrists burned from the friction, and my shoulders ached with the awkward angle.

Mr. Newton Reed, who didn't deserve the title of mister or the respect of his last name, would be known as Newt from here on out, because he was as slimy as the amphibian's name suggested. Newt observed the changes in Soren with extreme interest, as if the fatal development was a celebratory breakthrough. Struggling to stay on his feet, Soren bent at the waist while clutching his chest, face pinching in agony. His hands were already darkening, and his skin was slick with sweat.

"Congratulations, Dr. Barrett. I do believe he's dying," Newt said. "Soren, find a seat in the corner and stay." Soren stumbled over to a corner and settled on a stool. His legs lifted toward his chest, and his mouth gaped as if trying to drag in air. I wanted it to stop.

Satisfied, Newt approached me. "Now, there's only you left." The deranged boss leaned close and dragged a finger along my jaw.

I shivered. "Don't touch me."

He cackled. "Feisty. You and I are going to be good friends."

I glanced at Dad, silently pleading for help, but he dutifully continued his work as if he were the only man in the room.

With a pit in my stomach, I shifted and tugged at the plastic strip around my wrists. I couldn't cut the material with anything within reach. Even if I did, I had no idea where to go. Soren couldn't and wouldn't help me. My dad was under this creep's thumb.

There was absolutely nothing I could do to escape.

I needed help. But how would I make a call? There were no phones down here. Mine had been tossed into the woods on the jogging trail. Even if I figured out how to dial out, who would I call? Who could possibly be strong enough to stop Newt?

No matter what had happened between us, no matter how much I was pissed at Oliver's mind games, I wanted him to rescue me, but I didn't want him to end up like Soren too.

I couldn't get help.

I was a puppet. Trapped in this mess just like Soren.

One of the nondescript doors to the lab boomed as someone smashed it from the other side—another door I wouldn't touch with a ten-foot pole. I startled on my stool while trying to figure where it came from—which door to avoid.

Then another boom and another. The first door on the right, next to the bank of refrigerators.

The door burst open, and Newt frowned, but he stayed calm.

Oliver and Pierce exploded into the lab together. The biggest relief wasn't that I'd be rescued, but that Soren hadn't lied. Oliver was alive. Before I could relish that truth, their snarling faces settled on Newt, as if looking for their orders. Had the creepy boss man gotten to them too? Why else would they be working together? I was doomed.

Meanwhile, my dad kept working, ignoring everything.

Pierce carried a stake in his hand while Oliver had descended fangs and glowing red eyes, giving me a flashback to when he'd first shown me his true face at the ruined picnic proposal—back when I'd told Oliver to leave me alone, and he'd respected that.

"Newton Reed?" Oliver asked, dropping his offensive stance. "I shouldn't be surprised."

"My dear old friend." Newt smiled, but he didn't close the distance for a handshake or anything. "Quite serendipitous that you're here."

Oh, I was beyond doomed. This creepy monster and Oliver were *friends*. I...I didn't know what to think. Mostly, I just wanted to give up, go home, and cry for a while.

"What are you up to this time?" Oliver asked, throwing a glance at the refrigerators.

"A long time ago, you demanded to know what a 'witch chumming with vampires' wanted. I believe those were the words. Well, good news! Now's your chance." Newt's excitement would've been contagious if he weren't actively killing Soren. Or hadn't admitted he was a witch, inherently stronger than vampires and elves.

I didn't think 'doomed' was the right fit.

"Where's Soren?" Oliver demanded.

That little shred of hope I'd held onto went 'poof!' into thin air.

"He's indisposed," Newt said with a smirk and twisted his palm forward. An invisible force threw both the vampire and the elf across the room effortlessly. They slammed against the wall and fell into a crumpled heap.

I shouldn't have been excited for them to get their asses kicked, but knowing they weren't on Newt's side was an indescribable relief. Except...they were after Soren. Did they know I was here? Did they care?

Only one way to find out. "Oliver!" I called, but I think his name came out more like a squeak. I'd told them both to stay out of my life, so I didn't deserve their rescue. Even worse, my dad made a vampire weapon. Regardless of why they'd come—me or my ring in Soren's possession—I couldn't let the witch get the upper hand. "Be careful! There's—"

Newt jutted his arm in my direction, silencing me, while he casually strolled toward the still-heaping-on-the-floor Oliver and Pierce.

No! I yelled, but nothing came out. I fought the stupid plastic tie, ignoring the burning pain, but it wouldn't stretch. With gritted teeth and heart pounding in my throat, I walked over to the next row of cabinets and grabbed a disposable scalpel. I managed to slice myself several times trying to unwrap the thing and cut my ties. But I did it. I stifled a whoop of victory and rushed over to Dad. Finding whatever the witch did to me wore off, I whispered, "We have to get out of here."

"Daisy," my dad whispered, finally giving me attention. He gripped my hands in desperation. "The only people you can trust right now are the elves. You know about them, I hope?"

My eyes tracked to Pierce, who stood up with a snarl on his face and eyes glowing emerald green—the opposite of his usual bland and emotionless self.

I nodded.

"Good. Get out of here. Like your sister, run far, and don't ever come back. Don't ever stop moving. Go! Go now!"

"I can't leave without you." Tears pricked my eyes. I couldn't leave my dad. We had our issues, but he was still family, and I'd lost too much to turn my back on him.

"They need me to make the serum. I'm safe. Go now, before it's too late!" Dad forcibly pushed me back, and I stumbled over a chair and fell to the floor with a smack to my hip. Stunned, I stared in horror.

The witch effortlessly threw Oliver and Pierce again. This time they banged against the door where the thumping sounds had come from. Collecting themselves, they disappeared behind it to regroup, leaving me with a powerful witch and a dying psychotic vampire.

And a dad who wanted to sacrifice himself to save me from his creation.

Oliver

WE'D DUCKED INTO THE nearest room and pressed our backs against the door. My broken hand needed a minute to heal, and the elf and I needed a coordinated plan to slip by the witch.

And save Daisy.

It took every ounce of my strength to fight my instinct to go after her. Hence, the broken hand slowly healing.

"It had to be Newt," Pierce said, panting. "Weren't you friends a while back?"

"Before I knew what he was." I'd met Newt at a bar over a friendly game of pool. The bet grew sizeable, drawing in a crowd of spectators. In the end, Newt took the pot, but he'd said I could earn the money back. I'd needed the company more than the cash, so I'd brought him into my world. I never knew he was already in it. "It's been decades."

So, I never would've guessed the master Soren had referenced had been Newt. My little brother was a prick a lot of the time, but these recent shenanigans were too far, even for him. Now they made sense.

I didn't come here for answers. Daisy was out there, tied up, a prisoner. I needed to get her out of here, because the only thing a witch would want with a human carrying witchy DNA was to activate it for her. I wouldn't allow Pierce to decide Daisy's future, and I wouldn't let Newt either.

How was I going to beat a witch?

"What do we do now?" Pierce asked.

Needing ideas, I reached for the light switch and flipped it on. A hiss came from across the room. Knowing Newt, I expected any number of gruesome or pathetic sights. I extended my claws, ready to fight whatever else this lab had tucked away.

But I didn't expect this.

A woman with a snarling face and disheveled hair rested weakly on her knees in the empty room. Her thin arms were splayed apart by chains attached to the back wall, where claw marks had torn up the concrete. She wore nothing but a hospital gown, loosely tied, which revealed blackened veins snaking all over her throat, arms, and face. No matter how feral the woman appeared, I would never mistake that face. My heart stopped.

"Evangeline?" I asked breathlessly at the ghost I hadn't seen in decades.

"Do I know you?" That voice brought me back forty years to a memory I hoped I'd buried along with her body.

Chains rattled with her tired movements, and fever moistened her discolored skin. Vampires didn't succumb to illness, but she was clearly sick.

I rushed to her side and tried to free one blackened hand. "What happened to you?"

Evangeline Brant scrutinized me, and the moment recognition dawned on her features, I paused in my attempts at a rescue. Her face curled with unmistakable hatred. "Oliver Rockwell. I hoped to never see you again, and yet you continue to haunt me. Does my appearance make you feel guilt?"

She was going to have to be more specific. "I don't know what you're suffering from, and I can assure you I had nothing to do with it."

Evangeline lashed out against her chains. "Because of what you did to me, your friend Newt experimented on me for decades. I suppose it's fate that brought you here, since they'd finally succeeded in what they were after." She held up her blackened hand, lip curling in disgust. "And now you'll be next."

I couldn't leave Evangeline here to die like this, but I couldn't let her run free, either.

"I'd escaped this place a couple of weeks ago, leaving a trail of bodies from here to our old home. But your dear brother caught me and brought me back like a good little soldier. Not before I saw you with Daisy, and I wanted to tear her throat out right then. I couldn't kill you myself, but I told the witch about your little human. You should've heard the doctor pleading. It was pathetic."

Now I knew what to do with her, which was nothing. And Soren hadn't been responsible for all those animal attacks. I didn't understand why he'd taken credit, but he wasn't a lost cause.

But Evangeline was right about one thing. She was here because of me. "Evangeline, I'm sorry."

"Sorry? That's all you have to say? Get me out of here, and maybe I'll forgive you in a few more decades."

"You know I can't do that." I blurred away from her, returning to Pierce's side.

"I don't ever want to hear another word from you criticizing my relationships."

"Just... shut up. There's nothing more we can do here," I said.

"You're going to leave her like that?" Pierce asked.

"I have no choice."

Pierce spun his stake on his palm. "Do you want me to take care of it?"

"She's dying. Let's go." My focus was on Daisy. I ripped the door off the hinges and gripped it like a shield.

"Get back here and let me out!" Evangeline hissed behind us, chains rattling and metal straining.

Newt leaned in the corner, observing someone huddled up, and a scientist casually hunched over a microscope, completely ignoring the situation. I couldn't see Daisy. My stomach twisted in knots. "Are you ready to kick some witchy ass?"

Pierce gripped his wooden stake, and suddenly I wished we'd brought more firepower.

"Is that all you brought?" I asked.

Pierce looked at the primitive weapon in his hand. "This was a vampire assassination, not a witch hunt." He tucked it back into his pocket and unsheathed a gun from his back waistband. "Wood bullets."

"They don't need to be wood to kill a human," I admitted. "But be careful with his magic. I'm going after Daisy. You distract Newt."

Pierce palmed his pistol two-handed, and we charged. I leaped over the long counter and rushed across the room, seeking Daisy and using the door as a shield against a magic blast. I kept Newt in the corner of my eye to brace myself for an impact.

"Daisy!" I called, jumping over the next counter, and sniffing the air for clues.

Blood.

I tracked it to the other side of the scientist, whose human faculties couldn't follow my movements, and I kneeled at Daisy's side. She pressed a hand against her forehead, eyes pinched shut. Her wrists were sliced up pretty good.

"Are you okay?" I asked, heart pounding in my throat. If Newt had hurt her...

Daisy's big brown eyes opened wide in surprise. "Oliver?"

"I'm here." I took her hand and helped her to her feet, keeping the shield between us and the skirmish.

"You came for me?"

I smiled reassuringly. "Of course I did." I touched her cheek, but she didn't nestle into it.

"I'm sorry about—" Daisy started.

"I'm not sure how much Pierce can take. Let's get out of here," I interrupted. "We can talk later."

A crunch captured my attention. Pierce launched against the drywall, and his gun tumbled free of his hand.

"You!" Newt shouted, pointing at me. Perhaps the elf packed a few more punches than the witch had expected. That casual confidence was gone. Now he was raging. "I'd told you, if I ever saw you again—"

"Yeah, yeah, you'd kill me. Take a number," I said, holding Daisy in one arm and the door in the other.

The witch lifted his arms to the ceiling. "Release her and leave. This is your only chance. Otherwise, you'll be joining your lover, at least for a short while. I'll be needing a new subject."

Pierce rose, face puffy and streaked with injuries, and he collected his gun. He caught my eye and nodded. My turn to distract Newt.

I whispered into Daisy's ear, "Get down."

Daisy ducked below the lab countertop.

I taunted my old friend while strolling away from Daisy and keeping the door up as a shield. "If you want to chain me up, you'll have to do it the old-fashioned way. Come and get me."

At my feet, Daisy gasped.

Newt gritted his teeth and turned his back on me. He bent and whispered to the crumpled man on the floor. Then the witch stepped back, revealing his stooge. Soren. Alive, but barely, face pinched in pain, he was helpless against orders. Black spider webbing streaked his face, just like Evangeline's.

"Get him," Newt ordered, pointing at me.

My brother's empty eyes trained on me with a violence I hadn't seen in decades.

30

The Escape

Daisy

OLIVER TOSSED A DOOR over me. I ducked lower and covered my head just as a pistol fired. I flinched and gasped at the sharp sound. I peeked over the counter, looking for Dad, but Newt clutched his chest, agony written on his face. As the creepy witch collapsed, Soren rushed Oliver with a feral snarl. Once simply a monster in behavior, now he looked the part. Fangs descended, eyes glowed like cherries in the artificial light, fingers splayed like claws, and black lines snaked all over his damp skin.

I was no match for an angry vampire, and I didn't trust that door to do anything, but the gesture was appreciated.

While Oliver kept Soren busy, I slipped away from the door and rushed to my dad, who seemed oblivious to…everything. I tugged on his arm. "We have to go, Dad. Let's go."

He looked up from his microscope. "I have work to do. Please don't interrupt, or this will take longer." His refreshed obedience seemed to align with Newt's having given my father new orders. *'Back to work'.* It was literal. How long before it wore off again?

"We don't have time for this."

Dad sighed. "I'm busy. Do as you're told, and no one gets hurt."

I didn't have a magic cure-all in my pocket. In desperation, I tried to manipulate his orders. "Pack up your stuff. You can work from home."

"Daisy, you're getting in the way. Please, just sit down."

I grunted in frustration. What else could I do?

Across the room, Oliver wrestled against Soren's snapping jaws and swiping claws. My dad's vampire weapon concerned me. Soren had been infected with the fatal serum. Was it transmittable by bite or scratch? Or *touch*? I swallowed a lump in my throat and tugged on my dad's arm again. "What's the cure? Dad, what's the cure for this weapon you made?"

The gun fired again, and tears filled my eyelids.

Dad stared into the microscope, and fury burned through my body. All my life he'd dedicated himself to his work. I was always second...or third, or fourth. Constantly belittled for not upholding the Barrett family standards. But yet, that microscope and these test tubes had always been more important than us. Than me.

I didn't need Newt's spell to drive that point home, but it sure pissed me off. I swiped my arm across the counter, knocking trays full of red vials to the floor where they shattered on impact. I knocked over his microscope with a dull thump, and the crack of glass finally got his attention.

"Wait, what happened? What's going on?" My dad said, looking around in horror as if I'd finally woken him up.

"Can't you see what's in front of you?" I yelled at him, burning with anger.

"The spell's broken," Oliver shouted across the room.

The fight had ended. I rushed toward Oliver, dodging downed stools and lab debris. I found Soren bent over, blackened hands resting on his thighs. Both he and his brother panted.

"Newt's dead," Pierce said, rising.

"That'll do it," Oliver said.

I was relieved, and my attention shifted to what I cared about most. "Are you bit, scratched?"

Oliver said, "You don't have to worry about me."

"Dad," I pleaded. "What's the cure for the weapon you made?"

Dr. Greg Barrett looked all over his workspace and the surrounding floor. He turned to me with wild eyes. "The cure was right here. These tubes. What happened to my work?" He turned as if seeing the lab for the first time.

A sinking feeling punched my stomach down into my bowels. "The ones I broke?"

"What possessed you to...? Why would you...?" Dad furiously tried to salvage his workspace.

I turned Oliver's arms around and tipped his beautiful face, checking for wounds. Oliver seemed amused, but I wasn't. All his wounds had already healed, but I lifted his shirt to see if any serum had entered his system.

"Hey, not here," he said bashfully. "I'm as much of an exhibitionist as any other guy, but my brother and your dad are here. I do have standards."

"Now's not the time. Did you get any of the serum in you? Check your hands." While Oliver inspected himself with an inkling of concern, I called back over to my dad. "Does it transmit by touch?"

Oliver froze.

Soren slowly limped to the corner as if he carried a car on his shoulders. He breathed like a dying human, all raspy and wet. He dropped heavily onto the stool. His arms rested limply in his lap.

"I don't see any signs of infection," Oliver said. His fingers lifted my chin. "More importantly, are you okay?"

His kindness ripped away the dam of guilt. Tears welled in my eyes. "I destroyed the cure. I...I destroyed the cure."

We both looked at Soren. With vampire hearing, he knew. There was no way to save him.

"Don't worry about...me. I always knew...how this was going...to end." Soren gave us a sad smile.

I wouldn't be able to forgive some of the things he'd done. At least not for a while. But it wasn't all his fault. Like my dad, he'd been controlled. And he shouldn't have to suffer for it.

Oliver blew out a heavy breath as if thinking the same thing.

Pierce approached, sending me an apologetic smile, and said to Oliver, "Look, we can't leave your lover, no matter how much she hates you, and you owe me a staking." Pierce held up his stick.

Confused, I asked Oliver, "Your *lover* is imprisoned here?"

"Old history. Long story," Oliver said simply.

Fine, whatever. If it were old, it wasn't my business. I turned to the elf. "Since when do you fight vampires?"

Pierce blushed. "It's easier to show than explain, but you have to promise you won't be angry with me."

So he'd been messing with my head again. I wanted the truth more than I wanted to lash out. "Alright, I promise."

Pierce reached out and collected my hands. His eyes met mine and glowed green. Without any fanfare, images from a conversation sprang back into my memory. I blurted, "You're a vampire hunter! The two of you agreed to a truce, and you told me to keep my ring away from Oliver."

Which I didn't.

Oliver darted Pierce a bitter look.

"Why did you hide that from me?" I asked the elf, trying to contain my anger and somewhat failing.

"I'll take care of the prisoner," Oliver said to Pierce, ducking my fury.

Pierce watched the vampire disappear into a room. "The less you knew, the safer I thought you were. Oliver and I have a thing, but vampires can't be trusted, not even these two."

"I heard that," Soren's dry throat scratched out.

Pierce couldn't be trusted either, and there was an important part of my memory missing. "The night Soren attacked me, my roommate caught you with your hands on me. What did you do?" I glanced at Soren. Despite his condition, his hearing seemed fine. "But spare me the details."

Pierce sighed. "I healed you."

I stepped back, and my hand went to my throat. To the injury and its scars that should've been there. "What?"

"Vampires can heal unnatural wounds—stabbings, gunshots, paper cuts, blood drained from bites—but they leave behind scars. It's almost like their blood speeds up the natural healing process from weeks or months to mere minutes. Elves are better."

Soren scoffed.

"Our magic eliminates all injury entirely, and we leave behind no trace. We can also slow down disease progression to buy time to reach the hospital. I didn't want you to die from the injury Soren gave you, and I didn't want you to be left with a nasty reminder down your throat that Oliver's healing would've left you, so I took it all away. You were unconscious from blood loss, so I knew you wouldn't remember."

I wanted to hate him. I wanted to lash out at his violation of my person and hiding it from me, but...I couldn't. "Thank you," I said softly. I didn't have a single mark from Soren on me. And Pierce had always been named the best paramedic Boralis had ever had. "You heal patients, don't you?" It wasn't a question in awe of his ability. It was a soft accusation, as if he'd cheated to get where he was in life.

"Here and there."

I had to fight for every mark in med school while my dad breathed down my neck about it, and I'd still failed. Pierce had succeeded simply by birthright. Yeah, I was jealous. Since Pierce could heal with magic, I gestured at Soren. "Can you heal him?"

Pierce shook his head. "Not vampires."

My dad approached us. "All the doses of the cure are gone, but at Newt's request, his own blood contains the cure. If you can extract enough, it should work." Dad gestured at the body at our feet.

In a hurry, I grabbed an unbroken, clean vial off the counter and rushed to Newt's side. "Help me," I called to Pierce.

Pierce stood over me. "He's dead."

I began chest compressions on Newt. "Pierce, help me. We need to force his heart to pump so we can collect some blood. It's the only way to get a cure."

Pierce looked around the room. "No one needs it but Soren, and I don't see a reason to cure him." Pierce faced the dying vampire. "No offense."

"None taken," Soren said weakly, arms pressing against his middle in agony.

I kept pumping, arms rapidly growing tired. "Slice along his carotid and collect some blood."

"Desecrating a corpse isn't you, Daisy. Look at yourself." Pierce kneeled beside me, and his hands moved to gently stop my actions.

I didn't know the extent of my father's damage, and just because I didn't see effects of the serum in his system yet, didn't mean he was out of the woods entirely. And I just needed a dose. I had to have one. Tears welled in my eyes and the futile effort ahead of me. I swatted Piece's hands off mine. "Don't! Help me or go away."

Pierce sat back on his heels.

I wiped my tears on my shoulder while counting my compressions. And a dirty hand reached down to assist. An extended fingernail pressed into Newt's throat, and a line of blood seeped free. I looked up in relief but was surprised to find a disheveled woman with hair wilder than mine. Grateful for her kindness was an understatement.

"Hold the vial to collect it," I told her. "Get as much as you can."

Her dark brown eyes bore into me, and her lips quirked. "Thanks for the fix, love." Her eyes glowed cherry red, and that was when I noticed the spidery veins climbing up her throat. Her hand wasn't dirty. She had been infected too. With a smirk, she leaned down and bit Newt.

"No!" I couldn't stop pumping or the blood would stop, but this vampire was going to drain him. "Stop, please stop."

She lifted herself free, blood smearing her lips, and she sighed. Before my eyes, the darkness in her veins faded. Her face relaxed as if an exhausting pain had been eased. She got up and ran away barefoot in a hospital gown, which was untied, showing off her naked backside. It was a nice backside, too.

Oliver stood just out of reach, watching her go. The look in his eyes made me think she'd been his old lover? That didn't matter now.

"Oliver, help me. I can't keep the blood moving much longer," I pleaded, breathing heavily with the effort.

Pierce reached for my hands again.

"Touch me, and I will kill you." I didn't mean it, but I hated that he wouldn't help.

Oliver stared at the empty doorway as if he were considering chasing after her.

"Oliver, please."

After the longest moment in my life, Oliver crouched beside me. "Newt's not worth saving, Daisy. Trust me."

"Dad said his blood is the cure. I need to collect it. I think that vampire drank too much."

Oliver grabbed the vial and held it to the puncture wounds. Only a few drops came out. He used a clawed fingernail and opened the wounds wider. More drops came out.

"No, no, it's almost all gone," I said, whining. My compressions weren't effective. I was too weak and way too tired.

"Oh, fine. Move over." Pierce brushed me aside and took over. His movements were perfectly rapid and sufficiently rib-breaking. The blood pumped, and while I rested, Oliver filled the rest of the vial. Pierce stopped.

"No, keep going," I pleaded. "We need more than one dose."

"Why?" Pierce asked.

I took the vial and gave Pierce a meaningful look. "In case Soren isn't the only one infected."

I brought the vial over to Soren. The vampire looked at me with utter confusion. "What's that for?"

"I believe in second chances."

Soren groaned, and his face pinched, forehead dripping with sweat. The blackness was climbing up his chin. "I don't deserve that."

Agreed. "You probably don't, but I'm willing to see you prove me wrong."

Soren met my eyes. Guilt and pain crossed his face, and after a long beat, gratitude. I pushed the vial closer, and Soren tipped it into his mouth, swallowing it in a single swig. His face softened as the pain receded and the blackened veins retreated. Soren sighed. "Thank you."

"Don't make me regret that," I warned Soren.

"Pierce," I yelled while watching Soren's miraculous healing. "You better have another dose for me."

"Who's it for?" Oliver asked, resting a hand on my shoulder.

"We don't know how many vials of the weapon got out of here or who has them." And I needed a supernatural security blanket. I couldn't lose Oliver. Not after all this, and not even when I'd been mad at him.

Pierce held out a corked glass vial filled with blood, and I pocketed it. Never before had I felt such reassurance. With a smile, I said, "Let's get out of here."

Pierce led the way out, and Oliver helped his brother to his feet.

I paused at the door. "Are you coming, Dad?"

Dr. Greg Barrett's blank stare at the mess in the lab had me worried all over again.

"What is it?" I approached him and hooked my arm around his.

"Because of the nature of my work, I denied the request to install security cameras. But I don't know how they're going to respond to that." Dad pointed to Newt's body with two bullet holes and a torn-out throat. After the blood loss, his skin turned almost translucent, a pale shade of gray.

"That's not our problem right now. We need to get out of here." I tugged my dad's arm and rushed him out the door. "We need to find out if Newt released more of that weapon." I pulled the vial from my pocket. "I have the cure. Can you make more from this?"

Dad pocketed the vial in his white lab coat. "I'll see what I can do."

31
Trapped by the Sun

Daisy

WE SCRAMBLED ACROSS THE parking lot of PDI, security lights illuminating our path, where only a handful of cars slept soundly. I hugged Dad's arm as I brought him to his car as if I was afraid he'd drop over from exhaustion...or disappear again. Dad was the only family I had within reach, and I didn't want to be alone. Pierce stayed by my shoulder, smartly keeping a short distance between us. We finally reached Dad's commuter car, and he unlocked the doors with his fob.

My ex dropped into Dad's passenger seat. Since when did he claim shotgun?

Dad shrugged me off his arm and climbed in too. "Daisy, get in the car."

Pierce leaned toward Dad and echoed the order. "Daisy, get in."

I hesitated. I should get in the car, and I needed to talk to Dad about all this mess, especially why Pierce casually joined Dad without even asking. But I glanced over my shoulder at the sleek candy-apple red sports car, which I assumed had the 306 horsepower Oliver had referenced.

The car was pretty with its white racing stripes, but that was not what I looked at.

The vampire leaned against the shiny hood in a relaxed state, with his arms and ankles crossed, patiently waiting. His clothing was disheveled and torn, and his hair was a mess, but he wasn't rushing to get out of here. And he looked only at me. My heart fluttered.

"Daisy, hurry up," Pierce said.

Soren had already claimed the back of the two-door sports car. The passenger door was wide open.

An invitation. No pressure. No rush.

The chat Oliver and I needed to have was far more appealing. Yes, appealing was exactly what Oliver was. "I'm riding with them. See you at home."

As I walked away, Pierce called, "Daisy, I warned you about them. Look what they did to the place. You almost got killed. Come with us. Daisy? Daisy, come back here."

I swatted the air behind me, acknowledging his words and giving him my silent answer. If he wouldn't stop, he'd get a different kind of gesture next—a one-fingered salute. I strolled over to Oliver's car, and the sexy vampire's lips lifted. My stupid heart fluttered again at his intense gaze.

"Too crowded over there?" he asked playfully.

"Like a sardine can from hell."

Oliver chuckled and swiftly assisted me into his passenger seat. I checked on Soren, not trusting him yet. I didn't know him at all now that the spell had been broken. Soren sprawled across the back bench, arms folded over his chest, head shrouded in shade. He was closed off—definitely not in the mood to talk.

Dad's car motored away, and I was relieved to have them gone.

Oliver dropped into the driver's seat and fired up the deep, rumbling engine. A goofy grin pulled at my lips at the vibration beneath me. I buckled in, and after the latch clicked, Oliver tore off through the parking lot, shifting through the gears, and shoving me hard into the seat.

The grin stayed in place.

We zipped down the highway heading north, ignoring all posted speed limits, and since the early morning commuters typically headed south to the big city, traffic was thin.

Oliver glanced out my side window and frowned. "We're not going to make it."

"What? Why?" I looked behind us, expecting the dreaded red and blues, but all I saw was the encroaching dawn on a nearly empty highway.

"Speak for yourself," Soren said dryly with a quirk of his lips. He wriggled his fingers, teasing Oliver with...my Aunt Lisa's ring. My turn to frown. I shouldn't have taken so long to choose. One ring. Two brothers. If they fought over it now, I didn't know who'd win. And there wasn't time for fighting.

"I know a place. Hang tight." Oliver shifted into a higher gear and, after swerving around a vehicle, he took an exit.

While still relaxed in the back, Soren said, "We're in Peshtigo, like five miles from town. Use your lead foot to get the job done."

Pink and purple streaked the sky. Dawn would break within minutes, and the sun's rays would sweep across the land. I glanced at Oliver's white-knuckled grip on the wheel.

"This car doesn't happen to have that fancy window coating, does it?" I asked Oliver.

"Negative," he said, watching the coming dawn as if our car was in pursuit. "Affects the resale value."

Soren said, "Then you should've gotten two. One to drive like a vampire and one to admire. Not like you couldn't afford it."

I was annoyed at the victim blaming. I said to Soren, "Give him the ring back, and this won't be an issue."

The younger vampire scoffed. "For him."

"Then quit complaining about the detour," I said, exasperated. He sure didn't act his age.

Oliver took a few corners that had me frantically searching for the oh-shit handles above the door's window. There weren't any. The next turn screeched tires to turn onto a dirt road.

"There's not much out here. Where are we going?" I asked, glancing nervously at the sun's rays behind us.

The headlights lit up a small log cabin in the dense woods. Sunlight beamed through the tree canopy and glistened off the roof's morning dew. Oliver punched the brakes to a screeching halt. As he yanked the parking brake, he tracked the sunlight creeping lower and lower, heading down the aged logs toward the front door.

He wasn't going to make it. "Oliver, go!" I said as he tore out of the car, leaving the door open in his wake. I rushed out after him, but Soren remained in the back seat, as if this was entertaining. Jerk.

While Oliver searched around the cabin's porch for a key, the sun reached the top of the door, and I searched for something to use as protection against the sun. Spinning in place, I found twigs, pine needles, and a few large logs. Damn it. I ran to the side of the cabin and found nothing but an electrical box and a house-sized propane tank.

"Just break the door," Soren said, boredom on his tongue. "It's not like it's yours anyway."

With nothing else to protect him, I took off my shirt, ran up behind him, and held it up like an umbrella. The sun sizzled the back of Oliver's head and neck. Clothing wasn't made like it used to be. I tried to keep him semi-shaded while he yelled and flipped a potted plant that had long since died. Smoke danced above his head while the now stomach-churning sound of sizzling bacon turned my insides. The dirty key was there.

Oliver unlocked the door and disappeared inside in a flash. I still held my shirt over my head when Oliver faced me from the safety of the darkness.

"That's the second-best morning view I've ever seen," he said.

"I agree. Not bad at all," Soren said from behind me. I quickly put my shirt back on, face burning bright red.

Sun glinted in Soren's hair, and his shadow was cast along the dusty floor. "As much as this won't be fun, I'm out of here. Enjoy camping." Soren vanished into the woods using super speed.

"He's a jerk."

"And that's when he's in a good mood," Oliver added.

I shivered.

I'd been expecting a ride home to shower and sleep. In reality, I wanted to make absolutely certain Dad found a safe place for that vial of the cure and promised to make more. This place was cramped, filthy, and didn't appear to have running water. I held out my hand expectantly. "If you're healed, let's get out of here. I'll cover you while you run for the trunk."

Oliver blinked at me. "Did you just suggest that?"

It sounded like a reasonable plan. "Like Soren said, we're only five miles from town. I think you've handled worse."

Oliver handed over the keyring, and I climbed into the glorious vehicle, which I could admire in daylight. Slick leather seats. Cushion-wrapped steering wheel. I didn't realize how much I liked the feeling of power under my hands...not that I could afford a car like this in my entire lifetime. But since I got to pretend for a day, I was going to enjoy it. Then I checked for the trunk release, planning on backing up to the door, and that was when I noticed the big glaring problem in my plan.

Dejected, I got out of the car and shut the door. I could hike miles through the woods without a compass, but I shouldn't get lost around here. I'd be navigating my way across rivers and streams in my jogging shoes. Drinking dirty water. Nothing to eat for miles. Or I could spend the day with Oliver, alone in a rustic cabin.

That was an easy choice.

The vampire leaned against the kitchenette's countertop directly across from the door, arms and ankles crossed, patiently waiting. His toes were just out of the sun's reach. I bashfully closed the door, engulfing him in safety, and returned the keys.

"It's a stick," he said, assuming the problem.

"It's a stick," I confirmed, and should've noticed.

"I'll teach you," he said. I looked up at him. A warm smile lifted his lips. "Just not today."

I snorted. It was so hard to hold on to my anger. I almost couldn't remember why I was mad at him in the first place.

"I'm sure we can find something to do." Oliver rummaged through the kitchen cabinets.

Somehow I didn't think we'd find fresh limes in there.

The cabin was small on the outside and even tighter on the inside. The kitschy hunter theme was overdone. Moose and bear-themed blankets were tacked over the windows, blocking most of the light. The single full-size bed was covered in a camouflage comforter, and an end table held a bedside lamp with a black bear on it. A tiny folding table and chairs leaned near the door. I opened them up and set them in place. Then I searched for a bathroom. The first door was a broom closet, and the second, a tiny bathroom with enough space to turn around. I'd camped in RVs with bathrooms bigger than this. A sink, toilet, and a shower—perfunctory. The rugs and shower curtain were all camo-themed.

I tested the sink faucet, and it worked, surprisingly. Not wanting a full cold shower, I washed up to the best of my ability. As I dressed in my dingy workout clothes, I heard the dreaded sizzle, and I frantically finished dressing to rush to Oliver's side. He had a pan on the stove loaded with corned beef hash.

"Are you making breakfast?" A visual of the promised naked breakfast flashed through my mind, and a heat wave tore through me.

Oliver's lips lifted as if he could hear that. "It's not going to be gourmet with the choices here, but it'll be edible."

Oliver rifled through the cabinets and found a bowl and a spoon. He brought me the whole can and sat across from me without his own.

"Thank you," I said, feeling the need to express some gratitude.

Oliver leaned forward, hands clasped on the table's surface. "Doesn't take enhanced hearing to pick up on your stomach."

"I mean it," I repeated. "And not just for this. You saved my life back there." I paused and fished for what I wanted to know. "Whether you intended to or not."

Oliver reached out for my spoonless hand, but stopped himself short. "I needed help or perhaps...fodder." He gave me a small smile. "So, I'd promised the elf a chance to stake Soren, which was why he'd agreed to join me. I didn't know whether he'd be there. I also didn't you if you'd be, either. Understand this: I only thought of you—keeping you safe—and that meant neutralizing the threat first."

That was reassuring, but like me, he'd had a long night and he'd gone through the effort of cooking. I pointed at my bowl with my spoon. "You're not going to have any?"

"Vampires don't eat."

I set down my spoon, suddenly having lost my appetite. There was one downside to being trapped in a tight space with a vampire. I cleared my throat, wishing for my frailest body part to remain intact. "Are you *hungry*?"

Oliver flashed his dazzling whites. "I'm fine. You dig in."

That was a relief. Just like that, my appetite returned with a vengeance, and I didn't have to share. I shoveled in the steamy and satisfying mush while Oliver watched. When I'd nearly finished, he said softly, "Thank you."

I scraped together the last crumbs of meat. "For what?"

"I know Soren's a selfish ass, but he's my brother. I know what he's done to you, and despite that, I appreciate your having given him the cure. That says more about you than him."

"I've always believed in second chances."

Oliver met my gaze. "And I would've been ash if you hadn't blocked the sun for me."

"Why didn't you kick the door open like Soren suggested?" Seemed like an easy answer at the time. Would've spared me more exposure than I'd planned.

Oliver looked at his fingers on the table again. He said softly, "I'm not strong enough right now. So, I also need to thank you for helping when my own family wouldn't."

I didn't think he was referring to the cabin door. "Likewise."

Oliver tilted his head at me in silent question.

"You tried to give me my freedom, but all Pierce wanted was to control me. How could I respect someone who messed with my free will?"

Oliver dropped his eyes once more. Despite his confidence, he truly carried shame.

That was the reaction of someone feeling guilt. "What is it?" I asked, brow furrowing.

"Daisy, I've lived my life by two simple rules. The first led me to the lab—no harming my loved ones. The second forced me to protect you from our world. While tracking Soren, I found the gravely injured basketball player, and I fed him my blood to heal him, but I was too late. He'd died with just enough of my blood to begin the transition process. You were right—he was dead, but he also moved. By snapping his neck, I prevented him from attacking you and unleashing an out-of-control baby vampire into the city. I erased that memory out of obligation."

Having the truth was a relief, and his explanation seemed perfectly logical. "Soren explained to me how it worked. Although he didn't admit to killing my patient."

Oliver didn't lighten up. "Evangeline did."

Images of the wild woman with a crazy nest of hair and bloody medical gown came to mind, and I remembered Pierce had told me there were a lot of vampires out there, not quite worded that way. I shuddered at the thought. "The lab patient who escaped after sucking back the cure from Newt?"

Oliver nodded, clearly not wanting to go into his history with her. "There was another reason I took away that memory. I wanted to get closer to you. Since I'm being fully transparent here, I wanted my ring back, and I was willing to do whatever it took to get it." He gazed into my eyes as the memories of our bedroom escapades returned to my mind. "And I have no regrets."

As far as our bedroom activities, I didn't either.

Oliver kept going, and I wasn't going to stop him. "The night Pierce proposed, you said you hated him for interfering with your free will. The basketball player incident wasn't the first time I erased your memory. So if you want to hate Pierce for doing it, you have to hate me, too."

I blinked. The hypocrisy was insulting, and right now, trudging through the woods for miles wholly unprepared sounded tempting. I collected my dishes and got up, unable to look at him. I set the bowl in the sink, dug under the cabinet for soap, and washed the dishes with more vigor than necessary.

"Daisy, talk to me." Oliver was right behind me. I could feel his presence on my skin like an electrical current, and I was too close.

I fought tears from forming. I couldn't trust anyone. "Was it real?" I said while swiping the dishes clean with a washcloth.

"Was what real?"

I slammed the dish in the sink and turned around. "Us. Everything between us. Was it real, or were you only trying to manipulate the ring from me?"

Oliver stared me straight in the eye. I wanted him to see the pain he had caused me. I wanted the guilty to eat at him.

His hands touched my arms as if preparing to compel me, and I pulled away, eyes squeezed shut. "No. I want to hear the truth without you touching me, without looking me in the eye, so without any doubt, my head is my own."

"Daisy, if I'm compelling you, my eyes would glow. Same as Pierce's, but a different color. Now you know, and you can try to prevent it before it's too late. Look at me and see that I'm not manipulating you."

I'd figured out how it worked, but I also knew the time between realizing what was going on while still having the ability to stop it was inhumanly too short. But I wanted him to prove he wasn't betraying me again, so I looked. His pale gray eyes stared back at me.

But they glistened with tears. "I am going to show you the remaining memory I erased. Then you can decide what you want to believe about me. And if you never want to see me again, I'll dip out for good."

Emotion clogged my throat. I only nodded.

He captured my eyes, and the red glow returned too quickly for me to break free of it. "Remember the accident."

The pressure in my head exploded, and my heart pounded in my chest. I held my head between my hands as my history rewrote itself before my eyes. Images flooded my vision—pieces of the car accident I never knew were missing. Every one of those pieces featured Oliver's beautiful face.

I hadn't been strong enough to save myself. I hadn't dragged myself from the car and left my family to die. Oliver had busted out my window and...tore the door off the hinges. He'd saved me, but my family was already gone. It wasn't my fault I lived while they died. I couldn't have done anything.

Oliver had fed me his blood to heal me. Without him, I would've died too. On top of saving my life, he'd made me question what I really wanted, setting me on the path to figuring out myself, and breaking up with Pierce. Oliver had congratulated me on my graduation when no one else had. Oliver the vampire was my supporter, my hero.

As the pain receded, I straightened and calmed my breathing. I looked at the vampire, angry that he'd kept that from me. "Why did you make me believe I'd saved myself?"

"I wanted to show you how strong you could be."

"How noble," I said bitterly. That wasn't what I wanted to hear, deep down. But what was I looking for?

"Daisy." Oliver cradled my hands in his, and it took every ounce of concentration to allow it. "You remember the lab patient who'd escaped?"

I nodded.

"Evangeline Brant was my last serious relationship. Now you know how that ended. Please understand, humans and vampires don't mix. I'd learned that lesson."

"She wasn't human," I protested, breaking free of his grip.

He stared at me pointedly. Oh. She used to be and now she despised him.

"I erased myself to allow you to explore the future you wanted—to allow you to have a normal life."

While leaving me in the clutches of the brain-blasting elf? Oliver had erased the truth, which was the same as removing the choice from me.

The vampire dug into his pocket and opened a metal container—jewelry sized. "I meant to give you this as soon as I found you, but things were more chaotic than I expected."

With the dreaded sizzle, he lifted out a locket on a silver chain. The longer he held it, the more my stomach twisted.

"It's hurting you."

"It's supposed to." He offered it to me on his palm. "It'll stop vampires and elves from using compulsion on you. It guarantees your free will."

His hand continued to burn. Blisters formed. Smoke lifted in tendrils, and sweat beaded on his forehead. The pain must've been agonizing. Satisfied with his sacrificial suffering, I took the necklace and placed it over my head. Despite where we stood, guaranteeing my free will wasn't a hard sell.

A sad smile lifted his lips. "Don't ever take it off."

32

He's Back

Daisy

I'D TAKEN A NAP on the scratchy cabin mattress, but I still felt like I'd run two marathons and skipped sleep for a week. Oliver had crashed on the floor. When night fell, we'd silently returned to town, and Oliver pulled to the curb at Dad's house. The engine rumbled beneath me.

Hand ready to open the door, my mouth opened to say something, but I couldn't figure out which was most appropriate. My dad made a weapon to kill your kind, and I'm sorry? Your brother almost killed me but later decided to kidnap me for leverage, so we're even? Or you made me forget you snapped the neck of an innocent man, so I wouldn't discover what you were—what he was becoming? Or you blocked my memories of your heroism at my car accident so...I could have a better life without you and not get any say in the matter?

But that was in the past. What if things could be different going forward? I'd noticed his lips twitch when my heartbeat changed. I'd always wonder, was Oliver hearing my words or listening to my pumping arteries?

The necklace he'd given me was supposed to keep my head my own. But I didn't want to test it, so how could I trust it? I'd never be fully certain of what I knew was real and whether my decisions were my own choice.

And I didn't want to become Evangeline.

My witch roommates, my dad, and Pierce himself had all warned me. Vampires and humans didn't mix. That much was crystal clear. But it hurt. It hurt so much. I had to let Oliver go, and he knew it too, which was why he didn't say a word.

I climbed out of the sexy sports car, gleaming under the streetlights in the candy apple red of his hungry eyes, exactly what I'd expected Oliver to drive. Without further hesitation, I walked straight to Dad's house, no longer awkward about barging in unannounced.

Pierce Evansson appeared in the doorway, startling me. He must've crashed on the couch, waiting for me to return.

The rumble of the engine leaving the curb sparked both yearning—Come back! How could you give up so easily?—and plenty of anger. How could I be with someone I couldn't trust?

My fingers slid along the chain of the locket he'd given me as I avoided eye contact with the elf. I walked around him and ducked my head into the fridge. It wasn't hard to find the single cure vial courtesy of Newt's throat. It was intact and ready to make more.

"Where've you been, Daisy?" Pierce asked.

Oliver

THE SHELBY IDLED BENEATH my grip, waiting for the garage door to lift. I'd never been so grateful to be home. Pierce had Dr. Greg Barrett wrapped around his finger, and there was no telling how deeply the elf's compulsion nested in her mind. With Newt's spell broken, she wasn't in mortal danger any longer, so Daisy should stay safe. Giving her the necklace, so she could maintain her own free will from this point onward, was the best I could do for her. She had to decide what she wanted, but the playing field had already been tipped in the elf's favor. I tried to play a game I had no hope of winning.

The only loser was Daisy.

I went inside and dropped my keys in the tray by the back door, their weight unbearable. I needed a drink.

"You like that human," Soren said, leaning against the wall by the bar.

I wasn't in the mood to talk. "What are you doing here?"

"It's obvious. Isn't it?"

"That doesn't answer my question." I was covered in torn, bloody clothes, and I'd slept on the floor of a filthy cabin for a day with the scent of singed hair on me. Daisy had silently fumed at me, both before and after she slept. And after thinking on it, she'd still rejected me. So, I wasn't in the mood to entertain Soren, who was responsible for at least half my problems.

"Vampire's extreme emotions were so exhausting sometimes. Listen, I can see you don't want to hear it, but I'm sorry about how all this happened."

"Don't." I waved in dismissal as I passed by. I didn't need him to say it wasn't his choice to almost kill or to kidnap Daisy or rip out her best friend's throat. Compulsion used to be a vampire and elf ability. I wished it had stayed that way.

"There's something you need to know," Soren insisted.

"Then it can wait until I have a drink in my hand."

Soren grabbed my arm and spun me to face him. I only entertained his insistence when I saw remorse. I'd never seen it on him before, not even after he'd drained Evangeline and left her to die, just to make his point.

"This isn't easy for me." Soren shifted his weight, but he held my gaze. "I was forced to work for Newt after he captured me forty years ago, and I was the one who tracked down Evangeline and brought her to PDI for experimentation all that time ago."

"Yet you didn't tell me she was alive."

"Newt had forced my silence. She escaped a few weeks ago, and it took me too long to recapture her."

I knew where he was headed with this, but it was easier to hate him than to forgive.

"After I brought her back to the lab, you may have noticed the dead bodies stopped. She killed those people around town, not me, and then I was sent back to collect Daisy."

"But you would've killed her."

Soren squirmed. "I abstained for too long and got a little carried away. What was her friend's name? I am genuinely sorry for that."

"I'd pieced together most of that myself. Is there something truly worth delaying my need for a drink?" I was being dismissive, but my mood hadn't yet improved.

Soren shifted and rubbed the back of his neck. "The serum Evangeline and I had in our systems wasn't the end of the supply."

And that just accelerated my need. I slipped behind the bar, set a rocks glass on the wood, and opened a bottle of tequila. The good host in me hesitated. "You want one?"

"Aren't you listening to me? Getting drunk isn't going to fix this."

"Look, I don't care how Evangeline's alive...still. And the vampire weapon doesn't matter anymore. Newt's dead. Besides a small circle of us, no one else knows about it, so it's not a threat." I poured a double shot.

"It does matter. Come on, pull your head out of your ass. Who do you think made that serum?"

My fingers gripped the bottle too tightly, and it shattered. Tequila rained down on me, soaking my already ruined clothes. I gritted my teeth. Just great. A waste of perfectly good booze. "Daisy's dad, under a dead witch's spell. Case closed."

"I can see it's too soon to have a chat about the big fat elephant in the room." Soren glared at me, and I returned it right back. Nothing he'd said made me feel better. All of it was a waste of time, and I suspected whatever came next fit into that category just right.

I collected a new rocks glass.

My brother sighed. "Can I give you one piece of advice?"

"Feel free, but don't be shocked if I ignore it." I gulped down my next drink, relishing the warmth trailing down my throat.

"Daisy's a special kind of human." No kidding, I thought. "Go get her."

I scoffed. Being what I was had spelled doom for us before we even began. That was the only thing my brother had taught me well. "For her own good, I let her go. You should be proud you prevented another Evangeline. Mission accomplished."

Genuine anger pinched his face. "Daisy is certainly no Evangeline. She knew what you are and didn't send the pitchfork brigade after us. On the contrary. Can't you see that? You're pathetic. You're going to let an elf take her. God, not much is worse than that."

I counted a few breaths to calm myself. "She's wearing black nightshade...and vervain in case you get any ideas. You sound awfully passionate about a woman who means nothing to you."

"She said she believed in second chances, and despite all I put her through, she saved my life. That woman is capable of some gymnastic-level forgiveness." Soren paused while I considered his words. "On second thought, stay here. You don't deserve her."

I finished my next glass in a single swallow. Daisy was generous and compassionate, caring for those who didn't deserve it. Soren was proof, and I was a close second. After learning the sun ring would help me function and blend in, Daisy had given it to me, her most precious keepsake from her Aunt Lisa.

If I could have her, I would never let her go. I wanted her more than anything I'd ever wanted in my life. But she had witches for roommates, an elf with his metaphorical claws in her, and a dad who made a vampire weapon for an old enemy.

It was a battle sure to end in suffering, heartbreak, and probably a few deaths. But most importantly, she had to choose me.

A rattle of metal turned my head. My sun ring rocked gently on my bar, sparkling in the spilled tequila. I turned to face my brother, but he was gone. Soren was never known for being kind, and I stared at the ring while tears welled in my eyes.

There was still hope for him. The bastard.

Daisy

I CLEANED UP AND slept restlessly in my old childhood bed, but I awoke finally having a chance to feel normal again. Instead of carrying on as usual, I sat on a barstool at my dad's kitchen island, avoiding the elf's gaze by staring wistfully at the front door. I wanted to hate Oliver, but I didn't. Pissed, yes. Hate, not at all. In all honesty, after a relaxing hot shower, even the pissed wasn't sticking around.

Could I forgive his intrusion into my head? And if so, could I live with his being a vampire and all the gruesomeness that entailed? Could I forgive every time he had to take a life when I dedicated mine to saving people? In the van, Soren had laughed when I suggested Oliver fed directly from people.

I fingered the chain around my neck. Oliver had protected me from any and all future attempts to mess with my head by other vampires, by all elves, and even by himself. I wished I had Lily to talk to, but how could I drag her into this unbelievable world?

Assuming I could get her to show up for more than three minutes at a funeral.

"I made coffee." Pierce touched my shoulder, and I shrugged his hand away. As usual, the elf misread my disgust as soreness. "Are you hurt at all?"

I didn't care about the bruises or my shredded wrists. "No."

"Let me check you," Pierce said, lowering himself next to me.

Knowing he could erase scars and seemed truly concerned about my well-being, I allowed his touch. He tilted my face, checking both sides of my throat. A surge of anger made my hands shake. With shredded wrists, I swatted him away.

Oliver had said he'd used the elf as fodder and that Pierce only joined him with promises of killing Soren. So I figured their feud wasn't over, but that they'd come to some sort of understanding. I was wrong and insulted. "Is that all you care about—that the vampires don't win?"

"This has nothing to do with them. A lot went down in that lab, and I want to make sure you're alright. Can I search you for wounds?" At least he asked permission this time.

Dad clambered down the stairs and darted straight for the coffeepot without so much as a good morning.

I rose and glanced at the front door again, wishing Oliver would bust it down and sweep me off my feet. But it was daytime, so I was on my own.

Unlike the elf, I felt safe with Oliver, and I believed everything he did was in my best interest, whether I liked it or not. I needed to get out of here.

I said to Dad, "I wanted to make sure you're okay, and that the cure made it home safely, but I can't stay."

Dad sighed and brought his coffee over to the island. "Pierce, give me space with my daughter."

The elf-slash-vampire-hunter nodded and left the house, the door closing tightly behind him. Dad and I never had the best relationship, so I still couldn't relax.

Dad sat on the stool Pierce had just vacated, holding a steaming mug of coffee. He smiled kindly, but behind those eyes, all I saw was the cold, calculated scientist more concerned with reputation and accolades than hurting the people he was supposed to care for most—his family. Dad must've had a good explanation for going against his Hippocratic oath—this entire life—of common decency and respect for medicine and people.

"I did know, kitten."

"Know what?" I asked, already on edge. I hated that pet name. Always did. It felt so...patronizing, especially since Dad hated animals. But that wasn't a battle for today.

"Since you couldn't handle medical school—"

"Dad," I interrupted. I didn't need a rehash of my failings...of what he believed to be my failings.

"Daisy, I'm getting old. I'm not going to be around forever. Having a family was the next best thing for your stability, and Pierce wanted to provide that for you."

I scoffed in disbelief. "Yeah, I couldn't manage the hardest school on the planet. So what? I still graduated with a degree, have a career I adore, and pay my own bills as a grown-ass adult. And yet, you still can't respect me for who I am. Now I hear you and the elf have been plotting behind my back as if I were some asset to transact? Were you going to have him compel me into accepting his proposal?"

Dad tried to touch my leg reassuringly. I rose to avoid it, and he stood up to meet me. "Once I learned about the hidden world, and that Newt had plans for me, I spiked all the water bottles in the house with black nightshade and vervain, because I knew you drank them. That was my way of protecting you."

The herby flavor that only his water had, even when I'd bought the same brand to replace them. I was surprised he cared, but that wasn't enough.

"You two seemed great together, and Pierce couldn't compel you to do what he wanted. I made sure it was your choice." Dad smiled warmly.

But he hadn't vetted the elf completely. As soon as the witch blocked him from returning home, the spiked water ran out, and Pierce jumped into my head and took the wheel. If Dad really wanted my relationship to be my choice, he could've...told me the truth. "Am I supposed to say thank you? Because I don't feel like it."

"Sit down. Let me finish the story."

I wanted to be anywhere but here, but as long as Dad was being honest, I wanted to hear it. I returned to the stool, and Dad lowered himself next to me.

"Mr. Newton Reed had proposed a medical advancement for the safety of mankind. He wasn't a doctor, nor did he have research credentials, but that caught my attention."

His ego would've gripped onto that life a lifeline.

"After I wrapped my head around the hidden world, I believed the serum would save thousands of people, as he'd claimed. Here's where I misunderstood the intentions. I expected the serum to be used widely and invisibly in human food, rendering people inedible to vampires. They would seek other food sources. I never expected my formula to be made into a weapon that delivered a slow, agonizing death, so I refused. That decision cost your mother her life."

I'd always thought the coincidence was too suspicious—my and Abby's accident on the same day as my mom's. Hearing my suspicions confirmed was a punch to the gut. "Mom didn't die in a car accident?"

Dad shook his head.

Newt! I wished Pierce had shot him a few more times for good measure. Soren had been a puppy compared to Newt. Good thing the witch was dead.

Dad had lied to me this whole time about his work, his plans, about Mom's death—murder. I stood up. Disgust didn't scratch the surface.

"How could you keep something like this from me? I was walking around like the world was innocent and good, worthy of saving, and behind my back, you're working with monsters to create weapons and putting everyone you're supposed to love in harm's way." What else didn't I know? My sister had run off immediately after Mom's death. "Why won't Lily come home?"

"I told her to leave town for her own safety, like I told you in the lab."

Only one of us had listened. A shaky sigh escaped my lips, and I rushed out of the house. I needed to clear my head.

"Daisy, wait!"

33

The Race

Oliver

SOREN HAD LIVED BY the moon as long as I had, so I wasn't worried about how he'd manage without the ring. And I knew how hard it was to give up after a taste of the sun, which made me appreciate the gesture even more.

I slipped the ruby onto my finger. This ring was my mother's creation, which reminded me of her and brought her closer to me. It was priceless simply for that reason. I made a fist, locking the ring tightly against my finger, and I pressed it to my lips.

But the spell imbued upon it meant I was free. I could walk among the humans, not as a silent predator lurking in the shadows to pounce on my prey, but as a man with peculiar tastes, who craved the company of others. In all my endless decades, no one had accepted me for what I was.

And I was tired of being alone.

Evangeline Brant had ended in disaster, but I didn't have the heart to leave her in the lab to be discovered by security and carted off to a hospital, tested, prodded, marveled at...exposed. I hadn't forgiven Soren for what he did to her, and she clearly hadn't forgiven me.

After I had been selfish with Evangeline, I'd vowed, no matter the circumstances, I wouldn't be that selfish again. So, the one person I needed in my life would never become a monster like me. Which meant that whatever happiness I carved out for myself would always be temporary.

Witches and vampires were more volatile than oil and water. Combustible. Incompatible with nature. An eight-cylinder engine in a saltwater ocean. Impossible. If an event triggered Daisy's genetic witchcraft, then our time would be even more temporary than I'd hoped.

I'd been avoiding making a connection for years, but now, I would take temporary with her over nothing at all. Damned the pain. I'd take it all. And if I had to fight a war and grovel to the end of time...

So be it.

With burgeoning hope and a flourish of excitement, I rushed up to my bedroom and showered, washing away the blood and destruction, and I changed into my favorite custom-tailored suit—navy blue with a mauve dress shirt. I left the top buttons unfastened at my throat for a casual look and checked my shiny shoes for scuffs. Sophisticated but stylish, like an upscale Mardi Gras ball. I smoothed my dark locks in the mirror and ignored the week-old scruff on my jaw. Having already wasted the entire night drowning myself in booze, I grabbed my keys and headed to the garage.

The black nightshade and vervain locket would help her against Pierce Evansson, but it would be useless if the elf and doctor figured out what it was and removed it from her. Horrific to consider? Absolutely, but it wasn't beyond the nature of an elf.

And I didn't trust her father.

Rather than continue to fight against their smear campaign, I was going to defend myself and win Daisy's heart the honest way.

I climbed into my Shelby and fired up the throaty engine. I roared through town, commanding a wide berth on the road, and I stopped at the florist shop. Checking the time on the dash, I had a few minutes before closing, so I rushed inside and bought the exact same bouquet I'd given her at work in the breakroom. Ruby roses, golden sunflowers, and mauve blooms with greens accenting the flowers. They coordinated with my suit.

This time I remembered a vase, and I filled out the card. My hand shook with anticipation and nerves, like a young man worried about his date rejecting him. I snorted to myself. I was Oliver Rockwell, a business owner, luxury car driver, fine-suit-wearing hundred-and-eighty-something year old vampire.

Within minutes, I pulled to the curb at her dad's house, where I'd left her, where her car rested. I took the steps two at a time, holding the bouquet and squeezing the ring securely with my fist—which also stood for my brother's encouragement. I knocked furiously. After the long night we all had, I expected them to still be asleep, but this couldn't wait.

I knocked harder.

The door opened, and the scowling face before me was her father. "She's not here."

That I didn't expect. "Where did she go?"

"I don't know. She didn't leave on good terms, and I suspect you're the reason for that."

Being accused of placing Daisy's life in danger, whether or not that was true, sent a bolt of anger through me. My instinct was to compel the information out of him, but since he'd worked for a witch, I didn't waste the time. If he weren't Daisy's father, I would've snacked and snapped. Instead, I gritted my teeth. "What do you mean?"

"Vampires are the scourge of the world. Get off my porch."

Dr. Greg Barrett slammed the door shut in my face. My fists trembled with rage, straining every muscle and tendon, but I relaxed my hand before shattering the glass vase. I couldn't waste precious time on him.

I dropped into my car and sped off to Daisy's house. There were only so many places she would go.

Daisy

I COULDN'T STAY IN that house one more moment or I would've screamed. So I'd bolted out the door, and morning dew soaked my dirty shoes as I walked to the trail and found my phone. Dirty, but functioning fine. Then I began the long trek home across town. I needed to clear my head, and I couldn't trust myself to drive like this.

Thankfully, Pierce hadn't followed.

I'd wanted Dad to give me answers to things in my life that hadn't made sense, but I was left more hurt than ever. Rather than warn me about the danger encroaching on my life, he'd let me live in ignorance. But he'd told Lily to skip town for her own safety.

Never the favorite, never good enough, always belittled and insulted for my choices. But all the criticism from him was hypocritical. Because Dad cowed to the witch, my mother was murdered, I was attacked by Soren and nearly killed. Innocent people were scooped up along the way, including Megan's murder and Kayla's job-quitting attack, and Evangeline having committed all the 'animal attacks' on innocent people all over town. Dr. Greg Barrett, beneath all his puffy-chest superiority, was a coward. All Dad had to do was tell us the truth. We could've all left or protected ourselves properly. Obviously, a secret sprinkle of herbs in my water didn't help.

My fingers reached for the locket around my neck. At least now I knew it was there and when it wasn't. I could properly prepare myself.

Vampires might've been inherently dangerous, but it wasn't Oliver causing all my troubles. Oliver had given me protection against compulsion. He'd saved me from a selfish elf, from Soren's attacks, and from a witch's homicidal plan—I didn't want to know what was going to happen to me if Newt was unsatisfied in Dad's work.

Oliver had blocked my memory of him at my car accident to instill strength and courage within me. He'd blocked my memory of the basketball player to protect me from the hidden world I had yet to learn about and subsequently save me from a baby vampire's bite. Vampires, elves, and witches were a steep learning curve—but not as difficult to wrap my brain around as medical school.

And he was the only person in my life who didn't expect me to do more, to be more, like attain my paramedic's license. He cared about me just the way I was.

My walk turned into a jog, and I tucked the bouncing locket behind my shirt. A smile spread across my face. For a second, I wanted to turn around and get my car, but I couldn't waste those precious minutes. I had to get to Oliver as soon as possible. My legs pumped, and the air whooshing in and out of my chest was exhilarating. I was unstoppable, light on my feet, a breeze floating across the ground.

Dogs barked as I blew past their fences. Mail carriers hopped aside and nodded, but still I closed the distance. I'd find him trapped in his house by the sun, worried about me. I had to let him know I was okay—better than okay.

I rounded a corner, cutting through the wet grass, and I rushed down the block. At the bed-and-breakfast, I cut through the lawn and leaped up the stairs. I panted as my feet came to a stop. I tried the door, expecting it to be locked.

It wasn't.

He had been waiting for me to come to my senses. With a broad smile I couldn't shake, I pushed through the doors. "Oliver?" I called, turning in place.

No answer.

I rushed upstairs to his bedroom. Empty.

Huh. I went back downstairs and combed the main living areas. I stopped short at the bar.

A shattered glass bottle and tequila splashed all over.

A sinking feeling left my stomach in knots. Soren had tossed my phone off a trail when he'd kidnapped me. Not that I had Oliver's phone number yet.

"Oliver!" I cried.

He didn't have his sun ring.

Oliver

Since Daisy and daddy dearest didn't get along the greatest, I should've expected she went home, needing a solid sleep after tossing and turning on the lumpy cabin mattress during the day. I knew because I didn't sleep either, and it had nothing to do with the floor.

If I'd thought of that first, I could've saved myself a lot of unnecessary stress in having to face the man who'd created a weapon against my own kind. I walked away without killing him. See, I was evolving.

With vampire speed, I climbed out of my car and rushed up Daisy's front porch. I exhaled and raked my fingers through my hair, trying to straighten the disheveled strands for Daisy.

I cleared my throat, adjusted my posture, checked the flowers, and then I knocked.

And knocked some more. Come on, it was early, but didn't anyone ever answer their doors in a timely manner?

Allison pulled the door wide. "It's rude to show up unannounced." She then noticed the flowers in my hand, and her face paled. "Who are those for?"

"Daisy, of course. Can I come inside?"

Allison continued to block my entrance, and her defensive body language was setting me on edge. "What happened? What did you do? Where is she?" Allison asked, firing off questions with worry in her voice.

"I was going to ask you the same thing." I repeated in disbelief.

Allison braced herself against the doorway, panic curling into anger. "You were supposed to find her. That was the deal. If you didn't..." she trailed off and lifted a palm like she was going to cast a spell.

I held out my hands in plea. "Slow down. I *did* find her, and I dropped her off at her dad's, but she's not there now. You haven't seen her at all?" I raked a hand through my hair, this time not caring if I re-messed it.

"She never came home."

That elf. I had a score to settle.

Daisy

I SKIPPED UP MY front steps and barged through the front door. The excitement of finding Oliver waned as worry took root in my chest. Allison and Jamie had placed a spell on my house to keep vampires and elves out, back when I didn't know better, but I hoped they would've let him inside. With daylight on full display, he was trapped or ash.

He had to be here, sheltering from the sun, waiting for me.

"Oliver?" I called, moving from room to room, finding no one. I climbed the stairs to my bedroom. Nothing was touched. The bedding was smooth. The art on my walls was still there. I turned to leave when my eye caught on the drawing I'd hung from my aunt's belongings.

I approached the smiling faces drawn in charcoal. I didn't know who they were, but the initials in the corner, "O.R." and the date, 1870, made my heart stop. The style reminded me of what I'd seen Oliver drawing in his room, and the pictures on his walls. Could it be I inherited a drawing from Oliver's own hand? Once it was Lisa's treasured art, and now its value was priceless to me.

My house was empty. No Oliver, no roommates. Where was everyone? Something wasn't right. If only I would've stayed with him instead of checking on Dad. "Oliver!"

He had to be somewhere.

Or he was dead.

The broken glass at his house meant there had been a fight. Who would Oliver fight? His brother? Probably, but

I couldn't do anything about that, and I had to believe the younger vampire, after all he'd done, would be in some sort of apology mode. That left—

Pierce. I pulled my phone out of my pocket and dialed the elf. It rang and rang. No answer.

Something was horribly wrong. I felt it in my bones.

Oliver

I FULLY EXPECTED DAISY to be here, and likely not on her own accord, so I left the apology flowers in the car. That elf was going to pay for whatever he did to her. And if I found the protective locket gone? Truce nullified. With an immortal life and no obligations remaining to anyone, I would hunt him down until I tore his throat out, until he stared at me with total remorse, because I had none for a traitorous elf.

In a flash, he'd be visiting the Other Side, the afterlife for the supernatural, and he'd have company—his father Evan Logonson. The only thing giving me pause was Pierce didn't deserve the family reunion either.

I was extra grateful Soren had given me my ring back. Otherwise, I'd have been stuck in the shadows for another day, and this couldn't wait. I pounded on the door again. The heartbeat on the other side of the fiberglass was unmistakable. "Open up, elf. I can hear you in there."

I lifted my fist to pound again, but the door opened. Reminding myself he didn't deserve a swift end and a family reunion, I refrained from liberating his head from his shoulders on sight.

"What are you doing here, vamp?" Pierce asked with a bored tone.

"Where's Daisy?" My body was tense, and my chest heaved with restrained anger.

"I don't know."

"You lie." I pushed him back, slipping through the nonexistent threshold barrier, which meant no human lived here and that *Daisy* wasn't living here. That was a tiny relief.

I shoved him into an armchair, leaving the door gaping behind us. Even if the elf wanted to fly past me, his wingspan would be all too easy for me to capture, plus he wouldn't fit through the door. On foot, I was faster, and since I was older, I was naturally stronger. The elf had no choice but to obey. "What did you do with her?"

A cell phone rang nearby. We both turned our heads toward it. No way would I allow him a chance to request backup or send a message to move Daisy. "Ignore that."

"I don't know what you're talking about. She stomped off angrily from her dad's a few hours ago. Did you try there?"

Vampires couldn't compel elves, but fists could. My hand curled into a stone. I wanted to hit him so much it hurt. "Is that the truth?"

"I have no reason to lie to you."

"You have one big reason," I countered.

Like mine, his skin would sizzle at the touch of her locket, but that wouldn't stop him from gritting his teeth against the pain and taking it off, which would plainly demonstrate the kind of elf he was.

The cell phone rang again, and Pierce shifted to get up. I pressed a hand on his shoulder. "You stay right there and answer me. Don't make me tie you up."

Sweat broke out on Pierce's brow. Good. He deserved to squirm. "Daisy doesn't want me, and I couldn't force her."

Bad word choice, elf. "You tried to."

"Yeah, I tried. You can't fault me for being what I am."

But he faulted me for what I was. The hypocrisy angered me to no end.

A shadow spilled across the floor.

34
Coming Clean

Daisy

WHEN I'D FOUND THE broken glass in Oliver's house, I'd expected him to be in trouble. I didn't know why or by whom, but the elf's house was a decent guess. I planned to hunt down his captors and charge in like a raging bull—as much as a human woman armed only with defense against compulsion could. But this scene was not what I'd pictured.

It wasn't Oliver submitting in a chair about to get a serving of fist sandwich. I almost hoped Oliver would slug him once for me. Maybe twice. Brushing that appealing thought aside, the most important thing was Oliver was alive and breathing, and I sagged with relief. From the looks of things, he was pretty pissed off.

"What's going on?" I asked Oliver.

The vampire turned to face me, fist instantly dropping, handsome face shifting from pissed to relief. "Daisy?" he asked in a whisper.

"Are you okay?" I asked him.

Leaving Pierce sitting in the chair, the tall, dark, and smoking-hot vampire approached me. Sunlight streaked across his leg, and I screamed in panic. We'd survived too much for me to lose him now. I tackled Oliver to the floor and covered his body with mine. My face was inches from his, but rather than all the fun possible thoughts, I only worried about covering him, and since I was a fair bit smaller than him, I needed help. "Blanket, Pierce. Throw me a blanket now!"

Pierce stared. I always knew he was on the uncaring side, but this was harsh.

"Pierce, don't just sit there."

"Daisy, it's okay." Oliver's gentle words sounded like goodbye. He brushed the hair back from my face, and his pale gray eyes captivated me. His angled cupid's bow tempted me. I wanted his lips desperately. I wanted all of him.

Then I heard the sizzle. The dreaded stomach-clenching sound of flesh being burned. I was never going to enjoy bacon again.

"You can't quit on me now." I held back the emotion threatening to break me. "No matter what happened here, don't give up on me."

Oliver smiled. "As much as I like you on top of me, I'm not a fan of ex-boyfriends watching or my skin melting."

At once, the feel of Oliver's body pressing against mine sent a hot flash through my body, and the awkwardness of the uncaring eyes nearby had me shifting off him. Plus, my necklace was burning him.

Oliver chuckled. Oh, how I missed that sound. He stood and helped me to my feet. The sunlight reflected off his bare hands with no harm.

"I appreciate the effort, but I'm fine." He displayed his hand, and the sun caught the glinting ruby.

"But how?" The shattered tequila must've been the grand finale between Oliver and Soren. "You didn't—?" Kill him? I couldn't finish the question.

"Soren had a change of heart."

I blinked. When I'd arrived, Oliver was on a rampage about to pummel the elf. "With your fist?"

Oliver laughed. "That would've been my assumption too, but no. He handed it over voluntarily."

"Wow." I had been right about Soren. He *did* deserve the cure.

"Yeah."

Pierce cleared his throat.

I shot a glare at him. Yeah, it was his house, but after he conspired with my dad, he owed me. Ignoring him, I asked Oliver, "I'm sorry for tackling you. Did I hurt you?"

"Only my dignity."

I laughed, and that was my limit for my ex to eavesdrop. "Can we talk somewhere?"

"Yes, please," Pierce said, standing up and rubbing his face. He hid his defeat. I wanted to feel sorry for him, but I couldn't. "I'm not watching any more of this. Get out of my house."

"Let's go," Oliver said, guiding me with his hand at the small of my back.

I walked into the early morning sun with Oliver at my side. We meandered down the stairs, along the pathway, and stopped on the sidewalk next to his Shelby.

"I didn't tell you before, but I like your car," I said, gazing at the shiny red paint with a pair of white racing stripes running over the top of it.

"Without a driver, a car is an empty, pointless thing. Walk with me."

Obviously, this car was more special than he had led on, or he wouldn't have bothered with this specific rare model. "That's a cold point of view. I think cars are necessary, which is why some people have more than one."

Oliver darted me a look of horror as we strolled down the sidewalk, and that was when I understood the subtext. "But I'm a one-car kind of girl. I might not have chosen a candy-apple red antique Shelby, knowing what I know about...cars, but what's under the hood is more important than the paint job."

"What a car is extends beyond the pretty paint, and it can't help how it was made. That Shelby has the perfect façade to rope in drivers hoping for a test drive, but so many don't know how to handle the real power. There's an infinite road ahead, but so far, no driver could handle her suspension on the twists and sharp turns..." Oliver trailed off. The loneliness in his voice was crushing.

Finishing his unspoken thoughts, I said, "So, the car sits alone, worried the next driver will be consumed by the power, while wishing endlessly for that one special driver who can handle the whole package."

Oliver's misty eyes glanced my way and returned to our steps forward on the sidewalk. We turned a corner.

I continued, "Your car isn't scary, and it wasn't your fault I was ejected from the driver's seat. I wasn't equipped for all the special features of a car like that, and I handled some of them poorly. But I understand now." I glanced at the cracks passing underfoot. "Well, enough anyway, and I'd like to take another drive, if you're willing to open the door."

Oliver's lips lifted into a small smile, and we crossed the street to the next block, not far from my house. "There are a few things we must clear up before you buckle in again."

I smiled to myself. Things between us weren't over. "Name it."

"Tell me why you went looking for Pierce," he said.

I needed to hear his side first—the fascinating scene I'd walked into. "Why were you going to punch him?"

Oliver sighed and met my eyes. "I thought he took your protective necklace off and compelled you to submit. He wouldn't tell me where you were, and I was afraid he and your dad were up to something. Your turn."

"I went to Pierce's looking for you. I thought he hurt you."

Oliver waited for more explanation. I added, "Your house was empty, and I found the shattered glass. I figured you got into a fight with either your brother or Pierce. Since I knew where to find my ex, I went there."

We stopped in front of my gate. The same one where Soren had attacked me when I went for a jog, and later he'd killed Megan and my patient, and where my handsome rescuer had saved my life. A false sense of security is what I expected from it, and exactly what I'd gotten. Stupid gate.

"Now you tell me something," I said, hand resting on the gate. "You didn't personally know the basketball player, so why did you really go to Fully Loaded that night and pretend to be drunk?"

Oliver tapped his temples with a sly grin. "Vampire hearing. You told Megan you were heading to the bar, which I gave no thought to until I saw the ring on your finger. I wanted my ring back."

I remembered how charming he was, buying me a selection of drinks and walking me home, quite like this. "You planned to seduce it off me?"

"And I'm not sorry. I've walked this earth for over a hundred and eighty years. I've built a fortune, traveled the globe, and drunk enough booze to sterilize Las Vegas."

I cringed at the unwanted visual. "Is that supposed to make me feel better? Because it's not working."

Oliver gripped my hands with desperation, and he held my eyes. "No matter everything I've survived—places I've been, people I've met, enemies I've made—*you* are the best thing that's ever happened to me. I will keep you safe for as long as I live, because you are my forever, and that's a promise."

"Forever?" I asked flippantly, heart soaring with the beautiful words.

"Forever," he repeated, completely serious.

Taking that at face value, I asked, "Wait, you live *forever*?"

"Immortal." He stared intently into my eyes, and my heart fluttered. He was dead serious.

"That's a big commitment, and as of late, a big job," I said lightly and nervously chuckled.

His hands squeezed mine. Not hard enough to hurt, just hard enough to tell me this was his big confession. Butterflies tickled my insides. "I'm a one-driver kind of guy, Daisy. I love you, and I want you to take my keys."

Oliver quietly waited for me to continue, as if he'd explained his side and now he needed mine.

"I'm not afraid of what you are. Everything you've done was for my own good, for my protection, and I get that now, but I can't drive a stick."

Oliver studied me. "You mean that literally, or...?"

I admired his stunning suit, which complemented his skin tone perfectly. He was something out of a magazine—ethereal, inhumanly beautiful. He made me feel special, and I needed Oliver naked and kissing every inch of my body. I leaned in close, gazing into his gorgeous eyes. I palmed his jaw, covered in a five o'clock shadow. My thumbs rubbed the soft short hair.

He loved me. He would protect me, and I trusted he would never hurt me. His gaze moved to my lips as if starting to get the hint, and I said, "I trust you, and I love you. Shut up and give me the keys."

Oliver's lips fell upon mine, slowly at first, and deepened in need. I found his throat and kissed along his sensitive skin until he groaned, and I smiled in satisfaction. I gripped his belt, pulling him against me, no longer capable of waiting any longer. "Come inside."

"My pleasure," Oliver said gruffly.

Heart racing, I grabbed him by the hand and brought him up onto my front porch. I opened the door and rushed through, but Oliver's hand ripped from mine. The witch's spell kept vampires and elves out. "I forgot. You can come inside." I invited him in formally to break the barrier.

Oliver held up a palm, testing the invisible layer. "It's still up. This is a higher-level magic than your invitation."

I growled, full-on dog growl, and I turned to face the interior of my house. "Jamie? Allison? Either of you home?"

No answer. Damn it.

"Daisy, one of them has to drop the spell before I can enter."

I turned and called out to my roommates again, but no one was home. "Let's go to your house." I rushed back out onto the porch and gripped his hand, ready to drag him all the way to relieve the throbbing between my legs.

Oliver moved in a flash and turned me to face him. "Daisy, stop."

"What? Why?"

Oliver scooped me up into his arms. "I can move faster."

"That's the first useful benefit of your otherworldly life."

Oliver's eyes glistened with excitement. "Here I thought it was my endless stamina."

The throb pounded harder. I laughed. "If we were walking instead of talking, I'd already be spinning your wheels."

A devious smile lifted his lips.

35
Taming That Snake

Daisy

IN HIS BEDROOM, OLIVER set me on my feet. The bed was made, and the tower of suffocating pillows was primed for a fight.

"Now where were we?" Oliver said, lifting a devious brow.

I smoothed my hair after the quick vampire ride and sent him a sly smile. "Shifting gears." I tugged the hem of his shirt up and dragged my fingernails along his beltline.

"I want you to know I appreciate you following me on my car metaphors, but I'm concerned."

"Why might that be?" I slipped my hands around to his back and gripped the taut muscles under my palms.

"The transmission lever is down there." He pointed not-so-subtly down south.

I laughed. "Shut up and kiss me."

"Driver commands the radio." Oliver kissed my throat.

My head fell back, and my eyes closed in the ecstasy of his soft lips. "I like this game."

"Better than 'pin the tail on the donkey'?" he asked between kisses.

"So far," I teased.

Oliver growled, and with blurry vampire speed, he slipped off my shirt. "For someone who likes it hard, fast, and rough, you're moving tantalizingly slow."

"Are you in a hurry?" I cocked my brow at him and painstakingly unbuttoned his satin-smooth shirt, one slow button at a time.

Oliver shrugged out of his suit jacket and flung it aside, and I splayed the fancy shirt and admired the abs beneath.

"Depends. When's your next shift?"

"We have plenty of time," I said, gripping his wrist and checking his watch.

Oliver's lips pulled into a devious grin. "No, we don't."

Kisses rained down on my skin, and Oliver freed my bra with his magical fingers. My body arched into his, and he slipped my jogging pants free. In a growing frenzy, I unbuttoned his dress pants and freed his length. It bobbed happily at me, and I slipped his boxer briefs carefully over it.

"What was the occasion for the fancy threads?" I asked.

"I'd brought you flowers, but I left them in the car." Oliver kneeled, trailing kisses down my body to my thighs. "I'll have to buy you new ones, because I'm not leaving to rescue them from the hot interior."

"You dressed up to give me flowers?" I gripped his shoulders, and he lifted me up in the air and onto the bed. I bounced, and several homicidal pillows toppled onto me.

Oliver climbed up to face me, chest pressing against mine, swatting pillows aside. His skin sizzled where his chest touched the locket at my throat. I shifted it to my side, and we both fought the pillows together.

"She really does mean to kill me, doesn't she?" I asked.

"Nicole? Nah, vanity prevails over practicality every time. Don't take offense. Now, where were we?" Oliver grinned.

"Special occasion for the suit."

"Ah, right. Well, I intended to grovel endlessly for your forgiveness. Instead, I'll appreciate every inch of you while naked. Now, hang on tight for rough terrain. We're about to tackle a mountain." Oliver winked and kissed every inch of my skin, leaving one spot begging for attention last. When his mouth reached my sensitive clit, I cried out in pleasure overload.

The flicking of his tongue drove me up the mountain closer and closer with each pass, and my breath stopped as I reached my climax. Oliver didn't stop, didn't waver, just a machine set to a continuously smooth RPMs. "Oh, God, don't stop," I breathlessly begged.

"Your wish is my command."

I tumbled over the cliff, but I didn't find darkness. There was only light...and a warm surge of sensitive tingles. Oliver licked through those glorious waves, and when I settled, he looked up at me, resting his chin on my mound. "Did you call me God?"

I laughed. "I think I did."

"Okay then." Oliver kissed his way back to my throat and hesitated. His breath quickened, and his length pressed against my thigh. He stopped.

"What's wrong?" I asked.

"Nothing. Nothing at all." His lips took mine, and he positioned himself for entry.

Slowly, he pushed in and slid out, deeper and deeper with each gentle thrust, until I fully took in his length to the hilt. I groaned with fullness, and Oliver took a moment to collect himself again.

"Hard, fast, and rough? Or have you changed your mind?" he whispered gruffly.

"Hard and fast. Save the rough until after my shift."

Oliver smiled. "You're the driver."

The sexiest vampire I'd ever met delivered as requested. Rapid thrusts shook the bed and slapped the wall. I didn't care. Nothing in the world mattered but Oliver, and I wanted nothing but to make him happy, as he'd done for me. His passion was addicting. I could never get enough of him.

Oliver climaxed, arching his back and grunting with his own ecstasy. His glistening chest heaved with his deep breaths. He lowered himself onto my chest, careful not to crush me.

"Oliver," I whispered into his ear.

"Hmmm?"

"I love you."

He made a noise of contentment. "And I love you."

"Do you have any limes?"

"Downstairs at the bar."

"Good."

We fell asleep tangled in his bed as midday turned into afternoon. I never wanted to be anywhere but in his arms, but I had to get to work.

To be continued...

Dear Reader,

DIVE INTO THE NEXT chapter of Oliver and Daisy's story in **Vampire's Secret**, where Oliver's worst nightmare becomes a reality. And don't forget to check out **Vampire's Distraction**, the prequel short story where Oliver and Daisy first meet at Abby's wedding.

As an indie author, I'm thrilled you shared your time with me, exploring the crazy worlds and voices living rent-free in my head and keeping me up at night. Your reviews are very important to me, so if you enjoyed this book, please consider leaving some stars at your favorite retailer for the first part of Oliver Rockwell and Daisy Barrett's story, Vampire's Deception.

If you found any typos or errors, I blame my cat. Rat her out at: support@stephanieflynn.com.

Thank you for your support!

Also By Stephanie Flynn

Find my catalog at StephanieFlynn.com

Immortal Protector series

0.5 Vampire's Distraction

1 Vampire's Deception

2 Vampire's Secret

3 Vampire's Promise

3.5 Elf Bound

4 Vampire's Demand

5 Vampire's Destruction

6 Vampire's Conquest

Immortal Protector Side Tales

Deer Holiday

Love Claws

Depths of the Heart

Matchmaker in Time series

0.5 Minutes to Live

1 Seconds to Act

2 Hours to Arrive

3 Days to Hide

4 Years to Savor

Pirates in Time series

1 Pirate's Prize

2 Pirate's Treasure

3 Pirate's Plunder

Time Travel Romance Shorts

Fateful Time

One Crazy Time

If you like your urban fantasy without the romance, too, check out Stephanie Flynn's other name, Marie Flynn!

About Stephanie Flynn

Stephanie Flynn writes action-packed paranormal romance filled with adventure, suspense, and danger. She lives in Michigan, USA, with her husband and kids, and she spends her writing time surrounded by a herd of normal cats who bat everything off her desk, including her coffee. Check out her website for more books: StephanieFlynn.com